WHITE APACHE WOMAN

When Lobo Negro—Black Wolf—came to take her, he wore only moccasins and a short loin cloth. His muscular thighs were bare. The thin set to his mouth told her all she needed to know.

"No words of welcome for your new master?" he said quietly.

"You are the son of a dog," she told him levelly. "You can kill me, but you will never be my master."

She fell when he struck her, and as soon as she fell he was on top of her, his weight crushing her and one rock-hard knee pressing to get hers apart.

He untied her skirt and ripped it away, pulling it from beneath her and flinging it aside. . . he held her down and pulled her legs apart . . .

Quickly she bent her knee and clawed for the top of her moccasin. As her searching fingers found the bone handle of the knife, she ripped it free and struck swiftly at his throat.

Also by Kenn Smith

RIVER OF THE WIND

We will send you a free catalog on request. Any titles not in your local bookstore can be purchased by mail. Send the price of the book plus 50¢ shipping charge to Tower Books, P.O. Box 511, Murray Hill Station, New York, N.Y. 10156-0511.

Titles currently in print are available for industrial and sales promotion at reduced rates. Address inquiries to Tower Publications, Inc., Two Park Avenue, New York, N.Y. 10016, Attention: Premium Sales Department.

FLOWER OF GOLD

Kenn Smith

TOWER BOOKS   NEW YORK CITY

A TOWER BOOK

Published by

Tower Publications, Inc.
Two Park Avenue
New York, N.Y. 10016

Copyright © 1982 by Tower Publications, Inc.

All rights reserved
Printed in the United States

Chapter One

The desert, like some species of spider, can be beautiful in its ugliness. Like now, with the great orb of the sun resting on the western horizon as if exhausted, its screaming fierceness slowly changing to a soft rose hue while at the same time painting long shadows across the scarred land. Stark, without a hint of friendliness, and yet it seemed to beckon with a promise that couldn't be defined. For a moment, he felt like a moth before a flame.

He stood by himself, fifty yards away from the evening camp stirring behind him, and watched the scene with fascination. Cacti, some fat and bulging, some long-spined and ragged, and some with giant fingers stretching three times the height of a man, stood arrogantly aloof from the ragged, sandy floor. Mesquite and saw grass clinging tenaciously together in clumps and competing for the sparse available water in the sunbaked earth dotted the scene. And in the distance, red smokes of mountains emphasized the loneliness.

Except for broken rocks, seemingly dropped carelessly by some giant traveler centuries before, the land was flat for long dusky miles. But already, experience had taught him that the appearance was deceiving. The desert was actually filled with hidden depressions, from small gullies to deep arroyos that could hide men on horses. And this last surprise had been the downfall of more than one traveler through Apache country, from Spanish conquistador to American wanderer.

"Purty, ain't it, Lieutenant?" The dry voice coming

from behind him contained a hint of gravel and was pitched low.

Lieutenant David Foxcroft turned slowly and nodded, surprised as usual at the quietness with which the scout could move; he hadn't been aware of the approach of the other man. Buffalo Harrison was a large man, thick in the trunk and legs. However, his movements were smooth and fluid, seemingly effortless, and his moccasins made not the slightest whisper, where a trooper's boot would crunch and scatter.

"A man could lose himself here in more ways than one, Harrison," David said.

The scout grinned, a wry, onesided droop of his mouth beneath a thick mustache. "Heard a man say once that when the desert finally wins over a fellar, and it most always will, there ain't but one place left to hide. And that's to go crazy."

"A last refuge in madness." David nodded again and allowed his gaze to return to the scene before him. "I wonder how many men have faced that choice here?"

"Reckon quite a few."

"How long have you been out here?" David liked this Westerner, liked the quiet confidence of the man, and had been a little surprised to discover that he in turn seemed to return the respect. Especially since he was under no illusion himself as to the fact that he was a greenhorn Eastern Army officer with limited knowledge in how to survive in this hostile land, much less how to ensure the success of the troops assigned to his command.

"Oh, mebbe twenty years or so," Harrison drawled. "I forget. Time don't mean all that much out here. Drifted in from California one time hunting beaver; got tired of that and switched to looking for gold. Finally decided that scouting for the Army paid more regular than either one."

"How long do you plan to keep that up?"

Harrison grinned again. "Till my bones get too old to move, or an Apach lifts my scalp, whichever comes first."

David started a smile himself, then allowed it to die. "Our mission, the Army's I mean, is to pacify these Indians, Harrison. We must stop all the raiding and make this country safe for both Indian and whites. Personally, I expect to succeed in that mission."

"What you really mean, Lieutenant, is that we're gonna try to take the land away from the Apach. Push him off into some godforsaken corner and make a farmer out of him. But I can tell you right now, it ain't gonna work. The Apach is a proud man. And he's been living free ever since he came here a hell of a long time before this country ever seen a white man."

Harrison paused and allowed his eyes to sweep the horizon. "The Spanish tried to tame him first, and the Mex after that. They didn't even come close. The Apach is as wild as this land, Lieutenant. The only way he can be tamed is to kill him."

David changed the subject abruptly, suspecting from what he'd already heard that the scout was right. "You didn't find any gold when you were prospecting?" he asked.

This time, the slow grin spread across Harrison's face. "You wouldn't be thinking about that lost city I told you about, Lieutenant? Quivira?"

"Not really. Afraid I'm not much for believing in legends, Harrison."

The hint of sarcasm in his voice was ignored by the scout. "Lots of folks do believe in it, Lieutenant. That land ahead of us is full of the bones of men who came here looking for Quivira."

"An ancient city full of fantastic treasure," David quoted. "Built by a civilization lost to history and now guarded as sacred ground by the—what kind of Apaches did you say?"

"Chiricahua. Toughest Apach of them all, and that's saying a mouthful. Chief is a man called Cochise."

"And you really believe this city exists? That it's somewhere in the desert?"

Harrison turned and eyed him thoughtfully. "There's gold here, Lieutenant. Gold and silver; mebbe more than you and I ever dreamed about. And if anybody knows where it is, the Chiricahua do. They know this land, know it like it was a part of them. Which it is."

He swept a hand toward the horizon. "Apache boys—and girls too—are taught by the grownups how to live with the desert from the time they quit sucking tits. They learn how to find food and water where me'n you would die looking. And when the boys are big enough to walk, they're taken out and left by themselves for days at a time. They learn to depend on nobody but themselves. They learn, or they die. The Apach is as much a part of this land as that mesquite bush there."

"Then if they know where gold is, why don't they use it? With wealth they could buy anything they want. Why live a primitive life?"

"Cause it's the kind of life they perfer. It's their nature. The Apach likes to fight, and he likes to raid. Kind of an honor thing with him, to show how clever he is, and how tough he is. Also shows his contempt for the rest of us." Harrison paused. "Tell you what, Lieutenant, when you get to negotiating with Cochise, or any other Apach for that matter, you remember that. Most Apach will talk straight to you and keep his word when he gives it. He might even act friendly. But deep down he really don't think much of you. Not much at all."

David heaved a sigh. Before him, the sun was disappearing below the horizon, the shadows lengthening. "Well, just between you and me, Harrison, I'd be happy to leave this land to him. It and his lost cities as well."

A sudden thought struck him. "That other thing you were telling me last night, the Indian woman. Now there's a tale that does intrigue me. You wouldn't be laughing at a greenhorn, would you, Harrison?"

This time there was a different light in the scout's

eyes when he faced David. Amusement, but intermixed with a strange sort of longing. "I ain't saying you ain't a greenhorn, Lieutenant. Reckon you are as far as the desert goes. But that's natural since you just come here from the East. I learned long ago how to measure a man, though and I don't think you'll be a greenhorn long. Knew that the minute I laid eyes on you. You'll learn. And it'll be worth my while to teach you. Lots of men it ain't worth the trouble."

He paused a moment, but his deep-set eyes, overshadowed by heavy graying eyebrows, remained on David's. "Naw, I wasn't funning you about the woman. I seen her once myself when I rode into Cochise's camp with the Army to palaver. Reckon she was about the purtiest thing I ever laid eyes on. She had long hair, the color of real gold; a face that made you think of a spring morning; and blue eyes that give you the shivers when she put them on you. Even under buckskin, she had a figure that would make a man's balls ache. Tell you what, Lieutenant. Any man would give up just about everything he had or was going to get for that squaw. He'd crawl in the dirt to have her. Reckon I didn't sleep for a week after that time, just thinking about her."

David watched him closely. Harrison's reputation as a scout was the best. Tough, independent, and an excellent Indian fighter. But the quality in his voice was soft and wistful, like a small boy speaking of a gift he knew he could never have.

"Hair of gold? A blond Indian? Are you sure she's Indian?"

Harrison shook his head. "Don't rightly know. She walked like an Injun, and talked their lingo. She could be white; the Apach have been known to capture white women and treat them like their own. Or she could be a half-breed. I just don't know. It ain't considered polite to ask. Anyhow, she's the daughter of Cochise, and I'm one man who ain't about to mess with that Injun if I can help it."

David smiled. "I think this is one legend I've got to see for myself, Harrison. Does she have a name?"

"Flor de Oro. That's what they called her. Spanish for Flower of Gold, in case you don't speak Greaser. And damn if it don't fit. But you take my advice, Lieutenant; leave her be if you ever do see her. Touch her and Cochise will roast you over a small fire. And that's just the beginning of how you'd die."

Night was almost upon them, and with it, the chill that always surprised him. The change in desert temperature from hot, baking heat during the day to the need for blankets as soon as the sun dropped out of sight was almost unbelievable. But more than the chill caused his skin to prickle. *A woman that beautiful . . . A madonna of the desert . . . That would be something to see . . .* He decided that if there was ever the chance to see her he'd take it. Even at a risk.

Flor de Oro made her way toward the river, walking as she always did a short distance apart from the other laughing, chattering girls. Although three of them were also daughters of Cochise, the chief of the Chiricahua, and the rest she could call her friends, it had always been her nature to keep slightly apart. She adopted the habit almost from the time she came to live with the Chiricahua ten years ago and the squaws, both young and old, respected her privacy. The fact that she was of the white skin and her hair was yellow rather than the black of an Indian did not set her apart in their eyes, for she had been declared the daughter of Cochise, with both the privilege and the duties of such a daughter. It was merely the way of all Apache to allow a man—or a woman—to be what he wanted to be.

An Apache was expected to be free, independent of the wishes of others except in matters that were necessary to the survival of the tribe. Even the chief was limited in his ability to command. If his decisions did not suit a particular warrior, that man was allowed to take his possessions, including his squaws, and leave the tribe. If his decisions went against the desires of the majority, then the chief was required to change them or leave himself. No Apache lowered his eyes before another man. And a squaw, although she must obey her husband in every matter, faced him on an eye-to-eye level. Until she was married, she obeyed only her father and more often than not was inclined to test the mettle of the braves who desired her with scornful words.

Flor de Oro walked apart, slept in the corner of Cochise's lodge that was allotted to her, and performed the duties required of his daughter. But while the others gossiped around the campfire, she usually remained silent, answering only when spoken to directly. She was an Apache and proud of the fact. She could run like a deer, her knee-length moccasins protecting her from the spines of the cactus and the whiplash of brush; disappear in the desert floor as well as any brave; and walk for days on end with little food and less water. Anything expected of an Apache squaw, she could do as well as if not better than most. But still there was a difference within her. There would never be a time in which she forgot that she had once lived another life.

Cochise was her father, and she gave him all the respect and devotion that was required of a daughter, but in the long nights of winter she still remembered her first father; remembered his white hair, the burning eyes; and his last, straining words as he lay dying in her arms. "Child . . . forgive me. Live, Jennifer . . . Live . . . so that my soul will not burn in hell for what I have done to you. . . ."

He died. And she looked up into the dark eyes of the man who would become her Indian father. Looked, and saw compassion. She had been afraid then, surrounded by savages and holding her dead father in her arms. A white girl-child, nine years old and faced with the unknown. But Cochise had been gentle with her, lifted her up in his arms and walked away, talking softly to her in a language she hadn't then understood but was comforted by nonetheless. She cried that night in his lodge, but she cried for the last time. The next day she started learning to be an Apache, and fear was forgotten.

At the river, she joined the rest in removing the soft buckskin shirt she wore, loosened the belt around her waist to allow the second two skins it held in place to make a skirt to drop, and lastly stripped off her long moccasins. Naked, she waded into the water, and in Apache fashion she began first to wash her long hair, using the short root she had brought for the purpose.

A shout of laughter brought her head up and she smiled at Qua-tos, her youngest sister, a child of eleven. The girl was attempting to do a handstand under water but each time she kicked her legs in the air, she tumbled over and came up blowing spray. The rest of the girls screamed encouragement to her, their wide faces bursting with merriment.

Flor de Oro smiled and returned to washing her hair, grasping a section in one hand and gliding the root across it until the strands separated, then leaning to swish it rapidly through the water. It was a long process, and she didn't stop until she was sure she had not missed any part. Only then did she begin to bathe her body, rubbing her hands vigorously over the root and scrubbing them against her skin.

As she bathed, she thought of the coming day. Tomorrow was to be her wedding day and her last day with the Chiricahua. Her selected husband was a minor chief under Mangas Coloradas, chief of the Mimbreno. Cochise and Mangas had decided the marriage to strengthen the alliance between the two tribes. It was to be the second such marriage for that reason.

Flor de Oro had yet to see her new husband; he would arrive in the morning, and she wondered what he would look like. He would be a strong man, and a good provider, that much she already knew because he was a chief. Being a chief, even a minor one, was a position that could only be held by a strong man. And her father had told her she would be the first wife to this man, with all the future rights of a first wife. That helped. But still there was this strange feeling inside her, a feeling that was alien to an Apache. She somehow wished it could be a marriage of her own choosing. But such a wish was foolish. The marriage was decided as all marriages were, by her father, and that was that.

Another shout echoed behind her, a shout of warning intermixed with laughter, and she spun in time to see a snake hurled toward her. Catlike, she ducked and flashed a hand up to grasp the reptile in midair. She caught it not far behind its head, or she would have had to follow through with her arm and throw it from her in a continuation of its flight. But in catching it near the head where it could not turn to sink its fangs into her arm, she could hold it and look for another victim of the joke. She laughed herself and ignored the frantic lashing of the serpent in her hand as she coolly surveyed the giggling girls, who each ducked under water as her eyes fell upon them.

She made as if to throw toward one a few feet from her but then paused as the girl went under and waited. Just as she rose again with a whoop and a shake to clear the water from her eyes, Flor de Oro threw.

The snake made a loop in the air and its intended victim saw it with no time to duck. She could only throw herself backward and go under at the same time that it reached her. The rest of the girls screamed with laughter. However, the snake had had quite enough. Intent only on survival, it swam quickly away, easily outdistancing the frantic attempts of the Indian girls who chased it.

Flor de Oro finished her bath and returned to the bank to dry herself with her hands, rubbing them over her body and pressing away the water. When she'd finished, she redressed in the Apache fashion, pulling on first her moccasins, without which she could not run far through the desert in case of sudden flight from an enemy, and afterward holding the front and rear buckskin in place until she could secure her belt. Then, because her long hair was still wet, she left off her shirt, carrying it instead in her hand and walking down the riverbank to where she would be out of earshot of the noise the others were making.

She sat down on a large rock, folded her shirt for a pillow, and lay back with her hair spread over the rest of the rock to dry. She had chosen an angle away from the sun so that it was behind her and she could enjoy its warmth without having it on the backs of her eyelids as she rested.

With her eyes closed, her mind returned to the evening two days ago when Cochise had called her into his lodge and sent the others away. She had known for a long while that she was well past the age of marriage but had assumed that it was her father's decision to wait. Several braves had approached him for her, one of whom she had almost hoped would be granted the favor. He was a tall man, taller than most, and his arms were thick with strength. And although he was young, not much more than her own age, he had already proven his cunning by raiding a Mexican ranch and stealing a dozen sheep from under the noses of the owners. Another time, he had been chased across the desert by five Mexicans on horseback and laughed as he recounted the ease with which he evaded them. He had even lain motionless at one point, allowing the riders to pass within a few feet of where he lay exposed if they had only the desert eye to see him.

That warrior would have made a good husband. He was a man of spirit. And as she had stared at him frankly, allowing her eyes to travel up and down his body, the buckskin had moved quickly between his legs. He was a man a woman could expect much from.

But Cochise had ideas of more than the horses and gifts he would receive in exchange for her. Flor de Oro sat before him in the lodge and listened as he described the need for a closer alliance with the Mimbreno and of his great respect for Mangas Coloradas. "This chief has seen you, Flor de Oro," he told her gravely. "He knows that you were not always Apache. But he knows as well that you are now the daughter of Cochise as much as if you were born to my squaw. He knows of the affection I hold for you. And he knows that the heart of Cochise will remain with you no matter where your lodge is built. It is good that the heart of Cochise will live with the Mimbreno, for Mangas Coloradas is a great chief and the Chiricahua need his strength."

A thought had occurred to her as she listened, and it was not the first time it had occurred, of how it would be not to marry an Apache but to marry a white man instead. Since her father's death she had seen less than a half dozen, most of them all at one time when they had been invited to the camp of Cochise to make a peace agreement. The Americans had been older than she would have liked in a husband, and none had the cleanliness of an Apache, smelling instead of grease, dirt, and tobacco. But then she had to think that as there were young men among the Apache, there must be young men somewhere among the Americans. Could she possibly go back to the life of a white?

However, that thought had been only in passing. She was now an Apache, and the free life of an Indian was one that she liked. Besides, Cochise would decide her husband for her, no matter what. That was the way it should be.

When her father finished, she agreed and promised that she would never bring shame upon his name. She was the daughter of Cochise, she said proudly. Her new husband would walk tall before her because of that name.

The chief smiled, reached for her, and gave her a bear hug. Then he chuckled. "The desert will look with amazement at the strong young braves who run through it with hair the color of yours," he said. "It will think the Sun is their father!"

Flor de Oro smiled as she remembered his words.

The sun grew too warm and, lazily, she raised to a sitting position. It was time to return to camp; there were many chores she must do this day and, too, she must make herself ready for the wedding tomorrow. There would be new buckskins to finish. They must be rubbed with clay to make them white, with extra-long fringes added to signify the long life of the marriage. She must make a new band for her head, colored brightly with dye from berries. And before retiring to her blankets tonight, she must rub herself well with pine needles to give off a fresh scent when she met her new husband tomorrow. Lastly, she would sit for hours before the campfire and listen again to all the older squaws tell her of what is to be expected of a bride. Things she knew already, but it was tradition to be told on the eve of her wedding day.

A rock lizard joined her, perching on a smaller stone a few feet away, and she watched it with amusement. Its small warted body flexed in and out with its breathing as it watched her, and she flecked her tongue in imitation. Then suddenly, its head switched to a different direction and just as quickly it disappeared in a crack in the ground. She stiffened, knowing that she had not frightened the reptile. That something else had. Knowing, too, that she must discover the direction of danger before she made a move. The one second she hesitated was too long, as the man recognized her awareness and made his own move, leaping the few feet that separated them and crouching with a crooked grin on his face. His arms were spread in a dare for her to move in either direction, left or right.

Flor de Oro kicked her feet in the air, throwing them up over her head and pulling the rest of her body in a flip to land on the other side of the rock. But he was quicker. Before she had taken two running steps, his weight struck her from behind, forcing the breath from her as the two of them crashed to the ground. She struggled, both for breath and to free her arms as he pulled them behind her body and pinned them.

Her breasts were ground cruelly, scraping across the dirt with her efforts to squirm from beneath him. But her breath came back with a sob. She bucked upward, arching her back and twisting at the same time. But he was too strong. He locked both her elbows with his hands, pulled them together, and fastened her wrists with an iron grip. His other hand grasped her hair and yanked her head back until her neck strained with the effort.

The man pulled her to her feet, still holding her bent into a backward position, and pushed her into a stumbling run. The pressure on her neck was designed to prevent her from crying out unnecessarily, for even in her pain she knew a cry would be useless. There was no one to hear her but the other girls still in the water, and she was moving away from their direction. She fought for air and attempted to steady her legs as she ran. Better now to do as he wanted. Escape would come later.

He sensed her cooperation and eased the strain on her neck. But the grip on her wrists did not lessen as the pace of their running increased.

Short minutes later, they rounded an outcropping of rock, and she was surrounded by horses with grinning Apaches sitting on them. Her wrists and feet were bound and she was flung across one of the horses. Quickly the man who had taken her leaped up to its back and held her belt with one hand to keep her in place as he urged the animal to a run.

Flor de Oro gritted her teeth against the shock of the moving horse under her belly, braced herself as best she could, and waited. It would end sooner or later, better to put it from her mind now. Whatever happened, the Indian behind her on the horse would pay for this. She was the daughter of Cochise, and the chief would not rest until his honor was avenged. This man had made a foolish mistake and would eventually pay for it with his life. If he were lucky, he would meet a quick death in battle when he was caught. But if he were not lucky, she would get to enjoy watching him die slowly. That thought made riding the horse much easier.

Chapter Two

He was a tall man, six feet in stature, and stood straight as a reed. His chest was full and broad, thick even for an Apache, enabling him to run with the best of the young men, although he was thirty-eight years old. A Roman nose and deep-set black eyes balanced the wide face, but his firm mouth more often than not exhibited a gentle if not melancholy expression.

To the children of his tribe he was quiet-spoken and kind, laughing with them a great deal. Even a sharp tongue from a squaw was frequently ignored as long as the woman was wise enough not to tread upon his dignity. But the Chiricahua braves who willingly followed him into battle held him in awe, respecting him as only an Apache does another who is stronger, swifter, and more fierce in war. For he was the greatest warrior of them all—greater in the eyes of the Chiricahua than even the old ones who were legend. He was Cochise . . .

This time the face of the chief of the Chiricahua was far from gentle as he listened to the excited clamor of the young women crowded in a close group in front of him. His jaw grew more rigid as each fearfully added her own version of the capture, spilling words over one another like rushing water over break rocks. His chin rose higher and higher as he listened, and his black eyes glinted with the cold anger of a hawk about to strike.

A moment later, he raised a hand and the babble from the women ceased immediately. The glittering eyes singled out one of the older girls. "Did you know the man?"

"No," she said quickly. "He—we did not see him. They were gone when we went to look for Flor de Oro. But there were only the tracks of one brave."

When the women had first run shouting into camp from the river, a few warriors had been drawn to them in curiosity. Word had spread quickly, however, and now all the men were gathered around Cochise in a large circle, their eyes waiting for command.

Cochise didn't bother to look about him. "Ten of the swiftest with me," he snapped. "The rest will guard the camp. This may be a trick to draw us away."

Shi-la, an older one, stepped forward to thrust a rifle into the hands of his chief as Cochise started to move, and without debate among themselves, ten men separated from the rest of the group to follow him. There was no need to decide who would go, for the braves had competed with one another since childhood and each knew the other as well as himself. Each Apache could run for days across the desert without tiring; as youths, they had been trained to hunt deer by the steady, running chase. Once flushed, they would keep an animal moving, following doggedly each burst of speed, catching up as it tired, and forcing the deer to run again. Always it was the deer that gave out first, sometimes waiting in exhaustion for its inevitable death, sometimes already dead of a burst heart.

Cochise quickly reached the spot where Flor de Oro had been taken and paused to read the sign. He nodded with satisfaction that she had struggled as she should have. Then the fierce light in his black eyes deepened as they followed the dragging spoor of her feet where she had been forced to run. One man, the signs told him. But a large man, very powerful, with a long stride. The toes of his moccasins were turned up—which meant an Apache. But who? Not of the Chiricahua, certainly. The Mescalero? Perhaps the northerners, the Jicarilla . . .

He shook away the thoughts. Time enough to find

that out when he caught the man. And time enough to make him pay dearly if he were foolish enough to be taken alive.

His voice was low, not much more than a growl. "He will be captured if possible. If he does not surrender, leave him to me. Only prevent his escape."

A few cast glances at one another. Fearless as they themselves were, none would care to be the man who faced Cochise in battle. It would be like challenging the whirling, angry wind that sometimes roared across the desert.

Their chief knelt swiftly to pull his moccasins to his thighs. Each was made of a whole skin and normally folded down to just below the knee, the folds also serving to carry possessions: a knife, fishhooks, trinkets. But the real purpose of the folds was to enable him to to cover the whole leg for protection against brush and cacti on a hard run through the desert. The sole of the moccasin was sewn of skin with the hairy side out to protect the feet, and the toes were turned up for ease of running.

Then he set off on a ground-covering lope, and the rest fanned out behind him in an inverted V. The formation was designed both to prevent ambush and to enable each man to track sign in case the quarry doubled to confuse his trail.

Cochise led them only a short distance, however, before he rounded the rocks and discovered the hiding place where the rest of the raiders had waited with the horses. He stopped and snorted with disgust, and his anger deepened as he read the signs of their leaving. The stride of the ponies indicated that they were not being ridden hard, even in this beginning. The ponies were running, but not in a hard run. That meant the raiders had been sure of themselves and were saving their animals for a long trip. With care, and a knowledge of the *tinajas*, or seeps, natural tanks of water hidden in the rocks, his quarry could travel a great distance and still remain away from the known water holes. And they could travel faster than any Apache on foot. For him to start the search now would be useless.

The braves with him read the signs, too, and came to the same conclusion. They squatted around him, watching his face and waiting for a decision.

Cochise pointed to two of them. "Follow the trail," he said. "Do not return until you know where he hides or who he is. He is Apache, and he knows who I am. But I do not believe he will leave Apache land with her."

The two men indicated got up and left, trotting in the direction the horses had taken, and Cochise led the rest back toward his rancheria. He was glad that the raider was Apache, for that meant he could eventually be found. If he had been Comanche, he would be on his way back to the great plains, where his superb horsemanship made him a deadly fighter, equal to or even better than the Apache. It would take a war party of several tribes of the Apache to have even a small hope of success against the Comanche and their allies, the Kiowa. And that hope would be small indeed. But the raider had been Apache, the signs told him as much. And few if any Apache could find refuge with the other nations who had suffered too often at their hands. He would be forced to hide somewhere in Apache lands.

But why this raid? The tribes were generally at peace with one another. There was problem enough from the Americans. The Apache were being pressured more and more by the Mexicans and the Americans who moved into Apache lands and took parts of it for themselves. Perhaps someday soon there would be no more room in which to hunt and roam.

Traditionally, even in the ancient days when they first came down from the far north, the Apache had been raiders. Living as much from what they took from other tribes as what they hunted. And in the three hundred years since the Spanish had first arrived, the Apache had fought them as well as the succeeding Mexicans to a standstill, then raided their settlements as well.

But now the Mexicans had lost a war with the

Americans from the East. And the latter claimed ownership of the land, demanding that the remaining Mexicans and even the Apache knowledge their rule. A foolish desire as far as the Apache were concerned. A man did not own the land, he was a part of it—brother to the desert as well as the mountains. It was the way it had always been for the Apache, for he was as free as the land and the sky. For a man to try to claim the land, to stay in one small place without desire to roam at will and pour sweat into the dirt in order to raise food would be to place chains upon the spirit. And an Apache would rather be dead than be confined by chains.

The mind of Cochise ran over these things as he walked rapidly back to his rancheria. The raider was Apache but it was unlikely that he had the backing of his tribe in this venture. Flor de Oro was different from even the one or two other white women who lived with the Apache; her golden hair set her apart. All would know she was daughter to Cochise and to steal her would mean war with the Chiricahua.

No Apache chief had absolute rule over his tribe, and the majority would be against this raid unless the tribe wanted war with Cochise. Therefore this raider would have to be a renegade—living apart of his own chosing, or having been thrown out of his tribe for some reason.

Cochise stopped short as the answer came to him, causing the rest to murmur in surprise. He ignored them, thinking swiftly. The answer was simple. One man—a renegade Apache—was capable of defying Cochise, chief of the Chiricahua. One man had both the courage and the hatred. And he was unwelcome in any other Apache tribe as well because his unrelenting raiding and murder of the whites stirred hatred for all Apache and brought the bluecoats out constantly in punitive raids. Raids that always fell on the wrong Indians.

He nodded in decision and spoke the name aloud. "Lobo Negro!"

There was immediate agreement around him. The

warriors cast glances at each other and echoed his nod. "Lobo Negro!" The name went around them in a ripple.

The closest spoke to Cochise. "He was here five, perhaps six, days ago. When you were away. He was seen near the camp with three others, sitting on ponies and watching. When we came out, he ran away."

"Watching?" Cochise said.

The man nodded grimly. "They were watching the squaws. Flor de Oro was with them at the time. I remember."

Lobo Negro . . . A man as tall and as strong as Cochise himself. He was once a Chiricahua and might even have become a war chief, since he was intelligent and no one could question his courage or skill in battle. And as a raider, he had no peer. But only a few would follow him, misfits themselves, for he was thought to be possessed of a demon. He could explode with little or no cause and usually death would be the result.

No Apache feared death, and all would fight when necessary. But an Apache who fought without cause was a fool, for his death meant his squaws and children were left without a provider. There was no dishonor in avoiding a fight in which he was overmatched, or even in leaving one he was losing. Better to remain alive and try again when the odds were more in his favor.

Lobo Negro was different. He would fight at any time, for no reason other than the anger deep within him. Therefore, he was to be avoided.

Cochise moved on and at the camp he summoned all the warriors before his lodge. He told them of what he now knew and assigned runners to carry the news to all other Apache tribes. They were to know that it was now a duel to the death between him and the renegade. His honor demanded that Lobo Negro should die. There would be a reward of many ponies to those who found the hiding place of Lobo Negro. More if he were taken alive. For he, Cochise, chief of the Chiricahua, badly wanted the pleasure of that final fight for himself.

They had ridden for hours, a steady pace that only varied with the necessity of changing terrain or a rare pause on higher ground, which Flor de Oro knew was to search for signs of a chase behind them. The sun was hot overhead and burned her bare back in spite of years of living under it. Her bound wrists chafed, and being unable to brace herself in any manner to lessen the jarring movement of the horse under her caused the pain in her chest and stomach to increase unbearably. After a while, her brain began to cloud and she could no longer think clearly. It had taken all of her Apache courage not to cry out from the pain, and her mouth was salty with blood where she had bitten her lip.

The man mounted on the horse behind her was strong. In all the hours they had ridden his grip on her belt never loosened, and when she slipped, a combination of the movement of the horse and its sweaty back, he pulled her in place again without apparent effort. He seldom spoke, never to her, only to the warriors who surrounded him. And each time it was only a low, guttural command.

When the motion of the horse changed into a lunging walk, Flor de Oro forced her mind to clear enough to understand that they were climbing into mountains. A minute or so later he brought their mount to a halt and slid from its back. He pulled her down as well but allowed her to crumple to the ground at his feet, ignoring her as he moved away. Flor de Oro lay with her eyes closed, experiencing the hard ache in her stomach and chest where she had lain across the horse and knowing that worse was yet to come. The real agony would start when the blood began to circulate to her numbed legs and feet once more.

The pony was led away by another man, probably to water it, and she was left alone. Dimly, she heard the leader talking to the others, but sooner than she had expected, the stinging began in her lower body and quickly rose to a shriek. She fought the pain away, knowing she needed to remain aware of what was happening.

But she was forced to close her eyes and mind to the pain and with that, time slipped away. Later, when she opened her eyes once more, she was aware of a shape above her, blotting away the bright sun. She blinked her eyes and the shape moved, bathing her face with a cool, wet cloth. The sensation was wonderful and without thinking, she moved her head to place her mouth on its relief.

The cloth was taken away but returned immediately, much wetter. It was pressed against her lips and squeezed, allowing water to enter her parched throat. She sucked voraciously, afraid it would move again, and the water flowed down her throat too quickly, causing her to cough explosively.

"Gently, Flor de Oro," came an amused voice from the blur above. "I've gone to too much trouble for you to die before I have my reward."

The coughing helped to clear her mind and she found that she could focus her eyes once more. The blur was a man kneeling above her and with improved vision she recognized the warrior who had kidnapped her. The same cat smile was on his face.

He recognized her understanding and nodded in satisfaction before reaching behind him to wet the cloth again. Holding her mouth open with his fingers, he squeezed the cloth gently, and this time the water went down her throat without difficulty.

"How do you feel?" he asked when he stopped.

She didn't answer. With a clearing head the anger had returned, and hatred overcame the pain from her body. She glared at him.

But he only chuckled and playfully pushed her face to the side with his fingers. "The Flower has spirit. Good. That will make your conquest all the more interesting."

His chuckle faded as quickly as it came, his mouth slid into a crooked smile, and his dark eyes locked her own as he gripped her chin, forcing her to look at him. "That conquest will happen, Pretty Flower. Do not be in doubt of that. You now belong to me and will remain so for as long as I desire you. Fight if you will; I shall enjoy that as well."

She relaxed her straining neck muscles and rested her chin in his fingers. As she expected, he made the mistake of allowing his grip to loosen and a second later yelled with startled pain as her teeth sunk deeply into his hand.

He ripped it away and slapped her hard with the other, bringing tears to her eyes with the force of the blow.

But he had let her go and when her eyes cleared once more, she saw him squatting and holding the injured hand in his own mouth, sucking at the wound and eyeing her over it.

Flor de Oro noted with satisfaction that blood was seeping from the hand and staining his lips. And with greater satisfaction that the arrogant look was no longer in his face but was replaced with anger.

When he spoke, however, his voice was low and controlled. "Before I am through," he said from behind the hand in his mouth, "you will regret fighting me. You will crawl on your white belly to my moccasins and beg me to take you. Remember my words."

She spat at him.

He glared at her a moment longer before he stood up abruptly, dismissing her with his movement. But his moccasins made angry, twisting sounds on the hard ground as he stalked around her and out of her vision. She heard him call to another in a low voice and a moment later begin to converse in an even quieter tone. Flor de Oro rolled over to her other side, ignoring its effect on her bound wrists, and strained to hear.

He stood behind a large rock, and even though she stretched her muscles to the limit to raise her head, she could only glimpse a portion of his shoulder and back. And she could catch but a fragment of what he was saying. When she heard the word ambush, she knew this delay in the journey was for more than rest.

Evidently they were waiting to see if they were being followed and planned to do something about it here.

Then he moved out of sight and she relaxed to the ground again. Her captor knew who she was; he had called her name. Therefore he knew she was the daughter of Cochise and that he would not rest until she was retaken or his vengeance was satisfied. But then, she thought, this man had known that from the beginning and it hadn't prevented him from the raid. Who was he? And why had he taken such a foolish step? She shook her head; it made no sense.

He was too far away now to hear and it would be better for her to be as he left her. She rolled back to her original position and tested the bindings around her wrists halfheartedly. They were too tight to loosen as she expected, but then even if she were to get free she stood no chance of escape at the moment. Even if her legs worked well enough to run, the warriors had horses and could chase her down easily. She doubted if she could hide; they were Apache and also knew this country better than she. Her best course was to wait—wait for a time when the odds favored her more.

She closed her eyes to rest, but then a sudden thought occurred to her. She rolled over to press down on her right leg and felt with satisfaction the hard object under it. The man had not searched her, had not discovered the knife concealed in her moccasin; perhaps it hadn't occurred to him that a squaw would carry one there. Anyhow, it helped the odds. Perhaps he would make another mistake. She smiled thinly and hoped he would; it would be a great pleasure to cut his throat.

A few minutes later he was back and pulled her roughly to her feet. "Your chief has sent two trackers," he told her. "We now know this for certain. He expects them to discover where I have taken you. But I promise they will not be alive by morning. And when their bones are found, our trail will long have disappeared. You can forget Cochise from this moment, Flor de Oro. And the Chiricahua as well. None of them will ever hear of you again."

He waited for a reaction, but she kept her face turned from him, holding her head still but using her eyes to see if she recognized any landmark now that she was standing. Nothing was familiar. She memorized it all so that when she escaped she could find her way to return.

Her captor recognized what she was doing. With a grunt of anger, he stepped away and quickly returned with a cloth that he wrapped around her eyes and tied behind her head.

Flor de Oro waited, angry with herself for having allowed him to see what she was doing. A moment later, he knelt and cut the bonds around her legs. She felt a horse beside her and a hand gripped her thigh, just above the knee, another clasped her back and she was lifted astride the animal.

The leader mounted behind her, grasped her waist with one hand, and the horse began to move. Flor de Oro listened, straining, and could tell that fewer ponies were following them. Some had remained behind. She held a moment's sorrow for the warriors of her tribe who were tracking them, but quickly put it from her mind. They were Apache and would die as men. Perhaps they might even escape the ambush and report to Cochise. Either way there was nothing she could do about it. What would happen would happen, there was no need to dwell upon it.

This ride was done at a much slower pace than before. The ponies moved at not much more than a walk, and very often the labored straining of the animal between her legs indicated a hard climb. Even without that, she knew they were well within the mountains since they rode as often in shadow as in sunlight. Once, for a long period, they pushed through scrub pines, the long needles brushing against her legs in a prolonged whisper.

After leaving the pines, they climbed again steeply. The man behind her pushed her body almost to the horse's neck in an effort to aid it. A short level stretch and then they began a short twisting descent. Suddenly the sun disappeared completely from her skin and the sound of the pony's hooves echoed hollowly. She was in a cave of some sort, possibly a natural tunnel in the rocks.

It proved to be a tunnel as once again the warmth burst upon her and at the same time her mount broke into a halfhearted lope. The ride lasted only a short time before she could hear shouts of greeting. The man behind her let go of her belt and slid his hand up to remove her blindfold. "Home," he said. "Where even Cochise could never find you."

Flor de Oro blinked her eyes rapidly, and he waited patiently for her to clear them. When she could see, she found herself in a clearing of short grass and scrub. Flat land, but surrounded on all sides by steep cliffs making it the bottom of a bowl. Directly in front of her was a rancheria of a dozen or more brush huts. The few squaws and fewer children she could see had stopped whatever activity they were engaged in and gathered to welcome the arrivals with broad grins and much chatter.

One woman, a gray-haired old crone, approached the pony on which she was sitting. Her face was dark and seamed with age, but she retained all of her teeth and moved easily on thin legs.

"You have done as you said!" she cried to the rider behind Flor de Oro, grasping the halter around the horse's muzzle. "Who is greater than Lobo Negro? Not even Cochise, chief of the Chiricahua!"

Her captor chuckled and raised a hand to greet the rest. "Did I not tell you what I would do?" he boasted, loud enough for all to hear. "And have I not a prize worth taking? Stolen from under the nose of Cochise himself!"

The old squaw's eyes searched Flor de Oro's body from head to toe and returned once more to the man. "Too skinny!" she shouted, and slapped her leg in merriment at her joke. "This one will trip over her own bones!"

The man slid from his horse and then pulled Flor de Oro down to stand in front of him, before shoving her suddenly toward the crone. "Then feed her, old woman! Fatten my prize. For she will give me many nights of pleasure."

Flor de Oro stumbled from the unexpected push but quickly caught her balance and whirled to face him. But the old squaw was just as quick and grabbed her by the hair, yanking her head backward and straining her neck. "Ha!" she cried, reaching a claw to pinch her victim's naked breast. "This cow has bags too small to pleasure a mighty warrior. She's good only for work!"

"What do you know of pleasure, old woman?" he laughed. "Take her to my lodge and feed her as I said. Wash her as well so she will be ready for me. But—" he paused and his eyes mocked those of Flor de Oro. "Do not untie her until you are finished, I think. This one is not a cow. She's a snake and can strike very quickly."

The laughter on his face faded and he glanced down at his still wrapped right hand. "A snake," he repeated, and his mouth hardened. "It will be interesting to tame her."

The claw that had pulled at her breast dropped to one arm, the other remained in her hair, and Flor de Oro was propelled rapidly toward the ranchería. But then she was carried through it completely, past the wide grins and snickers of the women, and finally to a hut larger than the rest and set apart on the other side. At the low entrance, the old crone let go of her hair and pressed her head down, tripping her at the same time to make her fall forward into the hut.

She managed to keep her feet under her, however, and halfway across the dirt floor, spun to face her tormentor.

But the squaw had picked up a heavy stick propped just inside the hut and used to keep small animals out. She raised it and tapped it across her palm, grimacing with glee and leaning forward slightly. "So the snake will fight," she said harshly. "Try it, stupid one. Try it and feel my stick across your back."

By the time night came, she had been left alone in the hut for a long time. Inside, it was dark except where long flickering fingers of light entered through the open doorway from a small campfire a few paces away. From where Flor de Oro sat on some blankets in the rear of the lodge, she could see the old woman sitting cross-legged in front of the fire and alternating between dozing and rousing herself long enough to stir something she was baking in the ashes. Across from the woman were two warriors, sprawled full length and passing a clay pot of liquid back and forth between them. Probably the pot contained *tiswin*, although neither man showed the boisterous manner that usually accompanied the drinking of that brew.

Flor de Oro allowed her mind to play with the idea of escape. Leaving the hut would be simple. Using her knife, she could easily cut her way through the rear wall in a direction away from the camp. But she would not have time enough to get away, for every so often one of the warriors at the fire would rise and saunter over to peer into the hut at her. Obviously their leader had assigned them to guard duty. Her absence would be discovered by one in a short time, and the hunt would be on.

She decided to wait and face what she knew would happen soon. That the man the others called Lobo Negro, the Spanish name for Black Wolf, would come to claim his pleasure from her she had no doubt. He had made that clear in his boast to the others. Her first thoughts had been wrong, he hadn't captured her in order to claim ransom from Cochise. He'd done it from his own desire to prove his strength and cunning to his followers. Or even to himself; it made no difference in the end. He now considered her his possession, the same as a horse or a sheep he'd stolen in a raid. The only thing that stood between him and what he wanted from her was the knife she still had in her moccasin. The knife, and her own determination.

Only this morning, she suddenly remembered, she had felt doubts about the right of her Indian father to give her away to a man of his choosing. Conflicting

31

doubts caused by a long-ago memory of being a white girl-child. But she had no doubts about being taken against her will by a man who had no rights to her. No doubts at all. He would not find it easily done.

Her hands were free and as she watched the fire outside, she was grateful for that as she rubbed the wrists where the rawhide had cut into them. The old squaw had freed her after she had first been bathed and then had her hair combed. But the woman had growled to her that the warriors were outside and would come quickly to beat her if she made a move. Afterward she had been given food and ate eagerly. She had been hungry and not to eat just because she was in an enemy camp would be foolish. One cannot fight without strength.

When she finished the meal, the squaw brought her a shirt to put on. Not buckskin, but cloth, probably taken from the whites in a raid. She was glad she had it now, for the warmth of the fire did not penetrate into the hut.

She was alone, waiting on his blankets for the coming of Lobo Negro and a struggle in which she would kill him or be killed herself. Part of her was afraid, the part that was white she decided, the Apache in her could never fear death. Apaches believed that there was no life after death; individual life at any rate. One merely returned to the mother of life as a small stream joined a large river and lost its identity. Life does not end, it merely changes form and becomes part of another. She pushed the little bit of fear aside and prepared to fight. . . .

He arrived abruptly and the move was intentional. One moment she was staring at the fire and the next it was blotted out by his form crouched in the entrance. Flor de Oro made a startled reaction backward before she could stop herself and became immediately angry, because she knew that was what he hoped to provoke.

Her captor entered and stood upright. "So the Flower *can* show fear," he said softly. "Do not be afraid, pretty one. I tell you I will be gentle enough if you let me."

She didn't reply. Merely watched him closely and measured his strength. He was as she had first thought, as large a man as Cochise himself. The shoulders were as broad, the arms as thick, smooth in the Indian way with the muscles long. His chest may have been less deep but was wide nonetheless and it tapered to a narrow waist.

He wore only moccasins and a loincloth that was shorter than usual; it came only to his knees, and the muscles of his thighs were bare to either side. His long black hair lay loosely across his shoulders without a headband to hold it, and part hung in front to frame his face.

This face was slightly different from most Apaches', his chin was more square, jutting out like an overhanging cliff chiseled in rock, and the cheekbones were closer toward the front.

His eyes were deep-set and since they were in shadow with his back to the firelight, she couldn't read them at all. But the thin set to his mouth in spite of the softness of his words told her all she needed to know. There was no humor in the mouth—and no mercy.

"Are you not going to speak, Flor de Oro?" he asked, still in the same quiet tone. "No words of welcome for your new master as a squaw should?"

"You are the son of a dog," she told him levelly. "Your father was the beaver and you stink of the same smell."

He made a move with his shoulders and her head came up. "You can kill me," she told him. "But you will never be my master."

He nodded slowly. "We shall see, Flor de Oro. We shall see."

Then he did move, crossing to her and standing so closely that she was forced to move her head or have her face against his leg. His still bandaged hand reached down to caress her hair. She moved, and the hand closed in her hair and yanked her head back.

Flor de Oro reacted, reaching up to pull his grip free, but her hand never reached his wrist. She didn't see the blow coming, wasn't prepared for it. She felt only the explosion in her head as he slapped her hard across the face, driving her backward on the blankets.

As soon as she fell he was on top of her, his weight crushing her and one rock-hard knee pressing to get hers apart.

Flor de Oro's head rang with the force of the slap and she was dizzy. But still she fought. She tried to pull from under him, locked her legs and reached for his face with her fingers. But he blocked her arms, caught her wrists and pulled them together to hold them with one hand over her head, riding her thrashing body easily the while.

The steady pressure of his knee forced her legs to separate in spite of her struggles and he used his other leg to lock one of hers down. His knee began to punish the flesh of her inner thigh in an upward direction. The pain only increased her will to fight.

When his free hand began tugging at her belt to loosen it, his other slipped a little in its grip on her wrists. She jerked one arm free and brought her elbow down sharply against the side of his head.

He merely grunted from the blow and recaptured the wrist before returning to his attempt to free her belt. When he had it untied, he raised his weight to his top hand on her wrists and the knee on her thigh and ripped the skirt away, pulling it from beneath her and flinging it to one side.

Flor de Oro fought desperately; she was a writhing snake beneath his heavy weight. But he held her down and his free hand gripped her other thigh and pulled her legs apart.

She tried to butt his face with her head. He leaned away, out of reach.

She began to curse him as he fumbled with his own loincloth, his legs now between hers and holding them apart. Her breath came in short gasps from her labored breathing, and she used every ounce of it to curse him, first in Apache, then to her own surprise,

34

in English, a language she hadn't used since her childhood. It sounded strange to her own ears, but the words came easily as she called down the wrath of a God she had forgotten. She repeated the raving of her white father when his maddened brain had caused him to scream at the desert until his voice grew hoarse and spittle drooled from his lips.

Every muscle in her body was strained to its utmost, but the man still held her as he shifted his weight farther down in preparation. When he was in place, he let go of her wrists and dropped his hands to her hips in an effort to hold her still as he entered her. Quickly she bent her right knee and snatched her leg up beside him, her hand clawing for the top of her moccasin. As her searching fingers found the bone handle of the knife, she ripped it free and struck swiftly at his throat.

The man felt her movement in surprise, understanding it almost too late. He had only time to lift a shoulder and drop his head to protect his exposed throat.

The knife glanced across his shoulder and slashed his face, opening it from ear to chin. He yelled and threw himself away from her, rolling halfway across the hut before he stopped.

There he remained crouched for a moment, blood pouring from his face where the knife had laid it open. But only for a moment. With a scream of rage he dove for her and she dodged to one side and plunged the knife at his head.

She missed, and one steel hand locked her wrist. The weapon was sent flying across the hut as he charged her backward, falling upon her once more.

Flor de Oro fought with every ounce of strength she could muster, but she was tiring rapidly and was now struggling for air as well as from the weight of his heavy body.

Her attacker sensed her weakening and redoubled his own efforts until finally she could fight no more and he had his way at last, the free flowing blood from his face covering her own as he took her.

Chapter Three

Flor de Oro had lost count of the days that had passed since her arrival in the renegade camp. Most of them were best forgotten at any rate. The first few especially.

The man had returned for her the morning after he raped her, his face heavily bandaged from her knife wound and the blood-stained cloth wrapped completely around his head, making it difficult for him to talk. But he'd needed few words for what he intended. She was stripped of all clothing, her wrists were bound, and she was taken to a post planted near his hut and tied to a rope fastened to its top. Then as he and the men watched, the squaws beat her with sticks, getting in each other's way in their eagerness to strike at her.

It had taken her great effort not to cry out under the punishment. Several times she had passed out from the shock of the blows. Each time, however, they threw water on her, bringing her back to consciousness again, and continued the beating. Her body became a single bruise from neck to ankles before he stopped them. Afterward, she was left to hang there, drifting in and out of awareness throughout the day, her mind taking trips between the reality of the moment and fantasy of other times and places until at last it ceased to function at all. Dimly, she was aware of a great thirst the second day, and the pain in her arms overrode that of her back and legs. But she was given very little water, and no food at all. She could not remember being taken down.

When she had drifted back to understanding,

slowly at first, as if she were swimming upward through a heavy, clogging mist, she was once more in the hut and wrapped in his blankets.

Even then she could not steady her vision; objects—the entrance with daylight behind it, the man sitting beside her—were blurred. Double images that, try as she might, she could not bring together. Her body burned, as if she were being slowly roasted over a small fire. She moaned, the sound coming of its own accord, and she hadn't the will to stop it.

The man had moved at the sound. He crouched over her and wiped her face with a cool, wet cloth. A moment later the blanket was removed and he bathed her entire body slowly, wetting the cloth frequently. His touch was gentle and the coolness of the cloth a temporary relief wherever it touched.

When he finished, he covered her again and gave her some warm broth, holding a small bowl to her lips and supporting her head while she drank. He didn't speak, and when she awoke again he was gone, not to return.

Gradually she recovered and was able to dress herself and move about once more. As soon as she could stand without falling from the protest of her bruised legs, she was put to work. Small things at first, requiring little movement, and then as she grew stronger, heavier work was added.

The old squaw drove her in the work with shouts and more blows, kicking her when she staggered and fell under the load of wood or water she was forced to carry. But she was fed well and slowly her strength returned and her bruises, the ones the old crone didn't renew, began to fade.

Flor de Oro worked in silence, biding her time and ignoring both the curses of the squaw whose slave she had become and the taunts of the other women. Her face was full of a hatred that they well understood, however, and all of them kept their distance, abusing her with words only. She noted their reaction with satisfaction, aware that they were afraid of her. Even the old squaw made sure there was always a man close by when she used her stick.

Life in the rancheria was the same as any other; only its smaller size made it different from what she had known in the past years. There were no more than a dozen warriors and fewer squaws. The old woman, whose name she had yet to hear used, was the boss of the litter, and Flor de Oro decided that she was related somehow to Lobo Negro. Perhaps an aunt or a grandmother—she didn't think she was his mother. As for the leader himself, she didn't see him often, he stayed in the crone's hut for the better part of the day, moving her in with Flor de Oro.

She knew that arrangement wouldn't continue forever and understood that it had ended when the old squaw came in after darkness one evening and removed her own blankets with sly looks toward Flor de Oro. After the other woman had left, Flor de Oro sat on the blankets, trying to decide how best to fight him this second time. It would be even more difficult since she had not completely recovered, and even at her best she was no match for his strength.

But before she could make up her mind, he returned. This time his arrival was deliberate instead of abrupt. He squatted outside the entrance and looked at her for a long time before he entered.

Inside the hut he stood erect and looked down at her for a time, and in the dimness of the hut she could not read his face. It would have been difficult even in light, for one whole side of it was swollen so badly it distorted his appearance. The cut had been sewn closed—a painful process for him, she thought with pleasure—and then covered with a sticky clay that left the ends of the gut thread exposed.

As she watched, he reached up to touch his face with his fingertips while his eyes remained on her. Then slowly he moved over to squat with his face on a level with hers and with the closeness between them she could read his expression. There was anger in his look, but something else as well, something she didn't quite understand.

"So," he said, shattering the silence between them.

"You see you have left your mark on me."

He waited, but she neither answered nor looked away and finally he nodded, a barely perceptible movement of his head. "Had it been anyone else but you, no matter who, I would have killed them slowly. Do you know that?"

"Then kill me," she said.

"No. Whether you live or do not live is still my choice." He reached up to touch his cheek again thoughtfully. "This time I chose to punish you instead. And I will do that again, or worse, if you force me."

His dark eyes bore into hers, but she refused to look away from them. "I am the daughter of Cochise," she said. "You will have to kill me, for I will belong to no warrior except the one he has chosen for me."

"You are no longer a maiden," he said sharply. "No chief will accept a squaw he did not first claim, even the daughter of Cochise."

She didn't reply.

"Besides," he continued, "you are not an Apache. You are of the white blood. I knew that before I took you from Cochise. I knew all about you."

"I am the daughter of Cochise," she repeated. "None of the rest matters."

He shook his head. "No longer. You are only what I choose you to be. For as long as I desire it so. From this day on you will do as I say and become my squaw. My food alone you will cook and my moccasins alone you will mend. I have told it so to the others. And—" he paused significantly—"you will share my blankets."

He made a movement forward as he spoke the last and a spring coiled inside her.

Lobo Negro sensed the warning her body made and hesitated. "I will have my way with you no matter what you do to prevent it," he said, the edge returning to his voice. "You can only bring more pain to yourself."

She wanted to strike out at him, wanted it badly. But she understood the futility of fighting. She would lose to him, and more beatings would only delay her chance of escape. Slowly, she allowed the spring to uncoil. "You can do with me as you wish," she said instead. "But you still will not own me. And your life will never be safe as long as you allow me to live."

He nodded, his eyes glittering. "I understand that," he said. "And perhaps what is between us will make you all the more interesting."

She watched his face a moment longer, then suddenly turned on the blankets, twisted her legs around straight, and lay down with her arms at her sides to stare at the top of the hut.

She didn't move as he joined her on the blankets and began to stroke her body gently.

Mangas Coloradas, the chief of the Mimbreno Apache, was a man who had seen many summers. But his back remained straight and he moved his huge body easily on strong legs that gave no indication of his years. He stood, as courtesy required, at the edge of his camp and waited to greet his guests.

Cochise, chief of the Chiricahua, had asked for this council, but in deference to the age of Mangas Coloradas, and the respect in which he was held by all Apache, the meeting was to be held in his camp. The old chief waited, his arms folded across his enormous chest, and spoke words of welcome as each chief and subchief approached. All had promised to attend and since to an Apache his word was sacred, all arrived in the space of one hour.

There was Delgagito, the slender; Pounce; El Chico; Pedro Azul; Coleto Amarillo; and Cuchillo Negro as well as others less well known. Chiefs who had fought with and against each other but were now all at peace. Last came Cochise, and Mangas turned and walked with the chief of the Chiricahua back to the council circle formed in front of his lodge in the center of the Mimbreno camp. As host, he had his squaws pass around cigarettes—tobacco rolled tightly in oak leaves. The peace pipe was not the Apache way. They would smoke it at meetings with other Indians who offered it but only in deference to their hosts, much preferring tobacco in cigarette form.

When all were settled, and the small talk out of the way, Mangas nodded at Cochise, who immediately stood up to speak. The rest grew quiet and gave him their full attention.

"I have asked for this council to appeal for your help," Cochise said. "As you know, my daughter who was called Flor de Oro has been stolen from me. That she was once of the Americans is well known also. But she chose to remain with the Chiricahua and I caused it to be said that she was to be my daughter, the same as if she was of my blood."

Nods went around the circle but they remained quiet, waiting for him to continue.

"Now," he said, "the name of Cochise is shamed. I had promised her to Ko-koch-ne of the Mimbreno in order to make closer bonds between us. But before this marriage could take place, Flor de Oro was stolen from me by the outlaw Lobo Negro."

He paused and his mouth tightened. "This outlaw is now my sworn enemy. The honor of Cochise, chief of the Chiricahua, requires that I kill him. This I shall do. I will not rest until I meet him in battle."

Again they looked at each other and nodded. Cochise waited for the agreement to his words to be completed.

"But," he continued, "Lobo Negro hides like a snake from my anger. He knows of my intentions and he hides from me as a coward. Therefore I ask your help; not in my fight, but only to help me to find him. As the Chiricahua have been willing to aid you in your battles—" He stopped and looked at the young war maker, Geronimo, who had lost his entire family to a Mexican ambush at Kas-ki-yeh and then led three tribes back to exact a terrible revenge. "So now I ask that this help be given me."

He was finished and sat down for their discussion. Geronimo looked across the circle at him. "Does Cochise know the outlaw is still in Apache land?"

Cochise nodded. "That is my belief. I also know

that his raids on the whites cause all Apache great trouble. We have signed peace treaties with the Americans and we have kept our word and raided only below the border. But the Americans do not understand that Lobo Negro and others like him are outlaws from our tribes. They blame us and bring their revenge against peaceful Apache. Even as we talk in this council, they call on the bluecoat soldiers to make war against us until we are no more.''

His last remarks brought on a round of discussion. The growing strength of the Americans was a source of worry to all Apache. It was much later that the talk returned to his request. But all agreed. They would search for the hiding place of Lobo Negro and his band of outlaw Apache, and any movement the renegade made in their territory would be reported immediately to Cochise.

Later, when the feast prepared for his guest was served by the squaws of Mangas Coloradas, a warrior who had sat in the third rank found occasion to slip away. Lobo Negro, he thought, would be very interested in what had taken place and would pay well for the information.

The spy did not know the location of the hiding place of Lobo Negro, but he did know a white man who dealt with him on a regular basis, for he had accidently observed one such meeting and hung around for days after to satisfy his curiosity.

He would inform the American that he had a message and then wait near the town, but out of sight, for the outlaw to come to him.

Flor de Oro knelt before the pot of cooking meat she was preparing for Lobo Negro's evening meal and peered into its contents. The stew was almost done. She glanced up to see if the crone was watching—the other never allowed her out of sight except in the night when Lobo Negro shared her blankets—and saw that her back was turned for a moment. Quickly she spat into the pot. Then, satisfied with her small revenge, she reached for another stick to add to the fire beneath.

But the squaw had turned in time to see her act. With a howl of anger she grabbed her stick and swung it hard, striking Flor de Oro across the shoulders.

She swung again, screaming the while, but Flor de Oro dodged and suddenly realized the two of them were alone. The nearest warrior was over a hundred steps away. She pretended to stumble as she dodged the old squaw's swinging advance, then as the stick completed an arc, suddenly charged herself.

The crone was caught by surprise as Flor de Oro's body struck her in the side and the two of them went sprawling. Flor de Oro scrambled on top, grabbed her tormentor's gray hair in both hands and began savagely slamming her head against the ground.

The squaw screamed for help, fear a live thing now in her voice, and Flor de Oro shifted her grip to her throat. The cries were shut to a choking gasp. A moment more and her enemy would be dead.

She didn't have a moment left. The others had come running at the first cry and the hard body of a warrior, thrown at full tilt, knocked her away from her victim.

She rolled under him in an attempt to get free, but he locked a hand in her shirt to hold her, then began beating her with his other.

She didn't hear the command that stopped him, so busy was she trying to protect herself from the blows aimed at her head. But when he stopped, she followed his angry stare to its cause. The man was glaring at Lobo Negro, standing a dozen feet away with a rifle aimed at his chest.

"She must be taught a lesson!" the warrior shouted hoarsely.

Lobo Negro's reply was measured, but the command in his voice was evident. "The squaw belongs to me," he said. "You were told only to guard her."

The warrior hesitated, but the steadiness of the rifle convinced him and he finally lowered his upraised arm. Still, his grip remained on her shirt, holding her halfway off the ground. His head slowly revolved to look at the rest who had come to watch, and anger and embarrassment were evident in his face. "The great Lobo Negro is weak!" he shouted. "Because the squaw slave has hair like straw he thinks she should not obey or be punished. She makes a woman of him!"

Lobo Negro leaned to prop the rifle against a low bush, then covered the distance to where the other stood in a few long strides. His hand slipped a knife from his belt easily and the anger on his face matched the warrior's. "Draw your knife," he said curtly. "We will find out who is the woman."

The Apache holding her looked at the knife, then back to Lobo Negro's face as he measured his chances for a moment before making up his mind. Then he suddenly shoved her away from him and stalked stiff-legged away, his back toward them.

The old squaw still lay where Flor de Oro had left her, moaning with exaggerated pain. But Lobo Negro hardly gave a glance to her before his still angry eyes returned to Flor de Oro. "Come with me!" he snapped. And spun on his heel.

She followed, knowing that she had no other choice and feeling only regret that she had not had time to kill the old woman.

He led her to where the ponies were hobbled, pausing only once on the way to pick up a lariat hanging from the corner of a hut. The rest of the camp followed them both at a short distance.

Lobo Negro reached the nearest pony and bent swiftly to remove its hobble before turning to her. "Put out your hands," he ordered.

Flor de Oro stretched them toward him, her head up so that she could meet his still angry gaze squarely. He looped one end of the lariat around her wrists and pulled it tight. Then with a final glare at her, he bounded aboard the horse, grabbed its mane with one hand, and abruptly sent the animal into a startled run with his heels in its side.

The lariat tightened and nearly jerked her from her feet in spite of her anticipation of what was to happen. She was forced to run as fast as she could to keep from falling.

Round and round the camp he went, riding at a pace that drew every ounce of determination she possessed to keep from pitching forward and being dragged. That he intended that to happen eventually, she knew without a doubt. But she had no time to think, she could only concentrate on keeping her driving legs under her and dodging the obstacles he deliberately drew her toward.

He twisted the running pony around a high bush, holding the lariat in a manner that pulled her through it and caused its hard limbs to scratch her body cruelly. Then he did a quick turn on the pony, allowed the rope to slacken as he swept past her, and snatched it forward again. Flor de Oro stumbled as she whirled to keep up, only dimly hearing the shout of anticipation from the onlookers through the blood pounding in her ears.

Again he made the maneuver, and this time she did fall. And the unforgiving lariat dragged her turning and twisting on the ground for several paces before he pulled up only enough to allow her to climb stumbling to her feet once more.

He kept it up, riding in a circle around the camp until she began to fall with regularity. Each time she did, he would pause after dragging her a few yards and allow her to get up again. Then the run would begin all over.

Finally, when she could no longer run, only reel a few steps and fall, he let her lie and trotted the pony back to look down at her from it. His form above her shimmered in the sun and the ground seemed to heave under her, but she heard him ask, "Are you ready *now* to surrender, Flor de Oro?"

She twisted on the ground, rolling with the agony of getting breath. But she shook her head.

The lariat on her wrists tightened and she braced for its pull again. But then it slackened. Instead, he slid from the pony and dropped to one knee to gather her in his arms. Although they had stopped a distance from his hut, he carried her without apparent effort, holding her limp body against his chest and taking long strides. As they passed through the camp, he ignored the muttering that swirled around their passage, ignored it except for an angry glance for one squaw who dared to get in his path momentarily. At the hut, he squatted and crab-walked through the entrance to keep from putting her down before he reached the blankets on the other side.

There he left her, returning moments later with a water skin that he held to her lips with one hand while supporting her head with the other. "Drink only a little," he said. "More will make you sick."

Flor de Oro sipped the water, and he waited patiently until she had removed her mouth before allowing her head to lie back. He waited another moment and gave her a second drink; then he lay the skin aside and sat cross-legged beside her.

Her muscles were so tired her entire body was trembling, the legs jerking uncontrollably. He glanced down at them, moved closer where he could reach her better, and began to massage her legs slowly from knee to hip. As he worked, he kept his face toward hers to study her. "You understand I had no choice but to punish you," he said suddenly. "Had you killed Ta-ne-dako I would have had to let them kill you."

She couldn't answer, in part from exhaustion but also because of the unexpected change in his manner. His strong hands on her thighs brought a great deal of relief to her strained muscles and she was almost grateful to him. Almost . . . She fought away the feeling.

He completed his massaging of her legs and allowed one hand to gently rub her stomach, which was still moving rapidly up and down from her efforts in running. "Even now, not to run you to death weakens me in their eyes," he continued in a low, almost whispered tone. "They do not understand. But they do not know of what I feel. What the fire that burns within you does to me. Flor de Oro without that fire . . ." He allowed it to drop softly.

Even through the effort of breathing, she was fascinated by the light in his eyes as he looked at her. It showed a side of him she had never seen. And didn't understand.

"I do not wish to hurt you more," he said, moving his hand up to caress her face, tracing his fingers over her lips softly. "Give me your word you will not fight with any of them again."

She could only watch his face with amazement.

"Give me your word, Flor de Oro," he said again. "And I will see that you are left in peace."

She summoned the effort to speak. "I . . . will never . . . belong to you . . ." she gasped.

He shook her words away, a rueful movement of his head from side to side. "I am speaking now of saving your life, Flor de Oro," he said. "If you fight with them, injure one of them, I must kill you. Do not make me do that, beautiful one."

"I . . . will not fight them," she said, lost in the dark eyes that probed her own.

He nodded and smiled, the scar on his face twisting with the movement. For a long time he was silent, looking at her. "The other will come," he said finally. "I am warrior enough for even Flor de Oro."

Then he rose and left the hut.

In the town of Tucson, Milton Sattersfield owned a large warehouse and a house for himself that gave indication of his wealth. The house was often the center for gatherings of the better class of Tucson, but Sattersfield found it convenient at times to depart the town and visit a Mexican who worked for him and lived in a barely habitable mud-brick ranch house a mile or so outside of town. The Mexican's name was Ramon and he was a very discreet man. Each time his employer arrived unannounced, he would be very polite and welcome him as if the visit were expected. He would order his fat wife to prepare a meal for their guest, serve his best wine, the wine his employer gave him and which he never dared drink himself, and afterward apologize profusely for the unfortunate fact that urgent business called him to his brother-in-law's house a few miles down the road.

He would be told by his guest not to worry about it, that the other intended only to rest a few minutes and return to town himself. Then Ramon and his wife would both climb on the back of his mule and ride away into the darkness. Ramon did not fully understand what his employer's need for his home was, but since Sattersfield paid him two dollars a week for very little work and had a reputation of being very harsh with people who pried into his business, the Mexican found it easy not to be curious. He merely understood that he should play the host and leave for the night. And he did, paying absolutely no attention to his fat wife's grumbling the while.

After he was gone, his employer helped himself to another cup of wine and sat down in a wooden, homemade chair on the low porch to wait. But this time, Sattersfield's eyes narrowed quickly as he detected movement in the quarter moon's dark a short distance from the house almost as soon as he settled himself.

His hand slid down to loosen the large single-action revolver strapped to his leg and remained in place holding the butt. A second later, he drew it to aim it at the man approaching from the dark. "Hold it right there," he ordered tensely.

The Indian stopped, raised both hands with the palms out, and waited.

"Who the hell are you, Injun?" Sattersfield wanted to know in English. "What do you want here?"

"Friend," came the reply in a low voice. "Me talk."

"I don't know you, you thieving snake," Sattersfield growled. "So I don't want to talk to you. Get your red ass out of here before I put a hole in it."

"Me talk," repeated the Indian.

Sattersfield thumbed the hammer back, the click audible in the night stillness with the force of a gunshot. But the man standing before him refused to flinch.

The American hesitated. He had no compunction

about shooting an Indian; he'd done just that several times. In fact, when he'd first come to the territory as a young man he'd made a great deal of money by selling ambushed Apache scalps to the Mexicans at one hundred pesos for an adult male, fifty for a female, and twenty-five for a child's. But when the Army began building forts in the territory and began to negotiate peace treaties with the Apache, he'd found it even more profitable to freight in supplies for the troops at inflated prices. He'd grown rich at it, and it was far less dangerous.

No, he didn't mind shooting the Indian, but he figured the Apache understood that and wasn't scared. There had to be a reason for his confidence. Maybe he had a dozen more of the bastards hidden out there with rifles trained on Sattersfield. Which wasn't a good thought at all.

"Come here," he said, to gain time to think this through. He lowered his revolver to show his peaceful intention if anyone else were watching but kept it trained on the man before him nevertheless.

The Apache moved. He stopped again a few feet from the edge of the wooden porch. "Me talk," he said.

"Then talk, dammit!"

The Indian spoke rapidly in Apache, so rapidly it was a moment or so before Sattersfield could get a hand up to stem the flow. "Wait a minute, you blasted savage! I don't speak that lingo! Understand? No savvy!"

The Indian shrugged. "Me talk Lobo Negro," he said in English. "Him, me talk."

Sattersfield felt the hair on his neck rise. How in hell did this red bastard know about his deal with Lobo Negro? It had always been strictly between the two of them—an agreement made between two men who despised each other but found it mutually profitable. And the outlaw Indian had assured him that he didn't even tell his own followers why he came to see Sattersfield.

"I don't know what the hell you're talking about,"

he growled. "I don't know any Injun named Lobo Negro."

The Apache paid no attention. He turned and pointed behind him. "Me wait. You talk Lobo Negro. Sun come, me talk Lobo Negro." He made a circling gesture with both hands. "Big rock." One hand rose and made a chopping motion. "*Dos* rock. Me wait."

He turned suddenly and disappeared into the shadows.

Split rock. Sattersfield knew the spot the Indian meant—a huge boulder that had separated of its own weight centuries ago and now lay with its inner sides an almost perfect V. It was a quarter day's ride from here. An ambush? No . . . the renegade was too smart for them to warn him in advance, too smart to fall into such an obvious trap. The visitor had to be one of Lobo Negro's spies . . . or hoped to be.

But dammit, how did he know of this meeting place? Did the whole damn Apache nation know? Sattersfield decided he'd raise hell with the outlaw about that. Then decided he wouldn't. Lobo Negro was a dangerous man, with a raw temper. Someday, when he no longer had a use for him, he'd kill the Indian. But he'd make damn sure he had enough guns to back him when the time came. He settled back down to wait. However, the cup of wine beside his chair was forgotten and the wait was a long one. The quarter moon passed completely overhead and out of sight behind the ranch house before Lobo Negro appeared.

Chapter Four

There were two of them, athletic-looking even though they squatted on the ground. Long black hair flowed down their backs and was held out of their faces by brightly colored headbands. They crouched motionless in the center of a circle of soldiers, their arms bound behind them, and stared back at him without emotion. It was David's first time to meet an Apache up close since his arrival at Fort Buchanan and he inspected them with deep curiosity.

The best guerrilla fighter in the world, Harrison had told him. He could disappear in the desert right before your eyes, climb among the rocks and impossible cliffs of the mountains like a mountain goat, and strike at you when and where you least expected it. A man as tough as the desert he called home, who neither asked for nor gave quarter in a fight.

The soldiers kept their rifles trained on the two captives and looked at them expectantly, waiting for the order to do what they would already have done if the lieutenant hadn't ridden up at that moment with the rest of the troopers. David understood their look, but the thought of the cold-blooded murder of two bound and helpless men appalled him. His troopers were, for the most part, a sorry lot. Many were raw immigrants who still had a great deal of trouble with the language, and the rest were misfits who used the Army as security from having to make it on their own—or to hide from the law. He understood that he must be a hard disciplinarian to maintain control of such men. There were limits to how far he was willing to go, however, and murder was not within those limits. He didn't share the prevailing sentiment that an Indian's life was worth no more than a coyote's. Not yet, anyway.

He was on a routine mission from the Fort, a reconnaissance trip designed as much to familiarize himself and some of the newer men with the territory as to patrol the area protected by them. He had split his command a few hours before, taking Harrison with him and putting the rest under Corporal Tanner, an experienced soldier. They were to meet again at this location, and he had ridden up just as Tanner's men were about to execute the two captured Indians.

Tanner had hesitated only long enough to offer a terse report: "Two Apache, Lieutenant. We caught 'em carrying Army rifles." Then he turned to raise a hand to his men.

But David had stopped him with a short command.

After a long look at the Indians, he turned in his saddle to Harrison sitting beside him. The scout was watching him with a sardonic expression, and David knew the frontiersman was aware of how he felt. And obviously thought him foolish for thinking it. "Talk to them," David told him, ignoring both the other's look and the fact that the back of his neck was turning red. "Find out what you can."

Harrison held his gaze a moment longer and then shrugged and slid from his horse. He walked to within a few feet of the Apache as the rifles of the troopers lowered with disgust. On impulse, David followed him.

The scout began to speak in their language, a series of guttural pronouncements accompanied by hand signals. One of them replied at length, and Harrison spoke in English to David without turning. "Says both of 'em are Army scouts, Lieutenant. Got the rifles that way."

"What are they doing here?" David asked. "You ever see them before?"

Before Harrison could reply, the Indian spoke. "Defiance," he said in English, slurring the word. "Scout for that Fort." He nodded at his companion.

"Him, me."

For a moment, David thought he caught a hint of pleading in the dark eyes. But only a hint.

"What are you doing here?" he asked the man.

The Indian shrugged. "Come home," he said. "Soldiers no want no more. Sign treaty with Navajo."

David glanced at Harrison to get his reaction to the Apache's words, but to his irritation, the half smile had returned to the scout's face. "Could be telling the truth," he said softly. "Army has been using some Apach for scouts. Only way you can track 'em is to use another Apach to do it."

"Do you believe him?" David wanted to know.

Harrison cocked his head and shrugged. "Mebbe, mebbe not. It don't seem like the Army would let 'em keep good rifles if they had been fired though, does it?"

"Them devils are lying, Lieutenant," Tanner cut in. "They either stole those guns or bushwhacked some troopers to get 'em. Let's shoot the bastards and be done with it!"

David ignored him, his gaze fastened on the Indian who had spoken. Then he noticed that both captives had locked their eyes on him alone and decided that the other spoke enough English to understand. He had a problem. If he brought the captives to the Fort, his men would think him too soft and would be that much harder to lead. But dammit, he couldn't order helpless men shot!

He made his decision. "Bring them with us, Corporal," he ordered Tanner curtly. Then he turned and mounted his horse.

Later, as they rode in the direction of the Fort, he spurred his mount forward to catch Harrison, who rode alone a few yards before the column. The scout acknowledged his presence with a nod but kept his eyes on the landscape ahead of them. They rode in silence for a few minutes as David couldn't quite think of what he wanted to say.

Before he could, Harrison beat him to it. "You made a mistake back there, Lieutenant," he said

53

quietly.

"Why? Because I didn't murder two men?" David demanded. "What's the rush? If they're guilty they can be punished at the Fort after a trial. Why kill them without an attempt to discover the truth first?"

The scout glanced at him briefly. "Because out here you ain't got time for all them things, Lieutenant. You got to make your mind up quick or you liable to get yourself shot for delaying. Back East you got time for trials and investigations. When you fight Indians, you ain't."

"They were captives," David argued, becoming irritated with himself for doing so.

Harrison nodded in agreement. "Yeah, but now those two have you marked. They think you're soft for saving their lives. If it had been them with rifles at your head, you think they would have hesitated?"

He turned to give David a full look. "And your troopers think the same thing right now. Most of them troopers ain't worth a rattlesnake's bite as men, but they can fight when they have to. Only now they won't be very damn anxious to follow you into one."

David didn't answer and Harrison allowed the silence between them to continue for a moment. Then he raised an arm and pointed. "Fort's in that direction," he said. "But swing your men clear of that canyon yonder. Think I'll ride up on the rim for a look-in before I catch up with you again."

He started to lift his reins and then hesitated for a fraction. "Two Injuns ain't worth the price you just paid, Lieutenant," he said, and rode off leaving David to ponder his words.

The Indians were concealed just beyond the area where the trail emerged from under the shadow of a canyon wall. The choice of location for an ambush was deliberate. They already knew the Americans were well armed. Two guards, probably sharpshooters, rode on either side of the coach. The guards would be especially alert as the coach passed under the canyon wall with its myriad of hiding places. But the waiting Apache understood human nature and knew the guards, no matter how alert, would have a great tendency to relax with relief the moment they passed from the obvious danger zone. In that moment, the attackers would strike.

Lobo Negro lay in the shadow of a rock with his rifle ready. The rock was not large enough to conceal his entire body, but he'd taken care of that by covering his lower limbs with brown dust, rubbing it into both his skin and moccasins until they blended with the dirt. He lay motionless, his hearing attuned for the sound of approaching horses but his mind venturing over his problems.

Stealing the golden-haired one had caused bigger trouble than he had anticipated. He'd expected to become the deadly enemy of Cochise, and powerful as the Chiricahua were, he'd been willing to take the chance. But he had not expected Cochise to be able to stir *all* Apache against him; that thought had not even occurred to him. A serious mistake, it limited his ability to travel readily, restricting him for the most part to night movement and banning him completely from the use of any trails where he might accidentally meet other Indians. He was forced to get from one place to another through country so rough that the majority of Apache avoided it altogether.

The moment he was spotted by any Apache, no matter what the tribe, he found that he was trailed and knew that a messenger was dispatched to summon Cochise. He was forced to use all of his cunning to throw them off in time to avoid a confrontation with the Chiricahua chief. Or, if that failed, to kill them. Cochise was relentless, and Lobo Negro knew he would never give up the search. His only hope was to distract him to more pressing things.

But this latter need fitted in well with Lobo Negro's agreement with the American. He was intelligent enough to understand the motives of the trader—these attacks on the whites he carried out were to stir the settlers to absolute hatred for all Apache. Hatred and fear. Then they would scream to their government for more and more of the blue-coated soldiers. Soldiers who had to build forts to be supplied by Sattersfield and the rest. That trade made them rich. Lobo Negro understood what they were doing, and that the Apache nations suffered in the fights with the soldiers caused by his raids. But he was not a part of the tribes and owed them nothing. What happened to the rest was of no concern to him. In his mountain hideout he could continue to raid forever, even after the Apache were destroyed. For if Cochise and the rest could not find him there, what chance would the Americans have?

So a raid like the one he was about to make would divert Cochise. The man traveling in the coach, according to Sattersfield, was of some importance to the Americans, an official of some kind. His death would send them into a rage. Perhaps this time they would begin an all-out war against the Apache nations, and Cochise would have his hands too full to continue his search for the golden one.

Thought of her made the still healing flesh of his face itch, but he didn't move to touch it. And a mental picture of her in his blankets made his loins ache. Even though she lay like a stone each time he took her, he could sense the fire burning beneath him. That it was hatred was no matter. In time, she would tire of resistance and become his true squaw; and then that fire would burn bright for him. It was a time to anticipate.

His ears picked up a distant sound and he shifted his mind back to the present. His eyes found the warrior he had posted exactly opposite his own position, met with the man's briefly, and returned to the spot in which the approaching riders would appear.

His expectation of their moves was entirely correct as the coach and its guards rode out from under the threat of the canyon wall. The rider on Lobo Negro's side even turned in his saddle for a last glance behind him. Lobo Negro fired at that moment, and his bullet caught the rider in the side of his head and pitched him backward, his weapon flying.

Simultaneously the warrior across from him shot the other rider, but the man wasn't killed immediately. He fell from his horse, rolled through the dirt, and came up shooting. A shower of bullets and arrows from the hidden Apache cut him down quickly.

The driver of the coach had been slow to react. At the first crack of a rifle, his head had snapped around to the man Lobo Negro shot and he'd twisted desperately to the other side as the firing began on his left. Only then had it occurred to him to whip the horses into a run in a frantic attempt to flee.

Two Apache appeared from nowhere to grasp the harness on the lead horses in a running leap and then let their swinging weight force the animals to a dragging stop. The driver clawed with both hands for the pistol strapped to his leg, but before he could clear the weapon, an Apache arrow pierced his throat and he toppled from his high seat.

The Indians converged on the coach as one of its two occupants emerged from the interior with a revolver in his hand. He jumped to the ground and fired at the nearest warrior at the same time. His bullet knocked the running man down and the American whirled toward another. Lobo Negro killed him from a distance with a carefully placed shot.

The sudden silence was broken only by a plaintive wail from the remaining man in the coach. "Oh m-God," it said. "Oh m-God . . . oh m-God!" Each cry rose higher than the last.

The Apache surrounded the coach and through its wide-open dust flaps could see him sitting in the middle of the rear seat—a short, fat man in a strange-looking suit and an even stranger small-brimmed round hat. His eyes were wide, and sweat poured from his chubby face as he stared back at them.

Lobo Negro motioned and a warrior went in after the victim. The man screamed with fright as he was tossed out to fall rolling on the ground. He staggered to his feet and gave another, louder cry as the nearest grinning Indian slashed his fat behind with a long knife. The cut was intentionally not deep, but blood quickly stained his tight trousers.

Shouting Apache surrounded him with knives flashing, and the terrified victim's screams reached impossible heights as he dodged away from one cut only to back into another.

They continued the sport for over an hour, slashing him only deeply enough to bring blood without damaging his ability to run. The fat man's screams became insane and when exhaustion finally set in, a mindless babble. The Apache finished the job slowly, leaning over his writhing body on the ground and jostling one another with their efforts to find an uncut spot.

Finally they could no longer draw a response and looked to their leader, who had been watching from near the coach. Lobo Negro motioned for one of them to retrieve the man's hat and bring it to him and then, holding it in his hand, he approached the body and knelt beside it. There was still a faint bubbling coming from the man's lips, but his eyes were wide and lacked intelligence. Carefully, Lobo Negro placed the hat on the victim's head, jamming it down so that it would stay.

He smiled with satisfaction when he stood up. The gesture of the hat was first begun by Mangas Coloradas, chief of the Mimbreno, several years before. Since no Apache ever wore a hat, it signified that a body with one on its head was an enemy to them. If the fat man had been important to the Americans, placing the hat would raise them to a frenzy.

Afterward, he gave orders for the coach horses to be turned loose. He would have liked to have taken them with him for their meat, but with all Apache looking for him, the horses would make his movements too visible. That fact still angered him, but perhaps now it would not last much longer . . .

After he had reached the Fort with his prisoners, David had turned them over to the guard and written a report of the incident for Colonel Markham, the Fort commander. The latter had processed a request to Fort Defiance without comment, but David had read the disapproval in his eyes. Obviously the commander had agreed with Corporal Tanner and the troopers that the Apache should have been shot on the spot, no matter what regulations said.

Even when the word came back, two weeks later, that the two Apache had been telling the truth and were allowed to retain the rifles for future duty, the hostility from his troopers didn't lessen. The two Apache were released from the guardhouse and even taken on as scouts for Fort Buchanan. They were given a tent and camped just outside the Fort area, but their presence, David decided, only served to remind his men of the incident. He wished to hell they had been sent away.

It was quite obvious that everyone from the colonel to the mess cooks thought he had mishandled the affair. No one besides himself, and the possible exception of Doctor Henley, the post surgeon, and Harrison, gave any indication of considering the Indians as human beings. The scout camped outside the Fort himself and was often seen talking with the two Apache. But he had disagreed with the decision to save their lives, and David was beginning to wonder if he had been right all along.

Harrison's opinion didn't keep him from visiting David in his quarters in the evenings, however. He came two or three nights a week just to talk and with their discussions David began to acquire a knowledge of the territory that his fellow officers did not yet grasp. They talked about the history of the area and its possible future. Harrison spoke of the growing number of sheep herders and cattle raisers and predicted that after the Indians were gone, the two would finally clash over the grazing land. He spoke of the gold and silver that might someday be found there and only grinned when David mentioned Quivira.

"Why don't you go ask Cochise?" he inquired with a chuckle. "He might just lead you to it. Or for that matter, ask that Apache whose life you saved. Notice the way that Injun looks at you when he sees you?

Ain't often an Apach takes a shine to a white man, but when he does, he makes a hell of a good friend. That feller thinks you're tall medicine in his book."

David hadn't noticed and passed it off, thinking instead of something else Harrison had said. "What do you mean, after the Indians are gone?" he asked.

Harrison's smile faded. "The Apach way of life started to end the day we showed up," he said quietly. "They're doomed. We're going to kill all of them eventually."

"What about the reservations we're trying to set up?" David wanted to know. "Won't they work?"

Harrison shook his head. "Mebbe they would work with some Injuns, Lieutenant. But not with the Apach. He's too proud to be tied down in a small place and hand-fed by somebody else. He's had hundreds of years of being lord of this land and having everybody—Pinas, Navajo, Spanish, Mex—just about everybody, scared to death of him. About the only people he's come into contact with up to now who wasn't scared of him would be the Comanche. But they stay in the plains where good horsemanship makes them equal in fighting ability. They know better than to come down in the desert or these mountains. Both of these belong to the Apach and the rest know it. At least everybody did before we came."

"You don't think there's room for both us and the Apache?"

Harrison shifted his weight in the chair, settled into a more comfortable position, and shook his head slowly. "One day there'll be too many Americans, Lieutenant. They will all want land, and all of them will hate the Apach for being on it. They won't be satisfied until the Apach is completely wiped out."

"That's not going to happen," David said. "The Army's job is—" He was interrupted by a loud knock at his door.

He got up to open it and was confronted by a smiling Captain Henley. "Saw that walking pile of diseased buckskin headed your way earlier, David," he chuckled. "Decided I might like to join you for some of his lies." He held up a bottle of trader whiskey. "Even brought along the refreshments."

She had promised him she would not fight the others and the promise was worthwhile, for he kept his word and the rest of the camp left her in peace. Even Ta-ne-dako kept her distance, if not her silence. But Flor de Oro hadn't promised not to escape, would never make that promise, and the thought occupied most of her days. She went about her chores in his behalf as if she were truly his squaw, mending, cleaning, cooking, all done in silence whenever possible. Within a short time, shorter than she had hoped, the rest began to pay little attention to her and she found she could travel farther and farther from the camp without raising undue alarm.

On one such trip, going with some of the squaws and a few older children to gather berries, she discovered the key she was looking for. They were in a sparse patch of woods where the bushes were thickest, gathering both berries and acorns, when Lobo Negro and four others rode by them.

The other squaws hardly acknowledged their passing, caring only for the fruits of their return from a raid. But Flor de Oro watched carefully. She looked around and found herself a distance from the women and alone as usual. Quickly she stepped behind a large shrub, waited a moment to see if she would be noticed, and when she wasn't, followed the horsemen.

They were riding slowly, she had only to trot to keep up, dodging at the same time to stay hidden. In a few minutes, they rounded a protuberance in the wall and disappeared. When she reached the same spot, she stopped in amazement. The warriors were nowhere to be seen. Only after a closer search did she find the opening, a narrow slit in the rock that was almost obscured by a close-growing tree. The slit was a crack in the otherwise sheer face of the cliff made by some distant upheaval of the earth.

She was sorely tempted to enter it and find its opening on the other side, but she knew she had been away for about as long as she dared. Enough now to know where the opening was located. Unless Lobo Negro came back today to share her blankets, she would discover all she needed tonight. And she didn't expect him to do that. The hidden canyon was too distant from any place he would want to go for him to make the trip in one day. He never mentioned his absences to her. She found out about them only from the conversation that went on among the other squaws, talk that did not include her but was easy to overhear. She ran back to where the rest were and was relieved to see that none had seemed to miss her.

By nightfall she had lost most of the stoicism that was characteristic of an Apache. She was nervous and couldn't keep still. She busied herself with a small fire, cooked a meal she didn't want, and made two unnecessary trips to the stream, just to keep her restlessness from showing. Afterward she lay in the hut and impatiently waited for the campfires to die.

It was late before the murmuring of the camp ceased and the quiet sounds of the night took over. She exited the hut carefully, stood waiting for a moment to make sure no one else was around, and then walked with the silent steps of a deer around the edge of the camp.

As soon as she was clear, she began to run, a measured run that could cover distance without tiring her. It was difficult not to increase her pace, since behind her was slavery and before her freedom, but she knew she must travel far and carefully; masking her trail as she went, if she hoped to succeed in escaping.

Even in the dark of the night, she moved well. She had carefully marked the area on her return trip from the morning, and each rock or tree was familiar. She was traveling light, carrying only a small pouch of dried meat, a few berries, and a gut of fresh water. Whatever the land before her, she was Indian enough to find something to eat. That would be the simple part. Hiding from the chase that would develop in the morning whether Lobo Negro came back or not would be another matter. Ta-ne-dako would be the first to look for her, and when she didn't appear, the woman would go to the hut to find her. Afterward there were many warriors still in the camp, and they would quickly guess the direction she was taking and come after her.

She found the slit without trouble, entered it, and where the night had been dark, the tunnel was impossible. She had to feel her way along the side slowly, stumbling occasionally on its uneven floor. The thought of a drop off somewhere on the inside occurred to her, and she slowed even more, testing carefully with each foot before allowing her weight on it.

Once she followed a turn and ran into a blank wall, being forced to retrace her steps, and she began to think she would need the entire night to find her way through the tunnel. But finally her face felt the change of air before her eyes found the lighter dark, and a moment later she emerged.

The entrance was even better hidden than the exit. A leaning rock blocked most of it, and another, barely separate enough for a horse to squeeze between them. A man on horseback would have to know the fissure was there and even so, he would have to maneuver carefully to get through.

All around her were the mountains, which she could feel more than see. But she wasted no time straining to see. When she had first ridden in on the horse with Lobo Negro she had been blindfolded and nothing would be familiar anyway. But the sun had been at her back then, she remembered it well. And she knew from the direction of the tunnel from the camp that west would be ahead if she continued. She began to run once more.

The darkness was a problem; she stumbled often on the rough ground, often slipping as a rock rolled from under her moccasin. But she moved as rapidly as she dared and stopped to roll her moccasins higher only after brush began to snap at her legs. When the first rosy light of dawn edged up behind her, she was miles from the hidden canyon and still running well. The descent was smoother now, both because she was able to see and could pick her trail better and because she was entering more gentle slopes. It was time to hide her passage.

She looked for harder ground, preferably solid rock, which would leave no sign of her moccasins. She was especially careful to avoid any contact with brush or the patches of grass that were becoming more profuse. A broken twig or a bruised blade would be a perfect signal to the trailing warriors.

In the full light of morning, she stopped in the shadow of a rock and ate a mouthful of meat, taking a sip of water at the same time. Behind her were the mountains, before her the land with tough brown grass. Still there were dry shoals of rock that would conspire with her passage. In the hazy distance, she could see the beginning of the desert, unfamiliar to her at this point, but beckoning conspiringly, like a friend. She was at home in the desert, as much at home as any of the men behind her, who had been born to it.

Her birthplace had been a city far to the east, but she had only vague recollections of that and none of the mother who had given life to her. Her first real memories had been of a rough wagon drifting steadily west through farmland and prairie. Memories of heavily bearded men in rough clothes, bonneted women with hard faces, and her white-haired father with his constant talk to her of the Bible and of his mission to the heathen. All of those had faded with the passage of time; she rarely bothered to remember them anymore. The desert, the woods, and the wonderful lands of sweet grass had been mother to her, the difficult but happy way of the Apache, her teacher.

She took a deep breath to fill her lungs and started to run again.

It was late afternoon before they caught up with her. She had used all the skill she possessed to avoid leaving any sign for them to follow, but she was up against the best trackers in the world. And they had been mounted on ponies. Even so, she had run throughout all but the very high heat of the day, so they must have discovered she was missing before morning to be this close so soon.

She watched them come from her hiding place in the shadow of a mesquite thicket and at once understood her mistake. The warriors had not bothered to track her in the mountains where she had been so careful. They'd merely anticipated the direction she would take and ridden hard. Only when they'd reached the brown grassy flatlands with its striping of lava rock had they spread out and cast for her trail. If she'd taken a south or southeastern direction first, even though it would have been a much longer route, she might have thrown them off.

But it was too late to think of that now. She could only hope to conceal herself. Gently, so as not to disturb the shrubs, she pushed deep into the thicket and began slowly to cover herself with the loose, dry soil beneath. If she could stay hidden until night, she might still have a chance.

When Lobo Negro returned two days after her escape, Flor de Oro was tied hand and foot and lying in his hut. She had been given neither food nor water since her capture and now lay and listened to the excited shouts of greeting at his return. He would be quickly told of her escape and capture; the warriors would boast to him of their skill in finding her. And, she thought wryly, they would also tell him of following his orders not to harm her. But he would punish her again, she had no doubt of that. It didn't matter. No matter what he did, he would never change her mind on that score. Someday, somehow, she would get away and lead Cochise back here. She promised herself that.

It was a long time before he entered the hut. Dusk was approaching and the walls around her faded as the light inside grew dim. Still, she was able to see his face as he entered and sat down on the blanket beside her.

"So," he said, "you found your way out."

She watched him without answering.

"You are clever, Flor de Oro," he continued. "I knew that. I also know no one would tell you where it was, you had to find it yourself. I was curious how you did it, but then as I thought, I remembered where you were the day I left. You followed me to the entrance, didn't you? I showed you the way myself without knowing it."

He smiled at her. A thin, hard smile that didn't in the least disturb the livid scar across his face. "I have given this much thought since I returned. I should punish you again. But then, that will not change the mind of Flor de Oro, will it? No matter what I do, you will try again. So now I must find another way to bind you to me."

He waited, watching her closely, and the smile remained in place as she met his gaze with a direct look of her own.

"Ta-ne-dako told me how to do this," he said, after a bit. "It is also an answer that I like. She is sometimes a wise squaw, Ta-ne-dako. Wisdom often hides behind her sharp tongue. Her answer is simple. I must bind you to me with my blood. So now you will have my child, Flor de Oro. And another one after that. Many children you will bear for me."

He nodded in agreement with his own words and then slipped his knife free to cut her bonds. "A squaw bearing a child cannot run away very fast. Can she, Flor de Oro?"

Chapter Five

The dawn bugle woke David Foxcroft from a restless sleep. He opened his eyes and stared at the low ceiling above his head for some time before heaving a sigh and rolling his legs to the wooden floor. He'd been on post duty watch for the past three days, ending only last midnight. Rightly, he should have this day off, but he had orders to report to the post commander at eight o'clock. He could of course go back to sleep and hope he woke in time, but then that wasn't a good idea. Although Colonel Markham was usually a taciturn man, his tongue could blister the hide from an officer who failed even the slightest in his duty.

Probably, he was going to be given another assignment to settle some trouble in the area, or worse, to chase some raiding Indians again. Fort Buchanan was undermanned, as all of the western outposts were, and in the nearly a year's time since he'd come here, he'd been forced to do double duty. Regular patrols were sent out weekly, yet at the same time hardly ten days would go by without another group of fifteen to twenty men being dispatched to chase raiders. The settlers were constantly screaming for more protection from the marauders, but the Army was stretched thin, and there was pressure on Congress to bring even some of those back east again. Although news was scarce in the territory and nearly a month late, there were rumors of possible war, a civil war that would move them all back and leave the settlers to cope with the Apache by themselves.

He sighed. Chasing Indians, or sometimes Mexicans posing as Indians, was a difficult business at best. The victims who survived the raids were usually unable to identify anyone, not that it mattered to the rest of the Americans in the territory, who wanted all Indians removed, peaceful or not. At any rate, the pursuing soldiers usually found themselves chasing ghosts—or at best, capturing or killing Indians who had the bad luck to be in the area where the raiders were thought to be.

Guilty or not, the Indians often fought back, and fought well. He'd quickly lost his status as a greenhorn officer. Now his saddle and boots carried that well-worn look of a regular, and he had learned the territory under the Fort's jurisdiction almost as well as the acres his father owned back in St. Louis, where he'd ridden as a boy.

He'd also gained the reputation of being a fighter, he thought with satisfaction. A number of his troopers still considered him too soft-hearted when it came to taking prisoners, but none of them could question his courage or ability. He was sure of that. Twice he'd been ambushed by Apache, and both times he'd kept his head and fought clear with small losses. That, along with the fact that he'd never left a wounded man behind, had changed their minds.

He rose and pulled on his trousers and boots, buckling the belt but leaving his suspenders hanging, then went outside in search of some hot water for washing and shaving. The post sutler was a Mexican, and his wife did the laundry for the officers, so there was always hot water to be had in their store. He picked up a pail he kept hanging on the wall just outside his door and, ignoring the assembling soldiers in the courtyard, headed for the Mexicans' place.

After he'd eaten, he still had over an hour to kill before reporting and he spent the time in cleaning his weapons, both his rifle and the Army-issue Colt he wore strapped to his side. Finally it was time to go, and he crossed the courtyard to the colonel's office and knocked.

Colonel Markham was standing before a large map

of the territory pinned to one adobe wall. He didn't turn immediately as David entered but continued to trace a line with his finger on the map until he grunted with satisfaction. David stood at attention in the center of the room.

Markham was a tall, thin man with a slight limp in the left leg, the result of a musket ball he'd taken in the Mexican war. A wound that pained him still, it showed more in the compressed lips he habitually wore than in his limp. He turned and crossed to sit behind his desk.

"At ease, Lieutenant," he said. "Have you heard of this latest raid?"

David nodded. "Yes, sir. Two ranches on Bear Creek, I understand. Both families were nearly wiped out and the houses burned."

"Not just ranches, Lieutenant. Large holdings. One of the men involved has a brother who's a congressman from Illinois. There's going to be hell to pay when he hears of it."

"Perhaps then we can get the men we need to do this job, Colonel," David offered.

The colonel grimaced. "Not by hell we won't. All I'll get from the War Department is a telegraph telling me to mount a full-scale offensive against the Indians." His face looked as if he'd bitten into something sour. "A full-scale offensive—dammit, they'll demand I start a war I can't win with the few troops I have here!"

David remained silent.

"Lieutenant, a full-scale war is the last thing we want at this point. This man, Cochise, is nobody's fool even if he is an Indian. We start a war with the Apache and he'll gather all of the tribes together and whip our tail within a month. Do you know that?"

"Cochise is a good fighter," David said slowly. "But I believe he's smart enough to know he couldn't win in the long run. I don't think he wants a war any more than we do."

The colonel stared hard at him. "He may not have a choice. If we don't do something, anything, to slow down the complaints going back to Washington from the settlers, we're going to be ordered to do the impossible. Either that or the people here will organize the vigilantes again and try to do it themselves. The Army's in a bind, Lieutenant. We've got to do something, and do it soon."

"Yes, sir."

The colonel turned to glance at the map and suddenly swung back. "Have you ever heard of an Apache called Lobo Negro?"

David paused to think; the name wasn't all that familiar. But the colonel didn't give him time. "He's a renegade," he continued, answering his own question. "A wild Indian who lives apart from the tribes. I had a parlay with Mangas Coloradas a few days ago and he told me about this man. He says that most of the raiding is done by him and about thirty or so of his followers. I don't know whether to believe that wily old rascal or not, but he swears it's true. Says this Lobo Negro—Black Wolf in English—has a grudge against all Americans and doesn't give a damn what treaties we make with the tribes. He also told me he hates Cochise and would like to see the Army attack him."

He paused for a minute, as if thinking to himself. Then looked up from under lowered eyelids. "It may all be horse dung, but if it's true, we could do a lot to maintain peace by finding this renegade and hanging him. That's where you come in. I'm assigning you to track Lobo Negro down, if he exists, and bring him in. Dead or alive."

"Yes, sir."

"As of this morning, you're detatched from all other duty. Take all the time you need to prepare, but I want you to stay in the field until you find this Apache or prove to me that he doesn't exist. Do you understand?"

"Yes, sir. I'll do what I can. Do you have any idea where he might be found?"

The colonel let out his breath explosively and glanced at the map once more. "My guess is that he raids here and then slips back across the border into Mexico. If that's the case, you're to try to follow him there. Unofficially, of course, since we don't want any trouble with the Mexican authorities. Stay clear of their soldiers at all costs. Mangas says he may have a hideout somewhere in the Santa Ritas, you can start there. Find him, Lieutenant. Take twenty men and those Apache scouts you used before and find him. Clear?"

"Yes, sir. I'll leave as soon as I have something to go on. Maybe Konta can make some contacts and get a lead."

"Konta?"

"One of the scouts, Colonel. He was one of the two Apache who scouted for Fort Defiance."

The colonel allowed himself barely the ghost of a smile. "I see. I would imagine he does owe you a favor, Lieutenant."

"Yes, sir. Will that be all, Colonel?"

"Yes. Except that if this doesn't work, you can get ready to fight the whole damn Apache nation."

David saluted and left, feeling the commander's eyes on his back as he went out the door.

Outside, he paused on the plank walk and rolled his shoulders in exasperation. *Good Lord, now he had to go chasing ghosts! A man who may or may not exist!*

He stepped off the walk and crossed the courtyard rapidly, heading for the main entrance to the Fort. Konta's tepee was fifty or so yards to one side and he found the Apache sitting cross-legged in front of it, wiping his rifle with a cloth.

The Indian looked up at his approach, but said nothing until David had squatted beside him. "Good morning," he said then, the rag still moving slowly over the rifle stock. "You have work for me?"

David nodded. "Konta, have you heard of a man named Lobo Negro? An Apache?"

"I have heard of him."

"Can you find him?"

This time Konta's head moved slowly from side to side. "He is smart, like a fox. Many people would like to find this man. None have done it."

"Well, we've got to. I've been given the assignment to bring him in, and I want you to lead me to him."

The Indian's face remained expressionless as usual. It was a thing David could never get used to—the ability of an Apache to never allow you to know what he was thinking.

"Can you do it?" he asked impatiently.

Konta looked beyond him for a long time. Then he nodded slowly. "It can be done, I think. Lobo Negro is a fox." His eyes found David again. "He is also like the mountain lion. He will not let you take him when he is found and to kill him will not be an easy thing."

"My orders are to stop him," David said. "If he won't surrender, then I will kill him. We believe he is the cause of the trouble between the Apache and the Americans. If he is not caught, there may be war."

Konta nodded again. "Then we will find him. Or . . . we will let him find us."

"Find us? How?"

"I will send out some words. We will build a trap for him to smell."

"What kind of trap?" David asked.

But Konta only stood up, forcing David to stand as well. "I will put out the words," he said. "I do not know how long this will take. Then I will come to you."

"We haven't much time," David started to say. But Konta turned and walked away rapidly, leaving him to talk to his retreating back.

He was gone for a week and twice David had to report to the colonel to listen to a tirade. Both times, he explained the situation as carefully as he could and asked for a little more time. But he was beginning to wonder himself by the time Konta showed up again, knocking on David's door late in the evening.

"I have put out the words," he said as David let him in. "We can leave with the sunrise. If Lobo Negro hears these words, he will come to a place I have picked out."

"What makes you think he will? What did you say?"

The Apache hunkered on the floor a few feet from where David sat. "Lobo Negro is not of a tribe," he said. "The warriors that follow him no longer belong to a tribe. When some of them are killed, he needs more. He must find braves who think like him. Warriors who cannot live with the tribes because they have been sent away. I tell people who do not know me that I am one of these. I tell them where I stay. I tell them I am good fighter and that I want others to go with me on raids. That I have five braves who will go with me. If Lobo Negro hears of this, he will mebbe come for me to join with his warriors."

"You mean you think he'll come just to recruit more men?" David couldn't hide his disappointment.

"He will come," Konta insisted. "This Lobo Negro has great pride. He will come to boast of his raids and tell me I will get many goods if I follow him. He will boast of his strength and cunning."

His dark eyes found David's and held them. "And if he finds warriors who will not follow him but want to raid themselves, he will kill them. That is the way of Lobo Negro."

This time, David saw it. Konta was counting on jealousy as much as Lobo Negro's desire to increase his band. *Dammit, it might work at that!*

"All right," he said, and grinned. "We leave in the morning."

Konta got up and went out the door.

They rode out with the sunrise since David had already picked his men and had his supplies prepared, leaving only the need of informing the colonel, who didn't seem to mind being awakened at such an early hour, and assembling his troopers. The men were told to discard their uniforms and distinctive hats. They wore buckskins, side arms with full cartridge belts, and carried pouches heavily laden with ammunition for their rifles. They were also issued moccasins instead of their regular cavalry boots and spurs.

He led them out of the Fort and rode eastward for a

time before turning north. Konta held to a steady pace throughout the day and guided them into a brush-choked wash late in the evening for a dry camp, telling David it was important that they not be seen. Before dawn, they moved out again, twenty-two silent ghosts riding single-file across the barren land.

By midafternoon, the landscape had changed to rising country with peaks of broken rock on either side and filled with dips of shale and lava rock. Konta led them into a canyon that began with only a depression but quickly became a canyon whose sides rose higher and higher until it completely shielded them from the sun's rays. There was a stirring from the men at this point; none of them liked to travel with higher ground above them, and David had to caution them to silence.

Finally the canyon widened abruptly as if a giant hammer had smashed the sides in one great sweep. Konta stopped and turned to him. "Here we will wait," he said. "The soldiers must find places to hide in those rocks. From there they can cover the four sides. I am not sure which way he will come."

David allowed his gaze to sweep the area. It was a good choice for an ambush. The break in the canyon would give a traveler, even a suspicious one, the feeling of sudden freedom. And the rocks abounding in this area would afford both protection and concealment. He nodded slowly. "How do you know he'll come here?"

Konta pointed toward an overhanging rock jutting from a wall about ten feet from the canyon floor. "There is a cave there," he said. "It is deep and has been used before by Apache. I have made my camp in it."

"Does it have another entrance?"

The scout's horse moved restlessly of its own volition, and Konta had to soothe it with a word and a hand on its neck before replying. "There is only the one way. Your soldiers must not let Lobo Negro get to it. You will still have him trapped, but I will be in the

74

cave as well."

"That's risking your life," David said. "Is there another way? Why stay in the cave?"

Konta shook his head. "I must make it look like a camp to him. Lobo Negro will not come unless he sees an Apache camp. I will make a small fire near the entrance, but your soldiers must make no fires in the rocks. They must not move when they are hidden, except at night. This man is as the prairie dog who will watch everything before he comes in."

"All right," David said. "Set up your camp; I'll position my men."

He was a beautiful child, barely one moon of age, but already he struggled to lift his head, and his bright eyes looked about him as if he could understand. He had a well-formed body with no marks and the black hair and high cheekbones of the Apache. But his skin was closer to white than to red. He was good-natured and cried little except when he was hungry—which was often, she thought ruefully, mindful of her sore nipples his little mouth attacked as if he would draw out all her milk at one time.

And he was hers; the only thing that could push hatred away from her thoughts for a time and bring softness to her eyes. The others had come once out of curiosity, the squaws at least, and then ignored the child. Lobo Negro had held it and laughed about the blue eyes, but then he had been busy with other things and she was alone. Alone with her child.

Flor de Oro finished bathing him and smiled at his sleepy fretting at being disturbed with a full stomach to work on. Then she carefully dried him and placed him in his baby carrier. This was only a temporary holder; a better, stronger one would be constructed when he was three to four moons old.

To make him comfortable, he was laid on a soft bedding of well-massaged grass placed against the face of the carrier. Over the grass was a tanned, spotted hide of a fawn with the hair side up, and between his small chubby legs she had put soft shredded bark to drain the water away when he wet and keep his skin free from irritation. Lastly, she placed another fawn skin, the hair side in, over him, tucked the edges around his body and under his tiny feet, and laced it to the carrier.

The carrier had a top hood where she had permanently attached several pieces of squirrel fur for a pillow, as well as the tail of another on the outside. This last was to make him quick as a squirrel and a good climber. She wished she had the claw of a bear to attach too; the bear was good medicine and would keep him from sickness. Lobo Negro would bring her one if she asked, but she would never ask for anything, for to do so would be to acknowledge that she had become his squaw. Instead, she settled for the feathers of a hawk, to give him a clear eye.

When she was finished, she suspended the carrier from a low branch of a tree with rawhide strings and gave it a gentle push to start it swinging. The child's small frets ceased immediately; he gave a loud belch and went to sleep.

Flor de Oro watched him in amusement for a moment longer, then walked the few steps back to her campfire to begin preparing the evening meal. To her surprise, she was joined almost immediately by Lobo Negro, who squatted beside her and reached into the fire for a burning twig to light his rolled cigarette.

"Tomorrow," he said, after the brown leaf was burning, "you will leave the child with Ta-ne-dako and ride with me."

She looked up at him. "The child is too young. He needs my milk. Where must I go?"

He waved a hand. "There is another woman who has a child. She can feed two until I return. We will be gone two, perhaps three, days."

She didn't want to go. No matter what it meant, it wasn't something for her. He would never allow her to leave, especially now that she had borne his child. But there was no need to protest, he would do as he wished. She reached for a bowl and added water to the mixture she had started to stir in the cooking pot.

"I will be ready," she said.

She was up before dawn and fed the child as usual. She would have liked to bathe him again, but it was too early, the coolness of the morning would be bad for his exposed skin. Reluctantly, she handed him to Ta-ne-dako and followed Lobo Negro to where the horses waited. He had selected a pony for her, but unlike the rest, which had short rope halters looped around their noses for guiding by the rider, this one had a long lariat, which Lobo Negro held in his hand.

When she was mounted, he moved his own pony over beside her. His face was not the one he often showed to her when they were alone in the hut but the hawk look of a warrior.

"You will ride behind me and do as I say," he told her. "Do not make a sound that is not required of you. We may have to ride hard, or we may have to fight. Whatever happens, you will stay close to me."

The impulse was so strong, she couldn't resist it. "Why must I go?" she protested. "Are you going to see Cochise?"

He smiled a thin, crooked smile. "No, Flor de Oro. I have said you will never see Cochise again, nor any of your people. The ones we go to see are not of a tribe. I must convince them of the strength and cunning of Lobo Negro. What better way to prove this than for them to see the daughter of Cochise, who was stolen from under his nose?"

His smile widened. "It is a thought I should have held before. The golden-haired one will draw warriors to me more than any offer of goods I could make."

He turned then, gaving a command to the five warriors waiting and at the same time moved his pony out of the camp.

Once outside the tunnel, he sent one of the warriors to ride ahead as a lookout and the rest rode in single file with Flor de Oro placed just behind him. Her thoughts, as she rode, alternated between the possibility of escape that this journey might present, and the child she had left in the rancheria. Her baby could not have made this journey safely and would be a liability as well if concealment became necessary, that was obvious. But she was also certain that Lobo Negro considered the child a hostage who would prevent her from trying to escape.

Suppose there was a chance? Suppose a chance presented itself and she were able to run? Could she do it and take the risk of never seeing her small son again? Already, in the short time since she had left him, her arms were hungry to hold him again. Lobo Negro would understand this and use it to his advantage.

But if she did nothing, if she remained with the outlaws for the sake of the boy, what chance would he have in growing to true manhood? He would become a strong warrior, she expected that. And he would raid across the border in the Apache way. It was the other, the fact that he would grow up without a tribe as an outlaw, never to stand proud in the circle of his own people, that she would be forced to watch with sad eyes.

No, she could do neither. She could neither leave him with Lobo Negro in order to seek her own freedom without him, nor stay and allow him to grow up an outlaw. She wanted with all her heart for him to know the Chiricahua; wanted him to stand as a young warrior before Cochise and the elders and learn the wisdom of a man. That thought made her heart ache.

Somewhere ahead of them sounded the sudden bark of a coyote, and Lobo Negro raised a hand in warning. The others came to a quick and silent halt to listen and look.

That the sound was made by a man, she recognized as quickly as the warriors. It was a good imitation, but no human could fully capture the quality of an animal's cry, there would still be an echo to their attempt that no animal had. It was probably the scout ahead and he had spotted a possible danger.

Lobo Negro motioned again with his hand and immediately two of the men behind her slipped from their ponies and advanced on foot. The area they were in contained sandstone clifts with hundred-foot rips in their sides, and in between was a rough flooring with an almost total absence of vegetation. They were stopped in a pocket, a dividing between two buttes, and the pocket narrowed ahead of them in an abrupt climb.

The two braves went up the climb to the skyline, where they lay flat in order to peer over without being seen. After a look, one glanced back and held up a hand to wait.

Flor de Oro turned to Lobo Negro in question, but he ignored her to keep his eyes on the two braves ahead and for a very long time all of them waited before receiving another signal from the watchers that it was safe to proceed. Lobo Negro led the rest up to where the braves waited, bringing the dismounted warriors' ponies with them.

When they reached the waiting men, one of them pointed, and following his arm, Flor de Oro could see the faint whispering of far-off dust clouds below them. "Five riders," the scout told Lobo Negro. "White men."

"White men? Soldiers?"

The man shook his head. "They ride too fast. Too hard. Much afraid."

Lobo Negro grunted and pushed past the man, pulling Flor de Oro's pony along behind him. They began a slow descent on a steep slope, with many switch-backs and occasional gaps where their mounts were forced to jump a short distance and scramble for a footing on the other side. On those occasions, she would lay prone on the pony's back with her hands gripping its mane and her face against the side of its neck, urging it with soft words. Like the others, she rode bareback and had to turn her toes inward in order to grip the horse's middle to retain her seat as it scrambled.

The sun was near its height when they reached the floor below, and they as well as the ponies began to suffer from the heat. Flor de Oro wondered where the single advance scout had gone, she could see no sign of him ahead, and finally decided that he kept to the heights somewhere. She wished they had taken that route themselves, no matter how rough the ride. Here was like being at the bottom of a cooking pot; her tongue was dry and began to stick to the sides of her mouth no matter how she tried to work it.

At last, Lobo Negro called a halt for the afternoon hours and they sought shelter as best they could in the shadows of large rocks. They watered the ponies and drank a little themselves before sitting down to rest. Even in the shade, the heated air rising from the sandy rock soil was painful to breathe, and Flor de Oro rested her head on her drawn-up knees in weariness.

In the late afternoon, when traveling was once more tolerable, he had them moving again and didn't stop until nightfall. Even then, it was a dry camp with only a little water from the gut bags they carried and dried meat to chew.

Again, as the first rays of dawn deepened the normally red colors of the sandstone cliffs, Lobo Negro had them moving. She had spent a restless night, her thoughts on the child, and as she rode her full breasts demanded the relief of his searching mouth. They began to ache heavily, and she could feel the moisture seeping out and wetting her shirt.

There was a greater ache in her heart. For she had made a decision to try to escape. It was a course that would be dangerous and could leave her son without a mother if she were killed—or for that matter, even if she succeeded and then could not find him again. But it was a thing she must do. She must escape to Cochise and lead him and the rest to the hiding place of Lobo Negro. If she failed, her son would grow to manhood an outlaw.

Her breasts began to hurt more, and she slipped a hand under her shirt to expel the milk herself. But she could do nothing to release the tears held behind her dry eyes.

It was nearing midday again and Flor de Oro resigned herself to another long rest from the heat.

They were still in the sandstone country but now rode in a deep but wide canyon. Ahead of her she could see the heat-shimmering sides closing and had to look hard to be certain it wasn't a trick of her imagination.

It wasn't. As they advanced, the canyon did narrow, and Lobo Negro kept them moving into this possible trap in spite of the heat that was now sapping their strength. She was surprised but then suddenly remembered the single scout ahead and knew the canyon would already be checked.

By the time they entered the most narrow section she could see why he wasn't concerned. Its walls were too high and sloped inward at the bottom, making it difficult if not impossible for an attack to come from above.

This portion of the canyon was also short and quickly widened again into what was almost a cross canyon where each of the sandstone sides had collapsed.

The warrior she hadn't seen since leaving camp appeared ahead of them where the canyon opened, and Lobo Negro threw up a hand to halt. But the scout waved them on and in a moment or so they had joined him.

"The men you seek are in the cave as was told to you," he said to Lobo Negro. "I have seen only one near the entrance, but there are signs of the others."

The leader searched the area with his own eyes. "There is no one else?" he asked without looking at the scout. "You are certain of this?"

"I am certain. I lay on the ridge above us since the sun became high. I have seen no one but the man near the cave."

Lobo Negro grunted with satisfaction. "Good. We will talk with these warriors." He turned to the waiting men behind him. "Stay well apart," he told them. "I will approach from the center, but you will remain out of the range of their weapons if they decide to fight."

They moved to do his bidding, and he handed the

lead rope to Flor de Oro's pony to another to hold as they advanced.

A distance from the cave's dark entrance, shadowed further by an overhanging ledge, Lobo Negro gave another signal and the rest stopped while he continued on. Flor de Oro glanced at the warrior beside her and saw that he held his rifle stock in the same hand as the lead rope to her mount. Then she returned her gaze to the distance beyond the cave where the canyon continued again.

Lobo Negro stopped ahead of them and waited. Shortly, as if he had been watching, an Apache wearing only moccasins and breechcloth and carrying no weapon appeared in the entrance to the cave.

Lobo Negro raised an arm. "I am Lobo Negro!" he shouted. "Killer of Mexicans! Killer of Americans! The best raider of all Apache! I wish to talk!"

The man in the cave raised an arm in return. "I am Konta. Once of the Mescalero. What do you want?"

Lobo Negro took a last look around at the broken walls of the canyon and slowly urged his pony forward. To Flor de Oro's surprise some of the other warriors moved forward as well, seeming in their curiosity to forget their leader's command to stay back.

Lobo Negro had covered a little more than half the distance when he suddenly jerked his pony to such an abrupt halt the animal reared in surprise. However, its rider's attention was fixed, not on the cave and the man in the entrance, but on the jagged rocks above it. His head darted from side to side. Then he gave a shrill yell of anger and defiance and spun the pony, urging it at the same time into a squat-legged jump and a full run.

Behind him, the standing Apache dove headfirst into the cave as the cliffs above him errupted with gunfire.

Lobo Negro's warriors fired back in confusion, without clear targets to see, as their leader raced toward their ranks.

Flor de Oro's blood raced as the thought leaped into her head. Cochise! He had set this trap!

She shot her pony forward with a yell and a hard kick into his sides with both heels and at the same time leaned to grasp the lead rope in her hand and jerk it free, nearly pulling the man's weapon loose as well.

She gave another shrill cry as the pony stretched into a run and flattened herself along its back. "Cochise!"

The canyon walls resounded with gunfire and around her, puffs of sand and dirt leaped up, the stinging whine of bullets penetrating the clamor of blood pounding in her ears.

As she raced for the opposite side, away from the shouting warriors behind her, she saw Lobo Negro veer his horse in her direction to cut her off. He was close enough that she could read the rage in his face, but his shouts at her were lost in the gunfire behind him.

"Cochise!" she screamed again, and used her free hand to slap the pony's shoulder. The little animal responded, reaching down for a deeper burst of speed.

But it would not be enough. His pony was gaining, cutting the angle between them rapidly. She wouldn't make it!

She gripped the pony's mane harder, leaned forward more and pressed her face against his neck. "Run!" she yelled.

Lobo Negro was only yards away and now, above the noise of the guns and her pony's drumming hooves, she heard him cry, "No! He will not have you again!"

She saw his rifle come up, the barrel steading upon her as he rode—and his horse suddenly went down as if it had slammed into rope around its knees. Lobo Negro was pitched over its head and a moment later, both were out of her sight as she raced for the shelter of the canyon wall.

Flor de Oro twisted once to look behind her as she neared the wall and caught a last glimpse of him. He was on his feet and racing with long strides in the opposite direction, with dust clouds from the flying bul-

lets kicking up around his legs.
She was free! She had returned to Cochise!

Chapter Six

The headlong rush of her pony carried her deep within the canyon before Flor de Oro could bring it to a halt. She turned it and brought it slowly back, looking above in hopes of seeing some of the Chiricahua. Ahead, she could hear much excitement, a lot of shouting mixed with occasional rifle shots. By the time she came even with the entrance to the cave, she could see riders, almost obscured by the dust clouds they were making, racing in pursuit of Lobo Negro and his warriors.

Two ponies, Lobo Negro's and another as well as one warrior, lay dead before her in the flat. She was glad Cochise had horses himself; he would run them down, and she hoped he killed or captured all of them so that none could return to warn the others back at the rancheria. Then she could lead him there, she was sure she could return the way they had come here, and recover her son. That thought filled her heart with joy.

Not seeing anyone, she guided her pony toward the cave, still allowing it to walk slowly and recover from its efforts. But as she turned, the Indian she had seen earlier reappeared and walked toward her. He carried no weapon still except a knife at his waist. Still, she raised her hand in peace.

He was not of the Chiricahua; she didn't recognize him. But that was of no matter, Cochise must have combined with other tribes to continue the hunt for her. He would never have given up, for he was Cochise.

The Apache came close and his eyes were curious.

She stopped to wait. Behind him, the battleground seemed startlingly quiet after what had transpired only minutes before. Flor de Oro smiled at him. "Where is Cochise?" she asked. "Did my father go with the others in the chase?"

He advanced the few feet between them before he spoke. "Cochise? Who are you?"

She stared at him. *He did not know who she was? This was wrong! Why would he not know if he were with Cochise* . . . Doubt suddenly flooded her. Doubt that became an explosion as two more men appeared from around the rocks with rifles in their hands. *White men!*

Before her, the Apache spoke again. Except this time he spoke in English, a language that although it sounded harsh to her ears, she found she understood. "Who are you? What is your name?"

Anger replaced her surprise. *Americans! They were not with Cochise!* She whirled her pony to flee, but the Apache was quick. He leaped for the neck rope, caught it, and used his weight to stop the animal's attempt to run.

She kicked at him, then yanked at his hand, as behind her she heard one of the men yell, "Hold on! Don't let her get away!"

She couldn't dislodge him and quickly slid from the struggling pony's back on the opposite side to hit the ground running. But she was slow, not yet fully recovered from bearing the child, and he was a man. His hand reached for her back, grabbed her shirt, and snatched her from her feet.

Flor de Oro rolled, twisted out of his grasp, and tried to scramble up again. He was quick and strong, he caught one of her wrists, pulled her over, and placed a knee in her stomach to hold her.

"Stop!" he said. "I will not harm you!"

His words meant nothing, she continued to struggle until he was forced to use both hands to hold her flailing arms. "Stop," he said again. "You will not be harmed!" This time he switched back to her language.

Slowly, she gave in to his superior strength. It was

leader spoke again. "What happened?" he asked the Apache. "Why were you tied?"

Flor de Oro listened without appearing to do so as the Indian recounted accurately everything that had happened. How she had returned, how he had caught her pony, and the events that had followed.

When he had finished, the leader nodded. "About what I thought." He glanced at her. "Did she talk to you at all?"

"She asked for Cochise," the Apache said. "Before she saw the others. I think she believed we were Chiricahua when she ran from Lobo Negro."

"She's lucky one of my men didn't hit her," the leader grunted. He had a strong set to his jaw, and his eyes were deeply spaced around a high, unmarked nose. His face was longer than an Apache's, with no hint of roundness, but the part that his stubble of beard didn't cover was smooth and flawless. There were none of the pockmarks she had observed in the few other Americans she had seen.

"Ask her," he said slowly, "if she is the woman called Flor de Oro."

The sound of her name from his lips almost brought a reaction from her. She almost gave herself away.

The Apache repeated the question in her own language, but she didn't answer, trying instead to understand what this new development meant.

"She will not trust us," the Apache said after a moment, speaking again in English.

"Can't say that I blame her," the American replied. "Not after what just happened." He paused. "Tell her so that she will understand, that no one is going to harm her now. She has my word on it. And ask her if she belongs to the Chiricahua. Maybe she'll answer that."

She waited for the translation, then nodded slowly.

The leader kept his eyes on her but spoke to the Apache. "I'm convinced she's Flor de Oro, Konta. She fits the description too well not to be. You're an Apache, can you tell if she's really an Indian? Couldn't she be a white woman?"

Flor de Oro waited for him to answer; dreading what he would say. If this American thought she was white, he may never let her go back to Cochise and the Chiricahua.

But after the Apache's eyes locked with hers, she was surprised at his reply. "I cannot say," he told the American. "Mebbe. She is Apache in all other ways. I think she must be returned to Cochise."

"But dammit, Konta. If she's a white woman . . ."

The leader's face became angry as both of them stared at her. "She could have been captured as a baby," he said. "Maybe she never even heard her own language. But there's no way an Indian could have yellow hair and blue eyes!"

The Apache shook his head. "She must be returned to Cochise."

The American's voice hardened. "No. Not yet. Not until I make sure that's what she really wants. And that she isn't white."

He made a gesture with his hand. "At any rate, we'll give her something to eat now and make her comfortable for the night. After we get her back to the Fort, we'll send a message to Cochise and find out for sure who she is."

"You did not catch Lobo Negro?" the Apache wanted to know.

The leader grimaced. "No, dammit. We did kill two more of them, but the rest got away. Disappeared right before our eyes and we couldn't find a trace of them. Neither of the ones we killed was the man who rode up to you."

Flor de Oro lowered her eyes and her heart felt pain. *Lobo Negro had escaped. And now that he might think she was free to lead Cochise to his hiding place, he would be forced to move. She would never see the child again.*

Chapter Seven

During the night, Private Brewster made an attempt to slip away but was caught before he reached a horse. David ordered him tied to his saddle, the same as Tanner, and assigned two troopers to guard them on the way back to the Fort. The rest of the men were told to spread out enough to prevent ambush and still protect one another. Konta, as usual, rode ahead to scout.

Flor de Oro rode beside David, sitting her pony bareback with only a halter to guide it, and David found himself glancing at her often, intrigued by both her looks and her carriage. She rode with her back straight, adjusting herself to the movements of the pony without apparent effort, and resting her free hand on her hip like a man.

She was a slim girl but extremely well built, with high breasts and curved hips. He thought of Buffalo Harrison's comments about her figure when he'd described her long months ago and mentally agreed with the description. She was indeed a beautiful woman, buckskin or no. Her brown legs were uncovered nearly to her hips where the skirt was pushed up as she straddled the pony, and he could not keep his eyes from straying there often.

But it was her face that fascinated him the most. Her skin was smooth and clear; her cheekbones high and perfectly centering a full, sensual mouth. Her eyes were a deep, startling blue, with long lashes, and her long blond hair seemed to shimmer in the sunlight.

He half nodded in agreement with himself. A really

beautiful woman, in spite of the rough, soiled clothes she wore. Clothes that showed evidence of her struggle of the night before. He grimaced as he remembered Konta's description of that fight. Grimaced at the mental image of a man like Tanner attempting to rape her. But then, as he thought about it, he had to marvel as well, for according to Konta she had more than held her own against both of them for a while.

She was a puzzle. She must be white; he had already convinced himself of that. Probably she had been stolen by the Apache when only a baby or was the only survivor of a raid on some settler family. At any rate, she'd obviously grown up an Indian. There was nothing of the dependent white female in her actions. No hesitation, no coquettishness—her eyes met his squarely when she looked at him. And if there was fear in her, it damn well didn't show.

He suddenly decided that he was in love with her. And then decided that was certainly a damn fool notion.

She rode beside him without returning any of his glances except once, accidentally, when her head turned his way at the same time. He noted that she took in everything, her head constantly on the move. She was memorizing the area they traveled through, that was obvious. He decided he'd better warn his guards to be on the alert in case she tried to get away when they camped. Technically, she was a prisoner since she had been with Lobo Negro's band, but she had obviously used the fight to escape from the renegade herself. So what did that make her?

She had originally belonged to the Chiricahua, he knew that much from Buffalo Harrison even without being reminded of it by Konta. And the latter fully expected David to return her to Cochise. But he didn't want to do that. At least not until he could get her to talk to him. Maybe not even then. He suddenly tried to imagine her in a lace ballgown with her yellow hair done up in the latest fashion, then shook his head at the thought. Her bronzed skin would set an aristocratic Eastern ball completely on its ear!

She hadn't spoken a word, not the night before and none during the day's ride. On impulse, he moved his horse close to hers. "Want water, Flor de Oro?" he asked, without making a move toward his canteen. "You want water?"

The blue eyes turned on him briefly and looked away again.

David sighed and reached for his canteen. When he extended it, she accepted a drink, a small one, and gave it back. David smiled at her. "Good," he said, rubbing his belly. "Water good. Sun hot!"

She looked away.

He tried twice more to get a response from her before they camped for the night, even tried a couple of Apache words he'd learned from Harrison. But it was useless. She had no intention of communicating at all, either through suspicion of them or from some deeper motive of her own. Even when he had Konta talk to her in Apache, all the scout could get was one sentence. "I want to go to the rancheria of Cochise," she said. Nothing more. She wouldn't even acknowledge her name.

When they rode into Fort Buchanan the following day, she created a hubbub among the observers, as soldiers, the few civilians present, and even a few Indians stopped to watch their progress across the compound. David brought the file to a halt near the headquarters building with an upraised arm, then turned to Private McDonald just behind him.

"Dismiss the men," he ordered. "See that Tanner and Brewster are locked in the guardhouse, and tell whoever is in charge it's under my orders. They'll be dealt with later."

"Yes, sir." McDonald saluted and motioned with his arm to the others as David nodded toward Konta, who sat his horse a few feet behind the woman. "Bring the girl and come with me," he told him.

The Apache moved forward beside her, spoke briefly, and she immediately slid from her pony without argument. Both of them followed him to the plank sidewalk where a lounging Buffalo Harrison stood with a grin of incredulous surprise on his bearded face.

"Damn my hide, Lieutenant," he drawled as David reached him. "Where in the hell did you find *her*?"

David paused and matched the grin with a tired one of his own. "I'd say it was more like she found us, Harrison," he said. He half turned to find that she was watching him closely. "She's the woman you told me about, isn't she?"

"Yep. That's Flor de Oro, right enough. Ain't no other like that. Did you know she was stolen from Cochise a while back?"

"No. But then the renegades we were chasing were holding her captive. She ran away when we ambushed them."

Harrison's attention was still on the woman. "Well, I tell you what, my friend," he drawled. "Cochise has been turning hell over wheels to find her. And this here Fort just might not be big enough to handle him when he finds out she's here. You thinking of giving her over to him?"

David shrugged. "Not for me to say; that's up to the colonel." He started to add a comment, thought better of it and remained silent.

But as Buffalo Harrison allowed them to walk away from him, David heard him mutter, "I know what I'd do with her, Cochise or not . . ."

He knocked on the colonel's door and received a gruff reply from within. Markham was busy at his desk and took a long minute to look up. "Foxcroft! You're back! Did you succeed in . . . good God, man! Who is this?"

David saluted. "Her name is Flor de Oro, sir. I have reason to believe she lives with Cochise and his band."

"Is she white?" The colonel hardly noticed David; his gaze was fixed on the woman. "What is she doing here?"

"We captured—or rather rescued her from the renegades, sir. When we ambushed them, this woman ran away from them. I felt it best to bring her to the Fort with us."

This time the colonel's attention did switch to him. "Did your plan work? Did you get Lobo Negro?"

"I'm sorry, sir. We had only limited success, I'm afraid. Three of the hostiles were killed, but their leader got away."

"Damn!" The colonel's face reddened. "What happened? I want a full report."

David told him the story, including the chase afterward and how the renegades had disappeared. "I'm sorry, sir," he concluded. "We, my men and I, were just not equal to them in knowledge of the land."

"What about your tracker?" The colonel glared at Konta.

"He was serving as bait for the trap, Colonel, as I described. His horse was hidden a distance away. We couldn't afford to wait for him to join us in the chase. At least that was my judgment at the time."

Markham nodded. "You say this Lobo Negro spotted your ambush before he moved into it?"

David hesitated. "Yes, sir. But perhaps it was more . . . of a sense of danger he had. My men were well hidden. I don't believe any of them gave themselves away. He's . . . well, he seems to be a very capable leader. He was also smart enough to keep his people back as he advanced by himself to talk to Konta. We were lucky to get one of them during the fight."

"But he himself was within range of your fire?"

"He's also a very lucky man," David said quietly. "He should have been hit, but we managed only to shoot his horse from under him."

The colonel grunted and turned back to Flor de Oro. "Have you questioned the woman? Could she possibly lead us to him? Did you say she was white?"

"I believe she is, sir. White, I mean. But she refuses to talk to me or to Konta in Apache. She only seems to want to return to Cochise. I'm afraid she doesn't trust us, and with good reason."

The colonel raised his eyebrows in question.

"The two troopers who remained behind tried to

rape her, Colonel," David explained. "I returned in time to prevent it."

"Who were the men?"

"Corporal Tanner and Private Brewster. I placed them under arrest and intend to bring charges against both for their actions, and for being drunk on duty as well."

"They were drinking?"

"Drunk, sir. It seemed Corporal Tanner brought whiskey with him."

Markham's face reddened with anger. "You write up your charges, Lieutenant. I'll court-martial both of them and have them whipped on a wagon wheel. Tanner has tried my patience before; I don't know how that man was ever promoted in the first place."

"Yes, sir. May I ask what we should do about her?" David glanced toward the woman.

"Do? Humpt. If she's an Apache, she's a strange one. She should be allowed to go wherever she likes. But if she's white, I don't relish the idea of giving her over to savages. Are you sure she doesn't speak English? Any at all?"

"I don't think so, sir," David said slowly. "She gives no indication of understanding. May I make a suggestion?"

"Go ahead."

"I think we should hold . . . make a guest of her for a few days until we can communicate with Cochise. I'd like to go myself to talk to him. Maybe take Buffalo Harrison, if he'll go."

The colonel was eyeing her thoughtfully and David added, "It's my understanding that Apaches sometimes sell, or ransom, their captives. If we discover for certain that she's white, we should explore that possibility."

"Pay them to release a white woman, Lieutenant?" The eyebrows went up again.

"To maintain peace with the Chiricahua, sir. Cochise is reported to be a very proud man."

"I don't give a damn how proud he is," the colonel said sharply. "It would gall me dearly to pay for the release of a white woman he'd stolen. However, if she really is some sort of freak Indian . . ."

He moved around the desk and stopped a foot or so from the woman to peer into her face intently. "Do you speak English at all?" he asked her carefully. "Savvy white man talk?"

She stared back at him until he harumpted and turned away again. "I'll accept your suggestion, Lieutenant. But send Harrison alone. I don't trust that Indian, and if he knows you're the man who brought her in, it might turn him against you. Harrison knows how to deal with Indians. Meanwhile, find her a place to stay and get some rest yourself before reassuming your duties. Report back to me tomorrow morning."

"Yes, sir."

"And, Lieutenant . . ."

"Yes, sir?"

"I want a full report on my desk by six this evening. Also formal charges against Tanner and Brewster. Those two must be taught a lesson."

"Yes, sir." David saluted and left with Konta and the woman following closely at his heels.

Outside, Harrison was still waiting, joined by Captian Henley, and the latter pursed his lips as the woman came out the door. "Had to see for myself what everybody was talking about, David, my boy," he said. "Can't say that I'm disappointed."

David glanced at Harrison, but the scout didn't return the look. He was looking at Flor de Oro with the same wishful expression on his face that David remembered from the first time he had spoken of her.

"Doc," he said, still looking at Harrison, "I've got a problem."

"Nice problem," Henley agreed.

"No. I mean I've got to find her a place to stay. A place where she won't be bothered. Can you help?"

"You mean will Bess be willing to put her up, being I'm the only man with a wife on this post besides our good colonel. Well, my young friend, why don't we just go and ask her?"

"Thanks, Doc," David said. "Harrison, I need to

talk to you afterward. You mind waiting for me in my room?"

The scout turned and a sardonic smile slid across his face. "You figure I'm the man to go and palaver with Cochise, don't you?" he drawled. "Sort of tell him we got his daughter and mebbe we ain't gonna give her back?"

"I didn't say that. About not giving her back, I mean."

The scout chuckled. "But that's what you mean, Lieutenant, whether you know it or not. Might be you got an eye for this pretty gal yourself?"

David reddened. "I'll talk to you later. Will you wait?"

"Got any whiskey there?"

"Yes. A bottle in my trunk."

"See you later, Lieutenant." The scout stepped from the sidewalk and strolled away.

Henley watched him go. "I'll be damned," he said. "Don't tell me that old prairie dog is jealous?"

David was angry and didn't quite understand why. "Let's go, Doc," he said. "I want to get her settled. All right if I bring Konta along to interpret for us?"

Henley waved a hand and started off. "Hell, bring him along," he said over his shoulder. "Poor Bess might as well get to meet a whole tribe of Indians." His shoulders shook with silent laughter as he walked.

Bess Henley was a year or so younger than her husband, but life at a succession of frontier posts had somehow left more age lines in her face than in his, and her once brown hair was now heavily streaked with gray. There was humor in her face, however, plus a benign tolerence for her husband's unorthodox ways.

She was on her way back from one of the wells with a large bucket of water in her hand when she encountered them near the door to the quarters she shared with Doctor Henley. "Good Lord, Joseph," she exclaimed. "Who is this?"

"Indian squaw, Bess," he laughed. "I've invited

her to move in with us if you don't object. Just her. Konta here has his own tepee."

Mrs. Henley put her bucket down and pushed both her husband and David aside. "Indian my foot! I don't care what she's wearing, this is a white woman! Who are you, dear? Where did you come from?"

"David says she doesn't speak English," Henley told her. "And we're not really sure if she's white or not."

His wife gave him a short exasperated glance. "Joseph Henley, you're a fool. Anyone can tell this poor child is not any kind of Indian. And you call yourself a doctor." She peered closely at the shirt the woman was wearing. "Where's her child? Didn't she have it with her?"

"Child? What child?" Henley's startled look swept toward David, but the latter was just as shocked. He couldn't think of a reply.

By that time, Bess Henley had reached to touch the woman's arm and she patted it gently. "You come with me, dear," she said soothingly. "Don't be frightened. Joseph, she's recently had a baby, can't you see that? If she's lost it, no wonder she's in shock. David, where did you find her?"

"She . . . she was alone when we got her," he stammered. "We took her from some renegades. The ones we were after. I didn't see a child."

"Why didn't you ask her?" Bess Henley placed her arm around the woman's waist and led her unprotestingly toward her quarters. "Bring my bucket," she ordered no one in particular.

David picked it up and followed, but at the entrance she blocked them all with her body as she guided the woman inside. "Go someplace else and do something for a while," she told them sharply. "Get a drink of whiskey or something. I've got to help this poor child get cleaned up and then let her rest. She's worn out. You can talk to her later."

"But I've brought Konta along," he protested. "She doesn't speak any English. I want him to tell her—"

"Nonsense!" She took the bucket with one hand and pushed him away with the other. "She doesn't need to talk to anyone right now. She needs rest. Bring your Indian friend back later. After supper."

With that, she closed the door firmly.

Chapter Eight

To David's surprise, Buffalo Harrison readily agreed to ride into the Chiricahua camp to talk with Cochise. In fact, he seemed almost eager to do it. Nor did he seem particularly worried about any danger he might face, telling David that would come only if the Indian chief became unreasonable. That is, if he thought the Fort was holding the woman against her will. And in that case, his anger would be directed against the Fort itself, not against its messenger. He was, he said, merely going to talk.

He was also convinced he could persuade Cochise to let her come back to her own people, especially if he could offer him horses for her. And he would do as much as he reasonably could to find out her background, although that might prove difficult under the circumstances.

In the following days after he left, David was too busy to see much of the Henleys' young guest. He had gone back with Konta that first night but as he half expected, she refused to talk at all. She didn't seem frightened, merely suspicious, and no amount of persuasion from Konta could convince her to be otherwise.

He went back to his duties and tried to put her out of his mind. First, he had to present formal charges against Tanner and Brewster and then testify at their trial before the commander, Captain Henley, and one other officer. Afterward, he was given the task of supervising their punishment. Tanner was demoted to private, and both men received a dozen lashes across their backs while tied to the wheel of a wagon. They were also given ten days in the small adobe building used as a guardhouse. Brewster screamed in pain with the fourth lash of the whip and kept up a sobbing groan until it was finished. But the big ex-corporal bore the punishment in dark silence and when he was led away, he walked erect with a baleful look at David as he passed. He knew he was going to have to watch his own back as long as Tanner remained at the post.

By the evening of the third day after Harrison left, however, he was forced to give in to himself and walk to the Henleys' quarters, where he found Bess Henley sitting in one of two cane-backed rockers placed on the low wooden porch. She looked up and smiled as he approached.

"Hello, David. I wondered how long it would be before you came back to see us."

"Mrs. Henley." He touched the brim of his hat. "How're you?"

"What you really want to know, Lieutenant, is how is Flor de Oro," she laughed. "Sit down and I'll tell you. Be nice to talk to someone for a change. Joseph is off as usual on some business or other and I plan to allow his supper to grow cold. That man will never remember to be on time to eat."

He took the chair she indicated. "How is she doing?"

"Well, to tell you the truth, David, I don't really know. I believe she's a very troubled woman. She's caught between two worlds, so to speak. I can't get her to say a word, although I try to talk to her all the time, and Joseph too, when he's at home. There are times when I almost believe she understands what we're saying, and I have to wonder if she does vaguely remember a word or two from the time she was a baby."

"What do you mean—troubled?" he wanted to know.

Bess was silent for a moment, thinking. "Well, in the first place, she's recently had a baby. I'd rather not discuss with you how I know, but a woman understands such things. And I believe she's either lost it—I mean, it died—or else someone has taken it from her. There are times, David, when she doesn't realize I'm looking at her, that I can see a hurt in her expression. I can't explain it, it's sort of a sadness. Our young friend has a great deal of courage, but she's very human at the same time. I wish you could help her."

He nodded slowly. "Most of her life must have been pretty rough, living with Indians."

"No," she said in surprise. "I don't think that at all. I mean, I don't know a great deal about the savages, but that's not the impression she gives me. She obviously wants to go back to them and she seems like a very capable person, very well able to take care of herself. I was only thinking about recent events, like her capture by this renegade you were after. And the fact, as I said, that she's lost her child."

"But how can a white woman be happy living among savages?" he asked. "Even if she grew up there."

"You're thinking as a white man, David. She thinks, at least for the present, like an Indian. She doesn't understand what being white means."

She rocked for a moment, then stopped again. "I tried to get her to wear some of my clothes—I was going to alter them for her—but she would have nothing to do with them. She washed her own and put them back on. She seems almost afraid to do anything that would make her appear anything but an Indian."

"She's very beautiful, isn't she?" he said abruptly.

Bess Henley smiled at him. "Yes, she is. And you sound like a young man with more than an official interest in his Army duties, Lieutenant Foxcroft. You know, I believe if anyone can bring her out of this shell, you can. Would you like to talk to her? I could ask her out."

"Do you think she'd come?"

"There's only one way to find out." She rose and stepped to the door, opening it just enough to look inside. "Flor de Oro?" she called. "Come?"

A moment later, she stepped back and the blond

girl appeared behind her.

David stared. *Lord, she was beautiful!* Even in buckskins and moccasins, her slim figure would do justice to any woman. Her shirt now bore no traces of the dirt it had before, her face was scrubbed, and color was in her cheeks. The long blond hair was pulled back with a ribbon that held it in place behind her head.

"Flor de Oro," Bess said with a sweep of her hand toward him, "here is Lieutenant Foxcroft. Come to see you." There was a trace of amusement in her glance from one to the other.

The girl stood quietly, but her long-lashed blue eyes centered on his face and disconcerted him badly. He felt awkward, and his slight bow showed it. "Hello, Flor de Oro," he said stiffly.

To his great surprise, she nodded. Only a slight nod, a small movement of her head, but it was an acknowledgment.

His mind raced, searched for the Apache word for greeting, and wondered at the same time if he'd ever asked it of Konta. He couldn't remember, couldn't think of a gesture to use, and suddenly had an inspiration. "*Como está,* Flor de Oro?" he said.

A whisper of a smile crossed her lips. One slim hand rose until the fingers touched her chest between her breasts, and she nodded again.

David was elated. But then, dammit, his Spanish was limited to only a few words!

But he tried anyway. "*Habla español?*" he asked.

Her voice was low and soft, the blue eyes resting lightly on his face. "*No,*" she said. "*No entiendo español.*"

"Damn!" he said, and glared at Bess Henley in exasperation.

That lady raised amused eyebrows at him. "Well, at least you got a response," she said. "That's more than anyone else has done. I do believe the young lady likes you, David."

"You think if I go and get Konta . . ."

Bess shook her head. "I wouldn't push her if I were

you. She's got quite a mind of her own. Why don't you sit and talk to her while I go see about my husband's supper after all.''

"How in hell am I supposed to do that?" he demanded, forgetting for a moment he was talking to a woman.

Bess smiled. "I'm sure you'll think of something, young man." She took Flor de Oro by the arm and pointed to the rocker she had recently vacated. "Sit down, dear," she said, "and keep our Lieutenant Foxcroft company for me."

When Flor de Oro moved obediently to the chair, Bess gave him one last amused glance and went inside, leaving him standing alone and feeling absolutely foolish.

However, the blue eyes still regarded him from her sitting position and finally, for lack of anything else to do, he moved to the other rocker. She turned immediately to face him.

David sat for a long minute looking at her, then pointed first at her and then in a sweeping gesture toward the horizon. "Flor de Oro . . . go . . . Cochise?" he asked.

She nodded, and echoed. "Cochise."

"Damn I wish you wouldn't; or that you didn't want to," he said softly. "I wish you'd stay here. And I wish to hell you could understand me. I'd find a way to convince you." He was silent for a moment, watching her. "There's a wonderful life you don't even know about, you lovely creature," he said at last. "You would stun St. Louis society. I'd give almost anything to show it to you."

She nodded again. "Cochise."

"Yes," he said sadly. "You want to go back to Cochise. The Indians are something you understand."

He made a circling motion with his arms as if he were holding something close to his chest. "Flor de Oro . . . have . . . papoose?" he asked, slowly rocking his arms.

Suddenly the blue eyes darted away to stare at the

dirt in front of the porch. Her lips tightened.

David was alarmed. "I'm sorry," he said quickly and reached to touch her arm. "I didn't mean to hurt you. I was only—"

But she rose without another glance toward him and rapidly walked back into the house.

He sat for a minute in absolute frustration and then left, cursing his own clumsiness as he walked away.

For the next few days, he worked even harder: drilling troops, helping to direct further construction of buildings for the fort, and supervising the unloading of a supply train from Tucson. He made himself stay away from the Henley quarters and even avoided talking with the doctor on more than one occasion, knowing the discussion would turn to her. Once, he saw her carrying a bucket of water from a well and started to catch her to offer to carry it for her. But he didn't. She thought like an Indian woman and wouldn't understand. He stood and watched her until she went inside before turning away.

In the long evenings after the sun had gone down and he was alone in his own room, he lay on the bunk with his boots propped against the wall and thought about her. The image came easily to his mind, every detail was clear. Especially the one small smile she had given him.

He was hard at work when a trooper appeared, saluted, and told him he was to report to Colonel Markham's office immediately. David turned the task over to McDonald, now promoted to corporal to replace Tanner, and walked rapidly toward headquarters.

The commander was behind his desk, and sitting in a chair to one side with a moccasined foot propped casually on a small cabinet was a grinning Buffalo Harrison.

David had difficulty keeping his attention on the colonel as he reported.

Markham acknowledged the salute with a curt nod.

"Since you were involved in this affair from its beginning, Lieutenant, I thought it best that you be present now," he said. "I've sent for the young woman you brought in. We'll wait a minute or two for her to get here before we begin."

"Yes, sir." He couldn't help looking at Harrison. "You were successful? You saw Cochise?"

"Sat down and smoked with the big chief himself," Harrison drawled. "Although I wouldn't exactly say me'n him got to be buddies."

"What about Flor de Oro?" David persisted. "Did you find out who she was? Where she came from?"

"Lieutenant," Colonel Markham cut in sharply. "I believe I said we'd go into all of that when the woman herself arrives. I remind you that this matter could also affect the peace of the territory."

"Yes, sir."

"Incidentally, have you come up with another plan to capture this renegade?"

"I'm afraid not, sir," David offered reluctantly. "He wouldn't fall for that trick again, and I really don't know what else would bring him out."

The colonel grunted. "Well, he remains a problem as long as he's raiding the settlers in our area. We've got to do something about him. Have you thought of going back to where you lost him and having this Apache of yours try to backtrack to his hideout?"

"I've already asked Konta about that, sir. But he's certain the renegade will move his people to a new place and cover his trail well. He says Lobo Negro will be afraid the woman will get back to Cochise and lead him there."

"Cochise?" the colonel said in surprise. "What about us? Since we happen to have her."

David hesitated, then gave a mental shrug and plunged ahead. "Konta's also convinced that she'll do nothing except through Cochise."

"I see. Well, I'm afraid she won't get that chance," the colonel said, leaving David to wonder what he meant, because they were interrupted by the door behind him opening at that moment.

He turned as Henley stepped inside and held the door for Flor de Oro and his wife to enter, speaking over his shoulder at the same time. "Thought it best to bring Mrs. Henley along, Colonel. Our young guest seems a bit more willing to do what she asks."

"Of course." The commander stood up behind his desk. "Mrs. Henley, a pleasure to see you this morning."

"Good morning, Colonel Markham," she returned. "We're all anxious to hear the news."

"All right. Then we'll get on with it." He waved a hand in the scout's direction. "Mr. Harrison, tell them all you've told me."

David had stepped aside to make room for the three of them as they entered and from his new position he could see her face as Harrison, without bothering to stand, began to talk. Her attention was intent as the scout began to tell how he had ridden into the lands controlled by the Chiricahua and camped until he was suspiciously approached by some of the Indians. He had asked, he said, for an audience with the chief but still had to wait until the message was conveyed and answered.

Harrison was not one to mind an audience and entertained them with a complete description of how he was received in the rancheria of Cochise. How he was held apart from the center lodges until his wishes were discussed by a council, and only then was he taken to Cochise.

"I reckon he wasn't all that proud to see me," he grinned. "Even though I brought him good news, you might say. I got a strong suspicion he already knew this gal was here. You might keep that in mind, Colonel, in case there happens to be real trouble with his band. Ole Cochise keeps a pretty good eye on what goes on most everywhere."

Colonel Markham nodded without comment.

"What did he say about Flor de Oro, Mr. Harrison?" Bess Henley cut in, obviously losing patience with his drawn-out tale. "Does he insist on getting her back? Did he tell you who she was?"

Harrison slowly moved his gaze, not toward Mrs. Henley but to the girl. His heavy eyebrows lowered and he spoke slowly, almost to her alone. "No," he said. "He don't want her back. Not now. Not ever."

He switched back to Mrs. Henley. "She's—pardon the expression, ma'am—used goods."

Watching the girl, David saw a flash in her eyes. She understood! At least she understood the way he spoke. Then the thought hit him. *She wouldn't leave! She couldn't leave!*

Bess Henley's face had reddened with anger. "She was abducted," she snapped. "It certainly wasn't her fault!"

"Yesum. But that's the way savages think. Meaning no offense, Mrs. Henley, they think a woman . . . well, you know what I mean. Anyhow, he don't want her back. And he don't want nothing for her. She's free to stay here."

David had a suddenly eerie feeling. The girl's eyes had narrowed to pinpoints. Her lips were compressed. *By God,* he thought, *she does understand!*

He drew his attention from her reluctantly. "What exactly did he say to you, Harrison?" he asked.

"Well, Lieutenant, Cochise told me himself that he wasn't full sure she didn't sort of want to go away. Said she was supposed to marry this other Injun, some sort of chief in the Mimbreno tribe, and he figured mebbe she wasn't too happy about that. With her being white and all."

He grinned at their startled attention.

"He admitted to you that she was a white woman?" the colonel demanded.

Harrison nodded, his eyes slipping back to the girl's face. "She was stolen from a family up close to Santa Fe when she was a real young'un. Cochise said he didn't do it himself, but he knows who did. He took her away from the man that did it. He knows where she came from, and the way he describes the place, I'm right sure I can find it."

He turned back to Colonel Markham. "Why don't I explain all this to her in Apach? Tell her she ain't

117

wanted no more in Cochise's rancheria, and then mebbe she'll be more willing to talk to us."

"What do you think, Doctor?" the colonel asked.

Henley pursed his lips for a moment. "Well, she wanted to go back to the Indians, that was obvious. It's out of the question now, and I would certainly have been against it at any rate, since we know she's a white woman. Question is, can we convince her? If she's to be restrained, that is, taught to put aside the ways of a savage, we'll certainly need her cooperation." He glanced at his wife for confirmation, then added, "Mrs. Henley and I will do all we can."

Harrison spoke quickly. "When I said I could find where she come from, I meant take her back with me. Ride her up to Santa Fe and search for her folks."

The colonel shook his head. "I can't afford an escort for a mission like that, Harrison. My troopers are needed here. We'll have to make inquiries and if they're successful, have someone come here for her."

"Naw, colonel." The scout stood up slowly. "Ain't no need in all that. Most of the Injuns are peaceful enough, except for the renegades. I won't need nobody to ride with us. I'll see she gets there all right, don't worry."

"He does not tell the truth!"

Every other person in the room stared at her with astonishment, and Harrison's jaw dropped.

Flor de Oro's eyes were bright with anger as she glared at the scout. A moment later, she turned to David. "This man lies," she said with a knife edge to her voice. "I have no people in Santa Fe. I had only my father. And he is dead. Make him tell the truth!"

"My God!" breathed Doctor Henley.

Behind his desk, the fort commander moved his attention from her to Harrison and finally to David, who was still speechless. "Lieutenant," he said quietly, "I believe she's addressing you."

David shook his mind clear. "You . . . you speak English?" he stammered.

She nodded, and her eyes still flashed with anger. "You helped me with your soldiers in the cave. Help me now. He is lying about me. I think he lies about Cochise. Take me to Cochise and I will show he lies."

Her speech was slow, as if she had to carefully select each word. But it was clear and easily understood. He shook his head in wonder.

"Why didn't you tell us you understood?" Bess Henley interrupted. "Why wouldn't you talk to us before?"

Flor de Oro didn't answer. She kept her eyes on David.

He nodded slowly. "You were afraid, weren't you? Afraid we wouldn't let you go to Cochise."

She answered his nod with a short one of her own. "You will take me?"

Reluctantly he pulled away, out of the depths of the blue eyes, and glanced at the colonel. That officer merely returned his look, and David shifted at last to Harrison. "What about it?" he asked. "Did you really see Cochise?"

The scout's face was full of pure hatred. "You think I'm lying, Lieutenant?" he said in a voice that had a rattlesnake coiled in it.

David met his look squarely. "I'm asking," he said.

The scout moved suddenly, and both David and Colonel Markham tensed to stop him. But he only turned to his canvas saddlebags lying against the wall, bent over and fumbled with them a moment, then drew two blankets out and threw them at her feet. "You recognize these, gal?" he demanded.

Slowly the anger faded from her face. Her shoulders slumped as she stared down at the blankets.

"Yeah, dammit," Harrison growled. "They're yours, ain't they? Cochise gave 'em to me himself. You think I could have got 'em any other way?"

She didn't answer, her downcast eyes on the blankets, and Bess Henley stepped forward to touch her waist. "Flor de Oro," she said. "What do they mean to you?"

Her face was without expression. *The face of an Apache,* David thought suddenly. But her voice betrayed her; it was hollow . . . and distant. "He was my father," she said slowly. "He treated me as a daughter. I loved him as I loved my first father."

She paused a long moment, and David watched Mrs. Henley's arm slide around her waist and tighten.

"Now I have disgraced his name," Flor de Oro said at last. "He has put my blankets from his lodge. I cannot enter it again."

Except for the scout, who still watched her in anger, the rest were saddened by her voice. Even the colonel looked down at his desk and cleared his throat.

But then her head came up again and the defiance was there once more. The same expression she had held after he had stopped the troopers from raping her. She looked directly into his eyes. "I am no longer the daughter of Cochise," she said. "That is true. But I have no white family. Not here, not in Santa Fe. I will not go with this man."

"No," he said softly. "You sure won't."

"Excuse me." Henley interrupted the heavy silence between them. "Flor de Oro, you're welcome to remain with Mrs. Henley and me, I'm sure. For as long as you like." He cleared his throat noisily. "I believe no matter how long you lived with the sav—with this Cochise, after you've had a chance to adjust to . . . uh . . . our ways, you'll be glad you did."

"Thank you," she said. "I must—I have much to think about."

"Come, child," Bess Henley said, pulling her about. "Let's you and I go home."

The two of them walked to the door and went outside, leaving the three men alone. When they had gone, Harrison kicked his saddlebags toward the wall and sat down heavily.

"Foxcroft," he said, when he was seated. "I don't lie to any man. I don't have to. What I told you was what they told me in Cochise's camp. Don't ever question me like that again."

David didn't believe him. As much as he had liked this man, trusted him, and listened to him, he didn't believe him now. Harrison was lying. But why?

120

"No one called you a liar, Harrison," he said levelly. "Except the girl. But she's not going with you."

Their eyes locked. And whatever friendship there had been between them was lost with the look. Henley noticed it; David could feel him move closer behind him. But the colonel had his mind on other things. "That's beside the point," he said, turning to the map on the wall. "She's likely had other stories from the Indians she lived with. But Foxcroft's right, Harrison, it would be foolish for you and she to ride up there alone. I'll make the inquiries as I said. However, this could mean trouble if Cochise changes his mind. He's a powerful man among the Indians. Stir him up and we'll have our hands full."

He glanced around at them significantly. "And, gentlemen, we may not be here much longer. God help the settlers in this area if the Army has to pull out."

The doctor nodded, but David was surprised. "We're moving, Colonel?"

"Not yet," Markham answered. "But I wouldn't be surprised. The country is turning to war against itself, Lieutenant. Our southern states are demanding it. It will either be war, or we will become two separate countries."

He heaved a heavy sigh. "The war, if it comes, will be fought in the east, and we'll be ordered back to help fight it. There will be no one left to stand between the remaining settlers and the Indians. Judging the nature of the times, I hesitate to think what might happen."

"We may have more trouble than that," Henley cut in dryly. "Most of the people in this territory are sympathetic to the South."

The colonel nodded, and as they talked on, even Harrison seemed to lose his anger and drawled in amusement that he was hired to fight Indians, not Southerners. But David didn't take part and hardly listened. His mind was on the girl.

Chapter Nine

He was in love with the girl. That he was forced to admit. Before what took place in the colonel's office, he hadn't been sure and attempted to convince himself it was merely because he was a young, single man and she was a rare and beautiful woman. It had been ridiculous to consider anything else. He'd even suggested to himself that it was sympathy for a young woman caught in a difficult situation.

But all that was before she had spoken. It hadn't been the fact that she spoke in English either, merely the sound of her voice. That had been the missing ingredient. When she spoke and he could understand, a marvelous feeling had come over him; he'd wanted desperately to take her in his arms, hold her, and tell her how much he loved her. Until she spoke she had been beautiful, but as a painting by Michelangelo is beautiful. Lovely to look at but not meant to be touched; certainly not to be possessed. When she spoke, the illusion was shattered and she became a desirable woman.

He wanted to possess her—no, not possess her, to have her love. He wanted to be with her for the rest of his life. Wanted to hold her hand and walk with her in the evenings, sit across from her over a meal the two of them shared alone, and talk about things that meant something only to them. He wanted the touch of those cool lips on his own and—dammit! This was insane! Their worlds were too far apart and besides, she probably held him in the same classification she did Tanner!

No. She didn't think of him that way. He couldn't

believe that, not after the way she had looked at him. In the stress of that moment in the colonel's office when all that she had wanted for herself was slipping away and she stood alone among strangers, she had turned to him. He would never forget that look.

In the early afternoon, Buffalo Harrison rode out of the compound leading a pack horse behind him. David watched him go and if the scout noticed him in return, he didn't acknowledge the fact, merely lifting a hand in a casual wave to the patrolling guards. It was obvious he'd resigned as scout for the fort and was leaving for good. David felt a little sorry for him. The older man had made pretty much a fool of himself and had been embarrassed by the fact.

Whether Harrison had told the truth—or believed he told the truth—about Flor de Oro's background was immaterial. He'd wanted to take her away with him. David remembered the quality of his voice on the one or two times he'd talked about Flor de Oro in the past months. He realized there had been naked desire in those words. The scout was a tough and capable man, intelligent in his own way, and very good at his job. But he was an uncomplicated man. He'd wanted the girl for himself and made the mistake of taking her for a savage, a simple Indian squaw who could be easily handled if she had no other place to go. He'd botched it badly, and now he had too much pride to hang around.

But then he had to wonder also if Harrison had told the truth to the Chiricahua chief. Suppose he'd lied there as well? It was entirely possible. And if Cochise discovered he'd been lied to, the Apache might well go on the warpath to get her back, or at least to take revenge for the trickery. There was also Colonel Markham's worries about the possibility of war back east. If the Army was ordered home as the commander expected, Doctor and Mrs. Henley would go too. What would happen to Flor de Oro then?

Hell, it didn't make any difference what happened. There was no way he was going to leave her here by herself or allow her to go back to the life of an Indian.

123

Not if he could help it. After work tonight, he'd make another attempt to talk to her. Since he now knew she could speak English, perhaps she would react differently.

In spite of himself, he grinned. She must have thought him a pretty fool with his clumsy attempts to talk to her before. Using sign language, by God! He must have appeared ridiculous!

Well, by damn, she'd talk to him now. He intended to camp on her doorstep every evening until she did.

The doctor was waiting for him when he returned to his quarters; waiting with his boots propped on David's bunk and a cup of David's whiskey in his hand. He glanced up and grinned when the door opened.

"Hello there, my friend." He lifted the cup in mock salute. "Your stock is running a bit low; you need to resupply."

David closed the door and began to remove his belt and side arm. "Used to be plenty for me," he said. "It's my visitors I can't keep up with."

"Now I ask you, is that any way to talk to a man who's come to invite you to a good meal? I should think you'd be grateful enough to offer me a drink."

David had started to unbutton his tunic but stopped quickly. "Help yourself to the rest of the bottle," he grinned. "Fair trade for one of Mrs. Henley's suppers."

"And a chance to talk to the Henleys' young guest," the doctor observed into the cup in his hand. "I do believe everyone on this godforsaken post must be in love with that woman."

He tossed off the rest of the liquor and eyed David in amusement. "You are in love with her, Lieutenant. Don't bother to deny it. Plain as the nose on your face. But then I can't say as I blame you; she's a beautiful creature."

"I assure you, Doctor, my interest is purely . . . Oh what the hell. That obvious, huh?"

"That obvious," Henley agreed solemnly. "My

own Bess observed it the day you brought her in. Said you reminded her of a calf who'd lost its mama."

David crossed to the table and picked up the bottle, inspected its contents through the neck with one eye, and took a long drink himself. "I'm not the only one," he said after he put it down again.

"Like I just said, every man on the whole damn post," Henley agreed. "But I assume you're talking about our ex scout?"

"Then he did resign?"

The doctor nodded. "Quit cold. Strange how a woman could affect a man like Harrison. I would have thought him immune."

"She's quite a woman," David reminded him.

"Yes, she is. And by the way, my Bess is not just worrying about your having a good meal under your belt, my friend. Our guest asked to see you herself."

"Damn!" David exploded. "Why the hell didn't you say so?"

Henley grinned wickedly and stood up. "Wanted to be able to finish my drink before you rushed me over there," he said. "When you reach my age, Lieutenant, some things become more important than others. A drink of good whiskey, or even two, is—"

"Are we going or not?" David interrupted, rebuckling his belt.

The doctor sighed. "After you. And by the way, her name is Jennifer."

David opened the door. "Jennifer what?"

"Just Jennifer, as far as we know. She's polite, but evidently the only person she comes close to trusting at this point is you. To tell you the truth, I'm looking forward to our dinner conversation with a great deal of interest."

The adobe house assigned to Captain Henley as second-ranking officer on the post was large in comparison to the others. But still it consisted of only two full-size rooms, along with a storage area on the back. The rooms had a low ceiling and since one was used for sleeping, the other was made to serve as both cooking and living quarters. A small cast-iron stove stood in one corner with pots that emitted delightful aromas. A heavy plank table with wooden-slatted chairs around it stood in the center of the room, and a third rocker to match the two on the porch outside sat near the only window; various boxes, trunks, cabinets and shelves made up the rest of the furnishings.

When the two of them entered, Bess Henley greeted them over her shoulder from her position in front of the stove. "Hello, David. Glad you could come. Hungry?"

"Yes ma'am. Always happy to share one of your meals, Mrs. Henley. I'm grateful for the invitation."

"Good." She had already turned back to her cooking. "Why don't you get him a drink, Joseph."

Doctor Henley winked at David. "Excellent idea, my dear. Could use a little nip myself."

He opened one of the trunks, extracted a bottle, and crossed to a high shelf for two tin cups. "Sit down, Lieutenant. Make yourself comfortable."

David pulled a chair from the table, sat down, and when his cup was filled, raised it to his host. He was about to say something when the curtain covering the doorway between the two rooms parted and she appeared.

He stood up and stared. The buckskins were gone. She wore a dress with long sleeves, a high neck, and large, decorative ribbons woven throughout the front. If it had once belonged to Mrs. Henley, it had been well altered, for it clung to its present wearer very closely.

"Hello, Mister Lieutenant," she said.

"Lieutenant," he said. "Just Lieutenant. I'm not a mister—I mean, you don't need the mister—my name is David, Flor de Oro."

The blue eyes were drowning him. The room suddenly became very unsteady.

"I'm sorry," she said softly. "There are many things I do not understand. Mrs. Henley is helping me to learn."

That lady turned from the cooking. "Why don't

you put some plates on the table, dear. We'll be ready to eat in a moment or so."

"Yes," the girl said, and moved to comply.

David watched her as she went to a shelf for the plates and then, at Bess Henley's direction, for the tableware. Beside him, the doctor made casual conversation, but he only half listened and ignored his own whiskey. His eyes met hers often as she moved around the room, for she looked his way frequently—and not with short coquettish glances. Her own look was frank and searching, as if somehow she was measuring him.

When all were seated at the table with the blond girl opposite David, Bess Henley looked up over the steaming pot she had placed in front of herself. "Oh David, I forgot to introduce you all over again. This is Jennifer, I'm happy to say. Although I don't know her last name."

"Jennifer is a lovely name," he said, not looking at Bess.

"Thank you." She glanced at Mrs. Henley. "My full name is Jennifer McLean. It has been a long time since I used it. I am not used to saying it. I'm sorry."

Doctor Henley paused with a plate of beans in his hands. "Would you mind telling us about yourself, Jennifer?"

"But only if you want to, dear," his wife hastened to add.

She nodded slowly. However, she didn't speak and the silence built oppressively in the room. Henley shrugged and heaped his plate before passing the beans to David.

When she did speak, it was suddenly and in a rush, almost as if she were trying to hurry the words before she decided against it. "My father's name was Matthew. Matthew McLean. He was a mis . . . missionary. He died in the desert."

She dropped her hands in her lap and looked at David.

"You were crossing with a wagon train?" he asked, laying his own fork down.

She shook her head. "No. We had a wagon for a time. The horse died. Then we walked. There was only my father and me."

Her eyes dropped to her plate, and David glanced to Bess Henley for aid. But his hostess could only shrug her shoulders in a helpless gesture.

Mentally hoping he was doing the right thing, he decided to press on. "You say your father died on the desert, Jennifer? You were left alone?"

She shook her head again. "No. Cochise was there."

"Cochise? Then your father was with the Apache? I'm afraid I don't understand."

Slowly the blue eyes came up to meet his once more. "I will tell you all," she said. "Who I am. Who I was. You were a friend to me when I ran away from Lobo Negro."

She paused and David had to force himself to remain silent and give her time. The doctor and his wife had forgotten their own meal as well.

"If I tell you, I think," she continued slowly, "you will not like me. Per—perhaps . . ." She struggled with the word. "You will not be my friend. But—"

He could contain himself no longer. "Flor de Oro. No, I mean Jennifer. Nothing you could say will change that. I want to be your friend. All of us do."

She gave him a long, searching look. "But Americans do not like the Apache. I have been an Apache. I wanted once to be an Apache for the rest of my life. The way I was before was not good. Even though I loved my father, Matthew McLean, very much."

He was very tense, her nerves tight. He had to force his voice to remain casual. "How old were you when he died?" he asked as gently as he could manage.

"Nine years old."

"Then you don't really know what life as a white woman could be, Jennifer. All life is not the same." His glance took in both of the others. "Some white men don't hate Indians. None of us at this table do. And we want very much to help you as I said."

She was also nervous. He could see it in the tightness of her mouth and wanted to reach across the table and touch her.

"Then I will tell you," she said. "Your face is full of truth. Like the face of Cochise."

He nodded.

"My mother died when I was young. And my father—the other people where we lived, I don't remember very well where it was—they did not like him. He spoke always from his Bible and made them very angry. Some men came one night and made us go away."

David watched in fascination as the blue eyes clouded in thoughtfulness.

"Everywhere we went it was the same. He would talk and make people angry and we would have to leave. I knew even then he was sick. I mean, he was very troubled and blamed himself for my mother being dead. But he was my father and I loved him. I would cook for him and listen when he talked, even if I did not understand. Then one day he told me we must come here. That his God had told him to go and speak to the Apache.

"I was afraid. But he was my father. We rode in the wagon for many days and sometimes we did not eat. He did not always think to get food for us. When we met the Apache for the first time, they too were angry and would not listen to him. They would walk away, but they would not harm us.

"Then, I think they understood. My father became very sick in his mind. He would stand in the desert and speak loudly to no one at all. Only to the desert."

She took a deep breath. "For many days he would not even know who I was and would look at me without seeing me. He would talk only to his God. Then he would know me again and he would be kind."

Bess Henley had tears in her eyes. "But how did you find food in the desert, Jennifer? What did you eat?"

"The Apache brought us food. They would come in the night and leave it near our campfire. And they brought us wood for that as well. But they would not let him see them do it, only me. Afterward, when I lived with Cochise, he told me they thought my father had been filled with Spirits.

"Then one day he walked away from our camp and I could not bring him back to it. I could only follow behind him, and we walked for two days without stopping. When he fell and could not get up, I sat down beside him and held his head. The Apache came and built a brush hut over us to keep out the sun.

"Cochise came then, but I did not know who he was. He sat down in the hut with me and stayed there without talking for the three days it took my father to die. When my father was dead, he picked me up in his arms and took me home with him."

She paused and her chin lifted. "After that I became an Apache. Cochise made me a place in his lodge and told me I had become his daughter. I was sad at first, but then I became very happy and I wanted to be an Apache always. Still, I remember my father."

Doctor Henley coughed behind his hand, looked to his wife, and then allowed his gaze to sweep the room as if he were examining it for the first time. None of the others could think of anything to say as Jennifer placed her hands in her lap again and looked at David.

He struggled for words. "I'm glad your life with Cochise was not a hard one, Jennifer," he said at last. "But I'm even more glad we found you and took you from Lobo Negro. I want very much to . . . be your friend. I'll do anything I can to keep that friendship."

"Thank you," she said. "I will need a friend to find my new life now. I am strong and can work. I do not know what a woman does who is not an Apache. I have much to learn. I will work very hard to do this."

He didn't know quite what to say to that.

In the months that followed her arrival, David spent as much time with her as his duties would permit, and under the gentle tutelage of Bess Henley, the transformation of Jennifer McLean was nothing short of amazing. That she was intelligent was obvious; she absorbed information rapidly. With constant usage, her speech improved to the point that it was difficult for him to believe she had gone for years without using her first language. She even gave up the bold stride she had used as an Indian and adopted the shorter, more precise step of a white woman, probably due as much to the difficulty of the long skirts she now wore as to her imitation of Bess Henley.

When she was alone with him, she asked a thousand questions about life in the eastern cities of which she had only dim memories. Sometimes amused, sometimes touched by her naivete, and always a little discomforted by her directness, he did his best to answer.

She told him a great deal about life among the Apache when he was able to inject questions of his own, and David marveled at the insight he obtained. His knowledge of the Indians had come from Harrison and to a lesser extent from Konta. All of that, however, had been directed toward possible battle with the Apache. To learn of his homelife, his pleasures, and his beliefs, in fact his day-to-day existence, was to began to understand the Apache as a man.

That she adored Cochise, her Indian father, was apparent. But now she spoke of him with a tint of sadness in her voice, as if she were speaking of a parent who had died. On those occasions, David merely listened without comment, afraid to press her.

Nor did he mention her life with the renegades, although such information might be of use to him in his still assigned task to find Lobo Negro. If she chose to tell him, he would listen, he told himself. But to bring it up would be to summon what must be a painful memory. He couldn't do that to her.

He took her riding when he could find the time, renting a mount from the sutler since he couldn't allow her to use an Army horse. They rode miles from the Fort and stopped often just to sit and look about them. She delighted in telling him about the desert and laughed when she could point out things he couldn't see until she did. Once, she dismounted and challenged him to a foot race. When he accepted, with an amused eye on her long skirt, she promptly raised it to her thighs and easily outdistanced him. These were glorious hours for David.

In the evenings, whenever he could, he sat in the Henley quarters with the three of them and talked. The one problem that troubled the enjoyment of his days with her was the realization that civil war would take him away from her unless he put into completion a plan that was rapidly growing in his mind. A plan that depended on her acceptance.

He smiled wryly to himself as he thought about it. His mother and sister would be horrified. And his father too, in all probability. But then they didn't know her yet . . .

The situation in the East grew steadily worse. Many of the southern states seceded from the Union and the Confederate States of America was in full bloom. When the news arrived that a fort in Charleston harbor had been fired upon and was under siege by South Carolina milita, David knew the expected war had arrived.

Conditions at Fort Buchanan quickly deteriorated. Almost every night a few more soldiers, including noncoms, deserted to head east and join the Confederates in Texas. Double guards were posted but some of these disappeared as well. The trouble was that no one knew for certain where a man's loyalties lay until he declared them by his absence. The final blow came when two of the six officers at the fort left resignations in their quarters and also disappeared during the night.

Colonel Markham called an emergency meeting of the rest. When David, Captain Henley, and Lieutenant Pease assembled in his office, he faced them squarely and demanded to know their intentions one by one.

"I'm a Missourian, sir," David told him. "I realize there are strong Southern feelings in my state, but I understand it has not, and probably won't, secede.

My family is in business in St. Louis and we have never been slave holders. I have every intention of fulfilling my duties to the Army."

The Colonel's hard look softened slightly, and he turned a questioning glance to Doctor Henley, who merely nodded. "Ohio, Colonel. Loyal to the Union."

After the third man, Pease, had also declared his loyalty, Markham released a long sigh. "As some of you may already be aware, I'm a Viginian. But I believe in a strong Union. I think that's the only way our country can survive against the European powers who are waiting for just such an opportunity as this split may present. There's still a great deal of rich territory on this continent, territory that will end up in the hands of whoever is strong enough to hold it. A divided America will not be that strong. Therefore, gentlemen, much as it will pain me to take up arms against my native state, I intend to do just that."

He paused a long, thoughtful moment. "May God aid us in this struggle and make it mercifully brief."

"It won't last long, sir," Lieutenant Pease offered quickly. "The southern states can't be well prepared."

The colonel's jaw hardened. "Don't underestimate Southerners, Lieutenant," he said sharply. "We—they will fight very well, I assure you."

The officer reddened. "Of course, sir. I only meant in the matter of equipment. Most of the factories, weapon-makers and so forth, are located in the North. That's what I meant by prepared."

"Unless Great Britain or France decides to aid the South," Doctor Henley observed quietly. "If they do, we may well be destroyed as a country."

Each of them paused to consider his words and allowed a heavy silence to hold the room oppressively. David broke it with a question. "What about our situation here, Colonel? We're spread pretty thin now."

The commander shook his head. "An impossible job, Lieutenant. Indian attacks are already being stepped up in other areas, principally from the Navajo. Cochise and his people are beginning to do the same, and we'll be helpless to oppose him effectively if he goes completely on the warpath. I realize he may think he has every right to do so after that stupid Bascome incident at Apache Pass; no doubt he will consider war justified. I'd hoped to settle that with a new offer to him. However, there's no longer time for such delicate negotiations."

He glanced at the map behind him. "Besides, our position may well be untenable among the whites as well. In my own estimation, the majority of the settlers in this area are in sympathy with the Southern cause. With Texas in the Confederacy, I expect Southern troops from there to be sent to drive us out, and we can anticipate no help from the locals."

Turning back, he added, "If I were making the decisions, I'd pull all Union forces out of here for the time being. At least until we're strong enough to come back in force."

"But that would leave loyal settlers without any defense at all, sir," David protested.

The colonel nodded. "I'm aware of that, Lieutenant. And I'm certain those people are, too, and will make their own plans accordingly. And as I said, the Apache will take advantage of the situation. It simply can't be helped. We would serve no good purpose by remaining here and being captured by superior Confederate forces. I'm quite sure when Washington gets around to remembering us, they will concur and order us out. Therefore, prepare your men to depart as soon as we receive our orders from Colonel Canby."

There was some further discussion, in the main as to where they would withdraw, but David only half listened, impatient to be dismissed.

When he was at last, he went first to inform remaining noncoms and then hurried to the Henley quarters. Jennifer was sitting on the porch with a sewing basket on her lap when he arrived.

"Hello, David," she said. "I didn't expect you until tonight."

He was nervous in spite of himself. "Jennifer,

something important has come up. I need to talk to you. Will you walk with me?"

She placed the basket on the floor and stood up. "Where shall we go?" she asked quietly.

David reached for her hand. "Just walk," he said. "I want to be alone with you."

She moved beside him without comment as he led her behind the house and away from the compound. He stopped on a rise far enough from the fort that they wouldn't be accidentally interrupted.

"Jennifer, you remember I told you about the possibility of war back east?"

She gave him a quick nod. "I don't understand it. But I remember."

"I also told you I might soon have to leave here," he said gently. "And Doctor and Mrs. Henley as well."

The blue eyes rested calmly on his own. "Yes. I understand. You must go now?"

David nodded slowly. "Very soon. We've been told to prepare."

"I will be sorry to see you go," she said. "You've been a good friend."

"What will you do?" he asked. "I mean, have you thought about it?"

She looked out across the desert. After a long, agonizing wait for him, she turned back. "No, David. I can't return to Cochise, and I don't wish to live with any other tribe. I think I'll go to this town, Tucson. Perhaps I can find work there."

"It's no place for a woman alone, Jennifer," he said quickly. "You don't understand yet. You'll be taken advantage of there."

A hard little smile tugged at her lips. "I don't know a lot about towns," she said. "But I do understand what you are saying. I won't be taken advantage of easily."

"There's another solution," he said gently, reaching again for her hands.

The smile softened, and looking at her David knew she understood him also. What he didn't know was what she was thinking. He couldn't read her face and she remained silent, waiting.

"I love you, Jennifer McLean," he said at last. "I think I've loved you from the day I first saw you in that cave. And now I want you to come with me."

"To be your woman?" Her voice was very soft.

"No," he said quickly. "To be my wife. There's a great difference. I want you to learn to love me in return. Can you?"

"I have a child," she said abruptly. "An Indian child. Lobo Negro's."

He met her look squarely. "I know. At least I knew you had a child. I didn't know what happened to it. Bess Henley told me the first day."

"Knowing that, you would still want to marry me?"

"I love you, Jennifer. Nothing in the world can change that."

Slowly the blue eyes searching his own changed; he'd never seen them like that and suddenly his hopes soared.

But instead, she shook her head. "I can't marry you, David. And not because I don't love you, I think I do. But don't you see, I must stay here. I want my son back. He belongs to me. Perhaps Lobo Negro has killed him; I think that is possible, for he has a great deal of anger inside of him. I don't know if I will ever find out. But if I go away with you, there will no longer be even the small chance I will know."

"I understand, Jennifer," he said quickly. "But soon this territory will be at war, too. The Southerners will come first and then our army will return to fight them. And in between, I'm sure there will be war with the Indians. With all that, you don't stand a chance to look for your son."

"I must try. I must know."

His grip tightened on her hands. "Then come with me. Marry me. And when all of this is over, no matter how it comes out, I swear I'll bring you back and we'll search together. For as long as it takes."

She continued to study his face and David tried to

pull her into his arms. But she resisted.

"Jennifer," he said. "Come with me."

She shook her head. "I do love you, David. I'm sure of it. There is a feeling that has grown inside me since I've known you. I wouldn't listen to it before because I didn't know what you thought. But you ask me to give up my son . . ."

"Only for a little while," he said. "The war won't—can't last long."

"Cochise will still hunt Lobo Negro. Even if he has turned against me, he will still try to kill him. He'll never give up. If my son is with Lobo Negro when Cochise finds him, he could die in the fighting between them."

She was slipping away from him. He could feel it in desperation. So close . . . and she had said she loved him . . . "Jennifer, what could you really do? I know you understand the Apache ways, but you're only one woman. If you could save your son by yourself, couldn't you have done it before? When you ran?"

Her blue eyes flashed in anger. Alarming him. "I escaped only to get Cochise!"

"I know. I know," he said quickly, soothingly. "That's not what I meant. You thought you could get help. And you were right in thinking that. But now you won't have help. Let me do it for you, Jennifer. Just as soon as I can."

She shook her head. "You're strong, David. And you're very brave; I can see that. But you're not—you can't track an Apache. Or get him to fight you. Especially Lobo Negro. You don't know him."

"I said we would do it together, Jennifer. Remember? You'll be my Apache eyes. And you do know Lobo Negro. Don't you see it's the best chance you'll have?"

"You're right," she said abruptly, startling him with her sudden change. "I cannot do it alone."

Before he could speak, she added, "I will make you a good wife, David. When shall we become married?"

"My God! You really mean it?"

She smiled. A slow smile that began on the tip of

137

her lips and spread back to crease her cheeks. "An Apache's word is always good, Lieutenant David Foxcroft. You should know that."

And then she reached up to kiss him.

Chapter Ten

Lobo Negro sat on the ground a few feet from the fire with his back against a tree. Sitting far enough away from the small blaze to avoid looking into it. A warrior who did that was stupid; it would blind his eyes for precious seconds if he had to suddenly search for an enemy in the darkness. And he needed his night eyes, especially during these times. Cochise, or at least some of the Chiricahua, were still doggedly on his trail. They would continue until they caught up with him again or until he managed to move far enough away from these lands.

The new repeating rifle he'd gotten from the Tucson trader lay across his lap and he used a cloth to wipe it even cleaner. Before him, Ta-ne-dako squatted by the fire and stirred a pot of gruel made from caterpillars. Near her and always under her sharp eye, the boy played with a large tarantula, poking its hairy back with a chubby finger to make it move and at the same time confusing its flight with a stick.

The two of them were almost all he had left now. Only yesterday he'd had two warriors and one other squaw. But one of the men had taken the squaw and left during the night. Lobo Negro had seen him go but made no effort to stop him. A warrior who was not loyal was worse in a fight than no warrior at all. Now there was only the other one, standing guard on the ridge above them.

A week ago there had been four left, but two were killed in Mexico when Cochise had trapped him in a box draw. If he hadn't discovered the presence of the

Chiricahua in time, they would have been above him on the rim as well as in the entrance. Even so, he'd barely had time to escape. The two who stayed to delay the Chiricahua as he and the rest climbed out had been too slow with their own escape and paid for their slowness with their lives.

His anger returned as he thought about the Chiricahua leader. Anger that burned deeply in his stomach. Losing his hidden rancheria after the woman escaped had exposed him to the searchers and for each of the long months afterward he'd been forced to stay on the run. Like a deer with coyotes at its heels, he'd turned to fight when they closed in, only to run again as soon as he could. The long, running fight had taken its toll on his band and he'd been given no time to recruit.

The woman was the cause of his troubles. As he thought of her again, the anger burned even deeper. But at the same time there was also a weight in his chest when her face came into his mind. He thought of her in the nights and his body ached to have her beside him even though he told himself he no longer desired her. He hated the feeling and would always rise and walk until it was gone again.

Flor de Oro had made a fool of him before his followers. He had not believed she could leave her child or he would not have taken her with him on that journey. But she had.

He had nearly been caught when he followed her to where the soldiers lived. He stirred impatiently as he remembered the one opportunity he'd had to get her back. The two of them, Flor de Oro and the tall soldier, had been alone. He'd gotten close enough to use his knife on the American—knowing he could not risk a shot near the place of the other bluecoats—but suddenly she had spoken in the language of the whites and had raced away, laughing. The soldier had chased her in merriment and left him to curse in frustration.

He'd tried to follow, but he'd stayed near the soldier too long and had become careless with his attention on the two of them. The Chiricahua had been watching the fort, too. When they discovered him and attacked, he'd needed all his wiles to escape.

Even so, he'd been drawn back again. But when he had returned, she was gone. All of the bluecoats were gone, their houses deserted. He didn't understand why and had gone to the trader at Tucson to find out the reason. But this time he'd been ambushed by the Americans there and again barely got away with his life. That was another score he would settle someday. The trader had turned on him and tried to kill him. Someday, he promised himself, Sattersfield would pay for that.

Ta-ne-dako kept the fire very low to hide it. That meant the meal would take a long time to cook and he was hungry. He tucked the cloth back into his belt and carefully propped the rifle against the tree where it would be ready to his hand before lying back to rest.

He didn't understand why the blue-coated soldiers had left, and the mystery was even deeper now, for when he'd crossed back from Mexico into the lands of the Mescalero, he'd been surprised to see soldiers who wore a different coat, a gray one. They were riding west in long columns and carried a flag that was not the same one the American soldiers had been using. He had to find out what that meant.

Finally, the stew was ready and Ta-ne-dako put out the fire as she removed the pot and called softly to him. Lobo Negro moved to eat silently beside her in the dark and as soon as he filled his belly left to relieve the guard so that he could eat as well.

Major Ellis B. Clinchfield rode into Tucson at the head of a troop of Texas Mounted Rifles, their gray uniforms brand-new, their saddles and weapons sparkling. He led them down the street to the rousing cheers of most of its citizens. (Those whose loyalty still lay with the Union had either fled or were wise enough to keep quiet about it.) The editor of the *Tucson Gazette* had plastered the town with a one-page editorial proclaiming that ARIZONA IS NOW FREE AT LAST, and most of the yelling bystanders waved either a copy of the newspaper or a hastily made Confederate flag as they cheered.

In front of one high wooden-fronted building, a grandstand had been constructed and was decorated by long banners of the Stars and Bars. Clinchfield rode his stallion up to it, stopped, and stood up in his stirrups to raise his white campaign hat to the crowd. They had been loud before, but they went into a frenzy at the gesture; it took several minutes after he had mounted the platform before they quieted enough for him to speak. He used the time to shake hands with the half dozen dignitaries who shared the platform with him. Finally, after repeatedly raising both arms for silence, he was allowed to speak.

"Citizens!" he shouted. "In the name of Colonel John Robert Baylor, Commander of the Texas Mounted Rifles and now military governor, I hereby proclaim this the Confederate Territory of Arizona. Part and parcel of the Confederate States of America!"

The cheers were deafening and he was forced to wait again. Then he went on to tell them that the Union forces, although temporarily fortified around Santa Fe and Fort Craig, were on the run and soon would be pushed out of the territory entirely. That even now a large force was being recruited in Texas by General Henry H. Sibley to do the job. And that a representative of the territory would be elected and sent as soon as possible to the Confederate Congress at Richmond.

The crowd allowed him to speak only in brief snatches, and nearly an hour passed before he was through and had listened to the welcoming speeches from the town leaders. Afterward, his men were hustled off to various saloons to be plied with free drinks, while Clinchfield himself was led to a private room for more serious conversation.

Without the noise of the crowd to distract them, he was again introduced to the other men and one in particular struck him, a lean snake of a man named Sattersfield. Clinchfield considered himself a good judge of character and decided on the spot that this one would bear watching.

Brandy was served all around by a black waiter and over it, the major answered their questions. Some were about the possible conduct of the war, but most had to do with the territory itself.

"I can only tell you, gentlemen," he said, "that we fully expect to win this struggle. Our soldiers are the better fighters, and if you weren't already aware of it, the cream of the officer corps of the previous Army is now serving with the Confederacy. Our main problem is money and manpower. Our armies now forming are not as large as the Federal forces, and at the moment, are ill-equipped."

He took a long sip of his brandy to allow his words to sink in and continued. "The Northern forces have both arms and manpower in abundance. Therefore, we must strike swiftly and not permit this war to drag out. If we don't, I'm afraid time will allow their blockade of our seaports to take its toll. Equipping our armies rapidly, gentlemen, is where you come in."

"How is that, Major?" the mayor wanted to know. "Surely you're not contemplating supplying by wagon train?"

"No," Clinchfield said. "I'm talking about gold and silver. The wealth needed to purchase the arms and munitions we need."

The men in the room with him looked at one another quickly as he had expected, and Clinchfield allowed them the moments he knew they needed to evaluate the balance of supporting the Confederacy now with their money against the future wealth such an action might bring them. Then he added softly, "Gentlemen, these regions contain great mineral wealth, as well as vast acres of land suitable for plantations and the raising of cattle. Your major problem is workers, both to man the mines and the fields. Under the Confederacy, and its rightful policy of slavery, that problem is solved. You have countless Indians and Mexicans who can be, and should be, enslaved."

"What about now, Major?" Sattersfield interrupted. "The Apache doesn't make a very good slave. In fact, at the moment he's raising pure hell with us. The whole country is unsafe. Many of our mines have had to be closed for lack of protection. And as far as ranching or farming, only in the towns can a white family consider itself safe."

The major nodded in agreement. "The military governor has authorized you to organize a force of Arizona guards for the purpose of protecting your citizens. I assure you there will be no interference from the government in how you go about doing so."

A slow smile spread across Sattersfield's face. "Just exactly what are our instructions regarding the Apache?"

Clinchfield leaned forward to place his brandy glass on the table before regarding them deliberately. "Let me quote you Colonel Baylor's exact words in regard to the Apache. You are expected to use all means to persuade them to come in for the purpose of making peace, and after you get them together, kill all the grown Indians, take the children prisoners, and sell them to defray the expense of killing the rest. Buy whiskey and such other goods as may be necessary for the Indians and I will order vouchers given to cover the amount expended. Leave nothing undone to insure success, and have a sufficient number of men around to allow no Indian to escape."

There was general agreement among them at his words, as he had expected. These men understood that the Apache were an encumbrance, a past era of people who had lived out their age and now stood in the way of progress. The Indians were using valuable land to pursue a life that no longer had meaning.

The Washington government had followed a policy of moving them from one reservation to another and of spending large sums of money merely to feed them. It was a stupid plan that any intelligent man could see would never work in the long run. There would someday be no land on this continent that wouldn't be valuable to someone; then where would they go?

The only real solution was extinction for the Apache. Milder tribes would serve as slaves, but the Apache had to be destroyed.

Chapter Eleven

Jefferson City, Missouri was a busy little place. Its location on the wide Missouri River had been selected in 1821 as a site for the capital of the state, and it had grown in size and activity ever since. By 1839 it was in truth, a city. Nearly lost to the Rebels short months before, it had been saved, as was the state, more by the failure of the Confederates to follow up the Union defeats at Wilson's Creek and Lexington than by the slow maneuvering of Federal forces under General Fremont. Now it boasted both a pro-Union legislature and a supply center for men and materials for the Northern cause.

Captain David Foxcroft assisted his wife from the wagon before turning to tell the soldier who removed his saddlebags and her small trunk to carry them into the Blakely Hotel just opposite. He watched as Jennifer first bent her back slightly and then twisted from side to side to relieve the stiffness. "Long ride," he commented.

"Yes," she said, tugging at the jacket of her riding suit to straighten it. "And I'm hungry. Are we going to stay with someone here?"

"Uh uh. We'll get a room in the hotel where Private Williams is headed now. First town we've come to that was big enough to have one."

She studied the building intently until Williams entered the large front doors. "That's not someone's home?"

David smiled. His wife still had a great deal to learn; he was continually surprised at the things she didn't know. But the past few months, when he wasn't out fighting with Colonel Canby, had been enjoyable ones as he saw things, once familiar to him, freshly through her eyes. In Santa Fe, they had found quarters with the Army, and Bess Henley had been there for woman talk with her as well as to help her select the few clothes she now had. But when he'd received the orders promoting him and assigning him to General Fremont's staff in St. Louis, the two of them had said goodby and started the long journey through Kansas.

It had been a rapid trip with the two soldiers traveling with them, and the only stops they'd made had been to camp in the open or twice to stay in a farmhouse with friendly settlers. He realized she had no concept of a hotel.

"No," he told her. "This place has many rooms and they're there for the sole purpose of renting them to travelers."

"Like an inn?"

"Uh huh. You've stayed in an inn?"

Jennifer shook her head, still observing the passing scene with unconcealed interest. "My father wouldn't stay in one. He considered them wicked, I remember."

The other soldier, Boyle, had already moved the horses and wagon on down the street to look for a livery stable and David placed a hand on her waist to guide her toward the hotel. "Well," he said, "this place isn't wicked. It's only a place to get a room with a bed; a comfortable one, I hope. I'll get one for us and you can rest while I see about train tickets to St. Louis."

That brought her interest around to him. "We're going to ride a train?"

He stopped her in the middle of the wide street to avoid a passing carriage. "Yes. Think you'll like that?"

"Yes, I will. It sounds exciting."

"You're going to see a lot of exciting things in St. Louis, Jennifer," he told her. "At least I hope you'll find them exciting."

147

They reached the hotel and mounted the short steps to the entrance, where David held the door for her and guided her through into the lobby. Thinking of what he'd just said, he felt a flash of guilt. This staff job to General Fremont had without a doubt been his father's doing. He had that kind of influence. And when they got to St. Louis, there was going to be hell to pay when he told his father he didn't want a staff job; that he considered himself a line officer and intended to request a transfer to the fighting front. But then if he were successful, he reminded himself, Jennifer would be left alone with his family and he wasn't quite sure how that was going to work out.

They still didn't know he was married; he'd deliberately not sent a message to that effect. And when they discovered he'd married a woman who was as far removed from their idea of society and good breeding as she could possibly be, he'd better be there to defend her.

The lobby was crowded, both with men in business suits and the rough homespun. It took him a minute to get her to the desk, where Williams waited patiently.

"He says he's got one room left, Cap'n," the soldier reported. "But it ain't much of a room."

David looked at the clerk, who shrugged. "Sorry, Captain. Like you can see, the town's right active."

"Doesn't matter," David told him. "If it's got a roof and a bed, we'll take it.

"Yes, sir." The clerk spun the register around and offered a pen after first dipping it in ink. "It's small and three flights up, but like I told the soldier here, it's all I got left."

David wrote his name, caught himself, and added *and wife* behind it. By the time he'd finished, the clerk was offering him a large key. "Number 38, Captain. Up those stairs and all the way down the hall to the end. He glanced at Jennifer, who had her back to them, watching the crowd. "Sorry your missus has to climb those stairs," he added with genuine regret in his voice.

David smiled slightly, remembering she could outrun him easily. "I do believe she can manage," he told the man. "But thanks anyway."

"I'll just run these up for you, Cap'n," Williams offered. "Anything else I can do?"

"No," David said. "You and Boyle check back with me early tomorrow. I intend to wire St. Louis tonight; they may have different orders for you. If not, you'll bring the wagon on there as quickly as you can."

"Yes, sir." Williams picked up their luggage and headed for the stairs.

"Why are we riding the train?" Jennifer wanted to know as she climbed the stairs ahead of him. "Why don't we stay with the wagon if they're going to St. Louis, too?"

"There are two reasons, my dear," he told her. "One, I wanted the pleasure of providing that new experience for you, and two, I'm damn tired of a wagon."

"My husband is soft," she said with a giggle, stopping to look back at him. "White man lazy."

A heavy, red-faced man in a broadcloth suit too small for him squeezed past them on the stair at that moment, or he would have spanked her on the rear. "Get used to it," he grinned instead. "You're a society lady now. Your outdoor days are over."

She went back to climbing the stairs.

The room wasn't small, it was tiny, barely big enough to contain the one high bed against the wall and nothing else. There wasn't even a stand with a wash basin. He decided he'd order one anyway as he surveyed the room with disgust. "Damn," he said to her. "We might be better off in the wagon, after all."

Jennifer laughed and crossed to the bed, sat down on it, and immediately began to unbutton her shoes. But then she stopped and bounced experimentally. "It's too soft," she said. "Not at all like the one we had in Santa Fe."

David poked the mattress with one finger. It wasn't only soft, it was old and worn, the feathers giving off a dusty odor even under the blankets. He heaved a sigh and then noticed what she was doing. "Why are you taking off your shoes?" he wanted to know. "I thought you were hungry?"

She finished the buttons on one shoe and placed the toe of the other behind the heel to push it off. Then she looked up, sucked in her chin to her chest, and deepened her voice in imitation of him. "There are two reasons, my dear," she intoned. "One, you just said you were going out first and two . . ." She couldn't hold the deep voice and had to laugh. "Two," she continued through her laughter, "I just had another idea. We haven't been alone since we left Santa Fe."

Grinning at her laughter, David nevertheless felt a stirring in his loins. He'd had some experience with women before he went west, but not much. And he'd grown up in a society in which women expected to be treated delicately, considering sex merely a duty to their husbands, never to be mentioned among themselves, much less to a man. To have the knowledge that his beautiful wife not only enjoyed his making love to her but actually was willing to let him know she desired him was disconcerting. However, he was fast beginning to enjoy the idea.

"It's the middle of the afternoon," he said, still grinning. "Such things are done at night."

The blue eyes twinkled again. Challenging him. She reached up to unfasten the jacket.

"Oh God," he groaned, experiencing his manhood beginning to rise inside his trousers. "Jennifer, I've got to go and send a wire. And get our tickets!"

She was enjoying his discomfort. The jacket came off and she lifted her skirts to reach the buttons on the side of her other shoe. "Of course," she said with elaborate indifference as she flicked the buttons through the eyelets with a long finger. "My soldier husband is very busy. I must sit here all by myself while he goes about his soldier duties. Poor me."

His resolve was weakening rapidly. "Jennifer, I have to go!"

She removed the shoe and extended both stockinged feet to study them with great unconcern as she began to unbutton her white blouse.

David knew he was about to lose and thrust himself toward the door. With the knob in his hand, he said, "I'll be back as soon as I can." His voice was strained. "Believe me!"

She stopped him halfway through the door. "David!"

He waited, still facing away from her for a moment, then slowly turned. "Yes?"

Jennifer gave him a wide, promising smile and a barely perceptible wink. "Do hurry," she said softly.

He groaned again and closed the door behind him. By the time he was halfway down the hall he was arguing with himself. *Women were just not supposed to think like that,* one side said. *He should speak to her about it. The hell you will,* said the other quickly. *Foxcroft, you're a damned lucky man*!

He hurried down the street, grew irritable when it took him longer than he expected to find the telegraph office, and after he had sent his message and had given instructions for the reply to be brought to the hotel, became even more irritated when his question was answered that the railroad station was blocks away. Only his uniform and the fact the country was at war kept him out of trouble as he jostled passersby aside on his way back.

Jennifer was lying under the blanket when he returned to the room, and a quick survey on his part told him everything she'd been wearing was on the outside. Her dress, several undergarments, and her stockings were placed neatly over the footboard.

Heat began to build rapidly in him once more, even though he could feel the sweat from his exertions sliding down the side of his face. He closed the door and locked it.

Jennifer sat up in the bed, allowing the blanket to fall to her waist and confirming his thoughts about the clothing. The ruby tips of her breasts against the still brown skin drew his immediate attention.

"Good Lord," he said hoarsely. "Woman, don't

151

you have *any* modesty?"

She smiled and looked down at her breasts herself. "You don't like to look at your wife, Captain?"

"You damned right I do," he growled, sitting down on the bed and taking her roughly in his arms. He buried his face into the side of her neck where it met the bare shoulder and slid a hand up behind her head.

Jennifer moved against him, touching his ear with her lips. "Take off your clothes first, silly," said the cool voice barely managing to penetrate the blood pounding in his head. "You are *so* clumsy!"

She didn't enjoy the train ride as he had hoped, and he couldn't blame her. Their coach was crowded to capacity, uncomfortable, and dirty. Smoke from the small, struggling engine at the front constantly whipped through the open windows and made breathing nearly impossible. She didn't complain, but her relief in stepping down from it in St. Louis was apparent. David could also see that she was annoyed by the close press of hurrying people around them and decided wryly that in comparison to the open, free life she'd led, civilization perhaps hadn't stood up all that well, at least until now. He hoped to improve its image when he got her out of town.

But first he had a couple of things to do. Things, he admitted to himself, to help her in her first impression on his family. He had a moment's regret he'd not telegraphed ahead that he was married; it really wasn't fair to Jennifer not to have done so. But he hadn't, and now it was his responsibility to see that she met his family on an equal footing, at least in appearance.

There were several blacks scurrying about the platform assisting the arrivals with their baggage, and he selected one, a gray-haired man of medium height, and signaled him with an upraised arm. Beside him, Jennifer was still brushing vigorously at her clothes to remove the last traces of soot.

"Yes, suh?"

"Can you find me a carriage for hire?" David asked him.

"Yes, suh. Right away, suh. You jus' come with me."

David put an arm around her waist as the man picked up their luggage, as much to shelter her from the crowd as to guide her into following the man.

"Are we going to your father's now?" she wanted to know.

"Not just yet," he told her, leaning forward to block her from a hurrying man with two large carpetbags in his hands. "Couple of things I want to do before we go out there, and the first is to get us some money."

"Oh?" she said with interest. "How do you do that? Go to the Army?"

David chuckled. "Pay in the Army is always slow, darling. Even more so when a war's going on. To say nothing of being damn little in the first place. No, I'm going to a bank and present a draft on an account I have. I've a bit of money left me in a legacy."

"What is that?" She frowned in annoyance as she was brushed from the side that was away from him.

"A will. My grandfather left me some money when he died. I really hadn't any use for it until now."

He almost lost sight of the black man in the press and hurried her forward to catch up. When they were able to slow their pace again, she had another question. "Are you rich then?"

He smiled down at her. "We, my dear, Jennifer. Anything I have belongs to you as well. But no, we aren't rich. It isn't that much money."

The black man stopped by a cab, a nondescript carriage badly in need of repair to both its ragged top and the sagging frame. It stood harnessed to an even worse-looking mule, and the driver was a white man who appeared to be in little better shape than his animal. He sat hunched forward in a long black coat with splits in its sides. David started to object, then shrugged. St. Louis was garrison for General Fremont's fifty thousand men and also very busy with those who sought to do business with him. The Army would have taken up most of the better horses.

"Heah you are, suh," the black man said. "Right enough."

David nodded and produced ten cents to give him. "Thank you."

"Yes, suh." His luggage was placed in the rear boot and the man scurried away to look for another fare.

The driver hardly seemed to notice as David assisted Jennifer into the carriage, nor did he acknowledge his orders to take them to the Mercantile Bank. But when David was seated, the man gave a click to the mule and the animal lurched forward. Jennifer turned to watch from her side of the carriage.

"What do you think?" he asked her after they'd gone several blocks.

"Too many people," she said promptly. "Too crowded. Did you *like* living here?"

He chuckled. "I didn't live here. Not in the city. Besides, you're seeing the worst part at the moment. The central city is much prettier and a bit more spacious. It's an old French town, and some of the buildings reflect that culture."

He braced a leg against the odd swaying of the carriage. "My father owns a place a few miles north of here with about fifty acres around it—pretty land, with rolling hills. You'll feel more comfortable there."

When she turned, her face was serious. "David, your father is rich, isn't he?"

"Yes, I suppose you could say that. He also has a great deal of influence. But why this sudden concern with money? You never mentioned it before."

"It isn't the money," she said, giving him a peculiar look. "It's me. Besides living with Indians most of my life, I was poor as a white girl. I wonder what your parents will think."

He was silent for a moment, longer than he should have taken to reply. But it hadn't occurred to him that she would also think of that problem. He had to stop thinking of her as an unschooled Indian girl; Jennifer was very perceptive. "Oh, I'm quite certain they'll love you as much as—"

Her shaking head stopped him. "David, don't say things you don't believe."

"All right, Jennifer," he said quietly. "You're right, of course. My family is—well, they consider themselves . . . society, so to speak. My father expected me to follow him into business when I finished school. We had quite a scene when I decided to go into the Army instead. He thought it beneath me."

She continued to watch him silently.

"But the life he leads, that idea of business, didn't and still doesn't appeal to me. I thought a term in the Army would give me time to decide what I wanted."

He paused and then continued. "I won't lie to you, Jennifer. My family, especially Mother and my sister, Claudette, expected me to marry into what they often refer to as 'our class.' " He grinned at her. "I do believe Mother had already selected her choice, and not a bad-looking young lady either."

She didn't return the smile. "Am I going to cause trouble for you, David?"

"Jennifer, you're my wife. I love you more than anything in the world. No one, not even my family—especially my family—can change that. A long time ago I decided to make my own way in the world, and now you're a part of my life. A very big part, and don't ever forget that."

"I love you too," she said. "But I don't want to cause you trouble."

"Then let's not borrow it now," he said. "Give them a chance to meet you."

She nodded and returned to watching the street scenes they passed, and David lapsed into thought. Now he was a little embarrassed about what he'd planned to do. Knowing that she would be aware of why he was doing it seemed wrong somehow. But then, dammit, she was entitled to meet them on an equal footing.

Jennifer waited in the carriage while he went into the bank. It was crowded, but he was able to catch the eye of an official who hurried over. It was his father's influence, of course, the man having recognized him as the son of a man who held a great deal of the bank's stock. David answered his greeting quickly and then explained what he wanted, and in a few minutes was able to leave with five hundred dollars in new bank notes in his wallet.

Jennifer smiled at him when he reentered the carriage. "Now we're rich?"

"Now we're rich," he echoed with a grin. "And we're going to spend some of it on you. No, we're going to spend a lot of it on you."

"Me? Why?"

"Because, my dear wife, I want to. Don't argue with your husband."

"What am I going to buy?" she persisted.

"Clothes, darling. When we're through you'll be able to set St. Louis on its ear."

"And impress your family," she observed, her smile gone.

That hurt and he had to keep from wincing. "Remember what I said, Jennifer. You are the most important thing in the world to me."

Her blue eyes were bright with knowledge, but she surprised him by allowing her smile to return. "Then we shall make me a wife my husband can be proud of," she said. "I think I will spend all of your new money."

Madame Cussard of the dressmaking emporium of the same name took charge of her personally. The owner was a tiny, black-haired woman who would be hard pressed to weigh a hundred pounds. But she was a bundle of French energy and words.

"But of course, Monsieur Captain," she answered his query. "But of course. It will be done with the utmost speed. But not in haste. Certainly not in haste. It must be done with care. With careful attention to details. With correctness."

She cocked a birdlike head at Jennifer standing beside him. "Madame is lovely! A vision in her own right. But those clothes . . . *Alors*! They do no justice! None at all. We must create! For madame alone, to match her beauty, we must create!"

"And the rest?" he asked. "Millinery? Accessories, a hairdresser?"

She fluttered her hands. "It is done all the time. Leave everything to me. With such a beauty with whom to work . . . You will be delighted, Monsieur Captain. She will be ravishing, I assure you!"

David turned to see that Jennifer was regarding him with faint amusement. He bowed. "Mrs. Foxcroft I leave in your capable hands, Madame Cussard," he said.

"Please," she replied. "The captain will allow himself to become comfortable." She indicated one of the large padded chairs in the waiting room. "I will be privileged to have a brandy brought?"

"Thank you. A brandy would be fine."

She reached for Jennifer's arm, and a moment later both of them disappeared behind heavy drapes that covered one whole side of the room. David moved to the chair she'd indicated and hardly had time to make himself comfortable before a young woman appeared from behind the drapes with a tray on which was placed a large brandy goblet.

The girl crossed the room to set the tray on a small table at his elbow, curtsied, and removed herself as rapidly as she came. David leaned back, crossed his legs, and prepared to wait as behind the drapes he could already hear muffled voices in busy conversation.

For the next two hours, his solitude was interrupted only twice. First a woman with a large kit bag, whom he immediately took for the hairdresser, entered the front door and hurried through the drapes without a word. The second time, the same young girl appeared and shyly inquired if he would require another brandy. When he declined, she curtsied again and left.

A third hour, and then most of a fourth went by, and he was restlessly beginning to wish he'd accepted the second brandy. The murmuring behind the drapes continued, interrupted by an occasional high-pitched order from the emporium owner that he could almost catch. He sighed and recrossed his legs.

The girl stepped through the drapes. "Monsieur? Madame Foxcroft desires to know how many dresses she should select."

"As many as she wants," David said.

The girl disappeared, but was back in only a moment. "Monsieur, Madame Foxcroft wishes to inform you she has selected three until now. Will that be enough?"

David laughed. "For the time being, I suppose. She'll have ample opportunity to return later. You may tell her I don't believe I can wait through any more right now. Is she about finished?"

"Oh no, Monsieur. There is yet the dressing of the hair, and capes to be selected."

"I thought the hairdresser arrived long ago?"

The girl had an elfin face and large expressive eyes that widened with distress. "*Oui*, Monsieur. But it is not finished. And with the dressing and undressing . . . there are things that must be done last."

He sighed. "Very well then. In that case I'll accept another brandy."

"*Oui*, Monsieur."

By the time he'd finished the drink, however, Madame Cussard herself came out. "Monsieur Captain," she said, "I am not one to boast, but we have a masterpiece to show to you. A vision! Madame takes away the breath, I assure you!"

David stood up. "Then both I and my breath await," he told her gravely.

The little dressmaker's face was beaming. "*Alors*," she said. "Behold!"

With a long sweep of her arms she thrust back the drapes and he was suddenly looking at his wife. At least he thought it was his wife . . . the woman who returned his look would have been stunning at the court of a French king.

Her dress was full in the latest style, sweeping in

long, graceful folds down around her until it touched the floor. Green as an emerald but with glimmers of a lighter color, it pinched in unbelievably at the waist, and above that rose out again, intermixed with delicate lace. The bodice was low-cut, but the skin was hidden by a wrap of white silk that continued up around her neck.

Her yellow hair shimmered with highlights and lay in waves atop her head in a manner he couldn't believe. Her face had been powdered, but not to a white, only enough to soften the bronze of her skin to a delicate tint.

"Good Lord!" he breathed.

The vision smiled at him and moved into the room a few steps. Then she extended one arm and, holding the other gracefully poised in an arc, slowly turned completely around. "Do you like the dress?" she inquired.

"Like it . . . Jennifer, I . . . words fail me entirely."

"Did I not tell you, Monsieur Captain?" Madame Cussard wanted to know. "Is she not lovely?"

"The most beautiful woman I've ever seen," he said softly, still staring at Jennifer. "I have to be the most fortunate man on earth."

Long-lashed blue eyes smiled back at him, and she inclined her head gracefully. "Then I please my husband," she said. "I am happy."

Two more women came from the curtains behind her to beam widely as David took her hand and turned her around in front of him again. "Exquisite," he said. "I'm overwhelmed. How do you feel?"

The smile in her eyes became a gleam. "Do you really want to know?"

He nodded and the three other women moved forward in anticipation.

Her carriage would have done justice to a queen, her voice was low and decorous. But she said, "Once my people captured a very brave man and thought the manner of his death should equal his courage. He was sewn into a blanket of wet rawhide and placed in the sun. Rawhide is very strong and shrinks much when it dries. He made no cry even as his face turned black and his tongue was forced out of his mouth from the pressure."

She paused and extended a graceful finger of each hand toward her pinched-in waist. "I feel just like he did before he died."

David stared at her for a shocked moment, then caught the look of utter horror on the faces of the women. Madame Cussard in particular had turned absolutely white.

It was too much. He exploded with laughter; so much so he was forced to retreat to the chair again for support.

"My God!" he gasped, when he could. "What on earth am I going to do with you?"

Jennifer merely smiled.

He'd hoped to rent a rig for them and drive himself out to his family home, but there had been none available. Only one stable even had horses to rent but since he had no intention of allowing Jennifer to ride out astride a horse, he was forced to send for a carriage. Before he had taken her to the dressmaker, he'd found a boy from the last stable to ride out and summon one from home for him.

After some thought, he included the phrase "my wife and I" in the note and asked that they be met at the Empire Hotel. When the two of them left a still distressed Madame Cussard, who had been hardly able to make out a bill for him, and arrived at the hotel, they found the carriage waiting patiently. David recognized the driver, a longtime servant of his family.

The black man grinned widely at his approach and ran forward to take his luggage. "Mista Foxcroft!" he cried. "Your family shore gonna be glad to see you!"

"Hello, James," David said. "How've you been?"

"Fine, suh. Fine enough!" He touched his forehead in Jennifer's direction and bent at the waist. "How do, missus."

"This is my wife, James," David said. "James has

been with my father for as long as I can remember, Jennifer. He used to take me riding as a child."

"Yes, suh. I remember," James said, bobbing his head in agreement. "You was just in knee britches when I first knowed you."

"Hello, James," she said. "I'm happy to meet you."

"Missus. It's a pure pleasure. Just you let ole James get your things in this carriage and we'll be right on our way."

He began to load the pile of boxes into the back of the carriage, and David helped him after paying the lad who'd carried them for him. "Is everyone at home?" he asked as they loaded. "My father there?"

"Yes, suh. And powerful anxious to see you too, I reckon. They been looking for you for weeks now, I heard."

"Well, we'd better be moving then," David said. "Have you been waiting long?"

"Bout two hours, suh. Soon's we got the word you was in the city I put that mare into a trot I'll tell you."

He finished the loading, and by the time David had helped Jennifer into the carriage, he was in the high driver's seat and clicking to the mare. She started out briskly, probably aware that she was headed home once more and glad to be moving after her long wait in front of the hotel. James allowed her to pick her own pace through the streets but reined her slightly when they reached the open road to slow the swaying of the carriage.

They followed the sweep of the wide Mississippi, where even at this late hour they could see barge activity, at a rapid pace. The Foxcroft estate lay in the middle of the fertile land point made by the junction of this river with the Missouri, land that was valuable for planting. However, his father had chosen not to do so except for a few acres to supply fresh vegetables for the family and servants, his interest being solely in business. He'd left the rest of the estate in trees and rich green grass for his stable of horses.

The Foxcroft line had arrived in St. Louis only a few years after the city passed into the hands of the

United States following the Louisiana Purchase of 1803. They were of English stock, and like others who arrived along the same years, were disliked by the original French settlers—a fact that bothered old Ambrose Foxcroft not a whit. He was interested only in the enormous wealth that lay for the asking in the trade for furs. His son, however, had recognized the need for cultivating contacts with the still powerful French families and had even given his own daughter a French name. That political acumen and a shrewd business sense had eventually given Talbert Foxcroft great influence in the burgeoning city, second only to that of the Blairs, the most powerful family in Missouri.

The house sat on the crest of a small hill and was protected by numerous giant water oaks, which also helped obscure it from the curious who might travel the main road below. Only when a visitor rounded the final turn in the winding lane leading up to the house was its size and architectual grandeur apparent.

Graceful Corinthian columns lined the wide porch that ran the length of the house, supporting several delicate, spider-laced wooden balconies. The roof was a series of gables intermixed with slender turrets that contained many windows. Sculptured shutters around evenly spaced windows on the next two levels gave balance to the imposing front and disguised the fact that it was a very large house.

"There it is," David said as the carriage came to a halt. "Foxcroft Manor. Place I used to call home."

"It's beautiful," she said. "I've never seen such a large house. You must have loved it, David. Living here, I mean."

"Doubt if I ever thought about it," he replied and turned to look as the great front door with its brass ring knocker opened. But it was only Samson, the houseman.

He dismounted and helped Jennifer from the carriage, then greeted Samson. They left the two blacks to unload the luggage and went up the steps.

"Your family is in the drawing room, Captain

Foxcroft," Samson called after them. "They're expecting you, sir."

He guided her through the open door, across the large entrance room to a set of ornate doors on the right, and as they walked, glanced down to see if she were nervous. But Jennifer's curious eyes were taking in the room and the broad winding stairway with interest. His wife might be many things, he decided, but timid was not among them.

He opened both doors at the same time and allowed them to swing wide. Across the room his father sat in one huge wingbacked chair next to the fireless hearth, and his mother in a smaller one a few paces away. Claudette, his sister, looked up from the piano stool over a handful of musical sheets. "David!" she cried.

His father rose immediately and headed for him. But it was past him that David looked, to his mother's gaze, which was not on her son but on the woman beside him. A gaze that was neither startled nor warm.

"David! By thunder it's great to see you!" His father extended one hand to grasp his and the other to clasp him on the shoulder. "You look fit!"

"I am, sir," David said. "And you, too. It's good to see you again."

His hand was being pumped vigorously, but his father's pleased gaze switched to Jennifer standing beside him. David released it gently and stepped back. "Father, I'd like you to meet my wife. This is Jennifer. Once Jennifer McLean, now I'm delighted to say, Jennifer Foxcroft."

If there were surprise or displeasure in the older man he didn't allow it to show as he bowed to her. "My pleasure, my dear. Jennifer, is it? Then welcome, Jennifer, to the Foxcroft home." With his eyes still on her he added, "By heaven, David, I'm absolutely charmed."

"Sir," she said, "I'm very pleased to meet you. David has spoken of you often."

"Well, he certainly kept his own counsel of you," his father said ruefully, with a glance at David. "I

163

must have a word with my son about that. Come, young lady, allow me to present the rest of my family."

He extended an arm, which she accepted with a light touch, and the two of them left him standing.

"Edwina," his father said when they had crossed the room. "Look what your son has brought us. Jennifer, my wife, Edwina."

David caught up with them and watched his mother's eyes fasten on Jennifer's face. "How do you do," she said coolly.

"Mrs. Foxcroft." Jennifer returned the greeting with a slight curtsy. "I'm delighted to meet you."

He knew instantly that it was not going to be well. The two women had measured each other in a flash, he could tell by his mother's face and the trace of a stiffening in Jennifer's back.

His mother, always aloof in the best of circumstances, did not share her husband's ability to make people he disliked believe otherwise. She held herself apart always and considered formal entertainment the only social obligation required of her. Since even her own son was never at ease in her presence, what chance, he wondered, would Jennifer have?

Claudette broke the awkward pause by rushing to his side. "David! I'm so glad to see you!" But her eyes, too, were on Jennifer.

David grinned and draped an arm around her shoulders. "Claudette, meet Jennifer."

She slipped from beneath his arm and extended a hand toward Jennifer, but dropped it as soon as they touched. "How do you do," she said. "David was simply wicked not to tell us about you."

"He's been very busy," Jennifer returned. "Fighting the Southerners and so forth. But I'm happy to meet you, Claudette."

"Fighting?" his father interrupted, looking hard at David. "We've had a near thing here, nearly lost the state to them. But I wasn't aware of anything going on in the west. How serious was it?"

"It could have been worse, sir," David said. "We

were forced to move out of the entire southern part of the territory for a time, but Colonel Canby was able to regroup his forces and defeat the Rebels decisively at a place called Glorieta Pass near Santa Fe. Shortly after that they were compelled to retreat from the territory completely. California troops under a General Carlton were coming in as I left. I expect us to hold the area without difficulty."

"Good. Good. I'm glad you weren't injured. I want you to tell me all about it, and your difficulties with the aborigines there as well. Expect you have some excellent tales about that. But then we'll have plenty of time for such talk. I understand you've been detached to Fremont's staff here in St. Louis."

David permitted himself a small smile. "I presume you had a hand in that? I must admit it came as a surprise to me."

"I did take the liberty of mentioning your qualifications to a couple of Army people I deal with," his father said heartily. "They seemed quite interested as I recall. But then I imagine good staff officers, especially intelligent ones, are in great demand. The Army's expanding rapidly, David. They were grateful for the information.

"No doubt," David said wryly.

His father ignored the comment. "Of course, being with Fremont won't hurt your own future, son. It doesn't hurt to keep that in mind. He and Blair are at odds at the moment, but I fully expect the general to be a real power in this state after this unpleasantness with the rest of the South is done. He may even make another try for the presidency, and God knows he would make a better one than that awkward person, Lincoln. Remember we used to talk about politics being your future?"

"I remember," David said. "But right now I'm only interested in my duty as a soldier."

"Of course. And rightly so. But a wise man keeps his eye on the future, David." He looked at Jennifer. "And now you have responsibilities. This charming creature certainly deserves more than a soldier's pay to support her. Much more."

"I'm sure you're right, Father," David said. "But right now I would imagine she's as hungry as I am. Have you dined?"

His father laughed. "Ah, David. You know your mother as well as I do. She keeps me and the house on a tight schedule. But I'm sure Cook can prepare something for you. Right Edwina?"

"I'll give instructions," his mother said. "But I'm quite sure David's wife would like to rest and freshen herself first. She does look worn."

Jennifer's voice was every bit as cool as his mother's. "Thank you, Mrs. Foxcroft. You're *most* considerate."

Later, after the two of them had dined alone and had made only a little more conversation in the drawing room with his family, David excused them both by pleading a long day and his need to report early the next morning to headquarters. Once in bed in his old rooms, he lay with his hands behind his head and talked, telling her of his resolve to immediately ask for a transfer and why. He also told her it would cause an argument with his father.

"You must do what is right, David," she said quietly. "I hope it won't be for a long time."

"I know, Jennifer," he said, putting an arm around her and drawing her close to him. "But the sooner this war is over, the sooner we can go back to look for your son. Don't you see?"

"Will the Army send you back if you ask?"

"No, darling. I don't think so. Transfers are difficult enough to manage when you want to fight. They're impossible in times of peace. But don't worry about that, I don't intend to stay in the Army. I wouldn't have the freedom of movement we'll require if I were still a soldier. I intend to resign as soon as the fighting ends."

He rested his chin on the top of her head, enjoying the silky feeling of her hair. "Besides, Father is right. You deserve more than I can give you on a soldier's pay."

"I don't want to be rich, David," she said solemnly. "This is not a life I think I would like. But I do want whatever you want for us."

"Don't judge everything by Mother," he said quietly. "She's a difficult person, I know. But then, don't worry about living here either. I have no intention of remaining myself."

"Then what are we going to do?"

"I honestly don't know, Jennifer. I really think I'm interested in staying out west. I see enormous possibilities there."

He nudged the top of her head again. "That is, unless you become too accustomed to life here while I'm away and don't want to go back."

"No," she said, looking up at him quickly. "I want to go back as soon as we can."

He pulled her toward him and kissed her. "We will, darling. We will."

After she was asleep, he lay awake and thought; not about the distant future but of what life would hold for her in the next few months. For lack of a better idea, he had brought her into a nearly impossible situation. No matter how much she'd learned in her brief time since he'd met her, Jennifer would be adrift in the world in which his family moved. There were bound to be times of embarrassment for her and he wouldn't be around to help. His expectations had already been confirmed.

He felt sorry for the graceful, sleeping woman beside him and grave doubts that he was doing the right thing by leaving her to go and fight. Then suddenly he remembered the first time they had met in the cave. Remembered the look of savage defiance on her face and later, Konta's description of her fight with Tanner and the other man . . . what was his name? Brewster, that was it.

He was wasting his sympathy. If there was ever a woman who could take care of herself, Jennifer McLean was that woman. Jennifer Foxcroft, he corrected himself with a grin in the dark. Hell, maybe he ought to feel sorry for the poor fools of the so-called "civilized" East who crossed her too much.

And with that thought in mind, he drifted off to sleep himself.

Chapter Twelve

If there were another woman in St. Louis who could match the wife of Talbert Foxcroft in formidableness, it was Matilda Dobson, her spinster sister. Older than Edwina, she had a tongue twice as sharp and no reserve in using it. Jennifer was to discover that Matilda also possessed something that neither her sister nor her brother-in-law owned—a sense of humor.

In their first two meetings, which occurred when Miss Dobson called at the Foxcroft home, the older woman had been indifferent to Jennifer, ignored Claudette completely, and engaged in sharp discussion with Edwina. Jennifer was both surprised and suspicious when a carriage arrived late one morning with a message inviting her to visit Miss Dobson for luncheon. She started to refuse, having already grown extremely weary of the subtle snubs of the Foxcrofts in general and not wishing to extend the chance to another relative, but then she decided that any diversion might be a relief. She accepted.

When she arrived at a house half the size of the one she had left but still bespeaking wealth, her hostess surprised her by standing on its broad veranda to greet her. As the carriage drew to a halt, she even descended to the lowest step.

"My dear Mrs. Foxcroft," she said. "I'm delighted you chose to come. I've been looking forward to a chance to get to know you."

The driver leaped to the ground and hurried to offer his hand for Jennifer to step down. She waited until she was on the ground before replying. "Thank you, Miss Dobson. It was kind of you to invite me."

The older woman extended a hand and turned to lead her up the steps. "I'm going to call you Jennifer. Do you mind?"

"Please do."

"Good. And you must call me Matilda. I don't extend that invitation to many people." She paused on the veranda to offer her guest an appraising eye. "I've heard a great deal about you, young lady, and the real reason I asked you here today is because I've decided you need an ally. Let's become acquainted and find out if I can serve in that capacity."

It was a surprising statement, but Jennifer didn't feel disarmed by it. In the weeks since David had left, she'd found herself on the defensive in a situation she still couldn't readily define, much less know how to handle. Accustomed to directness, her inlaws' subtle maneuvering to set her apart from them was a difficult experience, a will-o'-the-wisp she didn't know how to challenge. Her father-in-law hardly seemed to notice her, and Edwina's icy politeness had only increased with Jennifer's best efforts. Even the servants took their cue from the mistress of the house, and any request of them was answered with deliberate slowness if it were answered at all. Somehow, she doubted that this woman would be any different.

"I'm not certain I understand what you mean," she said carefully.

Matilda nodded. "You will, my dear Jennifer. You will. We shall have a talk, you and I. A very frank talk. I've managed to acquire a reputation for frankness, I'm afraid. But first we much have luncheon. Come."

A young girl in a maid's uniform stood waiting to hold the door for them, and her hostess led her through it. Jennifer found herself in a wide hall, one side of which presented a large opening into a heavily furnished drawing room. Matilda, however, continued toward the rear.

"We'll dine in the garden if you don't mind," she said over her shoulder. "It's too beautiful a day to remain inside. I spend much of my time there. An old maid's pleasure."

As she talked, she led them down the hall the full length of the house to a door on the rear. Outside and down a series of curved steps, they found a brick porch that extended into a walled garden filled with flowing shrubs and flowers of every description. Its immediate scent as well as the multicolored scene forced Jennifer to pause at the top. "How beautiful," she said.

Matilda surveyed the garden herself. "Thank you. My gardener does an excellent job on the rest of the grounds, but I insist on having full authority here. Everything you see was planted at my direction. Not without argument from him, you understand, he's a very stubborn German."

A slight smile crossed her lips as she looked at Jennifer. "I'd even dig in the ground myself except that Karl would be horrified and would immediately resign. We're expected to retain our station, you know."

Jennifer glanced quickly at her but the smile was genuine. "Come," she said. "Our table is over here."

She took Jennifer's arm again and escorted her into a path that wound around several brightly flowered plants to a small wooden table with two chairs placed beside it. By the time she offered the first to Jennifer and was seated in the second, a different girl appeared with a large tray containing a tea service, bowls of freshly sliced fruits, and various sweet breads. The maid placed it on the table between them before handing each a sparkling white cloth for their laps.

"That will do, Mary," Matilda told her. "I'll serve tea myself."

"Very good, Madam." She withdrew as unobtrusively as she had arrived, and the two of them were alone again.

"You'll have sugar and cream?"

"Yes. Thank you."

Her hostess poured and then made conversation as they ate; for the most part talking about her garden, St. Louis in general, and her family in particular. Jennifer learned that Matilda's parents had arrived in the area shortly after the city became American and both were buried on the estate grounds, along with her brother, who had died of smallpox as a child. Since then she had lived alone.

Jennifer asked her why.

"You mean why I choose not to live with my sister?" Again the small smile crossed her hostess's face. "You should be aware of the answer to that by now, Jennifer. My sister is a cultivated witch. Edwina and I can only tolerate each other for an extremely brief time at best. Should I live with her and Talbert Foxcroft, I would eventually be forced to poison her."

She paused to pour them more tea and offer the sugar. "As for that pampered primp of a daughter of theirs, she should have had a hickory limb to her bustle years ago."

Jennifer smiled in spite of herself.

"You see?" Matilda said quickly. "I knew you and I were cut of the same cloth. I imagine you wouldn't mind doing that yourself." She paused. "Or whatever the Indians do to spoiled children."

Jennifer allowed her smile to fade and looked a long time at her hostess, who met her gaze directly.

"Jennifer," she continued after a moment. "I am probably the only person in St. Louis to whom your past life matters not a whit. In fact, I envy you the adventure. There was a time when I dreamed as a young girl of living on the frontier."

She sat back. "Ah, what a gloriously free life you must have had, my dear. Far away from the restraints of what we most piously refer to as civilization."

"The people with whom I lived had their own degree of civilization," Jennifer told her quietly. "Regardless of what others may think, I never considered them savages."

"Of course not. And you shouldn't. I'm afraid I don't know very much about the culture of the Red Man, but I have no hesitation in agreeing with you. We'll have many of these talks together I hope, and you can acquaint me with that culture. Will you?"

"As you like," Jennifer said. "May I ask how you learned about me?"

Matilda sipped her tea and then leaned forward again to place the cup on the table. "You, dear Jennifer. That's how I know. You are far too honest and direct, and when Claudette asked, you told her without hesitation that David found you living among the Indians."

Her smile became wicked. "I would have loved to have been present when that particular bit of news was conveyed to Edwina. She must have fallen into a terrible swoon. But tell me, why didn't she get it from David? I'm quite certain it was the first thing she would have asked him."

"David would try to protect me," Jennifer said. "But I'm not ashamed of what I am."

"Try to protect you? Good grief! If he did that, my nephew is not as intelligent as I thought. It's obvious he doesn't yet understand his wife."

"I don't want to cause him trouble with his family," Jennifer said.

"I can understand that. But what you don't realize, Jennifer, is that you have already done so. And it doesn't matter who you are. Edwina did not . . . shall we say . . . select you for her son. My sister is a woman who expects to control things, including the lives of her children. Talbert is completely wrapped up in his passion to make more money and is quite content to allow her charge of everything else. It wouldn't matter if you came from the finest family imaginable, you were not Edwina's choice for David. Therefore, you're the wrong choice. Don't you see?"

Jennifer nodded. "Now I do. I thought it was because I was not . . . cultured."

"Cultured! Good grief, child! Look at yourself. You're a classic beauty. Every inch a lady. Walk into any ballroom and you'd be the absolute envy of every woman there. And your manners—how ever did you learn those living with Indians?"

"I spent the months after I met David in the company of a good friend. Her name was Bess Henley and she was married to an Army doctor. She taught me most of what I know."

"She must have had a gentle background," Matilda observed. "You have learned extremely well. There's only one thing I would change."

"What is that?" Jennifer was beginning to think she might like this straightforward old woman.

Matilda eyed her intently. "I would advise you to forget what you cannot change, Jennifer. And not to worry about hurting your husband. I do believe I know David better than his mother ever will. He's a man of his own or she would have made him into a toading fop years ago. Merely be yourself, my dear, and allow Edwina to discover the steel from which her daughter-in-law is cast. That's what you should do."

"Then you think things will not get better?" Jennifer asked thoughtfully.

"I know so. When your David comes back, do you really think he'll want to remain in St. Louis? I don't. So what difference can it make what his family thinks of you?"

Jennifer shook her head. "No. He's already said we would go somewhere else. There's something we plan to do together." She started to tell what, but changed her mind. Not knowing why except that she couldn't bring herself to trust Matilda Dobson completely just yet.

"Then don't make yourself miserable trying to accomplish something you can't," the older woman said. "Be yourself, Jennifer. If you like, come and stay with me until David returns."

She was tempted. But David had expected her to remain with the Foxcrofts. "Thank you," she said. "That would be nice, but . . ."

"The offer will remain open," Matilda said during her pause.

Jennifer allowed the silence between them to grow as she thought about what the other woman had said. *Be yourself* . . . She felt a hard little smile tug at her own lips. *Why not?*

"I think perhaps you're right," she told Matilda suddenly. "If I can't change what they think of me, at least I can make it interesting."

Matilda chuckled, a deep, almost masculine chuckle. "I really expect you can, young lady. Interesting indeed!"

In the following months she put into practice her resolve not to be intimidated. Her verbal duels with her mother-in-law as often as not left her with secret satisfaction that the older woman could think of nothing else to say. And it took very little effort to frighten Claudette into avoiding her completely. To help occupy her time, she now had at least one friend in St. Louis, as at least twice or more a week the Dobson carriage called for her and the two of them were off to the city for shopping or the theater. A relationship, she could see, that pleased Edwina not at all.

Although the Foxcrofts entertained frequently, she was never invited. Occasionally, however, she would dress in her finest and invite herself, and found to her surprise that she was almost always the center of attention.

She knew that Edwina would never have allowed the news to spread that her son's wife had lived among the "primitives" as she referred to them, but the news had spread and Jennifer could only surmise that the servants were not as circumspect. Her entrance into any gathering at the Foxcroft home was cause for a sudden silence, and quickly she would find herself in the midst of a gathering of the younger men and even the few older ones brave enough to dare the wrath of their wives.

The conversation that centered on her was worded in polite, ballroom language, but repeated questions about "Life on the Frontier" and the bright gleam in the eyes of the men betrayed their real thoughts. Jennifer enjoyed meeting the looks directly when she answered, and found their discomfort at being matched by a woman amusing. She also discovered she could further confound them by defending Indians in general, without ever referring to her own life among them.

Such diversions didn't keep her from being bored most of the time, however. The days lay heavily about her until she came across another friendly face quite by accident. Wandering about the grounds on a bright sunny day, she found James, the driver who'd fetched her and David from St. Louis, grooming a magnificent black stallion. She stopped to admire the animal aloud.

"Yes, missus, he sure is," James answered, but eyed her warily at the same time, and Jennifer knew he'd heard the tales the other servants whispered about her. "This here King Henry's one of the finest ever seen in these parts. Mr. Foxcroft, he done paid a whole world of money for this horse."

She stepped closer and the stallion's head came up quickly, its large eyes rolling.

James was alarmed. "Better be careful, missus," he said quickly. "Ain't nobody but Mr. Foxcroft can ride this boy. Don't nobody but him and me even get close."

It was a beautiful beast, well muscled in its wide chest and slender of leg. Its satin black coat shone in the sun.

"How do you manage him?" she wanted to know, still admiring the horse.

James straightened and his own chest swelled. "I reckon he knows I'm only gonna take care of him, missus. King Henry, he like to have his coat rubbed and his hooves cleaned."

"Do you ever try to ride him?"

He was shocked at the idea. "Oh no, missus. Like I said, ain't nobody can get on this horse 'cept Mr. Foxcroft. And even he got a lot of trouble sometimes." His voice took on a regretful note. "He don't do it much anymore cause it's so much trouble. King Henry don't get much riding."

"But if he'll let you groom him, he should allow you to ride him," she persisted.

The black man shook his head vigorously. "Oh no, missus. King Henry wouldn't have no part of that!"

"Well, it's a shame," she said. "He's too beautiful a horse not to be ridden."

"I walks him," James offered. "And then I turn him loose in that fenced pasture there. Mr. Foxcroft don't want him with the rest."

She turned to see where he was pointing. "But that's too small. He can't really run there."

"Yes'm."

"James," she said on impulse. "Will you let me try?"

He was shocked again. "Missus, this King Henry would throw you something fierce!"

"Suppose I prove to you he won't? Would you saddle him then?"

"Missus, I surely can't. Mr. Foxcroft would skin me."

Jennifer shook her head. "I'll accept the responsibility. And you'll see first he won't hurt me."

"Missus, I just don't know . . ."

"Watch," she said. She took a step forward but then paused to look hard at him. "James, you must promise me you won't tell anyone what I'm going to do. I want your word on it."

He was plainly curious. "What you gonna do?"

"Promise?"

James slowly nodded his head. "Yes'm. I promise."

She faced the stallion and in a low coaxing voice began to talk to him in Apache. The way she had so often seen Cochise and others do. The stallion's head bobbed quickly and his eyes were wild as he listened. But gradually, as she persisted, he quieted. Jennifer stepped closer, continuing to use the same liquid sounds and rolling her voice in a soothing singsong. King Henry's ears turned forward sharply and he stood perfectly still.

She kept it up for long moments before she stepped forward again, one slow foot at a time, until she could reach up to touch his neck. The stallion didn't move as she slid her hand up and down, still talking in the same tone, and she paused to stroke his muzzle as well.

Slowly she drew his head down and slipped a hand behind his ear to rub the sensitive spot there, lowering her voice at the same time until she was whispering into it.

King Henry reached around to nuzzle her shoulder.

"Get a saddle," she told James, who was rooted in shock.

"Yes'm." He shook himself free and moved quickly into the stable, returning just as quickly with a blanket and a small, lady's saddle.

Jennifer eyed the latter in immediate disagreement, then remembered the cumbersome skirts she wore and shrugged. But when James put it on and attempted to fasten the girth around King Henry's barrel, she made him move it farther toward his rear.

Completely mystified, he complied and then stepped away. She raised her skirt and mounted, and King Henry only turned his head to look at her as she leaned forward to stroke his neck once more and speak in Apache. Then she straightened to smile at the black man watching her with wide eyes. "We'll be back shortly," she told him. "And remember, this is our secret together."

He slowly shook his head from side to side. "Missus, ain't nobody gonna believe old James nohow."

Her ride was sheer joy. Once away from the house with the trees to hide her from sight, she slid forward out of the saddle, raising her skirts and petticoats to her waist to straddle his broad back. Then she urged him into a run with a shrill Apache yell. King Henry responded with a high, pounding stride that whipped the wind across her face and sent her spirit soaring.

She returned almost an hour later, once again sitting demurely in the tiny saddle with her skirts down, and James was still waiting at the edge of the stables. He looked at the lather running down the stallion's shoulders and flanks, gave a small whistle, and when his gaze reached her face it was full of admiration.

He walked back beside her as she guided King

Henry to a dismounting step and slid off. "Remember," she told him. "Our little secret."

"Yes'm," he grinned. "And Miss Jennifer, you just tell ole James anytime you want to go riding. Jest any ole time at all!"

She left him still grinning and walked away with a light stride, feeling really free for the first time in months. Once in her rooms, she stripped completely, throwing the restricting corset aside with great relish. The remainder of the day she spent wearing only a loose shift with her hair down.

Summer faded into fall, the browning leaves and the freshening winds reflecting her feeling of isolation in spite of her twin releases of Matilda Dobson and the tremendous King Henry. She had received two letters from David since his departure, only one of which enclosed a brief note to his family, and was glad the Foxcrofts refused to ask her for details of him, since she was forced to admit to Matilda that she couldn't read the letters herself.

She had learned and learned well the manners and mores of civilization from Bess Henley, her husband, and finally Matilda Dobson. But learning to read was a different matter. If it had occurred to her to try, there wouldn't have been the means. Not being able was understandable but still she preferred that the Foxcrofts not be aware of that particular problem.

David was getting his wish to take part in the war. His letters described the battles he had taken part in, and dwelt as well on the suffering, the frustrations, and the setbacks.

The Federal forces had lost most of the early battles because of raw, untrained troops and overconfidence, the letters said. But there were already signs that the weight of better equipment, more manpower, and more modern weapons was beginning to make itself felt. When General McDowell and the Army of the Potomac began to move, David's last letter said, the war would change drastically. Perhaps he might even see her by Christmas.

Jennifer asked Matilda when the last one was written and was disappointed to learn it was almost a month old.

The hardest times of all, however, came in the nights when she lay in her bed and could not keep her thoughts from returning to the renegade camp and the small bundle of life she'd held in her arms there. She had not even given her child a name, hoping the two of them could return to Cochise first. Now she wished she had; it would at least be something to hold.

Was he still alive? Or had that anger that always lay close under the surface of Lobo Negro exploded in the death of her child when he returned to his band? Remembrance was fresh in her mind, waiting only for her to relax her guard and allow it to appear. Her son would soon be two years old if he lived . . . if he lived.

Tears often clouded the eyes of Jennifer Foxcroft in the night. But it was Flor de Oro who sat cross-legged in the dark and sang ever so softly in Apache to her lost child.

Autumn slipped into winter and Christmas and she'd had only one more brief letter from David. It offered encouragement about winning the war, but even in its few lines the encouragement was tempered with the sober assessment that winning might take quite a bit longer than he had expected. When Matilda finished reading it to her, Jennifer made her excuses and asked for the carriage to return home, where she went to her rooms and sat for several hours to stare unseeingly at the snow.

The husband she hardly had time to know was now engaged in a desperate struggle that could well take him from her at any hour and her son was growing up in the band of an outlaw, his beginning years without her presence making him a stranger to her. Both thoughts made her restless, and she found it difficult to control her moods. In either case, she could do nothing but hope for an early change in the situation.

David was a man and could take care of himself, but what about the boy? She allowed her gaze to drift toward the western horizon. Time was slipping away, she couldn't afford much more of it or he would be lost to her forever.

By early spring her restless desire for movement had increased to the point that as soon as she could ride King Henry again she was out two to three times a week. Since she was being virtually ignored by the Foxcrofts, leaving the house for long periods presented no problem. But to hold down the talk among the servants, she had James lead the stallion behind the stable to meet her. There she would mount him and ride to the nearest woods before sliding forward out of the saddle and giving him his head to run. She had become very familiar with the terrain and made sure she rode in the areas where she was least likely to be seen.

King Henry sensed her restlessness and responded with a nervous energy of his own. Each time they returned, he glistened with sweat, his great chest heaving with his efforts, but a day or so later when James had him waiting for her, he would be impatient to be off again, his hoof pawing the ground at her approach.

On one such race they were pounding down a natural trail between a series of oaks and tall spruce and headed for a large ravine that each of them knew was there. Jennifer gave him his head, even lay forward across his neck and spoke encouragement to him, knowing he loved the jump. King Henry flattened his ears in acknowledgment, and as they reached the ravine, bunched his muscles at the last possible moment and soared across it with room to spare.

She gave a cry of glee at the distance of his jump and King Henry flicked his ears in response. But as he did, another rider moved his horse from behind a spruce ahead of them and the stallion was forced into a startled veer to avoid a collision. Jennifer had to grip his sides fiercely to keep her seat.

They thundered past the stranger in seconds, and she caught only a glimpse of a tall man in a black suit and a wide-brimmed hat before he was well behind them.

"Wait!" he yelled. "Wait there!"

She leaned forward and called to King Henry and he lengthened his stride at her command. A minute later she glanced behind her to see that the rider had urged his own mount forward in an attempt to overtake her. She called to the stallion again and when she looked back the second time he was far behind, his horse no match for the powerful beast between her legs.

Jennifer rode for another mile, dodging between the trees, and then turned to take a widely different route back to the house, riding again in the saddle with her skirts down, much to the irritation of King Henry, who resented being held to such a sedate pace. But she was worried. Being discovered, no matter who the man might be, was a problem for them both. Edwina Foxcroft would be furious at her behavior when she heard of it and would in all probability insist that the horse be sold to stop her. She didn't really care what Edwina thought of her anymore, their relationship had gone beyond caring, but she didn't want to lose King Henry; he'd come to mean too much to her. By the time she returned, the worry had become a real fear.

However, a week passed and there had been no outcry. She had almost permitted herself the luxury of believing the man had been a passerby and knew nothing of the Foxcrofts when her fear was rekindled by a maid who knocked at her door with a message that the mistress of the house wanted to see her. The secret was out; she resigned herself to it.

Edwina Foxcroft was waiting for her in the drawing room, seated and wearing her usual haughty expression. She looked up as Jennifer entered but offered no greeting.

"You asked to see me?" Jennifer said, pausing in the center of the room.

Edwina's look indicated she'd bitten into something sour. "Yes. I wanted to extend an invitation to you."

"Oh?"

The older woman's words were forced. "We . . . the Foxcrofts, have been invited to a ball in St. Louis which will take place tomorrow evening. My husband has asked that you attend it with us."

"Why?" She hadn't expected this and was quickly suspicious.

"Why? Because you are . . . my son's wife!"

"Mrs. Foxcroft," Jennifer said deliberately, "that fact has been true since the day I came here. Why should it suddenly make a difference?"

From her face it was obvious that Edwina knew she was being driven into an admission. It was also obvious that it was an admission she didn't want to make. Jennifer didn't care. She waited, forcing the other woman to speak.

Edwina did, after a long moment, biting her words off as she spoke. "As I just said, my husband has asked it. I am certainly not attempting to persuade you."

"Then I choose not to go," Jennifer said quietly. "Is that all you wanted?"

Edwina didn't answer and she turned to leave but got only as far as the door.

"Miss McLean!"

Jennifer stopped and turned with great deliberation. "Mrs. Foxcroft, my name is the same as yours. Whether you like it or not."

The older woman's face was livid. She contained herself with visible effort. When she spoke, however, it was again in a controlled voice. "You have my apologies, *Mrs. Foxcroft*. I . . . I would appreciate it if you would reconsider your decision. My husband has made a specific request that you attend this ball with us."

Jennifer stared at her. *So! Talbert Foxcroft does hold the reins after all. Or at least the purse strings.* That was a surprise. "Do you happen to know why he wants me there?" she asked.

"I believe someone has requested to meet you," Edwina said icily. "I am merely conveying the request. I'm sure my husband would appreciate it."

"I see. In that case you may inform him I shall be happy to come." She turned and left the room.

The ball was held at the Campbell house in St. Louis, the home of a man who had become wealthy in the fur trade according to earlier information she had from Matilda. She rode there in the Foxcroft carriage with a coldly silent Edwina and an artificially cheerful Talbert Foxcroft. Their daughter had chosen not to attend—probably because she was going, Jennifer decided. She was curious who the person might be who wanted to meet her; even more so, why her presence would mean something of importance to her father-in-law. That it did was apparent. In the carriage, he went out of his way to mask the hostility between her and Edwina and she listened to his hearty conversation and answered politely whatever she was asked, allowing no hint of her suspicions.

The three of them entered the Campbell house together to join a very large crowd in the main ballroom, where Talbert took her arm and just as quickly his wife moved away to join some others, leaving the two of them to stand alone.

Jennifer walked beside him as he moved through the throng, nodding to those she'd met before, and giving her own polite greeting to those he introduced. But it became quickly obvious that he was moving her purposefully, if gradually, toward the end of the room where several high French doors led to a veranda outside. With her discovery in mind, she scanned the people ahead of them to see if she could pick out the person or persons he planned for her to meet.

All of them were as she expected, wealthy and polished, with none outstanding. None, until her gaze fastened on a tall man with white hair by one door who was in deep conversation with two others. Somehow she knew that he would be their ultimate destination. He would have stood out in any crowd. His white hair held not a trace of any other color, but the lean, totally erect frame beneath it belied the age suggested by the hair. His was a military, commanding stance, the attitude of a man used to being obeyed. A small mustache and a neatly clipped beard of the same color as his hair set off a thin, aristocratic nose and commanding eyes.

She spoke a greeting to someone else, brought her gaze back to the man, and suddenly realized the significance of the black suit he wore. *The man in the forest!* She had only glimpsed him then, but her impression had been one of a tall man wearing a black suit and boots. Mentally she prepared herself for the encounter.

A moment later they were in front of him, and his penetrating eyes found her own. "Ah, General!" her father-in-law said heartily—too heartily. "Good to see you again!" He pressed her arm forward. "You've met my son, David; I'd like you to meet his wife. Jennifer, may I present General Alex Hartman."

The small smile on his face was meant to be friendly, but it failed to reach his eyes. The look he gave her was the look of a predator. "I'm absolutely charmed, Mrs. Foxcroft," he said with a bow. "A most fortunate young man, your husband. Most fortunate to have captured the heart of such a beautiful woman."

Jennifer extended her hand. "Good evening, General Hartman. You're much too kind."

He took the offered hand and bent forward again to brush his mustache across it. "Only the truth, madame. Your husband described you to me when we were in brief conversation a few weeks ago in Washington; I confess then I took his words as those of a young man in love. Now I can see that he didn't exaggerate."

"Oh?" she said quickly. "In Washington? I had thought him elsewhere. News here is very slow, General."

His attention excluded her father-in-law she real-

185

ized suddenly, and Foxcroft was untypically silent.

"He was to be there only a short time as I remember, madame. Some military business or other. A friend pointed him out to me and since I knew your father-in-law, I made a point of introducing myself."

"I see."

Again the flicker of a smile. "I did promise to send his regards to you after he found out I was coming here, and now having met you in person, I relish my role as courier."

"Thank you. Is he well?"

"Quite fit, I would say. A soldier's life may be demanding but it seems to suit him."

"I'm happy to hear that," she said. "Will you by chance be seeing him again? I mean, will your duties take you close to where he is?"

Her father-in-law interrupted at last. "Excuse me, Jennifer. There is someone over there I really have to see. General Hartman, would you do me the honor of occupying my daughter-in-law for a moment?"

The general's look at her contained more than a little arrogance. He didn't move it to answer Foxcroft. "With the greatest of pleasure," he said.

Her father-in-law hurried away, and Jennifer half turned to watch his retreating back until he was lost in the crowd. The general's voice brought her back to face him. "To answer your question, madame, no. I'm not in the Federal Army myself. And my business will take me west, well away from the conflict."

"I'm afraid I don't understand. Aren't you a general?"

His smile was amused. "An honorary title at the present time, madame. I'm afraid my days as a soldier are no more. I held that rank in the Prussian Army under King Frederick and served my king and country for many years. However, all things come to an end. I have been requested to accept at least an advisory role in your country's present war but am forced to decline as much as I support the Northern cause. As I said, pressing business takes me west."

"I see."

He continued to watch her intently and the smile remained in place. After a long moment he added, "West, madame. To the territory from which you yourself came."

Her suspicions, no, her confidence, that she was being used by her father-in-law as a pawn in his business dealings were now confirmed. "General Hartman," she said quietly, "I believe you had reason to want to talk to me. Shall we discuss whatever it might be?"

He showed no surprise at her words. Nor did she expect him to do so. This man was different from most she had met here. He was a dangerous and powerful man, the glint in his penetrating eyes suggested a man who would forgo no means to achieve what he wanted.

"You more than meet my expectations, madame," he said. "I was already convinced that you were an unusual woman; there's more than a hint of steel in you. I admire that greatly. May I also add that you ride a horse better than most men I've known?"

She nodded. "You were the man in the forest."

"Yes, and not by accident. I had hoped to meet you there and talk to you alone. Unfortunately, I underestimated the magnificent steed you rode as well as your ability to ride him." The smile tugged at his lips again. "Very few people would have attempted that jump. They would have ridden around the ravine."

"How did you know I would be there? My father-in-law?"

"Yes. Foxcroft knew you were riding the stallion almost from the beginning. Only a stupid man fails to know what goes on in his own house, and I assure you, he is not a stupid man. If he chose to remain silent about it, it was for his own reasons."

Probably in hopes I would break my neck, she thought. "I see. May I ask again what you want with me?"

"Directly to the point, madame. As I said, I'm going to the territory shortly, but my business there is not important to our discussion. It should be sufficient to say that it could in the long run benefit your people."

"My people?" She raised an eyebrow.

"The Apache with whom you lived. The people led by your Indian father, Cochise. Are you aware that they are locked in total war with the settlers? Although they are more than holding their own at present, when this civil war is finished and soldiers can be spared, it's a war they are bound to lose. I hope to put a just end to their struggle before that happens; an end that will benefit both the Red and the White man."

"You do seem to know a great deal about me, General. I assume this mission of yours will not be without benefit to yourself. However, I'm not at all sure it is necessary. Cochise will take care of his own people. He's made peace before. And kept his word. He's a very intelligent man."

He shook his head, watching her intently. "Not this time, madame. He is in no mood for peace. A very young and very foolish lieutenant made sure of that when he tried to arrest Cochise after bringing him into his camp under a flag of truce. Violating, I might add, the most basic rule of warfare. Your chief escaped by slashing a hole through the tent and running away through a large crowd of soldiers. Our young lieutenant then compounded his error by hanging the Apache who didn't get away with their chief."

He paused, but she made no comment.

"Cochise, I'm told, has since sworn vengeance on all Americans and is doing an excellent job of getting it. I hope to convince him that he will eventually lose to superior forces and would be better off to make a just peace now. That is where you come in."

She shook her head. "I cannot help you, General. In the first place, Cochise will no longer talk to me; I am not welcome in his lodge. And in the second, I intend to remain here. I'm sorry."

A man behind her chose that moment to speak to him, but Hartman's sudden violent reaction and curt answer quickly turned him away with a muttered excuse.

The violence faded as quickly as it had come, but

she recognized it all too well. Lobo Negro had possessed that devil also.

"Perhaps I can change your mind, madame. At least allow me to try."

She nodded. "As you wish."

"To answer your first objection, I can prove that Cochise was misinformed about you; he believed that it was you who turned against him. I can see that he learns the real truth. Having done that, he will welcome you once more. And if you will consent to join me and the men I expect to meet out west, I'll see that you receive the reward you hold above all others."

He paused again and in spite of herself her hopes suddenly soared. "And that is?" she asked.

"Your son, madame. I have more than a little reason to believe he is alive and well. At least for the time being. However, Cochise is still close on the heels of . . . his father. The renegade's luck cannot hold out forever, and your son stands an excellent chance of being killed when he and his few remaining followers are cornered."

She fought down the panic in her breast and had to struggle to get out her next words. "My husband has promised to help me find him."

He shook his head. "That is a faint hope at best, Mrs. Foxcroft. Your husband is involved in a war that is going to last a long time. Only those who cannot see the truth believe otherwise. By the time this war is ended it will be too late for you. You're too intelligent not to understand that."

He was right. She'd known it all along, at least for the past long months. But she had refused to admit it to herself, knowing it was her only hope. Now she had another opportunity—a dangerous one—but still a chance. But how could she consider going away with this man? What would David think of her? Still, how could she *not* consider it?

"What do you expect to gain by this, General Hartman?" she asked to gain time to think. "I must know why you are doing it."

She could read in his face that he knew he'd won.

He was a man used to winning.

He nodded. "As I said, you're an intelligent woman. One who is wise enough to know that no one risks anything for nothing. Very well, madame. There is wealth to be had there in mining and trade. After the war is finished, many men now otherwise occupied will journey to the territory to seek that wealth. If I go there now and establish peace with the Apache, I'll be in a very advantageous position. A very advantageous position. Do you see?"

"Yes, I believe I do. But tell me, how do you know what Cochise thinks of me?"

"I can take you to a man who will convince you of what I say. Come west with me, talk to him, and I make you the offer that if Cochise still refuses to meet with you, I will send you back here under escort. And I will still see that your son is rescued."

"How do you hope to do that? If Cochise can't?"

"Because of what I know," he said softly. "I know a man who can contact this Lobo Negro. The only one who can. The renegade trusts no one, but he is badly in need of aid and will be forced to deal with this man. The bargain we will make is the return of your son to you. Believe me, it can be done."

When she didn't answer but continued to look at him, he added, "Your father-in-law is behind me in this venture. His money is backing me along with that of others. He's aware that I'm making you this offer and concurs with it."

"To rescue my son?" She stiffened. "I'm afraid I find that hard to believe, General."

"Of course not. You're too intelligent to be lied to. Your father-in-law merely knows that is the only way you can be convinced to help us."

She couldn't trust him. She knew that. He was a man concerned with his own ends, and her father-in-law would be more than happy for her not to come back. She would be placing herself in a trap and would have to be alert at all times . . .

And David! He would be angry, very angry to find her gone. But then, suppose she returned before he did? The man in front of her was right, it was going to be a long war. David had said so without meaning to in his letters . . .

Could she do this to him? Could she hurt him in such a way? She wanted to say no. Knew she should say no. But it was the only chance she might have to save her son . . .

"General, I must think about this. I'll give you my answer tomorrow."

His eyes were alight with triumph. "Good enough, madame. I'll call at one o'clock in the afternoon if that will be convenient. Now, may I get you some punch?"

Chapter Thirteen

The entire Southwest was aflame. The new military governor General James Henry Carleton's stated policy of purging the area of all Indians through either transportation to distant reservations or death had driven its intended victims to murderous fury. Along the upper Rio Grande, the Mescalero Apache struck time and again at isolated farming settlements, and west of there, Gila, Coyotero, Pinal, and Chiricahua had all but closed down the road from El Paso to Tucson, virtually isolating the latter town. The Apache were even raiding the settlements in the Santa Cruz valley south of Tucson, extending their forays into Sonora and Chihuahua, south of the border. North of the Gila River, Yarapais made life miserable for the miners around Prescott.

Atrocity stories stemming from the raids abounded in the territory, and the name mentioned with the most dread was that of Cochise. The chief of the Chiricahua had become a relentless enemy of all Americans, a man without mercy to his victims, and was reported to be everywhere at once. General Carleton issued standing orders to stop him at any cost. The Chiricahua, the orders said, were to be killed on sight no matter their age or sex. His orders were being reluctantly obeyed by the general's strike force leader, Colonel Kit Carson, but success was limited.

It had been a long journey for her. Jennifer was glad it was nearing the end. Once she left St. Louis, she had put all doubts about the wisdom of what she was attempting aside, knowing she must now concentrate only on the problems at hand. General Hartman had been the perfect host on the trip, seeing to her every possible comfort within the bounds of the haste with which they were moving.

When they arrived in Santa Fe, they had been met by a man named Sattersfield along with a large body of men, Mexicans for the most part, but also a number of heavily armed Americans. His was a small army of desperados, more than one of which eyed her in a manner that said she would stand little chance with them except for the protection of the leader. But Hartman left no doubt of her status when he issued orders that she was not to be molested, and two days later on the trail emphasized his order by personally shooting a man who was caught trying to enter her tent.

That tent was small and contained only a cot for sleeping. But she needed little space; she'd brought few clothes from St. Louis and most of those she'd left again in Santa Fe, retaining only a couple of traveling suits, shirtwaists, and underclothing. With great satisfaction, she also left behind the restricting corsets.

Five days out of Santa Fe, they stopped at noon and made camp near a river to wait. Hartman explained to her it was to effect a meeting with the man he'd told her about—the one who could reach Cochise. She asked no further questions but waited with less than patience, keeping for the most part to her tent.

Late in the morning of the following day, she heard the alert when the man was spotted coming in and hurried out to see for herself. When she saw the three riders, one American and two Apache, making their way through the camp, she recognized the man on the middle horse immediately. She didn't remember his name if she'd ever heard it, but he was the scout who'd lied about her to David and the others. The one who'd wanted to take her away with him.

A weight settled upon Jennifer as she watched. She had been a fool to come here! This was the man Hartman expected to deal with Cochise?

As he rode slowly past her on his way to where Hartman and Sattersfield stood in front of another tent, the man eyed her and grinned. He touched his hat. "Morning . . . Flor de Oro," he said.

She spun sharply and reentered the tent.

In a short time, however, he joined her there, following General Hartman, and the grin was still in place.

"Mrs. Foxcroft," the general said, "I'd like you to meet the man we've been waiting for. This is Buffalo Harrison. He's going to set up our meeting with Cochise."

"We've met," Jennifer said shortly. "This man is a liar. If you hope to use him to negotiate with Cochise, you've made a bad mistake."

The grin disappeared and the scout's eyes narrowed in anger, but his forward motion was stopped by Hartman's arm. "You're quite correct, madame," Hartman said into the tension between them. "If perhaps a bit blunt. Mr. Harrison has been guilty of that particular problem on occasion. But with good reason. And that is precisely why he can solve our problem. Would you care to explain, Mister Harrison?"

"You're doing the talking," Harrison said with an edge to his voice as his hard gaze continued to hold hers.

Hartman gave him an ironic glance. "Mister Harrison lied to Cochise for your own good, Mrs. Foxcroft. He knew if Cochise thought you wanted to return to him he would have attempted to rescue you. Since the fort commander at that time would never have agreed to your going back to the Indians, there would have been a fight. Harrison took the very wise course of informing the chief that you yourself didn't want to return. That you wanted to remain with your true people."

"You told him that!"

Harrison didn't reply and she shook her head. "Cochise wouldn't have believed you. Not without talking to me."

"But he did, madame," Hartman answered for him.

"Fortunately, some of the chief's people witnessed you riding in with your future husband and his men. Mister Harrison merely pointed out to him that you rode in of your own free will. That you were under no restraint of any kind."

"But I didn't!" she cried. "I mean, I had no choice!" *All this time he'd believed she deserted him.*

"That may well be," Hartman continued smoothly. "However, we are speaking of what Cochise believed at the time. Now Harrison has apprised him of the truth, namely that you wanted to return."

Jennifer shook her head. "I no longer do."

"Of course not. And you shan't. Cochise is an intelligent man, he understands that and he knows as well that you are married. But he again regards you highly and I believe he will talk to you."

She looked at Harrison. "Why should he believe you now? Since you lied to him before."

"I didn't tell him," Harrison said sharply. "I sent some Apach friends to see him, the ones with me now. They tell me he's willing to talk." He swung sharply to Hartman. "You through with me?"

"Yes, Mister Harrison. Unless Mrs. Foxcroft has any more questions."

Jennifer shook her head. "I've nothing to say to him." She thought about asking him why he also lied about the relatives near Santa Fe but knew it would serve no purpose now, and besides, she already understood the reason. He hated her now for rejecting him and making a fool of him in front of David and the others. He would only lie again . . . or worse. She must make sure she never gave him an advantage over her.

Harrison spun and stalked from the tent and Hartman waited until they could hear his voice a distance from them, calling to one of the Apache, before he spoke again. "I would be very careful in the future, madame. I'm afraid I didn't realize Mister Harrison's feelings toward you. He could be a dangerous adversary."

"Then why use him at all?" she asked sharply.

"What makes you think he won't lie to you as well?"

He chuckled. "The secret of dealing with all men, madame, is knowing their weaknesses. It seems Mister Harrison's value as a scout for the military has been lost due to an unfortunate attraction to the bottle. He realizes he is also growing a bit old to continue such a demanding life. I've offered him a last chance, so to speak, of financing a peaceful retirement. He could become a wealthy man."

She sighed. So much with which to contend. Every man had his price, and it was usually in gold. But then so did she have a price, only hers lay in the life of a little boy. No matter what, she had to see this through; she couldn't afford to turn back now. But would Cochise really meet with her? Or did he now hate her as well? They said he hated all whites, and she was white. Would she be risking her life in approaching him? This man standing before her believed Cochise would deal with her and he was not one to leave anything to chance. Therefore, the odds were good that Cochise would see her . . .

"What do you intend to do now?" she wanted to know.

"The Indians with Harrison have asked Cochise for a meeting, and he has agreed. At least we think so. It will of course be tricky, and we must move with great care. We'll break camp tomorrow and move to the appointed spot. If he arrives, you will ride forth to talk to him. Are you willing to do that?"

She nodded.

"Good. Then you and I must now discuss what you will say to him."

She raised a hand. "I won't betray him," she said. "Not even for my son."

"My dear Mrs. Foxcroft, I'm quite aware of that. Nor do I intend you to do so."

He paused and studied her intently. When he spoke again, it was with an apparent attempt at deep sincerity. A wasted attempt, since she already knew him too well for that.

"Please believe that I intend no harm to the Indians," he said. "For purely practical reasons—call them self-serving if you like—such a move would be foolhardy on my part. What we intend to do here will take great effort; effort that should be concentrated on the task, not in fighting with Cochise and his people. We simply do not want to work and watch our backs at the same time. As I informed you in St. Louis, if I can succeed in achieving peace with the Indians, this entire territory will be grateful to me. I will suddenly become a man of great influence, which will offer me latitude of movement. Do you see? The very last thing I want is to be an enemy to a chief of Cochise's influence."

It did make sense. For all the wrong reasons, of course. But then she had been east and now knew the power that lay there. When they finished the war and could bring their armies here, the Chiricahua would stand no chance against them. There must be peace in order for Cochise and his people to survive.

"What about my son?" she asked.

He nodded. "As soon as we've made this treaty with Cochise, we'll set about recovering him for you. Mister Sattersfield will see to it."

"How? What can he do?"

"He's the man I told you could reach the renegade. We'll offer Lobo Negro supplies and aid in slipping out of the territory to California. He's aware that remaining where Cochise can reach him will inevitably result in his own death. In return for his freedom and safety, we shall demand your son."

"And if Cochise refuses to deal with you?"

"Our bargain still holds, madame. Either way you will have your son. But I truly believe you will convince him."

"Perhaps," she said at last. "At least I can try."

"Excellent. That's all we ask. Now here's my proposal to him . . ."

She listened as he outlined his promises. The Chiricahua would be left in peace in their mountain stronghold and no whites would be allowed to disturb them. They would be given supplies each winter, including cattle, and offered contracts to furnish firewood such as they once had held with the Overland Mail. There would also be contracts to supply timber for the mines. In exchange, they would only be asked to discontinue their raids and allow the freight wagons to roll again through their lands.

He continued to supply details and she listened intently until he was finished, then repeated most of it for him to show that she understood. When he was gone, Jennifer lay on her cot and thought of the meeting; what it would be like to face her Indian father over the gulf that had grown between them. For the first time, she experienced a weakness and had to discipline herself to put it aside. She would do what she must for the sake of her child. But even so, she wished David were there to aid her.

Cochise's stronghold was located high in the mountains and no attempt by the blue-coated soldiers had yet been successful in dislodging him from it. His warriors boasted of their invincibility, but the chief of the Chiricahua had seen the power of the giant rifles the Americans called howitzers and knew in his heart that inevitably they would succeed. The dreams that haunted him told of a time when the Chiricahua would be no more.

Once, he had believed they could live side by side with the Americans, but that time was now long past. Too much blood had been shed, and there was only the matter of showing that the Apache could die with pride. And in doing so, he told himself grimly, to make them pay a very heavy price for the taking of Chiricahua land.

He held a council of war to discuss the latest move of the Americans. This new chief, the one called General Hartman, had extended an offer of peace, and as chief he was bound to present it to the others. When he had done so, he sat down and held his silence while they discussed it, smoking a long black cheroot and listening carefully. When they finished, they turned again to him for his opinion as he expected they would do.

"I do not know this man," he said. "I know only that he comes from the East and has many fighters with him. I do not trust him as I do not trust any of them. There are men of the town of Tucson with him, men who once worked with the graycoats to destroy our people. I think that they have not changed. I believe this man intends to destroy us also."

He waited for the murmur of assent to circle the seated men. "He has asked for a meeting; I think that we should meet with him. But we must be prepared for a trap. I would choose to ride forward to talk to him, but only in the open, while the rest of you prepare to fight."

He was immediately interrupted with a growl of dissent and raised a hand to still it. "I will never place myself again under a flag of truce. Nor will I enter the tents of the Americans. The meeting will be held in the open between me and their leader. He will suffer the same risks as I."

"Why meet at all?" one man wanted to know. "Why not attack?"

"Because they are too strong," Cochise said patiently. "Many warriors would be killed. It is better that we find out what they want first and then choose our course."

"Flor de Oro is with them," another warrior reminded him gruffly.

Cochise nodded. "She was once my daughter. Now she has turned against the Chiricahua who sheltered her. She is to be considered an enemy of the Chiricahua."

"The messenger said that she seeks to talk with Cochise," the man persisted. "She will attempt to reach the heart of Cochise."

The leader turned a hard gaze in the direction of the speaker. "If Flor de Oro attempts to betray the Chiricahua into the hands of their enemies, I will kill her myself."

They nodded in agreement. All, except for one man. Shi-la, the aged one who was closest to the chief of the Chiricahua and was often asked for his advice, doubted his words. He remembered too well the golden-haired maiden who had grown up in the lodge of Cochise and his pride in her. She had been the strong and silent one; Shi-la could not bring himself to believe she would betray the man she had so obviously loved. There was reason for her to be with the whites, reasons yet to be understood. He had taught her much himself when she was young; she had looked to him as an uncle and listened too often at his knee for him not to understand her.

Cochise had many things to trouble his mind; he had the responsibility of the entire tribe in his hands. But Shi-la had much time to think. And he wanted very much to talk to Flor de Oro again. He must look into her eyes and receive answers to the questions he wanted to ask.

It was decided. In the end, the chief of the Chiricahua was overruled by the majority and would not go forth himself to meet with the Americans. Another would go in his place while Cochise would stay back to direct the warriors if the meeting turned into a trap.

Shi-la was glad. Cochise had not told the others everything, only he and Shi-la knew that one of the warriors who traveled with the American called Harrison was there because his heart lay with the Apache.

The meeting with the Apache was to take place on a broad mesa shadowed by high mountains. General Hartman had brought only half the men, leaving the rest behind and explaining to Jennifer that it was a gesture of good intentions to Cochise. He was quite certain, he said, that Cochise already knew how large his party was, and leaving half in camp would prove he meant no trouble.

They reached the spot for the meeting by midmorning and settled down to wait. Looking around her, Jennifer did not have a good feeling about it. Even if he had brought only half his men, they were all heavily armed with new repeating rifles, double bandoleers of ammunition across their chests, and one or more side arms. And these men were nervous, she was still Indian enough to catch the scent of controlled and guarded fear. It made her nervous as well, but she put the thought aside as being only the uneasiness of men who knew the might be outnumbered in a possibly dangerous situation.

Waiting was hard. She sat on a rock near the spot where her horse was held and tried to ignore the many looks cast her way since her tent had been left in camp and she had no retreat in which to hide. Hartman and the one called Sattersfield stood together a few feet away and engaged in low conversation with each other. Low enough that she could not overhear them, but they too often glanced her way. The scout, Harrison, did not make the trip and she had to wonder about that as well. If he was the instrument of convincing Cochise, why was he not here?

It was hot already; the sun was high and uncomfortable because of the heavy traveling suit she wore. She'd removed all but one petticoat under the long skirt and still her legs felt smothered. How much better would it be to have a split buckskin skirt to give them air and freedom. A cotton shirt would also allow the light wind across the mesa to cool the perspiration of her upper body. Being civilized, she thought wryly, did have its drawbacks. Only an idiot would dress like this in desert country.

She wondered if Cochise would recognize her in different clothes and pursued that thought with a hand to her hair. It was done up with combs holding it in place. Slowly she began to remove the combs and when they were out, used one to free her hair until it hung loose as in the old days when she was Flor de Oro.

Her actions brought further attention from the men around her, and even Hartman turned to stare but quickly realized why she had done it and nodded in encouragement.

The general was still a mystery to her. She could understand readily a man like Sattersfield; he was interested only in wealth and the easy life it would bring to him. She didn't like him, but she understood him. He was a Western counterpart to David's father. The difference between the two, she recognized, was that where Foxcroft man pretended heartiness to those with whom he dealt, Sattersfield was dour.

Harrison, too, was easy to understand. On closer inspection after their initial meeting in the camp she could see the change in him. Alcohol or mescal had dimmed his once Indian eyes, the ones she remembered from the first time she saw him. And now his hands held a very slight tremor; she could almost feel sorry for him.

The man in the black suit concerned her most—worried her most. He was smooth and polished, his manner toward her was every bit the gentleman, but there was a coiled violence just under the surface of the polish. She had sensed it the first night she met him when he'd become instantly angry at having his conversation with her interrupted at the party. When he'd gotten angry, even in that minor thing, there was a light of instability in his eyes. That small flash had bothered her at the time, but she had forgotten it in the press of her own decisions. It was days later, well after she was already traveling west with him, before she understood the flash. It came to her at night as she lay on her cot unable to sleep. She had seen the same thing appear in her own father's eyes before he went mad in the desert . . .

That the rest of the men, hardened as they might appear, were afraid of him was apparent. And justifiably so; the man who attempted to enter her tent had been drinking and when captured was held by the arms, unable to resist. Neither fact had prevented Hartman from producing a pistol and, with deliberate aim, shooting him dead on the spot. There had been mutterings as the dead man lay on the ground, but since then none of the men dared look long at her.

There was more than a desire for wealth that drove Hartman, she decided. He enjoyed having power over others; she had observed him look slowly around after he shot the drunken man and could see that the fact that he created fear as well as obedience in the rest was a wine in his blood. He was a man who wanted to command; he acted constantly as if this were a right to which he was born. Understandably as far as it went, for he had said he was a general in a foreign army. But then that was another part of the mystery. She didn't know much about Europe, only what David had told her, but she had met a few people in St. Louis who, either themselves or their parents, had come from Germany, where Hartman had said Prussia was located. All of those people spoke with a recognizable accent. There was no trace of it in Hartman's voice. Why not?

A rider appeared in the distance, and every eye including hers was drawn to watch as he approached. All activity around her ceased as he rode up to the waiting men and brought his horse to a halt near Hartman and Sattersfield. He talked with them for only a moment before the general broke away and walked over to where she sat.

"He's coming," he told her. "Cochise and a large number of his band will be arriving shortly. Are you ready?"

"I'm ready," she said. And she stood up.

So it was to be, after all. So much time had passed since she last saw him; so many events to change her from the simple Indian girl he'd known. She was now married to an Army officer, a man who wore the blue coat he hated, and she was the mother to a child born of the renegade whom he's sworn vengeance upon. How would Cochise react to such a woman?

She was calm, her nervousness stilled by the arrival of a time to act. In her mind's eye she could see every feature of his face, especially the love that once was in his eyes. What look would those eyes hold for Flor de Oro now?

"We'll wait until they appear," Hartman continued. "Give them time to appraise us. After that, you'll ride forth with a few of my men with you, but you'll ride a bit forward of them so that he can see you clearly. It was a good idea of yours to let down your hair. He'll recognize you more easily."

"No men," she said. "Let me go alone."

"I can't do that, madame. It would be too dangerous and I consider myself responsible for your safety."

"Then come yourself. Only the two of us."

He frowned in annoyance. "My men are unsettled, Mrs. Foxcroft. They are extremely nervous; you can see that as well as I. My place is here to control them. One stupid move on their part, and this can erupt into a battle. Now please do as I ask."

Jennifer nodded. "Then have your men ride well behind me. I insist on meeting him alone."

"Why?"

"General Hartman, this meeting is your idea and I'm sure you planned it well. But Cochise is also a general and will not meet with men who are less than he. When I lived with the Chiricahua, women were often used as messengers between two warring tribes, as a signal of peaceful intent, but to send mere warriors to face a chief would be an insult."

"I see. And of course you're right. Stupid of me not to consider that. Bringing you here was the best move I could have made; your knowledge of these people is indispensable. We'll do exactly as you say, madame. I'll give the necessary instructions."

"And if Cochise agrees to consider your terms?" she asked.

"Then bring me the message. I'll meet with him where and how he chooses." He smiled broadly. "One general to another."

Someone called his name and both of them turned to look. Coming up from the south end of the mesa, as if appearing from the earth itself, rode a large number of Apache. They were spread out in war formation; she could see many battle lances with brightly colored cloth and feathers attached.

"I do believe it is time, madame," Hartman said softly.

The horse she rode, a dun-colored mare, had picked up the scent of fear from the men in camp and it was transmitted through its nervous, skittering step. Jennifer was forced to rein hard to control her. Still, the jerking head was an annoyance that kept her from concentrating on the Indians. That, and the fact that she would never become used to riding sidesaddle; it was a ridiculous way to travel.

Ten men were behind her, moving at the same pace but twenty or so feet to the rear. She didn't like the fact that they rode with rifles drawn from their scabards and resting across saddlehorns but didn't think there was much she could do about it. These men didn't trust Cochise any more than he would trust them; this meeting was going to be a very delicate thing. One wrong move from either side and she would be caught in the middle of a war.

Watching the distant, standing ranks of Apache, she tried to pick him out, and her gaze finally settled on a small knot of men separate from the others. He would be there, she decided, along with the war leaders. She guided the mare in that direction and a moment later three Apache moved out of the group and began a slow ride to meet her.

The man in the middle rode a large, high-stepping white horse that made Jennifer smile. If her Indian father had one real vanity it lay in the horses he chose to ride in the rare times he used them. He took an Apache's pride in the strength and endurance of his own strong legs, but when he did ride a horse, he loved to make a show of it. His must be the largest, and white, if at all possible.

Then something was wrong. She recognized a difference. The man who rode the white horse was too short to be Cochise unless he was bent with age, and too, his hair was almost all gray, unlike the black mane she remembered. This couldn't be him!

It wasn't. Moving closer, she recognized the three men, and none was Cochise. The gray-haired one riding so proudly on the white horse was Shi-la, whom she'd once called Uncle. She felt a great sadness. He had refused to meet with her. He would send Shi-la, but he would not himself talk with the woman he had once called daughter. She wanted to cry, but she lifted her head instead and held it high. So it would be . . .

A few more yards and she stopped the mare, reining it tightly to make the animal remain in one place to wait. She didn't look behind her to see if the men stopped as well but kept her eyes on Shi-la as he approached. He brought his own horse to a halt only a few feet away, near enough to cause her mare's head to jerk violently. Shi-la waited patiently until she had it under control again.

"It has been much time since we have seen each other, Flor de Oro," he said at last.

Her hopes suddenly rose, for there was no anger in his voice, only sadness.

"A long time, Uncle," she said. "My heart has been heavy, for I have missed the Chiricahua much."

"The daughter of Cochise is well?"

She nodded, and fought away the tears that wanted to come into her eyes. "I am well. Is . . . my father?"

"Cochise is like the eagle," he said. "His strength is that of the bear. But his people are hard-pressed by the bluecoats, and there is great anger in the heart of Cochise for the suffering they cause his people."

"I know," she said. "I have heard of this. Will you speak to Cochise of my love for him?"

"You are now the squaw of a bluecoat." It was stated flatly, but without heat in the words.

Jennifer nodded. "I love my husband as a squaw should. But I remember my people, the Chiricahua. My husband understands this and he carries no hatred in his heart for the Chiricahua."

"Why do you come?" he asked abruptly. "And where is your husband, the bluecoat?"

"He fights a great battle where the sun rises," she said. "There, the Americans are at war with one another."

Shi-la nodded. "They fight with those who wear the gray coats. These people were here once, and the bluecoats drove them away."

"Yes. My husband fought also in that battle. But now I will answer your question. I am here as a messenger for one who calls himself General Hartman. He desires peace with the—"

The warrior on Shi-la's right interrupted her with a sudden movement, bringing his rifle up sharply, his attention shifting behind her. His move was a second too late, as another rifle cracked and he pitched backward from his horse.

"No!" she cried. But her shout was drowned in an explosion of gunfire around her. The other warrior got off one shot before he too was swept from his mount, his chest erupting in blood.

Shi-la's stallion pitched skyward, hooves pawing at the mare which nearly danced from beneath Jennifer. He spun the horse in a desperate attempt to flee and she heard him curse.

"No!" she screamed again. "No, please!"

The mare bucked and it was all Jennifer could do to remain seated as before her despairing eyes, Shi-la rolled to the side of the white stallion to shield himself from the flying bullets. He had already been wounded, however, and his grip on the running horse failed, allowing him to fall free.

Jennifer wasn't conscious of leaving the mare's back, only of a stumbling run toward the fallen man, tripping over her long skirts as she desperately tried to reach him.

Shi-la rose on an elbow and turned as she knelt and gathered him in her arms. She leaned forward to shelter him with her body, as all around her men leaped from their horses and kneeled to fire at the Apache. Jennifer could hear the larger battle before her now, intermixed with the wild cries of the Apache. But she had time only for the bleeding old man in her arms.

The fight moved away from her as quickly as it had begun, the riflemen around her mounting their horses and following it, firing as they went. Still holding Shi-la in her arms, Jennifer knew without looking up that it had been a trap all along; Hartman hadn't left the rest of the men in camp, he used them to come up behind the Apache in an attempt to catch them in a crossfire. He'd had no intention of negotiating with the Chiricahua, he'd wanted to destroy them in one bold move. And she'd allowed herself to be used for bait!

Looking down into the eyes of the man she held, she read the same knowledge there. Flor de Oro has betrayed her people, the eyes said without anger, only hurt. She shook her head. "No," she whispered. "I did not know, Uncle. Please believe I did not know!"

The eyes probed her own, searching, and she wanted to cry with grief. "Please," she said again. "I was told the Americans only wanted to talk. I was given the promise of what they would do for the Chiricahua. I am a foolish woman . . . I believed their lies . . ."

She could hear horses pounding toward them. "Please, Uncle!"

He nodded weakly. His voice was low. "I believe the words of the daughter of Cochise."

Then she did cry. Tears of frustration and anger flowed freely as she gently laid him down and sought to find out how badly he was wounded.

She wasn't allowed to help him, however, as riders dismounted rapidly around them once more and she was jerked away from the wounded man. Two of them held her by the arms and a third pointed a rifle at Shi-la. She spun to face Hartman as he and Sattersfield rode up. The man in black had changed, the arrogant anger she knew he possessed now lay clearly exposed in his face as he stared back at her. Mixed with the anger was triumph.

"Most of your friends got away," he told her harshly. "My stupid men allowed themselves to be discovered before they were in position. But thanks to you we did capture the man we wanted most. Without Cochise to lead them, those savages will be simple to handle."

A flame of hatred burned brightly within her as she stared at him. Her captors felt it in her tension and tightened their grip on her arms. "You're a fool," she told him. "Cochise will now destroy both you and your men."

He laughed, a cold, merciless chuckle, and glanced down at Shi-la. "Your friend Cochise is not in a position to destroy anyone, madame. I'm glad he survives, however. I've a few questions he's going to answer for me."

Jennifer got a great deal of satisfaction out of her reply. "This man is not Cochise," she said slowly. "Do you think him so lacking in intelligence he would allow himself to be taken by the likes of you?"

He shook his head. "Clever as always, Mrs. Foxcroft. You meet my every expectation. But your small ruse will not work. You forget I have Mister Harrison and his Indians to identify your chief for me."

"Then bring them," she said shortly. "I shall enjoy watching your face when you discover your great plan has failed and Cochise still leads his people."

Her satisfaction increased as she watched doubt creep into his expression. He glanced at Sattersfield, who shrugged.

Jennifer allowed her own triumph to show. "You've made a very dangerous enemy, General. Cochise won't fight you the way you want him to; he'll trail your every move from now on, keep your men surrounded even though you'll never see him, and kill each of you one by one."

The men around her stirred and she repeated it slowly. "One by one they'll die. At night, during the days, anytime you least expect him, he'll strike. You're the one who has lost, General. You and these poor fools who follow you."

"Cleaver," he said sharply, looking at one of the men standing near her. "Mount your horse and find Harrison. Bring him here. We'll settle this."

"No need, General," the man said and pointed with the muzzle of his rifle. "Looks like most of our men are already coming back."

Hartman spun in his saddle and cursed violently. Then he looked hard at Sattersfield. "I gave orders that all survivors were to be pursued and shot! Don't your people understand simple commands?"

Sattersfield had been watching the approaching horsemen as well and slowly turned back to face him. "Chasing a few survivors is one thing, General. Riding hard after a full band of Apache is another. Can lead you into an ambush if you ain't careful. I don't blame them for quitting."

Hartman's voice was a whiplash. "My orders will be obeyed!"

She could see that even Sattersfield was afraid of him. The evidence was both in his face and his hand now straying toward the big pistol on his hip. But his manner was defiant. "Then you better give the right orders, General," he said softly. "Cochise won't give you much room for mistakes."

Hartman was rapidly losing control; his face flushed, he pointed to the man on the ground. "There is Cochise! She lies! Can't you see that?"

Sattersfield shrugged. "Let's see what Harrison says. If she's right, we got a world of problems."

"This man needs attention," Jennifer broke in as they stared at one another. "Will you let me attend him?"

Hartman returned his angry look to her for a long moment, then motioned to the men who held her. He released her, and she went to Shi-la.

He had been hit twice, one bullet had torn into his chest and another cut through the muscle of his left thigh. He was bleeding badly and was already losing consciousness. Quickly, she raised her skirt and tore off large strips of her last petticoat, and by the time the returning horsemen reached them, she had stopped the bleeding and had him tightly bandaged.

"Harrison!" Hartman called as she stood up again. "Come here!"

The scout separated from the group and rode up slowly. Jennifer followed his look as he took in the whole of them, including the man on the ground. His jaw twitched.

"Is this Cochise or not?" Hartman demanded.

Harrison shook his head. "Afraid you missed, General. This old Apach sure ain't Cochise. He's a relative though, I think."

"Damn!" Hartman exploded.

"I told you Cochise was a general too," Jennifer said quietly. "You underestimated him badly."

"Bring her!" He screamed the command. "And bring that savage, too. We'll get our answers from him, and she can watch us do it!"

Chapter Fourteen

Hartman moved his camp to another location, one that offered less chance of being attacked from more than one side, setting up his personal quarters in an abandoned ranch house. Once there, with guards posted, he lost no time in carrying out his threat. Jennifer was forced to watch as Shi-la was stretched out on the ground and red-hot iron applied to the soles of his feet.

The old man writhed in agony, but no sound passed his lips. When Jennifer refused even under threats to herself to ask the questions of him, Harrison did it. But at last she discovered what Hartman wanted to know as she was made to listen. Shi-la was questioned again and again about Quivira, a name she'd heard only from David. She knew from her husband that it was a lost city that was supposed to contain large treasures of gold and silver.

She protested that the old man didn't know of such a place, that none of the Chiricahua knew of it, but to no avail. Hartman was insane. She could clearly see that now. And the rest of these men believed there was a place called Quivira. Because of that foolish belief, because of a place that didn't exist, Shi-la was dying by inches. Even if he would talk, he could tell them nothing. They believed, and nothing would change their minds.

When the hot irons proved useless against the old man's stubbornness, gunpowder was placed on his bare stomach and set afire. Only a muffled cry came from Shi-la before he lost consciousness.

His tormentors brought him back with water

poured over his body as darkness fell and continued, building a fire to see by. The old man's shirt was bloodied by his reopened wounds, and Jennifer was exhausted by her own futile attempts to free herself from the ropes holding her.

The end drew near. Shi-la's voice was barely audible to her as he began his death song and Jennifer knew he no longer heard the questions directed at him, no longer understood anything but the pain. He raised his head in agony as they twisted his wounded leg until the bones snapped and suddenly his voice was stilled as an arrow came out of the darkness and penetrated his throat. His head fell back and she knew he was dead.

Pandemonium surrounded the fire as men dropped to their knees and drew guns to protect themselves; their startled yells brought the rest of the camp alive and gunfire resounded in the darkness. It was long moments before the firing ceased. There was nothing but darkness at which to shoot.

Jennifer lowered her head in relief. A Chiricahua had slipped into the camp and put an end to Shi-la's suffering. That could be the only explanation. She hoped the brave warrior managed to get away as easily as he had come.

She was jerked to her feet and taken into her tent, where she was left, still bound, to lie on the dirt and listen to the ongoing excitement outside. Only much later, when it finally ceased, did Hartman appear. He brought a lantern and held it high as he glared down at her.

"This is not the end," he snarled. "We'll get Cochise if it's the last thing I do!"

Jennifer watched him closely. He was trembling with rage and struggling to control himself. She wanted to tell him he had no chance, that better men than he had faced Cochise and lost, men who understood Apache ways. But he was unpredictable, there was no way to tell how he would react to her taunts.

He left and she was alone in the darkness. When he returned after a short while, he was a different man, one who had regained control. He hung the lantern on the center pole of the tent and bent to help her to the cot before standing back to talk.

"My apologies, madame, for losing my temper," he said. "It would seem that once again you are right. Your Cochise is a worthy opponent, quite as you said. I've made the mistake of allowing someone else to pick the men who serve under me and am burdened with fools because of that error. For them to have allowed one of the savages to penetrate the guard cordon around my camp is inexcusable."

"He got away?" she asked.

Slowly he nodded. "A very tricky people, your Indians. No one saw him enter and no one, it seems, saw him leave. However, I believe they will be more alert from now on."

"The Apache are like the night, General," she told him levelly. "They will come again, and you won't see them then either."

"Perhaps," he said. "I am quite prepared to lose a few men, they're generally worthless anyway. But that doesn't matter. I've suddenly realized I don't need to find Cochise at all. Stupid of me not to be aware that I held the key to Quivira all the time, but one sometimes becomes involved in planning a campaign to the extent that he forgets the obvious."

"There is no such place," she said. "This Quivira exists only in your imagination. Yours and the others out there. What makes you think it does? Who among you has ever seen it?"

"Quivira exists, Madame. There is too much evidence of it. Men have known of its existence ever since the Spanish came here centuries ago. I've spent too many years of my life studying every scrap of record available not to know it exists. I've made it my life's mission to find that golden city."

"You're not a general," she said. "I don't believe you ever were in Europe."

He nodded. "You're quite right. It's a guise I adopted long ago, finding early in life that men respect authority, need to be commanded, and are easily impressed with titles, especially European ones."

"Who are you?"

He shrugged. "What does it matter? I am who I choose to be at the moment. Many years ago I decided to shake the binds of abject poverty and climb to the heights of wealth and power. I educated myself to that, madame, and succeeded through my knowledge of the weakness of others. I am now on the verge of realizing my dream of becoming one of the most powerful men in this country. Soon my name will be legend. And you are, as I said, the key. When I control Quivira and its wealth, all men will look up to me in fear."

"You're mad." She said it flatly, without emphasis. "What good am I to you now? Cochise thinks I betrayed him."

"It doesn't matter. For you see, I have realized at last that in your life with him you were in a position to know the deepest secrets of the Chiricahua. You, madame, surely must know the location of Quivira. Foolish of me not to realize that simple fact. I had the key to that lost city in my grasp all the time."

"There is no lost city," she said wearily. "I never heard of it from the Chiricahua, only from Americans. You're chasing a ghost."

"You know and you shall tell me. Your Indian friend withstood the torture well, but I doubt if you can do the same. If I'm wrong and you surprise me, there is still another way. We will carry out our agreement and find your child. But then we will see if a mother can watch with sealed lips as her child dies."

She didn't answer, knowing it was useless. He was insane with a dream that didn't exist and nothing would change him.

Hartman waited for a long moment until he realized she didn't intend to reply, then said softly, "You have tonight to think about it, madame. Think well. There are many men in this camp who desire you. If by morning you still refuse to tell me what I want to know, I shall turn you over to them for their . . . shall we say, amusements? Think of it, madame. There's a great number of men out there."

Jennifer merely looked at him until he nodded once more and turned to leave, taking the lantern with him.

Well into the night she was still awake, thinking not of the morning and what it would bring but of David. The hurt would be great for him when he discovered what had happened to her, and afterward he would come looking for Hartman. She could only hope he wouldn't find him and would eventually go on with his life without her.

A ripping sound came from behind her and she held her breath, straining to listen. It came again, a slow, careful sound that took her moments to identify. She stiffened as she understood that someone was cutting the canvas of the tent. A moment later there was a presence with her in the darkness and someone bent over her to place a hand gently on her mouth.

Jennifer struggled briefly, but quickly realized that the hand was not harsh and that she had only enemies outside to whom to cry.

"Do not be afraid," whispered a voice in Apache. "I mean you no harm."

She relaxed and the hand was removed. She felt herself being turned over and suddenly the rope around her wrists was cut and she was free. The man reached down with one hand and found the ones around her ankles and cut them as well. Then he bent over her head once more.

"I will take you out of the camp," he whispered. "But I can do no more than that. I must stay here. Run, Flor de Oro. Run like the wind. You must save yourself."

"Who are you?" Her own whisper was strained. "Did you kill Shi-la?"

"He was a brave warrior," he said. "I would have ended it for him sooner but I had to wait for darkness. Now I do what I can for the daughter of Cochise."

"But why do you stay?"

"I must do what I am told to do. No more questions. Come."

He moved away and she reached for him. Her hand touched his back, felt the buckskin, and she grasped a portion in order to follow him through the cut he'd made in the tent.

Outside, it was somewhat lighter than the darkness in the tent but still she could not see his face, only his outline. He was Apache, and she remembered there had been two of them traveling with Harrison that first day. He must be one of them. Cochise had found a way to put his own man in the camp of the enemy and when this man had killed Shi-la, the Americans had gone looking for a raider who didn't exist. He had remained in the middle of them all the time!

With a warning hand on her arm, he led her through the sleeping camp. Three times they were forced to pause and crouch as a guard moved, and once they were almost discovered as a man stopped to light a cigarette. His own match blinded him to their presence, however, and he moved away, the glow of his cigarette marking the direction of his going.

A few minutes later, her guide stopped her. "The camp is behind us now," he whispered. "Move straight in that direction. You have time before the sun rises to gain distance. Cover your trail, Flor de Oro. For they will come after you. I will give you as much time as I can by seeing that they have something else to think about at the dawn."

"How—"she started, but he placed a hand over her mouth.

"A few of their guards will die this night," he said softly. "Tomorrow they will be afraid of attack. Only after the attack does not come will they again think of you."

"Thank you," she whispered and his hand touched her shoulder.

"If I live," he said, "Cochise will know the truth of his daughter. Go."

Her shoes were not made for running but she could

do nothing about that. The long skirt was a hindrance and she pulled it up to her waist, tying it by the ends to leave her legs free. True, the white of her pantaloons would be a signal even in the darkness, but she couldn't help that. She began a slow trot to allow her body and her senses to adjust to running in the dark and found that she would not be able to run as freely as she hoped since she couldn't feel the ground through the stiff shoes. Nevertheless, she increased her pace. As the first dawn gave her light to see, she would begin to hide her trail, but for now she must only put distance between her and the pursuit that would follow.

It was difficult to run in the confining clothes, and she had softened during the long months spent as a white woman, but even so the old feeling started to come back. She measured her breathing, pushing air deep into her lungs and swinging her arms to aid its passage. Often she stumbled in the dark, not able to see the ground under her running feet clearly, but her balance was still there. It was a good feeling; she threw her head back with exultation. She was free!

Twice she rested before the first light of false dawn began to give her vision. With its help she looked for lava rock upon which to travel, knowing its harshness would soon rob her of her shoes, but needing its silence to a tracker's eye to blind her trail. She climbed down an arroyo, up its other side through a slit, being careful not to dislodge anything during her passage, and spotted a grove of yucca, the bayonet tree. Flor de Oro smiled through her labored breathing, knowing that although the trees would be difficult for her, it would be impossible for a man on horseback to get through them. The razor-sharp leaves would cut the animal to pieces and leave her pursuer on foot as her equal.

Once beyond the grove, she was within sight of mountains and they, too, would offer shelter against the speed of horses. She turned and ran in that direction.

By the time she reached the foothills, she was tiring

badly and had to force her pace. Once she began to climb, however, she could move more slowly and rest more often, for she would be able to see behind her and know when they were coming.

When the sun was high with morning, she stopped to rest. Below her, the ground fell away in a long sweep and she could see a great distance. Flor de Oro leaned against a rock both to slow the pounding of her heart and to decide what to do. Her shoes were coming apart and her feet were numb. She looked down and saw signs of blood, but ignored it; there were more important things to think about. Soon she must find water, which meant looking for signs of a *tinja* since no cacti grew up here, and she had no knife with which to slice a portion and suck its lifegiving juices at any rate.

Also, she must decide her direction. She didn't know where she was, nor where to go. If she found a white settlement, it was likely that Hartman's men would find it too and take her away from whomever was there. But then if she found Indians, she might well suffer the fate of a white woman at their hands. She would have to call on all her learned skills as an Apache to survive, but she would do it. This chance had been given her, and she would make the most of it. She bent forward, took a long, deep breath, and began to climb again.

She found a *tinja*, surprising herself with the ease with which she discovered it, and drank her fill, being careful at the same time not to overdrink. Afterward, she lay on a rock and watched the trail behind her. By the time she was rested and ready to move again, she saw the rider coming . . .

It was only one man. The sun glinting from the rocks made it difficult to see him, but she forced herself to concentrate. He had to be a good tracker, guessing more than following her passage across the lava and through the zucca, therefore he had to be one of the Apache. One was her friend and would help her, but she could not plan for it to be him. Flor de Oro half closed her eyes, boxed one of them to concentrate on the faint speck in the distance, and saw that the rider wore a hat. He was not Apache, therefore there was only one other answer—a white man who thought like an Apache . . . Harrison.

He would be the volunteer, she thought with anger. None of the rest would dare venture out by themselves where they might meet with the Chiricahua, but Harrison wanted her badly enough to take the risk and he would be a difficult man to fool. What could she do to stop him? Without a weapon she stood no chance at all. The answer came quickly as she looked down the side of the cliff on which she lay. It fell away several hundred feet to a deep cut before rising again to a lower plateau. With a faint smile at her idea, Flor de Oro scrambled back to find some bushes, gathered them by pulling them out by the roots, and then removed her dress.

Harrison had bypassed the zucca, knowing the woman would only use it as a feint and guessing she would head for the mountains, but after an hour's casting about for signs, he started to have doubts. The mountain route was the most logical, she'd know she stood no chance against men on horseback through the flatlands. Her only hope would be the mountains, where a horse would be slowed to her own speed. But there was no sign of her passage . . . unless he'd missed it somehow. Patiently, he began to backtrack himself.

This time he spotted her trail and dismounted to make sure. There were only two faint depressions in the sandy soil, and the dry sides had collapsed to the extent that they could have been made by anything from a human foot to a mountain cat's paw. But when he gently moved grains of sand with his fingers, he found a trace of blood.

Harrison nodded to himself. She was Indian enough to cover a trail but she sure as hell wasn't dressed for this country and was already suffering. He walked back to remove a bottle from his saddlebag, pulled the cork, and studied the rising mountains before him as he drank. Trailing her would be slow, but in her condition capture was inevitable. However, if he could anticipate her path, he could shorten the chase considerably.

He was taking a risk by being out here in the first place, since the Apach would be spread throughout this territory to keep an eye on Hartman's movements. A fact of which all the rest were well aware; none of them had been willing to come with him, even under the general's threats. But he was gambling on a single issue—that Cochise would withdraw his band into his stronghold and plan his moves first. If he were right, he had two, three days, in which to find her before the Chiricahua came back. Wrong, and he would have to fight for his life.

Was she worth it? He took another drink and considered his own question. For over twenty years he'd searched for Quivira; he'd covered almost every mile of this damned land looking for it; spent most of his nights thinking about nothing else. Finally, he'd convinced himself it was too well hidden to be found without help from someone who knew its location.

The woman somewhere ahead of him must know the secret. Half Indian, half white, she was a prize worth having herself, but add to that the fact she was once the daughter of the chief of the Chiricahua and would surely know his secrets, and she meant wealth beyond belief.

He'd wanted her for both reasons ever since he'd first spotted her in Cochise's rancheria. An Indian squaw could be broken, like a horse could be broken, even if she had experienced the life of a white woman. And Harrison knew how to do that. When he'd thought he'd lost his chance at her forever, when that damn shavetail had gotten her, he'd gone into the bottle with his dreams and damn near killed himself doing it. Sattersfield had rescued him and it was the man from Tucson who'd come up with the idea of using her to get to Cochise. He'd contacted Hartman with his plan, and the general had persuaded her to come back. Back, he considered grimly, where he could reach her.

Until last night, neither Sattersfield nor Hartman had considered the fact that she might know the location of Quivira herself, because they didn't think like Indians. But he had thought of it and was willing to settle for part of the lost city's wealth just as long as he got the woman, too. The others wouldn't expect that of him and it would have been easy to accomplish once their attention was involved with Quivira. Once the city was found, he would have been able to gather what gold and silver he needed, take her in the night, and been in Mexico before they missed him. But Hartman had shot his plan to hell and gone when he allowed her to escape.

He decided on his course into the mountains and mounted the horse again. Only a few more hours in the saddle and he would have her. Eventually she would tell him what he wanted to know; he'd only to hole up and wait for her to break. Then he'd have both her and Quivira. That was one hell of a promise and worth any threat of Apach to get.

One last chance—all the pain and waiting would be worth it when he reached Mexico a wealthy man with that damned beautiful squaw . . .

Three hours later he discovered both the *tinja* and then the place where she'd lain and watched him. Harrison cursed softly. Now it would be harder since she knew how close he was behind her. She'd use every trick to slow him. He decided to lead his horse on foot, so he could read the signs better.

But suddenly the trail was easy to read—too easy. He stopped to consider what he saw. There were scramble marks where she'd climbed through cracks in the rocks, and nearly clean footprints on the level places, long dragging prints that zigzagged through the dirt. He was suspicious until further study told him why the trail was so clear. The marks indicated that she had panicked when she discovered him behind her. The woman was clearly running now, running like a rabbit would run under close pursuit. The trail darted about as if only fear were guiding her.

well under the torture, as well as any man. The only question was why? There was no one here to whom he wanted to prove his manhood except these Indians. And in the end, they didn't really care. His life was over, no matter what he did, so what real difference did it make how he died? Why make it harder for himself?

The dreams were gone. He'd never make it to Mexico a rich man. But then had he really ever expected to do so? Or were the dreams merely to offer some excuse for his having lived? Now that he could admit to himself that the dreams were no longer possible, curiously, it didn't really seem to matter. Nothing mattered, except to have it over and done with.

He rolled his tongue inside his mouth, doing his best to moisten it, since he wanted his voice to be clear and strong when he spoke. "You," he said in Apache when he was sure he was ready. "What are you called?"

The dark eyes of the Indian regarded him with amusement. "Why do you want to know?"

"I was a great warrior," Harrison said carefully. "Now that I am old and about to die I would want to know the man who led warriors to win over me."

The Apache nodded. "I am Shi-la-dia."

"Shi-la-dia," Harrison repeated slowly. "The old one we captured was named Shi-la."

The dark eyes glittered. "I know."

"He died of his wounds," Harrison said. "Did you know that?"

"Now I know."

Harrison spoke very carefully. He had to use just the right words or this man would think him a coward. "I wish to choose the manner of my death," he said. "It is a right I have given to others."

"The American is afraid of dying?"

He shook his head, difficult to do while lying on his side. "No. I am never afraid. It is only that I am old and choose to die with dignity. I ask this from one great warrior to another. In return I will trade information."

Shi-la-dia rose, walked over to kneel beside him, and Harrison noted that their conversation had aroused the others, who now sat up and listened.

"You will give us the information no matter how you die," the Apache said slowly, stretching his knife to just touch Harrison's throat. "You will tell us much."

Harrison didn't allow the knife to move him. "No," he said. "I am a warrior. I will talk only if I choose to talk. You know of me, and you know my words are true. You will enjoy my death, but you will not learn what Cochise wants to know."

The Apache studied him closely for a long time before he nodded slowly. "We know of you. You will tell us what these men who rode with you intend, and then perhaps I will kill you as you wish."

"No. I want the word of Shi-la-dia that I will die as a warrior should. With a bullet in my head. Then I will tell all."

His captor got up suddenly to walk away, and the others rose to follow him. They gathered in a group and talked with many glances in his direction as Harrison waited patiently for the outcome. He was already a dead man, why should he suffer a worse death for men he didn't know and didn't really care about? Sattersfield and Hartman were vultures; he owed them nothing. A minute or so later, Shi-la-dia came back and Harrison could tell by his manner that he had won. The Apache kneeled as before. "You have the word of Shi-la-dia of the Chiricahua. Tell us of the men who tricked us and tell us of the woman, Flor de Oro. Why is she with them and where are the bluecoats?"

"Let me sit first."

The Apache cut the rope that bound his wrists to his feet, allowing both to remain tied, however. Harrison rolled over and his captor helped him to a sitting position.

"The leader of the men is called General Hartman," Harrison said slowly. "He and the rest come in search of Quivira and treasures that lay there."

The Indians glanced at each other but didn't speak, and Harrison continued. "They come on their own, the soldiers will not help them in this fight. The one who took Flor de Oro for his squaw is not with them; he fights in distant lands."

"Then why does she come? For this treasure?"

Harrison shook his head. "She was tricked by the one called Hartman. He told her she must help him make peace with Cochise. That unless she did, your people would be destroyed by the soldiers. She did not want this to happen to the Chiricahua."

"Why? She is no longer of our people. She left the Chiricahua of her own choice."

"No," Harrison said. "That was not true. When she escaped from Lobo Negro, she thought she was being rescued by Cochise, not by the soldiers. When she was taken to the Fort, she was told Cochise no longer wanted her in his lodge because she had lain with the outlaw."

"This is true?" Shi-la-dia asked, half in doubt.

"It is true," Harrison said. "Listen, and I will tell you all of it."

He went over the whole story of how she had gone east believing Cochise had turned against her. How he and Sattersfield had gotten together and decided that she might be the key to tricking Cochise and had then contacted Hartman, and how that man had convinced her to come back to save the Apache. They listened closely and he knew they believed him in the end. Only when he mentioned Quivira did they look puzzled. He decided that only a few of the tribe leaders actually knew the secret, and suddenly wondered if the woman he chased out here to his own death hadn't really known either. That, he decided, would be a hell of a joke on him.

Finally, he was finished and they had no more questions. "It is time to put an end to it," he said. "I believe in the word of Shi-la-dia."

The Apache leader glanced around at each of the others and received nods in return. Without another word, he picked up his rifle and Harrison watched him point it at his face. In the second before his death, the scout was proud of the fact that he didn't flinch.

Chapter Fifteen

The sun was her enemy. Once through the mountains and headed south again, she had lost what little relief of shade and coolness they offered and had only mesquite and brush in which to shelter herself. Her shoes were gone now; they had been good ones, made for traveling, but for traveling in a wagon or carriage, not for walking through the edge of a desert. Her feet were swollen and bled constantly.

With only her shirtwaist and the remnants of her single petticoat for protection, the sun was cruel to her skin, swelling the area around her eyes and turning the rest a fiery red. Only her Apache knowledge had kept her alive, that and the ability to eat what the desert offered—insects for the most part, along with seeds, and a few plants. Food that would have horrified the white women with whom she had so recently lived.

Flor de Oro rested by lying immobile under some sparse shrubs through the high heat of the day, knowing she was giving up time to the man on the horse who trailed her but also knowing that to continue would cost her much more. She would die in this desert if she did not treat it with respect. The sun was an enemy to her dwindling strength; she would only sacrifice herself to it if she kept moving.

Resting, she thought about the man who followed her. He'd been fooled by her trick; she'd lain hidden in the rocks to watch as he read the sign she'd left for him. Only when he'd started back to find his way down into the gorge did she move on again. But the trick would merely delay him, he'd hurry back to pick up her trail as soon as he discovered the truth. He'd had plenty of time to do that by now; it worried her that in the three days since she'd seen no sign of him behind her. He was good enough to find her trail again, even though she'd taken all the pains she was capable of to conceal her passage. So there were only two other explanations: He was either delayed for some reason, or he was here somewhere and she couldn't see him.

Twice during the last days she'd stopped to watch for a time, picking a height where she could see far across the land. But there had been nothing to see that the desert couldn't claim. Where was he? Had he spotted her from a distance her aching eyes couldn't reach and was even now circling to lie in wait for her somewhere ahead? If he found her trail he would know she was moving toward the Gila and its life-giving water. Perhaps he waited somewhere in that direction? It didn't matter, she stood no chance except in heading for the river.

Flor de Oro rested and tried to think, but her mind was too tired to concentrate. It wanted to drift to other things, to thoughts of David, and her child living with the outlaw somewhere west of here. Sun shimmers on the sandy soil gradually formed into images that she had to force herself not to believe.

Lying flat and moving only one hand, using a minimum of effort, she dug with her fingers until she uncovered a stone buried deep enough to be cool to her touch. She pulled it free and cleaned the dirt gently away on her clothes, then put it into her mouth. Its coolness brought very little saliva and she knew she would soon have to find water. If not the river, then something else. Her body was drying rapidly; she had stopped perspiring long ago.

She wished she had thought to ask for a knife from the Apache who freed her, since with its aid she could get past the spiny protection of the barrel cactus and suck its wet center. But both of them had been in too much of a hurry to think about what she would do once she was away from the camp. That had been a mistake that she may well pay for with her life.

It was becoming harder to keep her mind aware, as both exhaustion and the heat pulled at her and begged her surrender. She thought of her father. This would have been how he felt in those last days. He had surrendered, given up his mind to the desert, and then allowed it to claim his body. She would not do that. She was too strong, and she had too much to lose. David . . . and the boy. She must only close her eyes for a short time to rest them . . . only a few moments' rest . . .

It was dusk when she woke, struggling back from the depths of a deep and cloying stupor that covered her mind like a smothering blanket. She didn't move until she was fully awake and aware that she had wasted most of the evening traveling time. Now she would have to make that time up in the dark. If she didn't, the man might be upon her by morning.

Her body protested each command, her skin threatened to split with each move, but Flor de Oro ignored both and made herself stand. The twilight played tricks with her weakened eyesight, but the sounds of the desert were normal. The insects sang their songs and a rustle a short distance away told her some small animal was moving—a desert rat probably, or a snake. Still, she waited long moments to make sure. She must not give away her own presence until certain someone else was not there in the dark.

When she was sure at last, she glanced once toward the stars for confirmation of her direction and began to move. Her legs protested and her balance took a long time to return, but she kept at it and in a few minutes she was moving almost at a normal trot.

The Gila should be ahead of her, but if she were wrong and she was farther south than she expected, then the San Pedro would take its place if she bore a little southwest. Even with her feet in bad shape she could make two more days. However, more than that was doubtful. She had spent too much time living the life of the white woman.

The muscles in her legs became more loose as she ran; she swung her arms to aid in her breathing and turned her thoughts away from the ache in her stomach. After half the night had gone by, when the moon was highest, she would rest and perhaps look for something to eat. For now she must run to cover distance. Tomorrow there would be the danger of the man seeing her. And tomorrow would bring the sun.

By midmorning she realized she was closer to a river than she had thought. The land was rough, but now it began to roll in hilly waves and the scrub had started to mix with small trees that needed more water than the desert would provide. Ahead of her she could see colors shimmering and knew that water could not be far away. But she could no longer run; her strength had gone more quickly than she had expected.

She drifted in and out, losing awareness of her surroundings for long moments and having to snap herself back. Her legs seemed to move of their own accord and her body belonged to someone else.

Suddenly she became aware that she was among cottonwoods as well as mesquite, and just ahead of her were slopes where the grass was green. She rubbed hard at her eyes, thinking she could actually see water glimmering somewhere up ahead, but then her mind refused to steady enough to be certain.

Flor de Oro stopped and sniffed, holding her head high, but her dust-caked nostrils were no longer functioning. Then a bird called, was answered by another, and her mind came back with the sweet sound. There was water ahead of her, she could see it clearly. But it was not wide water, only a stream, not a river. She stared hard, picking out its glimmer through the trees until her vision was blocked by a dark mass. It was water, but it was also danger, and the mass she didn't understand. She could no longer bring herself to care . . .

The stream was warm on its surface but free-flowing and therefore cooler underneath. Flor de Oro lowered her head into its soothing depths, forced herself to sip only a little in spite of an overwhelming desire to drink deeply, and finally crawled forward to immerse her entire body in its relief.

She drank a little more and then rolled over to lie still and let the moving water flow around her and numb her burning skin. It cooled her brain as well as her body, and after a few minutes she reluctantly sat upright and looked again for the dark mass she had been aware of from the first.

Downstream, only a hundred yards away, was a house. No, not a house, only part of a house, its rough plank walls completely burned away at one end and sagging at the other. Any life that might once have existed there had long since passed. She gave a grateful sigh and rested in the water.

When she had gathered her strength, she drank sparingly of the water once more before rising and moved toward the house. It had been built by Mexicans, she recognized the type as she reached it. Few Americans would have picked such an isolated spot and even if they had would not have taken the trouble to build a house. Apache would have put up a brush hut only. But the Mexicans came to stay and tried at the same time to avoid areas where they were likely to meet others. A search behind the house confirmed her guess; she could clearly see the broken ground where a garden had once been tended.

A short distance away, lying in the trees, she found the previous owner. His bones lay in a crumpled pile, the flesh long ago removed by animals and decay. There were no signs of clothing; whoever had killed him had stripped the body bare. She returned to the house and removed a few half-burned boards to get inside, and discovered that the fire had been put out by someone after it started. Probably some of the raiders who had attacked the owner had stayed to put it out while the rest chased the fleeing man. They would have wanted to save whatever was left inside for themselves.

There was little of value left now, a few broken clay

pots, shards of plates, and one badly smoked blanket. But she sifted through the rubble anyway and was finally rewarded in finding the broken blade of a knife. Its handle was missing, but there was enough left to make a weapon for herself, since she could easily use the blade to cut a limb and so refashion a handle.

Her greatest reward came an hour later when she discovered a hole dug in a bank and used to store food. The opening had been covered by boards and rocks with dirt piled above both. Twice she walked past it before she saw the depression in the ground that gave it away. Inside the hole were tightly sealed clay jars containing still usable flour and dried beans.

Her discovery meant all the difference in the world. With a knife she could use to fashion traps for small game, wood with which to build a fire, water and food, she could rest and rebuild her strength. And the piece of blanket would give her covering of sorts; not as good as a buckskin skirt, but infinitely better than the thin rags she now wore. Carefully, she removed one of the jars of flour and one of beans, replaced the boards and rocks, and carried them to the house. Then she went looking for the proper size limb with which to make her knife handle.

Before she could find the limb, however, the weakness in her body betrayed her again and she was barely able to stagger to the stream. She was dangerously close to collapsing and would have to rest for a while, perhaps as much as two days before she would be strong again. It was a risk she would have to take. Unless he had turned back for some reason, the man would eventually find her here but that couldn't be helped. She had run as far as her body would take her.

Her eyes ached badly. She bathed them slowly and drank a little more water before dragging herself to the bank again to sleep.

Two days later she was still alone and there had been no sign of pursuit. Food and rest had quickly brought back her strength, and with part of the blanket made into a skirt, the rest fashioned into short but serviceable moccasins, she had the feeling of being far less vulnerable. Having a weapon helped as much as the skirt.

If her new appraisal of her position were correct, this stream should flow into the San Pedro and once she found that river, she would be able to find the town of Tucson. It would, of course, be dangerous to go there since Hartman and his men might well have moved there too, but it was the only solution. No Apache could be considered her friend, not with the word out about the ambush of the Chiricahua and the part she had taken in it.

After she found the town she would have to decide what to do, whether to attempt a return to David somehow, or to seek help from someone there in tracking Lobo Negro once more. Both seemed impossible, but she couldn't worry about that at the moment. The only way to fail completely was to surrender. Cochise had taught her that long ago.

The warrior was standing so motionless and blended so well with the background behind him, she missed him at first glance. When she did see him, Flor de Oro stopped short and quickly measured the distance between them. It was too close to run; she would have to fight. She snatched her knife free.

But there was sudden movement to her right. Then to her left. She spun. There were five of them and they were all around her. Chiricahua . . . She recognized each man. These were once boys she had grown up with and now they were here to kill her. Defiantly, she crouched and raised her knife to face Shi-la-dia, who she knew would be their leader.

He eyed the small weapon in her hand. "It would be better for Flor de Oro to put down the knife," he said softly.

She shook her head.

Each man moved forward, the step of a mountain cat circling its prey, and she fought away sudden panic. *Flor de Oro must give account of herself. She must not die with dishonor!*

Shi-la-dia raised one hand slowly. "I give Flor de

Oro my word, the word of a Chiricahua warrior, that she will not be harmed," he said. "Put down the knife."

"Then why do you come?" she demanded. "You call me enemy, why should I believe you?"

"I will not harm you because I was told so. I was ordered to bring you to Cochise."

"And I will die there if I go." She tightened her grip on the knife. "Let it be now."

Behind her, she felt rather than saw a man move and spun to meet him, but was knocked from her feet by another in the moment of her turn. Flor de Oro fell beneath them both and struggled quickly to free herself as her knife was stripped from her hand. She had stood little chance against one warrior, and suddenly she was fighting four.

She gave up and was pulled to her feet to face Shi-la-dia.

"If you give me your word you will not try to escape, Flor de Oro, I will not have you bound," he told her.

She shook her head.

He shrugged. "Then it must be so. You will come with us to Cochise, who will decide your fate. There is much he wants to know from you."

He paused, and watching her closely for reaction, added, "The American who followed you from the camp of our enemies is dead. He will make no more war upon the Apache."

So Harrison was dead. That was why he hadn't found her. One less enemy to worry about. But it made little difference to her now.

Chapter Sixteen

The train station at St. Louis was crowded as usual and if any of the hurrying passengers noticed the heavily bandaged men in uniform who also dismounted from the train, they were careful not to let it show. The war had gone on far longer than anyone had expected and its costs were rising rapidly. Both in the higher prices and scarcity of goods, and in the men it was destroying. The civilians were careful not to jostle those soldiers with only one leg who clumsily manipulated new wooden crutches, or the blinded ones led by soldiers who were themselves heavily bandaged, and they gave wide berth to those who were carried on stretchers. But they didn't look at the men in doing so. They would grumble about the high prices, but they preferred not to think of the war's cost in flesh. Especially if they had brothers or fathers who wore the blue uniform of the Federal Army.

One of the wounded still able to move on his own was a tall captain of cavalry. His campaign hat was cocked by a soiled bandage wrapped completely around his head and covering one eye, and his left arm rested in a sling, but his legs were good and his right hand carried a pair of well-worn saddlebags. The captain made his way through the crowd inside the station, pushed through the doors to the street outside, and then paused to look up and down as if he expected to be met.

Only after careful inspection of the street did he wearily drop his bags and lean against the building to wait. He stood there long minutes before a portly man in a business suit and a well blocked hat noticed him and stopped short. "Foxcroft!" the man exclaimed. "David Foxcroft!"

Blinded from that side, David had to turn to see him. "How are you, Mister Johnson?"

The older man started to reach for his hand, thought better of it and dropped his own in a helpless gesture. "My God, David! It's not how I am, but how are you? What happened?"

Before he could reply, David was seized with a fit of coughing and had to bend over with the effort. He'd caught something in the hospital and his lungs ached most of the time now, but this cough was worse than usual and he took a long time to recover. When he straightened, he had to blink his good eye to clear it.

"Caught a bit of grapeshot, Mister Johnson," he said. "Nothing I won't recover from with a little rest at home."

"Does your father know you're here?" Johnson wanted to know. "I mean, do you need a ride home? I could summon my carriage."

"No," he said. "I mean about the ride. I sent word of my arrival and expect to have someone here shortly. Evidently they've been delayed. Thank you at any rate."

Johnson wasn't assured. He obviously wanted to do something but didn't quite know what, or how. He made another gesture with his hands. "Why don't you come to my office to wait then? I'll have someone check."

"I'll be fine, Mister Johnson." He grinned. "All I need is a chance to get home and see my family. Have you talked to my father lately?"

"Oh yes, certainly. See him almost every day."

"He's well I hope?"

"Yes, yes. Of course. Very good health. And your mother too; they were at a dinner I attended just last evening. He didn't mention you were coming home, however."

"Then you must have seen Jen—my wife, there

too. How is she? I haven't received too much mail of late."

Johnson's look was one of sudden shock, apparent even to David's one good eye, and he experienced an increase in the worry that had plagued him for weeks. "You did see her too, didn't you?" he asked.

"Uh, no. You don't know—I mean, no, she wasn't at the dinner. There were, I mean, most of the people there were your father's business . . . acquaintences." He was very nervous. "Uh, look David, I've a pressing appointment. But I'll be happy to send someone . . ."

David smothered an urge to reach out and take his arm, probe the nervousness, and discover the reason for it. But he would find out shortly at any rate, when he got home. "Of course," he said instead. "Don't let me hold you. There'll be someone along, I'm sure. If not, I'll walk over to the hotel and wait."

"Are you certain?" The man had already taken a step or two away.

"Good seeing you, Mister Johnson."

"Take care of yourself, David." A short moment later David was watching his retreating back.

He leaned wearily against the wall again. There was something wrong. He'd begun to feel it when he'd received his mail shortly before he was wounded, and none of the delayed letters had mentioned her. The note from his father and the long letters from his mother had been as if Jennifer didn't exist. She couldn't write herself, he'd realized that finally, she'd never been taught how. He planned to do that himself as soon as they were able to settle down together, but someone should have mentioned her, or written for her.

"Mister David!" The cry brought him from his thoughts abruptly and he glanced up to see James hurrying toward him. The black man almost stumbled in his haste.

"Hello, James," he said, when the other stopped in front of him. "Where's the carriage?"

"Lord, I'm sorry, Mister David! That mare I brung

done throwed a shoe! I just don't know how that happened! I sure keep a check on all the horses, but she done shook one loose and I had to leave her at the blacksmith. I knowed you would be waiting and I run all the way down here!"

"You didn't need to do that," David told him. "I've been a long time coming, a few more minutes wouldn't hurt. Is the mare being reshod now?"

"Yes, suh. Right enough. I told that blacksmith she had to be ready when I got back. Let's find you a place to wait while I go back and fetch the carriage." He was tired and the pain in his chest and shoulder was beginning to increase with the tiredness. It would be tempting to find a place nearby where he could have a drink and wait for James to return, but there was an urgency in him now, different from a few minutes ago, when he'd merely been anxious to see Jennifer.

"No," he said. "I'll walk back with you. No need to wait."

James shook his head with worry. "But Mister David. You're hurt. You sure don't need to do no walking."

"Nothing wrong with my legs," David said. "Come on. You can carry my bags for me."

The black man reached quickly to pick up the saddlebags, but there were deep lines across his brow as he looked at David. "You sure? Mister Foxcroft, he'll have my hide for making you walk."

"Then we won't tell him, James. Come on."

He started down the street and James fell in beside him, walking in a poised manner as if he thought at any moment he would have to catch his companion. It was irritating. The black man gave the appearance of a mother hen swooping over her baby chick. David put up with it for half a block before allowing his irritation to show. "James, I'm all right I tell you. Stop worrying so and let's get on to the blacksmith's."

"Yes suh, yes suh. I jest . . . that fighting is some bad, Mister David?"

"Bad enough," he said. "But then all war is bad, James. Be glad you're not involved in it."

240

"Yes, suh. I'm rightly that." He walked on another block before he spoke again. "Mister David?"

"Yes?" David gave him half a glance and almost stumbled from it. He was still having difficulty in moving about with only one eye.

"I reckon I got something to tell you. I was supposed to tell you when you was by yourself and not to waste no time doing it."

David stopped and turned so that he could see him. "Tell me what? And who told you to tell me?"

"Your wife, Mister David. Miss Jennifer told me herself to tell you." James had stopped too and the worry in his face increased. It was also mixed with more than a little fright.

Damn! There was something wrong! He forced himself to speak calmly. "What did she tell you?"

"She said for me to be sure to tell you to go talk to Miss Matilda. That you needed to go as quick as you could. If I was to pick you up when you come home, for me to take you there first. She made me promise that herself."

David was growing angry. Angry about something that he didn't yet understand. "Why should I do that?" he demanded. "Why can't she tell me herself when I get home?"

There was fear in the black man now; he could see it even with one eye. James took a step backward and lowered his head. "Miss Jennifer . . . she ain't there no more, Mister David. She's gone."

"Gone! Gone where? What the hell are you talking about, James?" Anger pushed him forward, and James quickly backed away.

"Please, Mister David. It ain't my fault!"

He controlled himself with difficulty. "All right, all right. I realize that. Now tell me what has happened. Where is my wife?"

"She's gone somewhere, Mister David. Gone back out yonder where the Indians live, I think. She went with somebody your daddy knows."

Gone west! Good God! Why? He was suddenly dizzy and raised a hand to his head. James stepped forward to grasp his coat. "You all right, Mister David?"

David shook him off. "I'm all right. What else can you tell me?"

"That's all I know, Mister David. Honest. 'Cept Miss Jennifer come to me before she left and told me to take you to see Miss Matilda just as soon as I could. I reckon that lady knows what to tell you."

"Then let's get on with it," David growled. The pain in his chest was gone now, replaced with a deep fire burning in the pit of his stomach. He turned and began walking as rapidly as he could, and James hurried beside him.

David said nothing else until they reached the blacksmith shop, where the Foxcroft carriage stood outside. The mare was ready, and he waited in the carriage while James brought her out and harnessed her between the double shafts. The black man mounted the seat with alacrity and urged his beast into a trot, showing the same urgency as his passenger.

He drove the mare quickly but carefully through the heavy traffic of the streets, dodging between the heavy freight wagons and pulling her curtly aside to miss the pedestrians who stepped into his path. In a few minutes, they were clear of the streets and hurrying down the road.

David leaned forward. "James, can you tell me what happened? Was there anything you could see that would make her want to leave?"

The black man shook his head but kept his eyes on the mare. "I don't know about that, Mister David. I don't figure what goes on in the big house is any business of old James. I jest tends to the horses."

He had no business pursuing it but he couldn't help himself. "Then why would she talk to you? She must have had a reason to talk to you. Where did you see her if it wasn't in the house?"

This time James did eye him reluctantly, turning only long enough to give him a worried look. "Miss Jennifer, she came to the stables a lot. She liked to ride

King Henry and I let her."

"King Henry?"

"Yes, suh. He's a stallion your daddy bought." This time James turned a different look, a look of pride. "There wasn't nobody could ride that big boy but your daddy and her. And your daddy had such a hard time of it if he quit. But Miss Jennifer, she could talk to him in a magic language and King Henry, he loved to have her ride him. I ain't never seen nothing like that in my life."

David leaned back in the seat. She would do that. She must have been miserable in the house. After living as free as she had, it would have been like a prison. And it was his own damned fault; he should have known better. He started to say something else, thought better of it and leaned back once more to wait. Matilda Dobson would have the answers if James were correct, and if he weren't, then by God someone at home would have them! He didn't yet want to think of why she left, or where she might be now.

He was sitting up anxiously again when James stopped the mare in front of the Dobson house and barely waited for the carriage to cease rolling before he dismounted. By the time he reached the door it was opened by a young girl.

"David Foxcroft," he told her. "My aunt is expecting me I believe."

"Yes, sir. Will you wait in the drawing room, sir?"

He nodded and entered the room she indicated as she left but didn't take a chair, standing instead by the wide double windows. A few short minutes later he heard his aunt down the hall, giving instructions to the girl to prepare lunch for them as she moved. He turned as she entered the room.

"My heavens, David! You're injured!"

"I'm all right, Matilda," he said. "Where is Jennifer? James said you would know."

She gave him a quick appraisal, her eye taking in both the bandage around his head and the sling on his arm. "Sit down, David. You don't look well at all. I'll fetch you some brandy and then we'll talk."

Before he could protest, she had left the room. He let out his breath explosively and settled down in one of the armchairs, allowing his legs to stretch out before him. Matilda was back shortly with a tray containing both a decanter of brandy and a glass that she placed on a table before pouring the latter nearly full for him.

He took it and drank a third in one gulp. "Thank you," he said. "That was just what I needed. That, and whatever you can tell me about my wife."

Matilda settled herself opposite him. "She is quite a woman, David. I like her very much, and we became good friends while you were away. You're a lucky man."

He nodded. "I hope I still am. But James tells me she's gone. Can you tell me where?"

"Yes I can, David. And I shall. But you are going to sit there and drink your brandy in silence until I'm finished. I will not appreciate any displays of masculine shouting or prancing about as I talk." She didn't smile as she said it.

He sighed and grinned for the first time. A weak grin that was all the fire in his belly would allow. "Still the same Matilda," he said. "Very well. But refill my glass first, please." He emptied another third and extended it.

She took it, refilled it, and gave it back to him. "As I said, David, Jennifer and I became very good friends. Probably the only one she had in St. Louis. Frankly, I think you ought to be horsewhipped for leaving her with your mother. I don't care if she is my sister and gave birth to you, that woman is the worst person I've ever known."

He started to answer but was stopped by her upraised hand. "I said for you to allow me to talk. We don't have all the time in the world. But then I hadn't expected you to be wounded, and that may change my plans."

"Plans?"

"For you to go after her, of course! But never mind,

244

let me tell you what happened. Jennifer was very unhappy here, you should have known that. However, she loves you and she would have remained in spite of everything, because she thought that was what you wanted."

He stirred restlessly, but another warning glance from the old woman stopped him. He sat back and sipped his brandy, gazing over the glass at her.

"Your father offered her a chance to go west again." Again the hand came up to forestall his questions. "It was one of his business deals, another scheme to increase his wealth. Something about gold mines, or silver, or something. A lost city that has some unbelievable treasure, I gather."

"Quivira!" He couldn't contain himself. "Good God! That's only a legend!"

"So you know about it? Well, legend or not, some general has convinced your father that it exists and Jennifer could help him find it. Your father and others are financing the trip. I don't know exactly how she fits in, but I understand she was to convince some Indian chief or other to tell them where it is located."

David groaned. "Cochise. He was the chief of the tribe she lived with. Did she tell you that?"

"Yes. She told me all of it. Everything. Jennifer is an honest woman. She's not ashamed of who she is nor of what she has been. I must tell you I admire her greatly."

"Did she also tell you Cochise now hates her? That he may well kill her?"

Matilda was immediately alarmed. "No! She said nothing about that. Why would he hate her?"

"It's a long story, Matilda," he said. "I haven't time. Who was this general?"

"He called himself General Hartman. Alex Hartman. I met him only once and I didn't like him. Nor did I trust him. I tried to talk Jennifer into waiting for you to return, not to go with him in spite of your father's urging, but she knew as we all do now, David, that the war will last several more years. And she was afraid of losing her child."

"She told you about that, too?"

"I said she is an honest woman. She doesn't believe in hiding her life. She didn't go with Hartman because of your father, she went because she thought it was the last chance she might have of saving the boy. She told me Hartman had promised her he could find him for her."

"They're using her, Matilda. I've got to find her before it's too late." He struggled to his feet. "How long has she been gone?"

"David, you're in no condition to go out there now."

"How long?"

Matilda stood up. "Two—no, three weeks now. But look at yourself!"

He was already headed for the door. "Matilda, the only thing that means anything to me in this crazy world is Jennifer. I'm going to find her again and kill that bastard who took her out there."

He reached the door and flung it open. "James!"

The black man was lounging in the shade near the carriage and darted to his feet. "Yes, suh!"

"Take me home! And hurry!"

"Yes, suh!"

Edwina Foxcroft couldn't believe what she was seeing. Of the two men who stood in the middle of the room shouting at each other, one was a man she had never seen before, even if she had given birth to him. His unbandaged eye contained a look of rage, and his free arm ended in a clenched fist. As a child he'd done as she wished without question, and later, as a grown man, he'd offered silence even when she knew he disagreed with her. He went about making his own decisions the past years he was home, but refused to defend himself when she scolded him. Never had she seen him in a violent temper. Suddenly, Edwina was afraid. The war had changed her son terribly.

"Dammit, you had no right to do that!" David shouted for the third time to his father. "You sent her to be killed! Just so you could make more damn money!"

"David," she said sharply in spite of her alarm. "I will not permit such language in this house."

He ignored her entirely. "Who is this Hartman?" he demanded of his father. "Where has he taken her?"

Talbert's face was equally red. "I will not be addressed like this by my own son, David. If you wish to discuss this matter in a rational—"

"Rational, be damned!" David shouted. "This is my wife we're talking about! Not some stupid business deal."

"When you have calmed down, David, we will—"

"I have no intention of calming down," her son interrupted again, and Edwina recoiled at the violence in him. His face had turned white with fury and he slammed his fist down on a table, causing a vase upon it to jump free and shatter on the floor.

"I want an answer now," he said. "I haven't time to wait. I'm going after her and you're going to tell me where to look."

"I will do no such thing!" Talbert was shouting now. "Your wife is in capable hands. And you're in no condition to travel. Look at yourself!"

Edwina's alarm increased as she could see David was controlling himself with great difficulty. She suddenly remembered that he had been fighting a war, that he had actually killed other men. It was a chilling thought.

"Father," he said, "you listen, and listen very closely. I already know how she was treated in this house. And I suspect that is part of the reason she was sent back west. That, and to be used to make money for you in some ridiculous scheme."

He paused and glanced her way. "It doesn't matter what happened here, for I will never bring my wife into this house again. But what happens to her out there does matter. I swear to you that if she is harmed because of your doing, the consequences will be terrible. *Now tell me where she is!*"

He moved forward as he spoke to stand only a foot

or so in front of his father, and Edwina watched her husband's face drain of color. She knew he was not a coward, but she could see that he suddenly experienced the knowledge she already held. Their son was beyond the brink of rationality. His words cut through the room like a knife.

"David, I . . ." he said.

"Tell me!"

"All right, all right." Talbert stepped back a pace and raised his hands in protest. "They are to make their headquarters in the town of Tucson. A man called Sattersfield is a business leader there. Once they make contact with this Indian chief—"

"Cochise?" David interrupted.

". . . With this Cochise, then they will move on to Tucson. You can find them there. But I still don't think you can make it out there, David. Let me get something to them by post."

Her son relaxed back on his heels, but there was still a tremor in his voice. A tremor, and what? Could it be hatred?

"Jennifer is to be used to contact Cochise," he said. "Do you know that he has disavowed her? That because of a misunderstanding, that Indian is as apt to kill her as not?"

"Why no . . . I mean, I wasn't told that."

"Or you didn't give a damn," David said harshly. "Let me tell you something else, Father. You and this Hartman are chasing a legend. Something that doesn't exist. And believe me, I've been in that territory long enough to know. Quivira is a city that never existed. You sent my wife possibly to her death for an idiotic dream."

"David, you're overwrought. I have it on the best authority, from men like this Sattersfield, who have lived there longer than you." But Edwina could see doubt in her husband's face as he spoke.

David spun suddenly and stalked to the door. He turned back to stare hard at his father before opening it. "I want two things from you," he said. "And I want them as quickly as you can get them. Tomorrow you and I will go into St. Louis and you will see that the bank presents no problem in allowing me to draw out what remaining funds I have. Secondly, you will use your considerable influence in seeing that I am granted a medical discharge from the Army without delay. It's the last thing I will ever want from you."

Edwina decided it was time she took a hand. This was going entirely too far. "David, I must insist that you rest and recover from your wounds. Your father will do everything that can be done to insure the safety of your wife."

He looked at her, a long, cold look that told her she had lost her son forever, then returned to his father. "Tomorrow," he said. And slammed the door behind him.

The train was crowded as always; he'd had to stand out of St. Louis and found a seat only by being quick at the first stop. A seat, however, that was shared by a burly man in broadcloth who reeked of whiskey and nodded against him most of the time. His ticket would take him to the end of the rail line. He thought it would be quicker that way, and his father had sent a wire there to have a horse and saddle waiting for him.

The three days at home had been difficult ones. He would have cut them shorter, but when he'd had time to calm down, he realized the necessity of resting and seeing a physician at least once. The bandage around his head had been changed to a smaller one and the doctor had told him he stood an even chance of regaining the sight in that eye. His shoulder was in fair shape and was wrapped tightly. As long as he didn't move his arm too quickly, the pain was livable. And also, he'd been given medicine for his lungs, medicine, he thought bitterly, that wasn't available in the field hospitals. Money made all the difference in the world.

The only thing he didn't have was his discharge. Other men more seriously wounded than he would be sent back into battle as soon as they recovered. Technically, he would be a deserter when he didn't return from his leave, unless his father's influence prevailed. David expected it would, however. He'd left no doubt of his intention not to return and, he smiled grimly as he thought about it, his father would make every effort to see that he received the discharge. He wouldn't want the family name soiled in that manner.

He could only hope he was in time to save her. And that he could find her when he arrived in the territory. She should have waited for him. But then neither of them had suspected how long this war would last, and now with time to think about it, he could well see why she couldn't wait. The boy meant a great deal to her—a child meant a great deal to any mother— and with her background there would be a fierce protectiveness as well. Jennifer knew if she didn't get to him soon it would be too late and he would grow up an outlaw. In fact, it might already be too late and the boy might not respond to her even if by some miracle she found him.

And, the thought was unthinkable but he had to consider it, if this man she was traveling with, this General Hartman, would not follow through on his promise to help her find the boy, she would try herself. Jennifer had a will of steel and she was absolutely fearless. She would not hesitate to travel on her own through the most savage of territory. Gazing through the window, he thought of the first time he had seen her, the look of utter defiance on her face. No, Jennifer would not stop to consider the odds, nor to think it beyond her ability as a woman. She would only think of the child.

His shoulder ached and he pulled a cheroot from his pocket and lit it to take his mind away from the pain. The man beside him had finally joined the two who sat opposite in sleep and he was, for all practical purposes, alone with his thoughts.

He had to have a plan of action. He couldn't just ride aimlessly around the territory in hopes of finding her and Hartman if they weren't in Tucson. His father had spoken of a meeting being set up somewhere between Hartman and Cochise, but he had been unaware of the details. She was to be used to negotiate with the chief; but surely they wouldn't expose her alone to the Apache. His father was also unsure of just what the meeting was supposed to accomplish; he only knew that some men other than the Sattersfield he mentioned had conceived that part of the plan. Who could that have been, and why did he think Cochise would be willing to play a part in their stupid search for Quivira?

Quivira . . . A legend that drove men mad. He suddenly remembered Harrison's words about the city so many long months ago when he'd first arrived in the territory. The scout had mentioned that some believed the Chiricahua knew where the city was located. That would be why they wanted to contact Cochise. To persuade him to take them to it. No, dammit! Not to persuade, to force. They would try to use her to trap Cochise and then make him tell them where Quivira was located. He groaned aloud with the thought.

She was fearless, but she was not wise in the ways of men, especially white men who were driven by greed. Men, he had to admit, like his own father. They would have given her some reason, some plausible reason, for making peace with Cochise, and she would believe it. And they had made her a promise she couldn't turn down, a promise to help locate her child.

Suddenly he had a terrible feeling that he was already too late, that whatever they were going to try had already been tried and she might be dead from it. Cochise was no fool, he'd proven that. Ever since the Bascomb incident had turned him fully against all Americans, he'd shown that ability. In the short time before the Army had to turn its attention to the Confederates, he'd matched his wits and generalship with the best they could offer and won. They'd not even come close to trapping him. And now this soldier of fortune hoped to trick a man like that!

He may well be too late. He had to accept that possibility. But he promised himself, a promise he would spend the rest of his life keeping, that if she were dead he would kill the men responsible for her death. Hartman, this Sattersfield, and the other, the man whose name he didn't yet know. They would pay. And then he would find the boy for her. He owed her that much.

At the end of the rail line he found the livery stable, and a horse was waiting for him as promised. So was a telegram from his father stating that the older man had been given assurances the discharge would be put through. David crumpled the message and threw it aside. He didn't really give a damn whether it was or not.

He traded his clothes at a general store for buckskins, bought some supplies, including extra ammunition for the rifle and side arm he was taking, spent a restless night in the hay of the stable, and left early in the morning. It would be a long ride, and this part of Kansas was still infested with both Southern sympathizers and outlaws who would be more than likely to ambush a man riding alone. But that couldn't be helped. A brush with them would only be a beginning of what he expected to get into when he arrived in the lands of the Apache.

Chapter Seventeen

The five Apache were traveling on foot and with only makeshift moccasins and still swollen feet, she was hard-pressed to keep up with them. To Flor de Oro's surprise, they quickly took note of the fact and slowed their pace. More often than not, one of them would take her arm to help her over the rougher terrain, and when they rested near any kind of water she was also allowed to soak her feet after they had drank. It was a manner much out of the ordinary in the Apache treatment of prisoners.

She wasn't relieved by their consideration, however; there was still no doubt what her fate would be as soon as she arrived at the rancheria of Cochise. That he had once loved her as a daughter would make no difference in that fate, for he was responsible for his people and she had betrayed the Chiricahua by bringing Hartman here. Her death for that mistake would not be easy, it would only be certain.

Why had she suddenly resigned herself to die, she wondered, lying awake and aware of the sleeping men around her. True, her chances of escape were slim at best since they kept her wrists and ankles bound at night, and one of them was always awake and on guard. But she had been in positions quite as hopeless before and managed to get away. Why did she not want to make the effort now? Was it guilt toward the people who had taken her in when she was a lost child and treated her as one of their own? She did feel she had betrayed them, and the fact that she didn't know it until it was too late made no difference. She should have been aware, should have read

Hartman correctly. But she had allowed herself to be blinded by the slim chance of finding her child.

She had betrayed her people; caused the death of an old man she thought of as an uncle; and very nearly trapped her Indian father, which could have destroyed the Chiricahua. Perhaps the feeling of lethargy she was experiencing now was a deep desire to pay the final price for her mistake. That, or the desire to meet him once more and tell him it had been a mistake, no matter the price she had to pay for doing so. She would stand erect to face him and say that no matter what others had told him or even what he might have seen himself, she still had a love for her people. And a daughter's love for him . . .

He wouldn't believe her. He couldn't afford to believe her and risk the safety of his people by doing so. She understood that. Still it was a thing she looked forward to saying, and perhaps in the long winter nights in his lodge when he had time to think, he would remember the way her eyes had met his and think that perhaps she had spoken the truth.

They were camped in a grove of stunted pines and thorn brush, lying in a shallow depression. On this second night of travel, her captors had built no fire for their single meal so she knew they were in lands not wholly controlled by Apache. That, and the fact that two warriors stood guard instead of one. When an owl hooted twice a short distance behind her, she was not surprised to see all the sleepers awaken instantly. It gave a second call, and each man silently and quickly disappeared into the trees.

Flor de Oro listened for long moments, but then allowed her head to rest again on the bed of needles she'd fixed before she was tied for the night. It didn't make any difference who else might be out there, or if there were anyone at all. She had no friends in this land.

Still, she could not help listening to the night sounds and didn't relax until the warriors came back one by one as silently as they had left, to lie down and fall instantly asleep again.

With the first false light of dawn, they were up and traveling again, and trotting along in single file, a warrior in front and another close behind her, Flor de Oro decided the danger of last night had been real. From the more than watchful manner of the men with her, there must be someone else here that they didn't want to have to fight. That could only mean a large party of enemies. Hartman? Or perhaps soldiers from one or another of the forts?

That last was an idea. Once before, she had been rescued unintentionally by soldiers—David's men. And she had found the man she loved when that had happened. Suppose she suddenly did something that would bring attention to them, yelled, or tried to run opposite from the carefully selected path they were taking? Would it be worth trying?

She thought about it for several running steps and then discarded the idea. It would only serve the purpose of hastening her own death. One of the warriors would slit her throat and the rest would split up to make the chase difficult. It would be an easier death than the one she faced, but in the light of day her mood was different. She was not quite ready to give up yet. And too, she still wanted the satisfaction of telling the truth to Cochise.

With the shelter of trees to protect them from the sun, Shi-la-dia made their rest stops brief and continued to travel even in the high heat of the day. They were starting a gradual climb as well and the land grew more familiar to her. She had passed this way as a girl. Ahead were some of the roughest mountains lying north of the border with Mexico, and that would be where Cochise had transferred his rancheria when he went to war with the Americans. It would take a very large number of the soldiers to dislodge him from their heights. If her guess was correct, his camp would be no more than another day's travel.

She slowed, took deeper breaths for a moment, and then picked up her pace again. The warrior behind her slowed as well and waited patiently until she was moving once more as he wanted. But she was begin-

255

ning to experience a dizziness and her legs were growing numb, causing an increase in the effort needed to move them. She hadn't recovered as much as she'd thought in the Mexican's hut, and too, her blanket moccasins were falling apart and her feet were bleeding once more.

It would be a relief to arrive.

Shi-la-dia ordered an early halt, much earlier than he should have, and she knew it was because of her failing strength, for two of the warriors continued to travel and soon disappeared from sight. The next morning they returned, bringing a pony with them and she mounted it gratefully.

Late in the same morning they climbed the last of the continuously ascending hills and began to follow a ridge. Flor de Oro could see sentries above her, watching their progress from the cliff heights, and knew the journey was nearing its end. She was not surprised when they dropped down a slope, rounded an outthrust of broken earth, and found the rancheria spread before them. She braced her tired shoulders and lifted her head. She would not show shame before the Chiricahua.

Shi-la-dia led her pony through the village, through the watching people, and she saw many familiar faces during her passage, most of which returned her looks without acknowledgment. He stopped before a lodge and motioned to the two women who stood there. "Take her inside," he told them. "Give her rest, water to bathe, and something to eat. And find her clothing as well. She will remain with you until Cochise returns."

So he was not here. There would be another long wait. She slid from the pony and followed the women into the lodge.

They brought her water with which to bathe and even helped her wash her hair. Her feet were treated with a powder ground from roots to stop the bleeding and aid in healing, and afterward, she was given new buckskins to wear along with a pair of very soft moccasins. She was even offered a headband. Dressed once more in acceptable clothes, Flor de Oro felt like a new woman. Suddenly death was not quite as easy to face as before, she wanted strongly to live and see David again. With such thoughts, waiting in the lodge with the two silent women became harder and harder.

By the time Shi-la-dia returned for her she was experiencing difficulty in concealing her impatience. He stopped in the center of the lodge and waited for the squaws to leave before he spoke.

Flor de Oro watched him for some indication of what was to happen but could gain little from his look. "Come," he said at last. "The council has gathered. You will be given a chance to speak to them."

"Has Cochise returned?" she asked, standing up.

"Come." He turned and passed through the opening.

She followed him outside and paused for a moment. The rancheria was unnaturally quiet. All around her squaws and children stood waiting and watching, their faces immobile but their dark eyes alight with interest. Two of the squaws standing near her held babies in their arms, and although they were younger than she, she remembered them. They had not even taken husbands when she left. Sadly, she thought of her own child.

"Come." Shi-la-dia prodded her, and she straightened her shoulders to walk behind him.

He led her to the center of the Rancheria where the council circle waited, seated on the ground. Seated, except for one man who stood with arms folded at the head. He was unchanged, she thought. Perhaps his hair had more gray in it, but he stood quite as straight and his arms were still as thick. When she walked into the middle of the circle and stopped opposite him, his eyes gave no indication that he had ever seen her before. Returning his look, Flor de Oro decided that his face was also sharper than before, with lines that were new to her.

A moment later, he spoke. "Let the words be heard

that accuse this woman," he said in a voice loud enough for all to hear.

An old man stood up slowly beside Cochise. Ah-koch-ne. He would have taken the place of the dead Shi-la as advisor to Cochise. "The woman is Flor de Oro," he said. "Once she was taken in by the Chiricahua and raised as the daughter of the great Cochise. She was stolen as a woman by the outlaw, Lobo Negro, and a great hunt was begun to bring her back to her people. But the Americans found her first and she refused to return to the Chiricahua."

She felt a great urge to protest his words, but held her peace. It was not yet time to speak.

"That she did not desire to return to her people who had treated her as their own was of no matter," Ah-koch-ne continued. "All Apache are free to choose their life and she was considered Apache. But she had been promised to a chief of the Mimbreno and in refusing to return she caused the word of Cochise to be broken, bringing shame on all Chiricahua."

No! I didn't refuse! She wanted to scream out the words and had to struggle to remain silent.

"She became the squaw instead of a bluecoat warrior who fought with our people. Then came her greatest crime." He paused again for a very long time, and the circle of men leaned forward to hear. "She returned to our lands with many Americans with guns and tried to betray the Chiricahua into their hands. Flor de Oro wanted to destroy the people who had taken her in."

His last words were no louder than the first, his tone did not change, but Flor de Oro felt the weight of them as crushing rocks falling upon her.

Ah-koch-ne raised a hand. "Flor de Oro would seek to capture Cochise and make slaves of his people." He stared at each man in the circle in turn before sitting down again, his mission finished.

She looked into the eyes of Cochise and found no mercy there.

"The council is fair," he told her. "You will now speak."

Her tongue was dry inside her mouth. She wasn't afraid, she felt only a great weight of shame. She would die now, but that was not the worst. Her name would always be spoken with anger among the Chiricahua, and they would believe she returned their love for her with treachery. That thought was hard to bear.

"I have done none of these things," she said slowly, then realized her voice was too low and repeated it more loudly.

"Then tell us why we should not believe them," Cochise replied.

She took a deep breath. This was her only chance. If she could convince even one man in the circle, if she could cause even a little doubt, perhaps someday the doubt would grow.

"I was taken against my will," she said. "Lobo Negro stole me from the Chiricahua and I fought him to return. Even now he bears the mark of my knife on his face. When the Americans trapped him, I believed it was Cochise and I escaped him in that belief. Only later did I discover who they were. When they took me to the fort, I would not talk to them even though I understood their language. I asked only to be returned to Cochise, my father."

She stared directly into his eyes. "But then my blankets were taken from the lodge of Cochise and I knew I could return no more. I knew I had brought shame to him because I had been made to bear the child of Lobo Negro."

This time there was a murmur among the squaws gathered outside the circle, and Cochise silenced it with a stern glance.

"So I sought peace for my sorrow with the Americans," she continued. "I took a husband and I bear him much love. He is a strong warrior who has no hatred for the Chiricahua. He has spoken of that many times to me. Now he fights a great battle in the land where the sun rises, but when it is finished he will fight no more. Not there, and not with the Apache. He has said this to me."

"Yet Flor de Oro returns without her warrior husband," Cochise said. "And she brings Americans who make no such promise."

"I am guilty of that," she said quietly.

The men in the circle stirred in anger, and even Cochise lowered his brow as he looked at her.

"But . . ." she said, and the stirring stopped. "I am guilty only because I was a foolish woman and believed the lies they told me. The chief who leads these men is called General Hartman. He said to me that he wanted to be a chief of all Americans here and to do this he must first be friends with the Apache. He would bring peace by making a just treaty with the Apache and setting up trade between them and the Americans. I believed his lies because I wanted very badly to help the Chiricahua."

She paused a long moment. The circle and the people behind it faded from her consciousness until only she and the tall man in front of her were present. "No matter what happens to me, I bear a great love for the chief who once called me daughter. And I bear a love for the Chiricahua. My heart is heavy because I have brought harm to them through my foolish mistake. I have no more to say."

For the first time she lowered her head. But quickly raised it again when he spoke. "If there is anyone here who would speak for Flor de Oro, let him speak now."

She was astonished to see Shi-la-dia slowly get to his feet and turned to face him.

"I believe the words of Flor de Oro," he said, returning her look. "When I was ordered to stay behind and watch the camp of the Americans, I took four warriors and followed them as they moved. In their first night of camp, we saw Flor de Oro flee. I was surprised at this and sent a warrior to follow her. Later, a man known to us as Harrison also came out to trail her and we followed him. By then I could see that she wanted to get away from all the Americans."

The mention of Harrison brought a fresh growl from the listeners and he waited for it to subside.

"Flor de Oro played a trick on this American in order to get away," he continued after a moment. "When he discovered the trick, he became angry and careless. We attacked at that moment and took him prisoner. I was preparing a death for him that would avenge the warriors he had killed when he asked for a trade. He said if I would give him a quick death, he would tell me everything about the Americans, including the truth about the woman he was seeking.

"I agreed, and he told me everything that she has now said. That is why I believe her words. He was the one who lied to Cochise and said she did not want to return. He said this because he wanted her for himself. Then he lied to her. He told me why these Americans came to our lands, telling me also that this woman did not know what they planned. She was tricked by the Americans, as she has said. This is what I have to say."

He sat down and immediately another warrior stood up. "When the battle began, I saw Flor de Oro try to protect Shi-la with her own body," he offered. "I do not believe she would have done this if she were an enemy to the Chiricahua."

He sat down as abruptly as he had stood and slowly she turned back to face Cochise. But his eyes told her nothing and her rising hopes faded.

"Who else would speak?" he asked, sweeping the circle with his gaze. "Speak now for or against her. Then we will decide."

There was no answer. But two men had spoken for her and that was more than she would have dreamed.

"Then I will speak," he said, bringing her thoughts back to him in a rush. "Once I thought this woman I called daughter had turned against me. I sent her blankets from my lodge because I believed that to be true. Now I think I was wrong. The man Harrison did not tell the truth, and I did not go to hear her words for myself. This council will now decide what is to be done with her, but Cochise, chief of the Chiricahua, will call her daughter once more."

She wanted to cry. It took every effort of will not to

261

allow the tears to flow or to throw herself at him and embrace him as she had as a child. He did believe her! No matter what this council decided, she had won!

"Go now," Cochise said. "Return to the lodge and the council will decide."

She turned slowly and walked out of the circle, concentrating on walking without trembling, and the crowd parted to allow her to pass. Only when she was alone in the lodge did she give in to her weakened legs and sit down on the blanket to hold her head in her hands.

Her wait wasn't long; it seemed only a few moments before Cochise entered the lodge, paused briefly, and then came to sit beside her on the blanket. He gave her a little smile and slowly nodded his head. "The council in its wisdom has decided that Flor de Oro tells the truth," he said. "I am glad."

It was too much to comprehend. His image began to blur as tears did form in her eyes; she could feel her limbs tremble.

"It is because Cochise spoke for me," she whispered huskily. "They would follow your decision."

"That is only true if they think their chief is right," he told her gently. "It is the way of the Apache. I could not save you if they thought me wrong."

"Then I am not to die?"

"No." He touched her arm. "It is the decision of the council to allow you to return to your people, the Americans."

"The Chiricahua are also my people," she said. "I am of two people, for my heart is also here."

His grip increased. "You have been a daughter of whom I am proud. You have suffered much pain and sorrow and you have shown courage in this. No Apache could show more. But it is a time to end that. Your life with the Chiricahua is over. Go from our land in peace and know that the heart of Cochise goes with his daughter."

"But—"

He stopped her with an uplifted hand. "It is the order of the council. And the order of your chief. The last order I will give you."

"I have a son in this land," she reminded him.

"I know. As soon as I can make my people safe from the Americans, I will find him. Already I know where Lobo Negro is hiding. I will kill this outlaw at last and then I will take your son to raise as I did you. The boy is Apache; he could not find his manhood among the whites, because they would hate him for being an Indian."

He released his grip and stroked her arm instead. "It is best for you and the boy. You have my word I will do all I can for him."

Perhaps he was right. She had made so many mistakes . . . But she couldn't give up on her child. Not yet. "Let me stay a little while," she said, looking up at him. "I can help you defeat this Hartman. I know how he thinks and what he will try to do."

He smiled. "My daughter would be a war leader? Would you advise Cochise in a battle? Do not worry of this Hartman. He is not a good war maker; already I have seen that. My scouts follow him even now and others have gone to gather help for us. Soon I will strike and he will be defeated."

"There will be more like him," she said quietly. "I have been to the lands from where they will come and have seen many times the numbers of the Apache. They will come to drive you from your lands and I feel great sadness for the Chiricahua because of this. I think you must take the people from these lands to save them. I thought about this much after I escaped from Hartman. That is, I thought about the others who will come."

"And where would you have us go?" he asked. "There is no place where the Apache would be welcome. It is better to fight."

"Cochise is a great warrior," she said. "But even Cochise cannot win against so many. Take the Chiricahua into Mexico, where the land is big and the Americans will not come."

"Your words have wisdom, Flor de Oro," he said

at last. "But the Chiricahua are not cowards to flee so quickly. We will see what will happen."

He stood up and she knew it was useless to argue further with him.

General Alex Hartman moved his angry glance from the Apache scout who squatted indifferently in front of him to Sattersfield. That the other man was also angry made no difference to him. "I tell you it may be our only chance to catch them before they scatter all over the desert!" he shouted.

Sattersfield shook his head. "And I tell you, General, it's too damn pat! Cochise ain't no fool. I just don't trust this damn Apache with Harrison gone."

"Harrison is dead," Hartman spat. "He was foolish enough to go after the woman without informing me and was killed for that mistake."

"We might just be making a bigger one," Sattersfield said quickly. "I tell you, Cochise ain't dumb enough to let us find his rancheria like this. Not unless he wanted us to."

Hartman glanced once more at the squatting Indian. "Are you sure the warriors are there too? You could make no mistake?"

The scout nodded. "All warriors there," he said. "Cochise in his lodge. He mebbe move soon. Get people ready."

"There, you see?" Hartman said. "A simple explanation. Your Indian chief knows he is outgunned and is smart enough to leave the field of battle with his troops intact. But I'm not going to give him the chance. I intend to attack the camp at dusk."

"Then you can attack by yourself," Sattersfield told him quickly. "Me and my men ain't riding down there. Not until I know for sure."

The man in black coiled like a snake and whipped an arm forward, finger pointing. "You will do as I say! I am in charge of this expedition! Disobey my orders and you will regret it!"

Sattersfield was taken aback by the outburst. For the first time he wondered if the man in front of him were completely sane. He started to object but stopped. Sane or not, Hartman had powerful connections back East, he'd already seen evidence of that. And the power of those connections extended to the Army that was presently in control of the territory. If those people turned against him, he'd have a devil of a time dealing with the Army. Like it or not, Hartman could destroy everything he'd built up. Damn the man anyhow!

"All right," he growled at last. "We'll ride in like you say. But we'll be damned careful doing it!"

Hartman's mood changed instantly from fury to cold disdain. "You need not worry. I've directed a hundred engagements such as this. The situation is prime for the classic Cannae maneuver Hannibal used to defeat the Romans. You will lead half the men down that west slope and attack from that direction, while I lead the rest from the east. His troops will be caught between us with no escape from our guns."

"If he's there," Sattersfield growled sourly. "If he ain't, we're leaving our backs exposed. I think it's best to stay together and come in from the front in force."

Hartman's lip curled. "Just the maneuver he would expect and prepare for. Which is obviously why no one has been able to defeat a simple Indian leader before I came."

Sattersfield eyed him a long moment, ground his teeth together, and then nodded. "How do you want to do it?"

Later, leading half the men toward the Indian camp from the west as he had been directed, Sattersfield had even stronger doubts. His men were extremely nervous, and although they moved with caution and were each well experienced in fighting Indians, the nervousness exposed their movements in little sounds and sights that would otherwise never have occurred. He expected at any moment that the alarm to be raised in the ranchería. Then, as he was almost into the position Hartman had assigned to him, he realized that the mere fact the alarm hadn't been raised brought the situation to a dangerous level. The Apache were too smart not to know they were there!

He watched the man on his right remove his hand from his rifle stock and rub it alongside his pants to dry it and realized his own palms were sweating. His nerves were tight. To relieve the pressure by doing something, he inched forward until he could see over the edge of the rock he was using for concealment. The Apache camp had all the appearance of normalcy. There were only a few men in sight, the rest were women, and they were doing normal things. Still, he wasn't reassured and from the annoying amount of stirring behind him, neither were his men. However, another few minutes and Hartman would be in place from his longer ride and the signal would be given.

Sattersfield's breath came in shallow draughts in spite of his best efforts to relax his chest as he listened. A moment later the crawling silence was shattered, not by a single signal shot, but by a thunderous roar of gunfire to the east mixed with the wild screaming of Apaches in battle. He immediately knew the reason, even before the Indian women in front of him threw off buckskin shirts and became warriors with suddenly produced rifles. It was a trap! Hartman had been ambushed!

The camp was deserted in an instant as the warriors took cover to advance and fire from concealment. His men answered the fire rapidly but had only a second's target as each Apache rose to fire and then rolled to another cover. Sattersfield searched frantically for a target and then spun around as to either side of him, new fire and yelling began. The damn place was alive with Indians! They had been waiting here, too!

He screamed an order to retreat as the rocks about him chipped and disintegrated from stinging bullets. The order was unnecessary, his men were already running for the horses. Sattersfield ran for his own life, stumbling as the dirt beneath his scrambling feet exploded in puffs of dust. His heart pounding, he grabbed for the nearest horse, caught its flying reins as it reared in fright, and swung aboard.

The horse reared again, its nostrils flaring and a frightened whinny coming from its wide-open mouth, as he fought for control of it. Seconds later he was lying flat along its back and urging it into a hard run. To hell with Hartman! Now it was every man for himself.

An Apache rose out of the ground ahead of him with an extended bow and he had only time for a snap shot before he raced past. His bullet caught the Indian in the face, it exploded in blood, and the arrow whistled harmlessly over Sattersfield's head.

Another Apache raced from behind a bush and made a desperate grab for him as he pounded past. Sattersfield clubbed him away and urged his straining mount to greater effort.

Horses were all around him now. Some contained clinging riders and a few had empty saddles. If he could reach the rise ahead of him, open ground was beyond, and there he would have a chance. The Apache would have to take time to gather ponies of their own and in that small amount of time lay his only hope of escape. That, and the prayer that the Indians would give up on the few men who got clear and turn to finish those who were still trapped.

He shot one more Apache before he topped the rise and raced into the open country with no more than a dozen men still with him. Gradually, the sound of the racing horses began to outweigh the noise of the battle behind him, and Sattersfield's hopes began to rise. Minutes later they were alone, and he eased back on his straining mount. Total effort would soon exhaust the horse; it would need all its strength to get away.

The men with him did the same and he risked a look over his shoulder. They were not being followed, at least not yet. He reined the horse in even more and steadied it into a controlled run, which gave him time to think. From the size of the ambush, Cochise had not been alone. He'd brought in at least one other tribe, maybe two. Hartman had never stood a chance in his damned Roman plan, and he'd compounded his mistake by dividing his own forces. Had they stayed together they might have had the firepower to stand the Indians off and withdraw in order. The man was a fool! He deserved everything he got—or was going to get if he were stupid enough to surrender to the Apache.

They rode throughout the night and by dawn they were miles from the battleground, still riding, but slowly and with great caution. Only with the first light, when he could see behind him, did Sattersfield allow them to slow to a walk. Riding the horse and exhausted from his efforts and the nervous reaction to the night, he made a resolution to himself. The dream of Quivira was over as far as he was concerned. Maybe that wealth existed, and maybe it didn't. At any rate it wasn't worth the risk he had taken. There were riches enough to be made in the manner he had always pursued; never would he become partner in this venture again.

With the emergence of dawn, small fires were being lit in the camp by the squaws for the preparation of an early meal. That is, all but three fires. These were prepared to cook something else. The three surviving white men lay heavily trussed on the ground to await those fires being brought to the proper heat. When it was time, the men would be suspended above the fires upside down, their heads only inches from the glowing flames that would slowly cook their brains as they jackknifed in agony. It would take hours for them to die.

Flor de Oro stood beside Cochise to watch the preparations as one of the victims, a man clad in black, returned her gaze with a frenzy of hate. She felt a stirring of pity, even though he had done his best to destroy her and the Chiricahua, and had the roles been reversed, would have held no pity of his own.

She turned to Cochise. "I would ask a favor," she said slowly.

He nodded. "I know what it will be," he said. Then

when she didn't reply, continued, "Flor de Oro would ask that these men be killed quickly. But it is the white blood in her that would ask. That is proof my words of before were true, you are no longer of the Apache way."

She nodded slowly. "Can it not be done?"

"No. My people have suffered at the hands of this man and his warriors. Some of them have died. Now he and the others must pay. The Chiricahua expect it."

He was right she knew. Two years ago she would have been Indian enough to watch the torture without cringing, but now the thought was more than she could bear. The split in her was growing, she would always remember the way of the Indians with fondness, but she could never go back to being an Apache. With one final glance at the white-haired man lying on the ground, another to the tall Indian who watched her with knowing eyes, she turned away and walked back to his lodge.

For long hours she sat alone inside and tried to think of David. And to close her mind to the screams from outside. . . .

Chapter Eighteen

The only help he had gotten in Tucson was from a doctor who shook his head slowly and told him he was a walking dead man. "You need rest, Foxcroft," the physician said. "Your lungs are clear, but that shoulder is in bad shape. You keep moving it and you may lose the use of your arm."

David had ignored the advice, knowing that time was running short. Fortunately, his eye was also improving; he could see blurred colors with it, not images but melded shapes that fused into one another. This doctor also thought it would eventually come around. He discarded the bandage for a black patch that gave him a wild look. That, and his near angry questions, caused the men to whom he spoke to back away from him.

Only one, a man who worked for a trader in town, the same one his father had mentioned, Sattersfield, gave any indication of ever hearing of Hartman. The man's eyes had narrowed in suspicion at the mention of the general's name and he wanted to know why David asked. The quick explanation that he was promised a job by Hartman didn't satisfy the man and he muttered an answer that he was somewhere in the territory and may show up in Tucson sometime soon. David decided he couldn't wait for that possibility. He traded his horse for a strong-appearing roan since his own was trail-worn from the hurried ride from Kansas, and headed for Fort Breckinridge at the junction of the San Pedro and Arivaipa Creek.

There, he was frustrated again. The major in charge of the fort had no information of Hartman and told him no one but the Indian agent assigned to the territory had authority to make a treaty with the Apache. He was also suspicious, and David knew that his story would be checked and inquiries would be made to find out if he were a deserter. He didn't give a damn what the major did. It was a large, rough country, and she was in it somewhere with a man who was chasing a legend. A man he knew nothing about but one he had to assume would only use her for his own ends. Dammit, why hadn't she remained in St. Louis until he could come with her!

He answered his own question. She didn't remain because she was Flor de Oro as well as Jennifer Foxcroft. She had a mind of her own and the independent will to follow it through. God, he loved her so much!

Riding out of the fort, he was startled to hear his name called and spun in the saddle to see a horseman riding toward him. An Apache—it took him a moment to recognize the man—Konta! He was never so happy to see a man in his life.

Konta reined his own horse to a halt and raised a hand, his round face beaming. "Lieutenant," he said happily, "I did not think to see you again."

"Konta, you are a pleasure for my eyes—for one eye at least. How are you?"

The Apache shrugged. "I am good, Lieutenant. I have a horse. I have work. What does a man need?"

"You're a scout for this post?"

The smile disappeared from his friend's face. "There is much trouble here, Lieutenant. When a warrior works for the soldiers, he can never go home." He shrugged again, a droop of his shoulders. "I do what I do."

David thought rapidly. He needed help, that was certain. And Konta, if he were willing, would know what was going on and where Hartman might be. Information that the Indian wouldn't volunteer to the fort commander unless he were asked. "Konta, can we talk?" he asked.

The Apache nodded. "The lieutenant is my friend.

He is welcome to my camp." His dark eyes locked on David's own. "My life belongs to the lieutenant. I remember this always."

David sighed. "Mine may well belong to you now, Konta. And you can forget the lieutenant part. I'm not in the Army anymore. It's just David."

Konta grinned. "Come," he said, and wheeled his horse.

David followed as he rode a short way down the creek, around a bend, and pulled up in front of a brush hut. With only a glance at the awkward way David moved his left arm, the Apache shouldered him aside and unsaddled the horses himself, hobbled them and led the way to his hut.

"Sit and rest," he commanded. "I have some *tiswin*. We will drink and then we will eat."

David leaned his back against a tree, stretched his legs, and relaxed. The beer was warm but good. Its soothing effect spread slowly through his tired body and made him sleepy. He watched as Konta built a small fire and placed a pot over it, suddenly remembering how hungry he was.

Later, after they had eaten, Konta squatted on his haunches as he rolled two cigarettes from leaves, handed one to David and asked, "Why do you come?"

The cigarette was of strong tobacco; it made him more drunk than the *tiswin*. He gazed at possibly the only friend he had in the territory, an Indian, but a man he respected. "You remember my wife?" he asked. "The woman the Apache called Flor de Oro?"

Konta nodded.

"She is here with a man called Hartman. General Hartman. He is looking for Quivira."

Again Konta nodded.

"You know of him?" David sat erect.

"I know," Konta said. "He came with many men and attacked Cochise and the Chiricahua."

"Attacked? There was a fight?" *And she was in the middle of it!*

"They wanted to capture Cochise," Konta continued, gazing at him through the smoke of his cigarette. "But Cochise and his people got away. Soon there will be another battle with this man, but the Chiricahua will not be alone, many other tribes will help."

"Doesn't the Army know about this?" David demanded. "The major didn't say anything about it to me."

Konta grinned. "The soldiers have only the eyes of the scouts," he said. "We do not think they need to know of this battle."

In spite of his worry, David answered the grin. "You're going to tell the major *after* Cochise wins, aren't you?"

Konta's grin widened.

David brought himself back sharply. "Konta, my wife—Flor de Oro—is with Hartman. If he is killed, she may be killed, too."

The Apache shook his head. "I have heard there was a woman with this Hartman but she ran away after the battle. She traveled alone until she was taken by the Chiricahua. I did not know who she was."

"You mean Cochise has her? But he'll kill her."

The dark eyes continued to rest on his face and David felt close to panic. "Listen, I've got to go there. To Cochise's camp. Do you know where it is?"

"Cochise will kill you. He is at war with all Americans."

David leaned forward, ignoring the pain in his shoulder as both his fists tightened. "Konta, I've got to go to his camp."

The Apache nodded. "We will go. I can take you."

"Will you be risking your life? I mean, since Cochise knows you have been working for the fort?"

The eyes of the Indian never wavered from his own. "He will know I work for fort," he said softly. "But we will go. You must rest now and sleep. When the sun rises, we will ride a long way."

David sighed. It was a terrible thing to ask of his friend. This man was willing to place his own neck in certain danger for him, and he had no right to allow him to do it. He had no qualms about risking his own life for her, he could do no less. But to ask Konta to sacrifice as well?

It was a long time before he slept.

With the first rising of the sun, the rancheria of the Chiricahua stirred into activity. The wives of Cochise had offered her nothing to do and even seemed to resent her willingness to help, so finally Flor de Oro gave up and walked to the water hole to bathe. She ate in silence with the squaws, wandered about idly for a time, and was grateful when he summoned her once more. Cochise sat before his lodge and motioned for her to sit beside him.

"It is time for Flor de Oro to leave," he said, after she had settled herself. "I have told the others that it is better for you to go back to the Americans. Shi-la-dia will take you to where you can see the town of Tucson, and then you will enter alone. I bring you here to say goodby to my daughter."

"My eyes will run like the river," she said. "My love for Cochise is great."

"It is best," he insisted.

She nodded. "I am an obedient daughter. When shall I leave?"

Cochise stood up and she followed him to her feet. She wanted to cry as he took her in his arms and held her for a moment, then released her. "The heart of Cochise will travel with his daughter," he told her. "Go now. Shi-la-dia is waiting."

"I would like to come back someday." She was reluctant to leave in spite of his order.

Cochise shook his head. "Your ways are no longer the ways of the Apache. Do not look back, Flor de Oro, when you leave the Chiricahua. One cannot travel far or well with his eyes behind him. Go."

She turned, walked away, and didn't look back.

Shi-la-dia and one other were waiting for her at the edge of the rancheria with ponies, and Flor de Oro swung aboard the smallest to follow without conversation as he set a steady pace toward the west. It was only when they sought shelter for the midafternoon rest from the sun that they talked.

She thanked him for standing up for her in the council, but he waved a hand to brush her words aside. "I told the truth," he said. "It was my duty."

"Shi-la-dia is a great warrior," she said. "He will someday be a war chief as was his father."

His sudden glance at her was suspicious, but her face contained only admiration, and slowly he settled back into his resting place with his back against a rise in the grassy ground. But she noted that his chin was raised and he flexed the muscles in his arms when he folded them across his chest. Noticed, and smiled to herself.

"When will Cochise seek out Lobo Negro?" she asked, after a long space of time had passed. She said it casually, as if she were only half interested.

"When we have defeated the Americans. Or have made peace with them." He spoke with his eyes still half closed against the heat, but Flor de Oro could tell there was awareness in his voice. He was not a man who would be easily fooled.

"That will be a long time," she offered. "I have been to the East and know how many Americans are there. They are like the drops of water in a river, so many they cannot be counted. I fear for the Chiricahua when they come."

"We will fight," he said. "The Apache will not be defeated."

She waited a while and then nodded. "I know you will fight well, but never have the Apache faced so many. And they have guns that can speak from a distance to kill a dozen warriors at one time. I hope Cochise will decide to go into the lands of the Mexicans for the sake of the Chiricahua. But if he does, Lobo Negro will go free from his revenge."

"Cochise has sworn to kill him," Shi-la-dia said shortly.

"But Cochise is a chief," she replied quietly. "He must first look after the safety of the Chiricahua and their women and children. It is his responsibility."

Shi-la-dia sat up to look at her.

"Shi-la-dia is a mighty warrior," she told him, returning the look. "He would gain the favor of Cochise if he captured Lobo Negro and brought him in. Then Cochise could punish his enemy and still look after the people of his tribe."

"And Flor de Oro would see her child," he said harshly. "I am not a fool that I am so easily tricked."

"It is not a trick," she said. "I make a bargain. Cochise knows where the hiding place of Lobo Negro is and I think so does Shi-la-dia. If you would take me there, together we could capture him. I would have my child and Shi-la-dia would gain much favor in the eyes of his chief."

"No."

"It would be easy," she continued, as if she hadn't heard him. "Lobo Negro hates me and once he sees me his thoughts will be on me alone. I will place myself where he can see me and when he comes, you will be there to capture him."

The young warrior settled back and closed his eyes to ignore her. But much later, when she had begun to be afraid he meant what he said, he spoke. "I am better with a rifle than most. And I can track any man . . ." He said it to himself, so low that she hardly heard him. But it was enough and Flor de Oro smiled.

They climbed slowly into the mountains and as they drew near the stronghold of the Chiricahua, David's stomach tightened. He was familiar enough with Apache ways to know they were being watched and when they were suddenly surrounded by the Indians who trained rifles on them, it came as no shock. He relaxed and folded his hands on the saddlehorn.

Konta spoke rapidly in Apache, and David understood little except the name Cochise. The Apaches talked briefly among themselves for a moment, then two of them advanced to take his and Konta's weapons before moving them out. An hour later, all of them rode into the camp of the Chiricahua.

Hostile faces were all around them, a few muttered

curses in Apache reached his ears, but he kept his head straight and ignored the sounds until he was ordered to dismount and his horse was taken away. He and Konta remained in a circle of muttering Indians for a very long time before it was broken and a tall man walked through it to stand before them. It was the first time he had seen Cochise; he looked at him curiously.

The chief of the Chiricahua eyed him in return with contempt. "Who are you?" he demanded. "Why do you come here?"

He spoke in English and David was glad of the fact. He didn't want this to have to go through translation.

"My name is Foxcroft," he said. "I was once a soldier at the fort called Buchanan. I am not a soldier now. I have no anger for the Apache."

"Then why do you come?"

"I look for my woman. She is called Flor de Oro by the Apache. She was once the daughter of Cochise." He said it slowly and carefully. And watched for a reaction.

Cochise's expression didn't change. "The woman called Flor de Oro is not here. We do not believe there is a white man who does not wish harm to our people. You say you come in peace, but others have said this as well and then tried to destroy us. Why should I believe you?"

Not here! Oh God, where could she have gone? He threw an agonizing glance toward Konta but the other was standing quietly, watching Cochise, and didn't return the look.

David took a deep breath. "My words are true, Cochise. I mean no harm to your people. I seek only to find my wife. If you know of her and will tell me, I will go in peace and do my best to see that others of my race do the same. That's all I can do."

He had been sure she was here. And like a fool he'd ridden into the camp and probably sacrificed both Konta's life and his own on that assumption. Damn, how stupid could he be!

Cochise stared at him without an ounce of sympathy in his gaze. "I have sent the woman away," he said. "Because you are her husband, and I do not think you will make war on the Chiricahua, I will let you leave again."

He glanced at Konta. "But you will go alone. This man has led the bluecoats against us. He must suffer the fate of all enemies of the Chiricahua. Go now, and do not come back here again."

He turned and started away.

David had only a moment to make his decision and didn't hesitate. "Wait!" he cried.

Cochise paused to look back at him.

"This man is my friend. He placed his life in my hands to bring me to your camp. I will not leave without him."

Cochise's mouth twisted. "You are a fool," he said curtly.

"That is the way it is," David returned. And stood there watching as the Chiricahua chief stalked away.

Chapter Nineteen

It was a high, narrow bench of land, flat enough in places but at the same time filled with treacherous cracks of soft dirt that could give way under a horse's hooves and plunge both the animal and its rider down the steep slopes. Brooding above the bench were overhanging cliffs, and across it thin but hardy wind-dragged pines struggled to maintain a precarious grip on life.

This was an exposed area, but Shi-la-dia had said it was the only way up and warned that they might easily be seen in spite of all precautions.

He had been hard to convince, it had taken her a day and a half, but once persuaded that he would be doing this thing for his chief (as well as his own glory) he had given the task his full attention. Lobo Negro was somewhere above them, he said, perched like an eagle where he could command everything he saw. Unlike that bird, however, he couldn't fly away. He was trapped on his perch. Each time he tried to come down, the smoke signals would immediately rise to warn those below and he would be driven back. Cochise had placed him in a prison as surely as if he were in a cage. Every Apache in the territory wanted to put a bullet or an arrow in him.

He was alone, Shi-la-dia told her, he had no warriors left to help him. He didn't know if the child was here, he said, but if he were, there were only the two of them. Flor de Oro felt no sympathy for the outlaw, only a deep fear that her son might be suffering as well. He would have kept the boy, she was convinced of that. Not out of love for the child even though he was of his own blood, but out of hatred for her. This would be her last chance to save him.

"How much farther?" she asked.

He shrugged, keeping his eyes on the way ahead. "I don't know. Perhaps he will find us before we find him. We must be ready."

A whisper of sound touched their ears, and both Shi-la-dia and the other warrior whirled to face it with rifles raised. They waited, poised to fight, but found nothing and finally relaxed. "He will not be easily tricked," Shi-la-dia said at last.

They moved on cautiously and Flor de Oro thought about the coming fight. Her plan was a simple one, as all good plans were simple. Soon the two men would drop behind her and travel on foot while she led their ponies. Lobo Negro would see her, but if they were lucky he would get close enough to make sure of his shots or try to capture her. She was banking on that. With his attention on her, Shi-la-dia and the other would have a chance to move against him.

The plan called for the outlaw to still have some feeling for her even if it were only hate. Whether it was that or the other, his desire to possess her again, he would want to capture her. Then he would be careless. Even if he didn't recognize her in time and shot her, the act would locate him for Shi-la-dia and mean his own death. For the latter was a good warrior, and smart in his own right. Smart enough, she hoped, even for Lobo Negro. Either way her son would be freed; she had to offer him that chance.

The trail narrowed and twisted out of sight around an edge. Shi-la-dia stopped, slipped from his pony, and crept forward to peer around the blockage for a long time. She and the other warrior waited patiently until he returned.

"This is as far as we can go together, I think," he said when he came back. "He could have seen us before, but not enough to know who we are or how many. After this, he would know."

She nodded. "I will ride on alone."

He shook his head. "No. There is too much light.

280

You must go in the shadows where he cannot see you well. We will rest here until the sun is behind the mountains."

He was right, of course. In clear light, Lobo Negro could readily see that the ponies with her were riderless even against the coloring of the cliff. With shadows, he couldn't be sure and perhaps would only expect them to have riders. But the shadows would also make it harder for him to identify her. Thoughtfully, she raised a hand to spread her yellow hair across her back.

When at last they began to move again, the trail widened but climbed sharply and her mount had to scramble in places. Sometimes it was difficult to make him move forward and still retain control of the two she was leading at the same time, and also, the shadows that would disguise her made the trail more difficult to read and a misstep that much easier.

Shi-la-dia and the other were somewhere behind her on either side, moving along at her pace, but she didn't expect to see either of them again until after the forthcoming fight. On this rough terrain, they could move as well if not better than she; she had no worries of their being left behind.

Flor de Oro moved cautiously and slowly, alert to everything about her, and emerged finally onto another bench, a wide and deep one covered with stunted trees and broken rock. This bench was, she decided, pausing to scan the area, where he would be waiting if he had spotted her. She took a long, deep breath, then spoke gently to the pony to start him moving again.

The silence of this high place was nerve-tightening, she shook away the feeling of being watched and tried to appear purposeful. Suddenly, the silence was shattered by a yell somewhere to her right, a short, surprised yelp that was as quickly cut off as it had occurred, and she whirled in its direction.

The quiet returned—a tense quiet that made her tremble with anticipation. It had to be him. He was here. Somewhere in the rocks and trees he had found, or been found by one of the warriors with her.

She had a sinking feeling that he had found the other, that he hadn't been fooled by the ruse and had gone after them instead of her. The cry had been one of surprise and sudden pain, and had stopped too quickly for its owner not to have been killed.

She waited, nervously scanning the area, and drew the only weapon she had, a knife Cochise had given her. She wished desperately she had a rifle.

Nothing stirred. She slid to the ground and held the ropes to the horses in one hand, the knife in the other. The silence was oppressive now, nothing moved, not a breeze to stir the branches, not a bird in sight. It was as if the mountain itself held its breath as the two remaining warriors stalked each other among the rocks and trees. Two men, with all the cunning and skill of centuries of Apache training behind them, sought to kill each other. One was an outlaw, the other a hunter. Even the ponies she held sensed the danger and stood with heads high and nostrils testing the air.

A long time passed, measured for Flor de Oro in the dying light of the sun now settling below the mountain and wrapping the dusk around her. The handle of the knife in her hand became slippery with her nervousness; she removed it long enough to dry her palm on her skirt. And waited.

He was moving around her; she knew it even though there was no sign of his movement, and hunting for Shi-la-dia, who was hunting him in return.

Two shots, almost at the same instant. She whirled at the sounds and saw a man leap to the top of a rock several hundred yards to her left. He fired once more at something beneath him, then flung up both arms at the quick reply and fell backward, too quickly for her to see who it had been.

Lobo Negro? She said a quick prayer and hurriedly tied the ponies to a branch before moving in the direction the man had fallen. Using all the cover she could find, she reached the area and slowed, listening. Nothing . . .

It took her long, cautious minutes to find the fallen warrior, and when she did, she wished she hadn't. Shi-la-dia lay on his back, with blood covering his chest. She didn't need to check, she knew he was dead. His rifle was missing, flung away in his fall, or taken away, it didn't matter which. Slowly she straightened to stand erect.

He appeared, as she knew he would, stepping from behind a rock and standing there to regard her contemptuously, the scar on his face visible even in the fading light.

"So," he said softly. "Flor de Oro has returned. I knew you would come back some day for the child. I have looked forward to that day."

He held both rifles loosely in his hands; she looked down at them and allowed her knife to fall away from her hand slowly. It was ended. And she had lost.

His camp was only a little higher up; they reached it before darkness closed in, and he made her sit while he rebuilt a fire in front of the cave he was using for a home. Then he took the ponies aside and hobbled them as she watched. Only when he returned and stood before her with a mixture of hate and triumph on his scarred face did she break her silence.

"Where is the child?" she asked. "May I see him?"

He shook his head. "He is hiding," he said. "The boy has learned to do that well since you left and set Cochise against me."

She was weary, a draining tiredness that came as much from her loss of hope as from the long journey to this place. "I did not do that," she said from the weariness. "The day you took me from the Chiricahua, you set Cochise against you. Don't you understand that? And he will still come someday. You cannot escape him."

That angered him, as she knew it would. "I am Lobo Negro," he snarled. "No one, not even Cochise, can defeat me."

Flor de Oro looked around deliberately. "No one?" she said. "Where are your warriors? Your squaws?

Where are the followers of Lobo Negro?"

"Others will take their place! When I leave here, there will be many who will want to follow Lobo Negro! Once again my name will be feared!"

He was different now, she realized. Not only in the lean, half starved appearance of his once powerful body, but in the hunted look of his eyes.

"May I see the child?" she repeated.

He waited a moment, as if still wanting to convince her of what he could do, but then turned and gave a shrill, sharp cry, the call of an eagle.

Flor de Oro followed his look, her heart suddenly in her throat and her hands gripping her arms.

There was a small rustle outside the firelight and a moment later the boy appeared. Small in stature, a miniature Apache warrior in breechcloth, moccasins, and a headband holding back his dark hair. His skin was as brown as the desert floor and his blue eyes regarded her with suspicion and mistrust.

He was like the prairie dog, she thought, moving so cautiously and poised to flee at the slightest hint of danger. Nothing like the happy child he would have been in the rancheria of Cochise. Her heart swelled in sympathy and love, and she wanted desperately to extend her arms toward him. But that would only make him run away again.

Lobo Negro watched her with cruel amusement and she knew he would send the boy away again with a quick command unless she remained where she was. She could only wait for his decision.

The child moved slowly to his father's side, eyeing her the while, and only when he stood with his father's hand on his shoulder did he seem to relax into a boy.

She brought her look up to Lobo Negro's face and could not hide her pain. "Tell him." The sound of her own voice was strained.

He shook his head. "A trade," he said. "I will give my son only to my squaw. You have the choice."

She knew what he wanted her to say. And she knew it would be the only thing he would accept. Without his consent, his order to the boy, the child would never be hers again, for he had no remembrance of those first days in which she had nursed him. Nothing less than a complete break with her past, with David and all the rest, and complete surrender to the man who stood before her, would return her son to her arms.

Still the words came hard. The weight of them sapped her will to resist. "I am the squaw of Lobo Negro," she whispered. "To do as he commands."

Chapter Twenty

They had been two days in the Chiricahua camp and still he had no idea of what their fate would be. Try as he might, David could not approach the stoicism of his companion; he found the pressure to move overwhelming most of the time and had to rise and pace about the confining space in the lodge. Konta had no such trouble. When he wasn't stretched out and sleeping, he sat cross-legged near the open doorway and observed what goings-on he could see from his restricted view.

David paused in his pacing and bent over to peer out himself but could see nothing to interest him, and the attempt made his bad eye ache. He straightened to rub it. Vision was slowly returning to the eye, which actually made it worse because the sight was blurred, with occasional streaks of clarity, causing it to interfere with the use of his good one. His shoulder was better too, painful only if he attempted to move it too quickly. The dizziness that had plagued him all the way from St. Louis was gone.

"Konta, we've got to find a way out of here," he said, squatting beside the Apache sitting at the entrance. "If we don't, I'm going to blow apart from this waiting."

"Cochise will let us go soon," was the surprising reply.

"The hell you say! What makes you think that?"

Konta didn't look at him. "I think about this much. If the Chiricahua wanted to kill me they would not wait this long. I think because you will not go without me, Cochise will let me go. He hates the Americans, but he will not kill the husband of Flor de Oro. He has too much love for her."

David let his breath go in an explosion. "I hope you're right," he said. "But why is he waiting?"

"He waits for news of her, I think."

"News of her?"

This time Konta turned to look at him. "Cochise will send warriors with her. He is waiting for them to return."

David thought about that for a minute, started to reply, but a movement just outside the lodge caught his attention and distracted him. A Chiricahua brave was approaching purposefully and he watched as the man stopped in front and motioned to them. "Come," he ordered.

It was a relief. He stepped through the opening and stood erect. Konta joined him, and the two of them followed the brave who was already moving away.

"What do you think now?" David muttered as they walked.

Konta shrugged.

The Apache led them around two more lodges and into the circle area that was the center of the rancheria. There he stopped and motioned for them to wait.

Their presence in the circle drew immediate attention and David found himself surrounded by what appeared to be most of the tribe. Some of the faces he looked at were openly hostile, but the majority were only curious. Unconsciously he straightened his shoulders to appear indifferent, but winced at the sharp thrust of pain the movement brought to his wound.

Cochise chose that moment to step from his lodge and advance a few paces to stand before him. When he spoke, it was in a voice dark with anger. "Do you tell the truth when you say you are no longer of the bluecoats?" he demanded.

David reacted slower than he wanted to, but managed to keep his eyes level with those of Cochise. "I speak the truth," he said. "What the Army does is no longer my business. I'm here to find my wife."

The Chiricahua chief paused for a long moment and David had the uneasy feeling that the dark eyes he looked into were probing deep within his soul. It was difficult not to move his own.

"If I allow you to go," Cochise said at last, "will you still seek her?"

It was an invitation that brought him a step forward. "Tell me where she is, let me and my friend go, and I promise to do what is in my power to help your people," he said. "I want only to find my wife."

"I do not know where she is," Cochise said. It was an admission of reluctance, obvious only in the change in his voice. "I think she is with the outlaw."

"Lobo Negro?" David couldn't believe it. "You let her go back with him?"

This time anger deepened Cochise's stare. "Do not speak foolish, American! I would never give her to my enemy. I sent warriors to take her to Tucson."

"But—"

Cochise stopped him with a movement. "I sent her to a safe place. But Flor de Oro chose not to go there. She chose instead to go after her child and my warriors disobeyed me by taking her where she wanted to go. Since they have not returned, I believe they have been killed by Lobo Negro."

David wanted to scream, to curse him. *By God, back in the hands of that devil!* "Where is Lobo Negro?" The words grated against the back of his teeth.

The Apache regarded him only a moment longer. "I will tell you where the outlaw is, and I will let both of you go in the hope you can find her. It is all that I can do."

There was more than anger in his voice, it was tinged with frustration. "The bluecoats are coming here," he continued. "I must move my people to a safer place and once again I have no time to seek the outlaw." The dark eyes holding David's own narrowed to steel. "A chief cannot always do as he would want, or I would long ago have killed Lobo Negro. I think now I will never have time for this. So I will tell you, American, how to fight Lobo Negro.

How to find him and what you must do to defeat him. Then you must go and do what I cannot. Now you will come into my lodge and we will talk."

Under different circumstances the eagle nest of Lobo Negro would have been a good place to live for a time. At least until the winter forced them from its heights. The blue sky surrounding her gave an appearance of friendly comfort, its passing cotton clouds seemed near enough to reach out and touch. The air was clean and fresh, nearly enough to lift her heavy spirits. Flor de Oro sat on a rock for most of the morning and watched the drifting clouds, occasionally allowing her gaze to fall away to the scene beneath, the place from which she had come.

She had surrendered to the outlaw on that first day, surrendered in the pain of that moment of despair when Shi-la-dia and the other were killed and she'd first seen her son. But that had been a temporary feeling. In the days that followed, her strength had returned little by little. She could not give up in spite of the hopelessness. A dozen things had occurred to her, piling one upon another until she had difficulty in sorting them out. If Lobo Negro would relax his guard for only a moment and give her a chance at his knife or his rifle, she would kill him and take the boy away. Or if Cochise would only come as he said he would some day. If hunger would drive the outlaw down from the mountain where she might find opportunity to escape . . . If. If. If. Her head ached with the thoughts.

Her life seemed suspended in time, and the strangest thing about the last few days was Lobo Negro's attitude toward her. True, he would sometimes taunt her in harsh words, taking pleasure in telling her that she was again his possession and soon would bear him many more children, but most of the time he offered her only a morose silence, ignoring her as if she didn't exist. She had gone about her tasks quietly, waiting for him to make his move, but he did nothing and she would occasionally glance up and catch him watching her with a surprising expression on his face. An expression that was almost tender. She shook that thought away; it couldn't be that, he hated her too much.

Why was he different? He had not forced her to his blankets. In fact, he'd not even touched her since that first day when he brought her here. He'd given her a blanket and made her sleep in the rear of the cave while bedding down at the entrance himself so that she could not get out without disturbing his sleep. Why was that? He taunted her that she would once again give him pleasure, but he was yet to force her to it.

He was gone most of the day, either to hunt for the scarce food available on the mountain or to guard against attack, she wasn't sure which. He was a shadow that disappeared and reappeared with abruptness, she could never be certain when. But she knew without trying that she stood no chance of slipping away while he was gone; Lobo Negro would find her before she was halfway down the mountain.

She sighed. There were no solutions. Not yet, anyway.

Her thoughts were interrupted as she became aware that she was being watched. She could sense a presence behind her. The boy? Carefully she turned so as not to frighten him away.

He squatted a short distance behind her, a small brown body beneath an intelligent face. This time, when she looked in his direction, he didn't rise and leave as he had before but continued to watch her.

Lobo Negro had not told him she was his mother; at any rate, he may not understand that concept in the life he'd led. He'd merely been told that she was a squaw who would live with them. The boy didn't trust her, would not reply when she spoke to him, and kept his distance from her when Lobo Negro was away. Most of the day he disappeared himself, leaving her to wonder what he did to amuse himself through the long hours.

Without moving further, she spoke softly to him.

"Will you come to sit with me?"

He didn't acknowledge he'd heard.

"I thought I saw a lion down there," she said, trying to project worry into her voice. "I was afraid it might come into our camp. Perhaps we should find something to defend ourselves."

His steady gaze flickered down the slope, then immediately back to her.

"No," she said quickly. "Over here." She turned and pretended to look down in another direction. "There! Was that him?"

It was too much for his curiosity. She heard him move but didn't look around. A moment later he was beside her and peering over the rock slope. Flor de Oro waited, not daring to move.

The boy looked hard, even crept closer to the edge, and finally blue eyes turned back to her. "No lion," he said. They were a man's words in a baby's voice.

She nodded slowly, as if paying great heed to his words, the first he'd spoken to her. "He is intelligent, the mountain lion," she said. "Perhaps he is circling us. Should we go back to camp?"

He turned to look again, a long, searching look, then rose and walked away. But after a few steps he stopped and waited with his head turned toward her. She got up to follow.

Once more in front of the cave, he found a long stick and squatted with it across his lap. Flor de Oro sat down beside him and was pleased when he didn't move away.

"You are a brave warrior," she told him solemnly.

He didn't reply, but she watched as his small hands on the stick tightened.

"All brave warriors have names," she offered after a while. "Do you have a name?"

He shook his head.

"But what are you called?"

"Boy." It was more a grunt than an answer.

"I am called Flor de Oro," she said.

He nodded without looking at her.

"Perhaps I could give you a name. Could I do

that?"

"Boy," he said with finality.

She tried her best, but the temptation became overpowering. She couldn't resist reaching out to touch his small shoulder and as she expected he got up immediately to walk away. "Go look for lion," he said.

She watched in frustration as he disappeared in the rocks.

The two of them lay on a low ridge with their horses tied well out of sight and watched the columns of men moving across the desert. It was an impressive sight, one that might have inspired David at one time in his life, but that was before he'd seen similar columns cut to pieces in battle. And it had been before he'd had the experience of being in an Apache rancheria. It wasn't only men—savages—that these columns were going to attack, it was an entire populace, including women and children. When he spotted the Howitzers being pulled by teams of horses he knew Cochise and his people stood no chance at all. It was suddenly a very ugly picture.

He pointed out the guns to Konta. The Apache grunted in agreement with David's unspoken words and the two of them waited in silence until long after the last column was a dust cloud in the distance before returning to the horses. Even that large body of troops would have scouts circling it and David wanted no encounter to delay them now. He knew where she was at last, and Cochise had assured him that the renegade wouldn't move for a while, at least until he learned that the situation had changed. He wanted to reach Lobo Negro's hideout before the outlaw knew he was free to leave.

They rode throughout the afternoon with only short breaks to rest the horses, continued through part of the night, finally made a dry camp, and were moving at dawn.

By midday they were climbing cautiously up the mountain. Somewhere above them, Lobo Negro waited, a wolf driven to bay who would fight with all the savagery of that breed. Add to that his cunning and the fact that many men born to this land had already failed to kill him, and the task seemed impossible. But he would do it. He had to do it.

As they climbed, Konta trailing him by a short distance, David concentrated on the area around him, his senses alert for anything that might be the least out of the ordinary. But at the same time a small portion of his mind ran over the things Cochise had told him in the long conversation in his lodge before they had been released. The chief had described this area to him until he felt that he knew it as well as if he'd been here before. And then he'd spent time telling him what to expect—no, what to anticipate—from the outlaw. It would be a cat-and-mouse game with the roles constantly reversing. The hunted would become the hunter and only the smarter, or luckier, man would win. The wisdom of Cochise, he hoped, would offset the advantage Lobo Negro held over him.

A sudden signal behind him, a whisper of sound that he would have missed if his entire body had not been attuned with caution, caused him to rein the horse sharply and lift his weapon. David waited and searched the scene before him with his good eye.

Konta moved up beside him and pointed.

Following his arm, David found what had stopped the Apache. On a ragged edge of cliff several hundred yards ahead of them, a clump of brush clung tenaciously. A normal thing at first glance, except that the rest of the area around it was bare of similiar green. He strained to see and cursed the fact that he had only one good eye to use.

"What is it?" he whispered finally.

Konta leaned toward him. "Brush not living," he said. "Look at ends."

This time he saw it. The tips of the close-packed brush were of a slightly different color, they were starting to brown. The shrubs were dying, they had been moved. In a few more days it would be obvious, but before then, he guessed, they would be replaced with fresh. It was a lookout post, a good one, and from it most of the area below could be seen without revealing the looker. Had he continued a few more feet he would have ridden from the trees into an open area where he would have been a target for anyone in the brush.

"We leave the horses here," he told Konta. "From now on we move on foot but far enough apart he can't ambush us both."

"But we watch each other," Konta warned.

David nodded. "Yes. Don't give him a chance to pick one off without risking being shot by the other." That had been one of the warnings Cochise had given him. Operating out of sight from each other, for whatever reason, would be to lose their advantage of numbers.

By midday she had been alone a long time. The boy seemed to do whatever pleased him, receiving at the same time very little attention from Lobo Negro. He may well be off hunting the mountain lion she'd pretended to see, and he was young enough not to understand the danger had it been real. How much longer would he have survived if she'd not come?

But then, what had her coming changed? He would still wander alone over the mountain unless she could reach him some way. How could she do it? What could she say that would reach her child who was now little more than a wild animal?

Movement in front of her reclaimed her attention sharply. The boy was returning, but there was something different about the way he climbed through the rocks. He moved slower, and when he reached more level ground, she could see why—he was limping badly. She jumped up in alarm.

But by the time she was on her feet she remembered, and waited for him to make his way to her by himself. When he had, she looked down into a small face struggling valiantly not to cry.

"You're hurt," she said, doing more than a little struggling of her own not to sweep him up in her arms. "What happened?"

He wouldn't look directly at her, but she realized he'd intentionally stopped within her reach. "Fall," he said.

He was as agile as a squirrel, but she could guess what had happened. His baby sense of judgment had failed him and he'd tried something beyond his ability to accomplish. It was her fault, she'd convinced him to look for a mountain lion that didn't exist and he'd concentrated on that rather than on what he was doing.

"Come," she said, not touching him. "It is a squaw's duty to take care of the wounds of a warrior."

She got a blanket from the cave and spread it near the entrance where she would have light, helped him to lie down on it, and then went for water with which to clean his bloody left leg.

With the blood washed away, she inspected the leg closely. It was badly bruised and had two long gashes running from thigh to knee, but no bones were broken and the cuts had bled freely. She cleaned the cuts carefully and pretended she didn't hear the several times he choked off a sob as she worked. But then there was nothing in the way of herb medicine to place on the wounds, she could only wrap the leg tightly in a strip she tore from the bottom of her shirt, and then wrap that again in a piece of blanket to hold it still.

When she finished, she placed a hand gently on his small shoulder and felt it trembling from his efforts not to cry.

"A warrior needs rest when he is injured," she told him. "Sometimes it is a squaw's duty to hold his head in her lap so that he can rest better."

He didn't reply, but when she moved behind him he didn't turn to look at her, merely held his head up. She sat down and carefully drew him toward her until his shoulders rested against her leg and his head was in her lap. A few minutes later, he still didn't object when she drew him even closer and wrapped her arms around him.

Holding him at last, Flor de Oro felt a tension within her release. It had been so long a time. . . .

The two of them spent an hour moving cautiously on the lookout post, only to find it empty as they had half expected. There was no sign that anyone had ever occupied it. David slipped carefully back from the edge of the cliff before he stood erect, making sure that he didn't become an outline against the sky. Never stand alone, Cochise had told him. Make him always have to find you against something else such as a tree or a rock. And never remain there long enough for him to be certain of the difference.

Konta joined him in the shelter of a fallen tree. "I think he will not be far now," he said in a low voice.

David scanned the area with his good eye. Just behind the lookout post was a wide, deep bench of land covered with broken rock and stunted trees, a place that was open but at the same time filled with crevices in which to hide and attack. "Got any ideas?" he asked.

"No. This mountain belongs to Lobo Negro. He will find us before we can find him. We can only be ready when he does."

"Then let's go play," David said grimly. "We'll leave the horses where they are. No use going back for them."

Without waiting for a reply, he made his way down a short slope and advanced along the bench, using every bit of cover he could but still feeling as if a thousand eyes followed his moves. A dozen yards away, Konta echoed his progress.

It took him nearly an hour to move only halfway across the bench and still nothing stirred ahead of him. David paused and looked in Konta's direction. The Apache caught his movement and gave him an inquiring glance, and in that instant his head exploded in blood. A split second later, David heard the crack of a rifle and instinctively flung himself to one side.

The rifle barked again at the same time he moved

and scattered rock and dirt where he'd been. Desperately he threw up his own weapon and searched for the shooter.

Nothing but silence met his search, and there was neither movement nor smoke to mark the killer's location. The rifle he was using had to be one of the new repeaters to have been fired so rapidly, and it used smokeless powder.

He cursed softly and glanced at the motionless body that had been his friend. Only a quick glance—Cochise's warning about remaining too long in one place came back to him and he slid around the ledge of rock beside him. Just in time—the hidden rifle sounded again and part of the ledge chipped where he'd been.

David rolled over, crouched for a second, and ran for another rock. This time Lobo Negro was slower in firing and he caught the flash against a shadow of rock to his left. He fired twice in that direction and raced for another cover.

He remained there only for seconds, trying to steady his rifle for another shot and calm his nerves at the same time, then moved again, scrambling for the shelter of a group of broken pines. He made it and was surprised to find that his movements did not bring another shot from the renegade.

With his back against a fallen log, another shielding him from the front, he waited. He may have hit his enemy, but the odds were against it since he never saw him. More likely, Lobo Negro was on the move now and circling to get a shot at him from a direction he least expected. He had to think, outguess him, and be ready for the unexpected.

Slowly, and with much patience, she had continued to gather him into her lap until she held him as she wanted, and he had not protested. For all his wild life he was still a very small boy and in the pain of his wounds she had become a haven as she had hoped. Now he slept cradled in her arms with his head against her breast. Flor de Oro looked down into the small sleeping face and lost the problems of her existence. He was her son and she held him, and for now that was enough.

The sudden sharp crack of a rifle, followed quickly by another, jerked her back to the present. She twisted to see. It couldn't be far away, the sound had seemed almost on top of her.

He wasn't hunting, he wouldn't have fired twice if he were. He was attacking someone, or someone was shooting at him. Cochise! He had come at last!

Gently she laid the boy down, careful not to disturb his sleep. The rolling peal of the rifle came again. She stood up, searching, but there was nothing to see. The fourth shot was quickly followed by two more that carried a different sound. It was a battle! Someone else was on the mountain! Could it really be Cochise? Her hands tightened into nervous fists. She had made that mistake once before when she was with Lobo Negro, what if she were wrong this time? But then what difference did it make? No matter who it was, they offered her a chance to break free once more.

She waited, listening, but no more shots were fired. Waiting was a thing she could not do. She glanced down at the boy, saw that he was still sleeping, and began to move in the direction of the shooting. It would be dangerous, but she could not remain here and wait for the outcome. If she could help in any way the risk would be worth it.

The shots could not have come from more than five to six hundred yards away, she could reach the spot in only a few minutes and stay under cover at the same time. Lobo Negro would not expect someone to come from behind him.

Do not stay in one place, Cochise had said, no matter how well you are hidden. He will find you. Move carefully, make the ground a part of yourself, and know each time before you move where you will stop.

David left the pines and crawled forward on his hands and knees to a cluster of broken rock. The effort brought screaming pain to his shoulder, but he ignored it and concentrated on making sure no loose rocks or gravel gave him away. With his back against a boulder, he turned to face the trees, knowing Lobo Negro would not have remained near the spot from which he had fired.

A moment later he caught movement on his left, a flash of human, and fired. His bullet kicked up dirt just ahead but Lobo Negro rolled away to his right and disappeared behind a rise of ground. That had been a mistake. Cochise had also told him the outlaw was right-handed and would have a tendency to move to his right when suddenly exposed. He should have fired in that direction instead of leading him with the shot.

He decided to crawl in the opposite direction. The outlaw would circle the trees and probably come up again from this side, expecting David to move left toward the spot where he'd been seen. Do the unexpected, Cochise had said, make the logical move and he will be waiting for you.

A dozen yards away, he stopped again and slowly raised his head to look between two rocks. Nothing. Then there was a whisper of sound in the pines followed by a hard rattle. David smiled grimly. It had been a thrown rock, the sound had been too violent, and Lobo Negro was too good to have made it accidentally. He was supposed to fire at the sound and give his own position away.

He rolled over to his left again, took a quick glance into a wide gully to see that it was clear, and dropped into it. The gully ran parallel to the pines and would make excellent cover from someone circling them. Even better, there was a lot of loose rock piled in it a short distance away that would block sight of his own progress until he reached them.

A small sound behind him caused him to whirl, ready to fire. Something was back there! He waited, feeling the sudden drumming of his heart inside his shirt. Damn! How could the outlaw have gotten up behind him so quickly?

The sound wasn't repeated, but he could not have been wrong, there was someone, or something, there and he couldn't afford to ignore it. Cochise had said the outlaw was alone but he couldn't be sure of that now. He had to do something about this new threat. He moved carefully back up the gully, stopping every other step to listen and look behind him. If Lobo Negro was in the gully with him and someone else was at the other end, he would be caught in a crossfire. Better to get clear of it and look for another shelter.

He crawled up the side and slowly raised his head to see over. Just as his good eye cleared the top he spotted a brown form scurrying from a rock to a clump of brush. David jerked his rifle forward and leveled it. That brush would offer no protection from a bullet.

He fingered the trigger, trying to decide exactly where to place his shot, just which side the man would be lying on, when he saw movement again. An instant before he fired, he caught a flash of gold, and lifted his rifle. Jennifer!

She darted to another shelter behind a rock and he lowered the weapon with shaking hands.

But he had been in one place too long, he heard the bark of the rifle behind him at the same instant that a hammer blow struck his back and tore him loose from the slope. He had only the recollection of falling. Then blackness closed in.

She knew she was close to where the firing had been and took refuge behind a clump of brush, stretched on the ground for a moment in its shelter, and immediately decided it wasn't a good place to pause. Quickly, she bunched her knees under her and darted toward a rock, barely reaching it to crouch when another sharp explosion jerked her attention to the area ahead of her. She had only a moment's view of a white man as he rose up from the ground, curled backward, and fell from sight. But the moment was enough in which to recognize him. She screamed.

Without stopping to think, she ran in the direction

he had fallen, crying his name. She covered only half the distance to the spot when another figure stepped into her view and leveled a rifle at her, his outline only a blur because of the sudden tears in her eyes. But she knew who it was, and knew he would kill her if she didn't stop. She didn't care. That was David who'd been shot. Her mind whirled with the thought. David!

Her legs were made of lead, she was running, she was conscious of that, and should be moving quickly. But the distance seemed so terribly long and she had the sensation of swimming against a swift river.

"Stop!"

Flor de Oro heard his command, but only dimly, from far away.

"Stop or I will kill you!"

David's rifle lay on the ground just ahead of her, dropped there when he'd fallen backward. She wanted it. Wanted it to shoot the man who'd killed her husband. Pain and rage competed inside her.

"Stop!"

She flung herself foward, snatched the rifle and rolled, expecting to feel his bullets tear into her as she rolled. But when she came to her knees, he was still standing with his own weapon leveled toward her.

The rifle in her hands was unfamiliar, it took precious seconds to grasp it correctly and aim it, and in those seconds, Lobo Negro lowered his own.

He was no more than a dozen yards away; she could see him clearly, and in the instant the heavy rifle in her hands exploded, she saw anger . . . and hurt, in his face. Then the face disappeared as he pitched backward from the force of her bullet.

Flor de Oro crouched, frozen in shock at what she had done. He could easily have killed her, even now she should be dead. But he had lowered his weapon and allowed her to shoot him. She stared unbelievingly at the body sprawled before her until he raised his head for a moment to look at her and then dropped it back again. The action broke her paralysis and she rose and walked toward him slowly, holding the rifle ready in case it was a trick.

It wasn't a trick, his chest was covered with blood, and as she looked down at his face staring back at her from the ground, a new trickle of bright red slowly released from the corner of his mouth and ran down across his scarred cheek.

He was dying. She knelt beside him to look into the already dimming eyes. "Why?" she whispered.

Lobo Negro tried to raise his head, but the effort was too much for him and he dropped it wearily back. His mouth moved, bubbling the blood, and she reached impulsively to wipe it away with her hand, cradling the rifle in her lap. "Why?" she whispered again. "You could have killed me."

The anger was gone from his eyes, replaced by a dark sadness. He tried again to speak and she leaned forward to hear. "Flor de Oro," he whispered through a mouth twisting with the effort. ". . . If I had once possessed you."

At last she understood and stretched her hand once more to touch his cheek. "It would never have been, Lobo Negro," she said softly. "I would never belong to you. Go now in peace. For there is no longer anger between us."

The eyes died as she watched, staring beyond her into nothingness. Flor de Oro closed them gently and stood up. She had lied to him in the moment of his death, lied because she would always remember him with anger in her heart. But it would be a different kind of anger, the fire had turned to bitter ashes.

David! She turned quickly and ran to the spot where he'd fallen. His body lay crumpled in the bottom of the gully, his face hidden under one arm. She slid down beside him, moved the arm, and cried with joy when he groaned.

"David, my darling." The words were wrenched from her. "Please live!"

As gently as she could, she straightened him and pulled up the buckskin shirt. But there was no blood, only an old wound, purpled and swelling.

It couldn't be! He'd been shot. She'd seen him hit!

David groaned again as she turned him over. The new wound was in the same shoulder, but the bullet had struck a glancing blow, ripping a ragged furrow across the flesh. She cried aloud with relief. He would live!

She traced the wound with her fingers, carefully pressing the sides together. It was not serious, shock had done more damage than the bullet; striking his already damaged shoulder, it had knocked him into unconsciousness. But he would live; her David would live. She hugged him close and allowed her tears to flow freely as she did.

David and the boy. She had them both. She looked up at the sky that had almost been her friend this morning and it was truly smiling this time. And in the distance below the mountain, the desert that had once been home to her offered a symbol to her future in its vastness.

No, she told the sky silently through her tears, you will no longer be my home. Flor de Oro is no more. Jennifer Foxcroft has her own family now.

PASSION'S TREASURE

Marsha Gibson

Price: $3.25
0-505-51805-8

Category:
Historical Romance

Virtually penniless at her father's death, beautiful Caryl Winthrop left the security of her home in England to take a job as governess in South Africa. Her employer's brutal advances, however, forced her to flee once again—on a merchant ship bound for the exotic Pearl Islands.